W9-BRI-501

*New beginnings are a
gift of life —
Treasure them*

Jane Dews

2002

SUNRISE
Jane Dews

©2001 Gardenia Press

Sunrise
Copyright © 2001 by Jane Dews.

Library of Congress Number:
ISBN Number   Softcover: 0-9678895-3-7

All rights reserved. No part of this book may be reproduced or transmitted in any form or by any means, electronic or mechanical, including photocopying, recording, or by any information storage and retrieval system, without the written permission of the publisher, except in the case of brief quotations embodied in critical articles or book reviews.

This is a work of fiction. Names, characters, places and incidents are either the product of the author's imagination or are used fictitiously, and any resemblance to any actual persons, living or dead, events, or locales is entirely coincidental.

This book was printed in the United States.

For inquiries or to order additional copies of this book, contact:

Gardenia Press
P. O. Box 18601
Milwaukee, WI 53218-0601
USA
1-866-861-9443
www.gardeniapress.com
orders@gardeniapress.com

CHAPTER ONE

Jacqui moved away from the window overlooking the canyon. She appeared almost oblivious to the orange and purple splendor splashed across the endless Arizona sky by the sinking sun. For one awful moment she felt that she was in danger of losing herself again, moving back into time— to feelings she didn't want to feel, resurrecting memories long buried, and asking questions for which there were no answers.

She had known it was inevitable when she found the porcelain goose in the antique store in Sedona the day before the wedding invitation arrived. It wasn't a coincidence that the goose's proud, silly stare was exactly like the one Rhea prized—the one shattered that unforgettable night so long ago. It was easily explained; there are no accidents in the universe.

The invitation lay on the kitchen counter between the telephone bill and the supermarket circular as if it were of no more consequence than either. And, as Jacqui reached for it for what must have been the thousandth time, she was tempted to toss it into the trash along with the flier with prices that expired the day before.

Instead, she slipped the elegant invitation out of its matching envelope and ran her fingers over the raised yellow rose, framed in a gold oval, that had become Sunny Houston's trademark. Unbidden memories of the exuberant Sunny flooded back. Once they had been close—another lifetime ago.

Another time. Another place. Almost five years ago. Time to reassemble enough of the odd shaped pieces of her life into a workable pattern once again. The invitation was an intrusion. Unwelcome.

Home was now a low, rustic house, small, but with an air of spaciousness, clinging to the rocky canyon wall. She had put down roots here—roots like the sturdy cacti that she was so fond of, desert yucca and strawberry hedgehog and the great old saguaro with the waxy, white blossoms that guarded her door.

She, who used to boast that she didn't have anything that couldn't be disposed of in a day, now owned a house with custom designed, handcrafted furniture, Navajo rugs and a growing collection of southwestern art, paintings and sculpture and Indian artifacts. She, also, claimed the most spectacular sunsets in the whole world were visible from her redwood deck.

And, she had a job she loved or rather, jobs as Jonathan was prone to correct her. "Jacqui," he was fond of saying, "hasn't decided what she wants to be when she grows up."

It wasn't true, of course. It seemed that she had always shouldered adult responsibilities. Her work was satisfying. She loved coaching girls' basketball, teaching a couple of night classes in psychology at the university, and counseling a few private patients from time to time.

Jonathan had been aghast when she turned down the full time tenure track position in psychology at the University.

"You can't do it, Jacqui! Think of all the years you worked to get your doctorate."

She had reminded him gently that she didn't need his permission. She had her own. And if the past had taught her anything at all, it was that she was the best judge of what was ultimately right for Jacqui. It was impossible to explain to him how the girls at the school gave her a daily infusion of their vital energy and that she couldn't function without it.

Nor did she need Jonathan's permission to go to New York for the wedding—if she chose to go. He didn't like the idea, but since he was already committed to being in San Francisco that week, she didn't see any point in telling him that if she did go, it was something she had to do alone.

"I can't believe you actually know Sunny Houston!" Jonathan exclaimed. "Why didn't you ever mention it? If a former roommate of mine were a celebrity, you can bet I wouldn't keep it a secret."

"She wasn't a celebrity then. Her name wasn't even Sunny Houston. We just happened to live in the same house. I was working on my Ph.D., and she was a waitress. We didn't have too much in common."

"There's something you're not telling me," he insisted. "The hottest young star on Broadway is marrying a congressman and invites—no, implores you to come to the wedding—and you can't decide whether or not to go. You know, Jacqui, sometimes I just can't figure you out."

Jacqui placed the invitation back into the envelope and shoved it into a drawer. Donning sweats and running shoes, she decided to run the canyon road before Jonathan came back. If she hurried, she could make it back before dark. At least it would rid her of some of the tension, and if there was anything she didn't need, it was another tense night with Jonathan.

Jacqui loved to run, and for several minutes, she was able to shut out everything but the sound of her own breathing and the dull thud of her running shoes on the pavement. Running, she could pace her thoughts as easily as she paced her stride. Running along the canyon wall was the only part of her day when the universe seemed to make perfect sense.

She knew she was in danger of losing Jonathan. She saw it in the hard set of his jaw when he talked about the job offer in California. Sooner or later, he would go. Theirs had been a comfortable union, born of mutual interests and shared affection, but it lacked the passion of a great love. She had come to that realization sooner than he, perhaps, because she had once known a great love.

Jacqui dropped to one knee at the crest of the canyon, breathing hard. She rested there as the darkness slowly overwhelmed the sunset. When she started back down, the decision to go to New York had been made. It was time to face them all again. It would have happened sooner or later with or without the wedding. It was time, as she had long suspected, to try to recapture that essential part of herself she had left behind five years ago.

CHAPTER TWO

JACQUI
HOUSTON - FIVE YEARS EARLIER

Jacquiline Wilder, barefoot and still in her short red robe, leaned on the balcony railing overlooking the sunlit pool. It was not even close to noon yet, but the day was oppressively hot. Only an occasional breeze stirred the potted palms and ruffled the fringe on the umbrellas below.

A dozen tanned young bodies languished around the pool, and Jacqui noticed that the tall iced drinks were flowing freely. The alluring water was inexplicable empty except for one couple, joined by their hands, drifting side by side on inflated mats that bobbed up and down in rhythm. As she watched, their hands slipped apart, and they glided to opposite corners of the pool. The indifferent pair seemed neither to notice nor to care.

She suddenly hated the artificiality of it all, the shallow friendships that formed around the pool, the inane conversation that ensued—as if anyone really cared where you worked or even if you did—and what sign of the zodiac you were born under, and if you were going to Cancun over Labor Day. It was just something to talk about on the way to the bedroom.

She reached down and picked up the newspaper and retreated to the dim coolness of her apartment. She poured herself a cup of strong, black coffee and climbed back into bed with the paper.

Uneasy Peace in Beirut. President Predicts Economic Upswing in November. Astros Bow to Atlanta.

Her mind was not on the headlines. She put the paper aside and sighed. The memory of Spence and another Sunday morning tugged relentlessly at her consciousness. She tried to push it away, but it would not go. She rubbed her finger tips slowly across the smooth sheet, remembering the feel of her fingers on his shoulders, sliding her hands down his muscular back. She remembered how she used to kiss the back of his neck and nibble on his ear while he playfully pretended to push her away.

"God, I hate Sundays," she realized aloud, reaching for her coffee. It was cold.

She shouldn't be here doing this to herself, she thought regretfully. She had to stop believing somehow that life would never be good again. "I am still and receptive to life," she affirmed. "I allow the essence of life to flow through me into all that I do and think. I know that my life is what I have made it, and there is no power on earth than can change it except me."

Abruptly, she swung her long legs over the side of the bed and sat up. She was not alive. She no longer accepted life. She was full of bitterness and resentment. Even the apartment bore the brunt of her displeasure. It seemed utterly impersonal with its oyster walls and draperies, so like a thousand others she had seen. Too many people had lived there—none long enough to leave the imprint of their true personalities. The thin walls had witnessed no real living, only the shallow facades of hollow people passing in the night and never touching in any way that mattered. And, if a miracle should happen, one groping hand finding another, however briefly, the jealous fates snatched it away.

"Stop it! Stop, right now! You do not believe in fate," she told herself. "Each of us creates his own fate."

The air in the apartment had become stifling. Jacqui quickly showered and slipped into a sundress. She brushed her long hair and pulled it back from the face, winding it into a knot, and attaching a spray of silk flowers. It gave her, she had been told, a faintly exotic look.

You have so many looks, Spence had said, standing behind her one night as she brushed her hair, *and all of them beautiful.*

Jacqui looked at herself critically. Whatever Spence had seen was gone. She felt ordinary, even drab, most of the time. She retrieved a pair of sandals from the closet and stuffed her wallet into an oversized tote bag that contained her notebooks. The university library would be open soon. She might as well grab a bite somewhere and get to work. Work was the only balm for her wounded spirit, although, the enthusiasm with which she had begun her thesis had long since faded.

She had been studying the various ways that victims of abuse coped with their experiences in hopes of devising more effective treatment plans. She had interviewed hundreds of abuse victims, and she was in the final stage of putting it all together. She wasn't sure what she would do when it was finished. Take a trip to Europe? Look for a faculty position in psychology? It didn't seem to matter much. But, one thing she did know with certainty, she was going to get out of that apartment. And soon! Her lease expired next month, and she had hesitated about signing another. But, what was the alternative? Another apartment? Buy a condo? What difference did it make? They were all pretty much the same. She had to get away from that awful sameness.

Jacqui backed her little red sports car out and headed down Chimney Rock Road. Something would turn up if she were receptive. The right choice would be made. She would find another place to live

CHAPTER THREE

JILL

Jill Turner sat sweltering on a Metro bus as it wound its way through the Montrose area of Houston in the middle of the afternoon. The air conditioning definitely was not working, and the windows would not budge. A not uncommon condition, she had been led to believe during her brief stay in the city. Jimmy had hated everything about Houston. He had dubbed it Dante's Inferno, and his opinion had not changed, especially after his van was stolen. They had taken a bus that night back to the cramped, dingy apartment they were renting by the week. When Jill went to the kitchen to make them a sandwich, the biggest cockroach she had ever seen scurried across the cabinet and disappeared into a crack behind the sink.

Now Jimmy was on his way back to Arkansas, and she was all alone. "You are the most stubborn girl in the world." His angry words had been flung at her in frustration when she refused to board the Greyhound bus with him to go home to Arkansas, paid for with the money his parents had wired.

He was right, she thought. She was stubborn. And all his arguments were valid. She had no clothes; they had been stolen with the van, and virtually no money—except for the hundred dollar bill hidden in her shoe—the one she hadn't told him about. "I won't go back," she declared. "I won't go back and admit defeat. I can just hear my mother saying I told you so."

"You don't have any other choice," Jimmy had argued. "We

don't have enough money to pay another week's rent, and I can't find a job. It's the same story everywhere I go. You have to have experience. I don't know how you're supposed to get any experience in this crummy place if nobody will hire you. And now we don't even have the van. It's crazy, Jill. I was crazy to let you talk me into coming here."

When she didn't answer, he took her by the shoulders and shook her savagely. "You can't stay here alone. You'll end up murdered," he predicted. "This place if full of crazies."

Jill could see tears in his eyes. She knew he really loved her, but she couldn't go back, and she knew he wasn't strong enough to stay. She turned away from him as he boarded the bus alone. His dismay turned to surprise as the bus pulled away. Jill could tell by the look on his face that he expected her to change her mind— right up to the last minute. She wondered what Jimmy would say to her mother and what her mother would say when he arrived without her. She felt tears come.

Now she was on a Metro bus looking out the window at marvelous old houses, some converted to shops and restaurants. Some had been wonderfully restored, others were shabby. The bus slowed and came to a stop. The driver nodded to Jill. This was her stop.

Fear gnawed at her. She had a momentary lapse of self confidence. She should have gone home with Jimmy. She should have swallowed her pride and gone home. No! She would make this work, she vowed as she stepped down from the bus, steadying herself against the rail. She flashed the driver a smile of thanks for his help, and the bus pulled away. A summer breeze stirred the air around her perspiration-soaked blouse and cooled her.

The neighborhood had improved rapidly. There were magnificent old houses with manicured lawns and huge shade trees. Jill pulled a hand-drawn map from her pocket and glanced at it. Her aunt's house was only a block away. How could she refuse Jill a place to live for a while just until she got on her feet?

She remembered proudly that she had a job—starting tomorrow. Jill had walked boldly into a chic restaurant-bar, the Aloha, in a downtown hotel and asked to see the manager. He had given her a cool, appraising look—the kind she had learned to expect from men—and hired her. She foresaw no problems. She was smart, and she would catch on quickly.

Jill noticed the clientele in the bar, mostly men, professional types in dark suits with briefcases, and, she imagined, although it was too dark for her to see, clean fingernails. The few women were smartly dressed. Jill shook off her fear and knew that she, too, would be a part of this new world. It would be different and exciting. Maybe Jimmy's leaving was a blessing in disguise. He would never have allowed her to take the job.

Her aunt's house was just as she remembered it, a ten year old memory. She laughed at the door knocker, a ferocious lion's head with a ring through its snarling teeth. It had fascinated her as a child. She drew up the memory of her aunt as she had been five years ago at Granny's funeral, tall and elegant in a designer suit, standing with her handsome husband among the dowdy relatives.

The door opened cautiously. The lady with the pretty unlined face and dark curly hair was unmistakably her aunt, but she was shorter and considerably plumper than Jill remembered.

She began with uncertainty, "Aunt Rhea, I'm Jill. Jill Turner, your niece."

"Jill, of course. Come in." The greeting was warm. "My goodness, let me look at you. You've grown up. What are you doing in Houston? Why didn't you let me know you were coming?"

She embraced Jill with a radiant smile, and she smelled faintly of lilac scented soap.

Jill breathed a sigh of relief. Everything was going to be all right; she had a place to live.

CHAPTER FOUR

CAROLINE

Caroline Cortero glanced nervously at the clock on the wall of the Houston Public library. She had been there a long time. It was one of the few places where you could loiter for hours without attracting attention. All you had to do was find an empty table, stack reference books in front of you, and scribble on a note card periodically.

Rick should have been there by now. With a sickening dread, she knew that something had gone wrong this time. He had been too lucky. She had a momentary flash of him lying dead in a pool of blood on the blistering pavement of a parking lot in the middle of the afternoon. But Rick knew the terrible risks he took. A wave of nausea rose and crested in her throat. Some days the morning sickness lasted all day long.

She leaned back in the chair and covered her face with her hands as if resting her eyes. The nausea passed. She glanced at the clock again and pulled her oversized pocketbook closer to her. It was almost as if it had become a part of her. She could never be without it. And she could never be without the little cylinder of mace on her key ring. It, too, was an extension of her.

Rick was not coming. She would have to proceed without him. What would happen to her and the baby she carried if he never came back? Ironically, she was not sure if the thought was a wish or a fear. She loved him, of course. At least she loved parts of him. But the brutality that was always just below the surface of his tenderness, she hated. He was good to her most of the time.

And, he would be good to the baby. He had promised that they would go away, make a new start, maybe in Florida. She loved the sun and surf, and they would lead normal lives. She believed him. It had been promised in one of his tender moments.

Caroline gathered up her note cards and stuffed them into her pocket. The knot of fear in her chest dissolved. Everything would be all right. She had only to follow Rick's instructions implicitly. With the bag clutched tightly against the baby and her finger on the trigger of the mace, she walked up Louisiana Street to the Hyatt Regency Hotel. She entered the plush, flower-filled lobby through revolving doors.

It was Rick's idea. "They never look for you," he said, "in a suite in a luxury hotel, sipping champagne high above the city lights."

Usually, she waited for him in a public place until the money exchanged hands, and then they checked in the hotel together. A different hotel each time. But this was the first time he had failed to show up within a reasonable period. "If I'm not there, go to the hotel and check in without me. Register under the name we agreed on, and don't open the door to anybody. I'll be in touch as soon as I can."

Two policemen were standing by the registration desk. Another was waiting by the glass elevator. Sheer coincidence? She couldn't take the chance. She turned and walked casually across the lobby and out the side door, emerging again on the street. She walked briskly for almost a block before she summoned up the courage to look backward. No one was following. On Main Street she boarded an outbound bus and rode nervously all the way to the Holiday Inn out by the Astrodome. She went directly to the bar and ordered a glass of seltzer with a twist of lime.

Her hands were shaking badly, but alcohol could harm the baby. She sipped the drink slowly watching the television set above the bar. Suddenly, she gripped the bar to keep from falling off the stool. A homicide was the lead story. An unidentified man had been shot in a downtown parking garage just minutes after witnesses overhead a violent quarrel.

The identity of the dead man had not been established, but she knew with a dreadful certainty that it was Rick. She fought to keep the shock from registering on her face.

Rick never talked about his deals, but she knew he had been more apprehensive than usual this time. You just hold on to that bag and wait for me.

She finished the rest of the drink. Above all, she had to appear normal. The identification would come. Rick had served time in a federal prison. She stared at the television set, unseeing. There was nothing to connect her to Rick Cortero. Of that she was certain.

She paid for the drink and walked slowly out of the bar. "I'm Caroline Kelly again," she said to herself, and it rolled easily off her tongue. She had been married to Rick Cortero for three years, three turbulent years. She was sorry that he was dead, but she was relieved that it was over.

She knew that she would have to disappear. But how hard could that be for a pregnant woman in a city of two million people? Especially for one with a hundred thousand dollars in small unmarked bills in a nondescript bag slung over her arm.

CHAPTER FIVE

RHEA

Rhea Roberts Gregory sat angrily twisting a cocktail stirrer at the bar in Nick's Fish Market. The chic, expensive restaurant in downtown Houston was located in the same building where her former husband, Carter Gregory, III, maintained an impressive office with a gorgeous, young secretary. Rhea had just left that office, and neither the elegant atmosphere of Nick's nor the double scotch she had downed seemed to ease the seething fury churning inside her.

A once close friend, having lunch in the restaurant, saw her come in. "Isn't that Rhea Gregory," Liz Howard asked. "God, I hope she doesn't see me."

"She didn't even glance this way. She headed straight for the bar," Laura Massie, her companion, said.

"Maybe she's drowning her sorrows these days instead of talking them to death. I haven't heard from her in months. She's been a basket case ever since Carter walked out on her."

"Didn't Carter and your husband used to be partners?"

"Yes, but Ben and Carter went their separate ways a couple of years ago."

"Does she still live in that big, old house in Montrose?"

"As far as I know. She told everyone who would listen that she didn't get a dime in the divorce. Only that house."

"It's a lovely old house," Laura said.

"It is," Liz agreed, "full of antiques and oriental rugs and such. They bought it when they were first married, and Rhea has been collecting furniture and redecorating and restoring that house as long as I can remember. It really is the only thing she cares about."

"If she doesn't have any money, how can she continue to live there?"

"Ben said that Carter wanted her to sell the house and buy a townhouse. He wanted her to use the money to retrain herself for a career, which would have been the sensible thing to do. They don't have children, and there is no such thing as alimony in this State. The last time I went to see her, she spent the whole time telling me what a bastard Carter is."

"I wonder who the other woman is?"

"What other woman?"

"Oh, come on, Liz! There has to be another woman. But I will say this for Carter, he is discreet. There hasn't been a whisper of gossip."

"You may be right. What else would make a successful man like Carter want out of a twenty year marriage to a woman like Rhea? I mean, she is the original little Suzy Homemaker, plump and pliable."

Rhea saw Liz Howard and her friend out of the corner of her eye, laughing conspiratorially She sighed and hoped they didn't see her. She couldn't talk to anybody now, especially Liz. She drained the glass of scotch and ordered another grimacing. She didn't even like the stuff. Scotch was Carter's drink. Carter, the unfeeling bastard! What was she going to do now?

That, my dear Rhea, is your problem, he had said. I told you from the beginning that you couldn't afford to live in that house, but you refused to be reasonable. I'm sorry you don't have any money. But I just bought a new place of my own, and I'm short of cash myself. The twenty thousand I gave you is all you are going to get. Period! That house was worth far more than your share of the community property. I'm sorry, but that's the way it is. And you had better face it.

The bastard!

The bartender set the new drink in front of her. Rhea traced a line around the rim of the glass with one finger. Nobody understood what that house meant to her. She had twenty years of her life invested in it. Perhaps, it was impossible to understand unless you had grown up in a place called Cullendale with the scent of paper mill in your nostrils. *Smells just like bacon and eggs to me,* a local cafe owner said, but to Rhea, living in Cullendale carried a stigma, like being poor white trash. Cullendale was a microcosm; only mill people belonged. It was a closed society, and once you got in, you hardly ever got out.

But Rhea had attacked her high school studies with the single purpose of getting out of Cullendale in particular and the State of Arkansas in general. And, by the time the ink was dry on her diploma, she not only had a scholarship to a Texas university, but a place in the work study program that would pay the rest of her expenses. She purchased a one-way ticket to Dallas and boarded the bus leaving her tearful mother and bewildered younger sister.

Now, twenty-four years later, she still felt like that scared young girl boarding the bus with nothing but a dream to sustain her. But she was not eighteen any longer; she was forty-two. The dream had been shattered more than a year ago when Carter came home unexpectedly in the middle of the day and announced with almost no warning, *I want a divorce.* And nothing, not reason, nor tears, nor pleading, and not even the threat of her suicide would dissuade him. He wanted a divorce. And he got it, she thought bitterly.

Her family was no help. Cullendale as she had known it was no more. It had been annexed by nearby Camden, but the paper mill remained the main source of employment for the whole area, and the odor was as noxious as ever. Rhea had not been back for more than five years—not since her mother's death.

Her sister had married a mill hand, and they were light years away from her in lifestyle and experience. She dutifully sent them Christmas cards every year and enclosed generous checks for the children, but she hoped fervently never to go back to Arkansas again.

Rhea asked for her tab and gasped at the amount. She paid it with dismay, watching her dwindling resources dwindle further. Mercifully, Liz had not seen her. And as she walked through the tunnel to the parking garage, she mentally counted her money, thirty dollars in her bag and eight hundred sixty-nine in her checking account, hardly enough to get her through the month. Then what would she do?

Driving home, Rhea noticed that the air-conditioning in her

car did not seem to be cooling adequately. It probably needed coolant But she would have to swelter. From now on, no money would be spent for anything not absolutely necessary.

There was a knot of fear in the pit of her stomach. She had not really been scared until now. She had believed that Carter would relent. She had devoted her whole life to being his wife. Nothing was too much trouble to make things pleasant and easy for him after a difficult day at the office or during an important trial. After all these years, he had spurned her efforts; she had been abandoned.

Even the sight of the house, her symbol of defiance, failed to cheer her. Usually it gave her a sense of pride to return to this gracious old mansion that had weathered time and hurricanes and the assaults of progress. She was really going to lose it, she thought sadly, and she was very close to tears. This magnificent old house, classified as Georgian Revival, stood across an expansive esplanade with towering oaks. The neighborhood had managed to survive the urban plague that surrounded it despite the fact that there were no deed restrictions there.

Rhea put the car in the garage and turned on the sprinklers to water the lawn. If only it would rain the way it normally rained in Houston in early summer, she wouldn't have this expense. She gave the house one last loving look before she went inside.

She didn't know how she was going to manage it, but, somehow, she would find a way. This house was too much a part of her to ever let it go.

She went directly up to her bedroom and peeled off her sweaty clothes. She put an extravagant splash of lilac scented bubble bath in the tub and turned on the tap. "God help me," she said aloud. It occurred to her that she had not prayed in a very long time, and although she was not a religious person, she repeated the words again and convinced herself that she felt better.

After she dressed and went downstairs, she heard someone knocking at the front door. As she looked out, Rhea saw a smiling child-woman in faded, tight jeans with honey blond hair tumbling around her face. She had the clearest, bluest eyes that Rhea had ever seen.

"I'm Jill," she said. "Jill Turner, your niece."

CHAPTER SIX

The morning sun streamed into the sitting room through double doors that opened out onto a flagstone terrace with a view of the rose garden. Rhea sat sipping her coffee on a wicker settee among ferns and folk art and contemporary paintings. This was one of her favorite rooms, comfortable and unpretentious. She had decorated it on a shoe string when she first acquired the house and through the years, she had changed it little, adding a more expensive touch here and there as Carter's law practice flourished, such as the proud porcelain goose staring at her now with disdainful eyes.

It was as if the whole world, with the possible exception of her niece Jill, disapproved of everything that she had done since Carter's unexpected and awful announcement that he was moving out. She had been forced to tell Jill, of course, that she and Carter were divorced when it became apparent that her visit was not a casual duty call on an aunt she hardly knew, but that in reality she was alone in Houston with no funds and no place to live.

"I couldn't throw her out," Rhea said to the goose and smiled in spite of herself. Now on top of everything else, she thought, she was reduced to talking to a silly porcelain goose.

She poured herself another cup of coffee from the gleaming silver and glass carafe she had picked up long ago, tarnished and stained, in a forgotten flea market. She was good at spotting treasures among trash, and it was one of her favorite things to do, browse garage sales and flea markets and junk shops, especially in rural Texas towns. She loved antique shows, too, and touring historic homes. And she liked working in her gardens. The roses needed attention. Later, she promised them.

Jill was still asleep. Her horrible job kept her out until the wee hours. And that skimpy costume that was supposed to resemble a sarong hugged her voluptuousness and exposed her long, lithe legs in a way that left little to the imagination. However, as Jill pointed out, the tips were fantastic. Where else could someone without training or skill or experience make that kind of money? She had pressed two hundred dollars into Rhea's hand at the end of the first week, confident that in no time at all she could save enough for a down payment on a car.

Rhea had to admit that having her in the house was not unpleasant. Jill was so full of enthusiasm and laughter. There hadn't been any laughter in the house for a long, long time. Rhea smiled as she remembered Jill coming down the grand staircase to stand with her arms outstretched under the massive crystal chandelier.

"Oh, Aunt Rhea," she exclaimed. "I want to be married in this house in a long white dress with a train. I want to come down this staircase with the music playing. Will you let me?"

"Of course I will. I always wanted to see somebody married in this house. You'll be the most beautiful bride in the whole world."

Jill had hugged Rhea warmly, and they went upstairs to sort through closets to find Jill some clothes. Rhea never discarded anything. All the clothes from her younger and slimmer days were still hanging neatly in plastic bags in the closets of the spare bedrooms— the house had five bedrooms, hers, Carter's, and three others.

It was then that the idea of renting the bedrooms occurred to Rhea. If she enjoyed having Jill in the house, why not other young people? Somewhere in this vast city, there had to be other nice youngsters like her niece who would adore living in this gorgeous old house the way Jill adored it. Who wouldn't? They could use the pool, small though it was, the washer and dryer, the kitchen.

The house was convenient to downtown, to two universities and a community college. She would have to choose her tenants carefully. Someone quiet, cooperative, and good humored. The rent would have to be high—as high, perhaps, as a moderately expensive one bedroom apartment in the area, but, for someone unburdened by furniture, who wanted a quiet, comfortable, beautiful place to live, it would be worth it.

It was not an easy task, she soon discovered, to find someone suitable. She discarded the idea of placing an ad in the newspaper; thinking that too many undesirable people might respond. The roommate service she picked from the yellow pages was not very encouraging. However, about a week later, they sent over a cool, reserved young woman in her mid-thirties, very well dressed, who explained that she was a recent widow who had just arrived in Houston and was working as a registered nurse at St. Luke's Hospital. She readily agreed to all Rhea's ground rules, chose the smallest bedroom at the end of the hall, and paid Rhea two month's rent in advance.

Rhea phoned St. Luke's and confirmed the woman's employment and informed Mrs. Caroline Kelly that she could take occupancy of the room as soon as she wished.

With Mrs. Kelly's money and Jill's contribution to the household expenses, Rhea began to breath a little easier. She still felt that she was clinging to the edge of a cliff by her fingernails but at least, she was still hanging on.

The ringing of the telephone interrupted Rhea's reverie. She put down her coffee cup and reached for the telephone. She felt her back stiffen as she recognized her former husband's voice.

"Have you given any more thought to selling the house?" he asked her.

"No, I have not!"

"Rhea, be reasonable," he pleaded. "What are you going to do?"

"That, my dear Carter," she replied, mimicking his inflection at their last meeting, "as you pointed out, is my problem."

"Rhea, I want to help you."

"How strange! I definitely failed to get that impression. Is there another point to this call?"

"Yes, I've moved into a new condo, and I'm sending someone over to move my library."

"You mean you are stripping my library, leaving me an empty room. I don't think so."

"What do you mean? Those books are mine. I collected them over the years. They mean a great deal to me."

"Yes," she agreed, "the books are yours. Take them if you insist, but leave everything else. The furniture, including the bookcases, belongs to me."

"If I insist? Rhea, you don't even read. You can turn the library into a sitting room or something. You have an attic full of furniture. I want my desk and the bookcases and the leather chairs."

"No," she said firmly. "They are mine."

"Damn it, Rhea, be reasonable."

"I have been more than reasonable," she said angrily. "The divorce was your idea, but the property settlement gave me this house and all the furniture. Buy your own. And don't send any movers today. I'm busy. Call next week, and I will let you know when I will be available to supervise the packing of the books."

She put the receiver down none to gently and when it immediately began to ring again, she walked away. She might have more time for reading, she thought defiantly, now that she didn't have a husband to cook and clean for. The thought, however, brought her no comfort. She was very close to tears as she entered the library and stood looking around.

Above the massive leather topped desk that she had found for Carter at an estate sale more than ten years ago hung an arrangement of photographs, primarily of Carter and herself in earlier, happier days, Carter in his football uniform, she in her graduation gown, both of them together on their first cruise ship. She could feel the tears sliding down her cheeks. It wasn't meant to end this way. There should have been children, grandchildren someday. She had kept her end of the bargain, had loved, honored and obeyed. It wasn't fair.

"Aunt Rhea, is something wrong?" A gentle arm came around Rhea's shoulder. "I heard the phone ringing," Jill said.

Quickly Rhea brushed the tears away. "Oh, Jill, I'm so sorry. I forgot you were asleep. I shouldn't have let it ring so long. It wasn't important."

"It was Uncle Carter, wasn't it?" Jill asked.

Rhea nodded. There was no point in lying to her.

"And it still hurts, doesn't it?"

"Yes, it does," Rhea admitted.

"What you need," Jill suggested, "is to get out of this house, lovely though it is, meet people, and get a job."

"Oh, don't think I haven't thought of that, believe me. But what on earth would I do? I have a degree in home economics and interior design that is twenty years old. The only job I ever had was in the college bookstore."

"If I could find a job anyone could."

"Jill dear, I'm a little heavy and a little long in the tooth to be a cocktail waitress."

Jill laughed. "That wasn't what I had in mind. Let's get dressed and go out to lunch," she said impulsively. "My treat. Together, we'll think of something."

"Jill, neither of us can afford to go out."

"We can afford lunch. Besides, things are looking up for both of us."

Jill's enthusiasm was contagious. Rhea put the encounter with Carter out of her mind and went up to shower and change. When she came back down, she noticed that Jill had washed the carafe and coffee cup. She seemed more than willing to help with the household chores, in fact, seemed to enjoy keeping a gleaming polish on the furniture which she touched almost reverently.

Jill appeared in a pale blue wrap dress Rhea had given her that seemed as if it had been designed for her perfect figure. She wore a pair of high, white sandals, obviously new, and her honey colored hair glimmered with pale blond highlights from her afternoons around the pool. She looked older than her eighteen years, sophisticated and confident. But, at times, in her faded jeans and an oversized old shirt of Carter's, she looked much, much younger, dreamy and vulnerable.

"I'm holding you personally responsible for her safety and well being," Rhea's sister Ruth had threatened when she telephoned the day Jill showed up unexpectedly at the door.

Ruth had insisted that her daughter come home immediately, but Jill had refused. Ruth blamed Rhea, of course. If she had not extended a helping hand, Jill would have been forced to come home where she belonged, Ruth charged. Rhea didn't tell her about the Aloha Room and the skimpy costume and the tips. Poor Ruth would probably have a stroke if she knew.

"Where shall we go for lunch?" Jill asked. "Would you like to see the Aloha Room?"

"Not today," Rhea answered quickly. She wasn't ready for that yet. "I know a place not far away that I would like to show you. It's a house, much like this one, only larger, of course, that has been converted into a European style hotel. The restaurant is excellent, and the luncheon menu is not too expensive for us. I'm sure you'll love it. Carter and I used to go there often. It was one of our favorite places."

Jill readily agreed, and Rhea telephoned for a reservation. On the way over, she pointed out local points of interest, historic homes, The University of St. Thomas, and finally Le Columbre D'or where they were greeted with courtesy and warmth.

Jill chattered happily through the lunch, entranced with the food and fresh flowers on the table that matched the pink napkins while Rhea thoughtfully sipped a glass of white wine and only nibbled at her shrimp salad. Her mind was busy at work, trying to figure out how to rent the remaining rooms, how to find herself some kind of job, and how to get Jill out of that awful Aloha Room and into classes at St. Thomas.

And late that afternoon after Jill had gone to work, Rhea stripped the house of all the photographs of Carter and packed them in the attic. Then she took the employment ads from the classified section of the newspaper and went up to her room.

CHAPTER SEVEN

Caroline Kelly awoke to a field of bluebonnets on the wall opposite her bed. The painting was, perhaps, the thing she liked best about this cool, serene room, something to feast her eyes on, something to calm her. She needed the calm after her chaotic nights in the emergency room with the trauma, the pain, the anguish, and the frustration. And she needed it for the panic that rose in her throat when she thought of Rick Cortero.

There was a time before Rick when nursing had given her a sense of fulfillment, a place to belong in a lonely world, a useful satisfying place. No longer. She had lost that place, and she was afraid she could never find it again. Burnout, the experts called it when they spoke glibly about low pay, long hours, low status, difficult patients, a loss of control, and the inability to cope with one more crisis. It had happened to her just before she met Rick, and she had allowed him to fill the emptiness she felt, never dreaming that he would take over her life.

Now she was back, coping once more, but everything had changed. Nursing was something to fill up her time, the hospital a place to hide where he would never think to look for her.

Rick was alive—his incredible luck still holding. The panic had started the day she saw the policemen in the hotel. She had known for the first time in her life a moment of sheer, unreasonable terror. Or had she? Caroline often thought of that day. Had it really been panic or had she seized the first desperate opportunity to escape Rick and the life she had unwittingly been drawn into?

Yes, Rick's incredible luck might still be holding, but hers would run out if he ever found her. She knew that beyond a shadow of a doubt. He told her once in graphic detail what would happen if she ever left him, twisting her arm behind her back until she cried out in pain. No woman leaves Rick Cortero! But she had, and she had taken his ill-gotten drug money, one hundred thousand dollars of it, now tucked away in a bag in the corner of her closet behind her new uniforms.

She refused to think of him any more. She sat up slowly on the side of the bed and stretched. She felt refreshed here, restored somehow. It had to be the effects of this peaceful old house and, perhaps, the people in it. Rhea and Jill were really very nice, wholesome in a way she had forgotten people could be.

It was the middle of Sunday afternoon. She had finally acclimated herself to working nights and sleeping days. Jill also slept in the mornings, but hardly ever as late as she. A queasy feeling prompted her to throw on a robe and start for the kitchen to prepare her customary tea and toast for breakfast.

Jill would probably be out around the pool, since Sunday was her day off. Later Caroline would join her. Soon she would not be able to fit into a bathing suit.

As Caroline stepped out into the hall, she heard an unfamiliar voice. Rhea was standing at the top of the stairs with a tall, strikingly beautiful young woman whose dark hair was caught up with red silk flowers at the nape of her long, slender neck. She was wearing a white sundress embroidered with splashes of red hibiscus blossoms across the skirt. The ample white bag she carried bore the same design. Expensive, Caroline thought. Everything about her looked expensive from the flawless porcelain skin to the polished toenails in the white leather sandals. Caroline tried to retreat to her room. Too late! Rhea saw her and beckoned.

"Caroline Kelly meet Jacquiline Wilder. She will be moving into the room next to yours."

"How do you do," Caroline said stiffly and apologized for her robe.

Rhea explained that both Caroline and Jill worked late hours and often slept late in the morning.

"No problem," Jacqui smiled. "I'm a night person by choice. I hardly ever come alive until noon myself. This is a marvelous house. I can't wait to get unpacked. I love your furniture. You'll have to give me a history of each piece."

"More than you'll ever want to know," Rhea promised with a little laugh. "Antiques are my passion."

Caroline excused herself and left them talking at the top of the stairs. "I believe every room should be used," Rhea was saying, "and that each one should be filled with the things you enjoy. If there is anything in your room you don't care for, tell me. I'm sure I can find you something you like better."

"Oh no," Jacqui replied. "I love it just the way it is. But I could use another bookcase. I have an awful lot of books."

Caroline agreed with the new girl, it was a lovely house, and she wouldn't change a thing in her room.

The kitchen had magnificent cabinets and arched stained glass doors leading to a sunny breakfast room. Caroline took her tea and toast there where Rhea had thoughtfully left a single freshly cut, perfect red rose and the morning newspaper.

Rhea was still somewhat of an enigma to Caroline. She had this great house and what appeared to be valuable furniture and paintings. She drove a fairly new car, newer than Caroline's, and she wore very nice clothes, if somewhat matronly. She did not have a job, and she was renting rooms as if she needed the money, cleaning the whole house herself without the aid of a domestic, and caring for the expansive lawn, mowing, edging, and watering. Jill helped, of course, but, apparently, she, too, had been there only a short while.

Jill poured out her life story their first afternoon around the pool—how desperate she had been to leave the little town in Arkansas where she had grown up and how she had persuaded Jimmy to come to Houston with her. It was almost Caroline's own story of how she had left Louisiana, except that she had been older and trained in nursing, and there had been no Jimmy in her life. Eventually, there had been a married doctor before she finally left nursing. It was during that turbulent period that Rick had come into her life.

Methodically, she washed her cup and toast plate and put them away. She was working graveyards, the eleven to seven shift, and she had agreed to work weekends. One day was pretty much the same as any other to her anyway. When she started back up to her room, the new girl had changed into a pair of shorts and was carrying a large box up the stairs. Even that she seemed to manage with grace. She flashed Caroline a wide smile which was returned without any warmth.

It was not something she could put her finger on, but somehow she knew that with the presence of this tall, sophisticated stranger in the house, the character of the quiet, safe place had been forever altered. It produced an anxiety that Caroline did not know how to cope with, and she hurried past Jacqui and fled into her cool, blue room.

Late in the afternoon she summoned up the courage to go back down to the kitchen for something to soothe her queasy stomach again. By then, the house was quiet. The new girl and her little red sports car were gone. Caroline had watched her leave from the window. Rhea's car was gone, too.

Caroline poured herself a tall glass of cold milk and began to relax. After all, she had planned to stay here for only a few months, three or four at the most. By then, she would be visibly pregnant. She would quit the hospital and find herself another place to await the birth of her child. Her child. She had never been able to think of the baby as Rick's or even as theirs. Only hers.

After she had eaten, Caroline went into Rhea's sitting room overlooking the rose garden. She chose a paperback book from a small stack tucked into a wicker basket. Rhea had pretty much given her free run of the house, encouraging her to use the pool, watch television, use the laundry, and enjoy the gardens. She had never been much of a reader except for romance novels where everybody always lived happily ever after. At this point in her life Caroline needed desperately to believe that was possible.

She returned to her room, settled into the wing back chair, elevated her feet, and started to read. She was only vaguely aware that Rhea and Jill had returned. She heard the closing of a door and muted voices in the hall.

Later there was a rapid knock on the door, and Jill's voice startled her. "Caroline, are you there?"

She put down the book and opened the door.

"We're having a glass of champagne," Jill explained. "We'd like you to join us. You have a couple of hours before you leave for the hospital."

Caroline smiled. It was impossible not to be charmed by Jill. She was wearing a pair of jeans, and, with her blond hair caught up in a ponytail, she could easily have been mistaken for a fourteen year old.

"I've never tasted champagne before," Jill said gaily. "I wonder if it will make me do wild and crazy things."

She hopped up on the banister, balanced precariously for a moment and slid expertly to the bottom while the astonished Caroline watched from the top of the stairs.

"You don't need anything to make you do wild and crazy things," Caroline said. "I would break my neck if I tried anything like that."

"Did I tell you," Jill asked, "that I'm going to be married in this house? I'm going to come down this staircase in a long white gown with a train."

"Not on the railing, I hope," Caroline laughed. "That would give the wedding guests something to remember."

"Say! That's not a bad idea. Why didn't I think of that?"

Just then Caroline heard voices in the sitting room. Rhea and the new girl! She had entirely forgotten her presence in the house. Too late! She could not very well retreat to her room. How would she explain it? A few sips of champagne and a quick exit, she promised herself.

"I've been saving this for a special occasion," Jacqui was saying as she opened the bottle. There was only a small pop as the cork came out easily.

"You do that so well," Rhea acknowledged. "Choosing wines and uncorking bottles was my husband's job. If I can get the bottle open, the champagne erupts, and I lose half of it."

"There's a trick to it," Jacqui explained as she filled the crystal stems Rhea had provided. "You grasp the cork in one hand and slowly twist the bottle away from the cork. Most people hold the bottle and try to twist the cork."

She handed Jill and Caroline each a glass, picked up the other two, and wordlessly handed one to Rhea.

"Shouldn't there be a toast?" Jill asked eagerly.

"Of course," Jacqui answered. "Would you like to propose it?"

Jill solemnly raised her glass. The others followed suit. A sheepish grin spread over her face. "I can't think of anything to say," she confessed.

"Let me," Jacqui offered with a laugh. "To this marvelous house and to you, Rhea, for letting us share it."

Rhea flushed with pleasure as they all took a sip of champagne. Jill immediately made a face.

"It's an acquired taste," Jacqui assured her.

"Yes, it gets better with time," Rhea added. "and don't worry, you have plenty of time."

The conversation flowed smoothly, as if they had all been friends for a long time. It might easily have been taken for a reunion. While the others finished the bottle of champagne, Caroline took only a few sips and made herself a quick cup of tea before rejoining them.

Jacqui and Jill were deep into a discussion of feminism with Jacqui asserting that women were actually biologically superior to men. "Not only," she declared, "do we live longer than men, but we have lower death rates in almost every country in the world at almost every age and from almost all causes of death."

"But men have more dangerous jobs," Jill protested. "And they have more stress in their lives."

"Not necessarily true," Jacqui countered. "During the first year of life, male babies are thirty percent more likely to die. Doesn't that sound like females are biologically superior? Stress factors could not account for male infant deaths."

"But I don't want to be the stronger sex," Jill complained. "I want a strong, handsome husband who will take care of me and give me a house like this one, and babies. And I'll devote the rest of my life to making him happy. After I sow a few wild oats, of course."

"I don't know about biological superiority," Rhea interjected. "I'll leave that to the scientists. But I do believe that every woman should make a life for herself separate from her husband. She should learn to take care of herself economically and emotionally. I let Carter be my whole life, and I was devastated when he wanted a divorce."

"You're going to be fine," Jill told her. "You said yourself that Uncle Carter would come to his senses in time and come back home."

"Yes, I believe he will."

"Do you want him back?" Jacqui asked candidly.

"Of course, I do," Rhea replied. "I still love him. But even if I didn't, what alternative would I have? We've been married for twenty years. I don't know anything except being married."

"I hope you get him back if that's what you want," Jacqui said.

"But everybody has alternatives. You just have to learn to recognize them. I guess, in a way, we're all starting new lives. Maybe we can help each other. I will be getting my Ph.D. in psychology. I'm almost finished with my thesis. I guess that means I have to think about finding a job. I've sort of become accustomed to being a professional student."

"At least you'll be prepared," Rhea said bitterly. "I've been looking for a job for weeks. I'm getting very discouraged."

"What kind of a job are you looking for?"

"I'm not particular at this point. I can't afford to be. I've never worked, and I don't have any skills."

"Of course, you have skills," Jacqui said. "Look at this house. You are a marvelous decorator. You're creative and artistic. You know antiques. Go to work in someone's shop, get some experience, pick their brains, then open your own place."

"Oh, Aunt Rhea," Jill cried, "that sounds perfect for you."

"Do you really think I could?" Rhea asked tentatively. "I haven't seen a job like that advertised in the classified ads."

"Because it isn't advertised, doesn't mean that it doesn't exist. About eighty percent of all jobs are never advertised."

Caroline listened to Jacqui offering to help Rhea with a resume and giving her advice on how to use her experience as a volunteer for charitable organizations to aid in a job search. As she listened to the talk around her, Caroline felt more like a spectator than a participant. Yet her planned exit had been forgotten. She was thinking that it had been a pleasant evening when one of Rhea's many clocks began to chime, and she realized that she barely had time to dress and get to the hospital before the shift change.

CHAPTER EIGHT

Rhea dreaded going home for the first time that she could remember. It had not been a good day. Carter's movers had come early in the morning, and, in a couple of hours, all his books had been packed and loaded into a waiting van. Then Rhea had simply closed the door to the study without even bothering to dust the empty shelves. Somehow with his books gone, Carter's leaving seemed final.

She did not give in to the tears welling up in her eyes. Instead, she went upstairs and changed into a navy blue silk shirtwaist that minimized her plumpness. She took more care than usual with her makeup and with her stubborn dark hair that managed to look slightly tousled even in the best hairdresser's hands. Then she slipped into a pair of plain navy pumps and surveyed herself in the mirror. Almost satisfied, she added a single strand of pearls to her throat and touched her lips with a slightly darker shade of lipstick. Then, firmly grasping the list of antique dealers, she steadied herself for another frustrating day of job searching.

By late afternoon she had visited six shops, talked to four owners, her gas tank was almost empty, she had skipped lunch, and she still did not have a job. Discouragement weighed heavily upon her shoulders as she cut through an area of Montrose just blocks from her neighborhood where porno shops, massage parlors, gay bars, and topless clubs flourished It was an area that she usually avoided, if possible. Today, it didn't seem to matter.

She pulled up to an intersection with a four-way stop sign and applied the brakes. Almost instantaneously she heard the squeal of tires behind her. She braced herself for the jolt as a silver Corvette slammed into her back bumper.

Rhea swore.

The lone occupant of the Corvette, a slender, tanned young man with serious eyes approached her apologizing. "I'm sorry. I'm really sorry. It was my fault. Are you okay?"

He looked so honestly contrite and sounded so earnest that Rhea forgot about her annoyance. She inspected the damage; it was minimal. The Corvette with a broken headlight had suffered the worst of it.

The late afternoon heat was stifling. The navy silk she had chosen so carefully clung to her sweaty body, and she felt drained and spent. She brushed a lock of damp hair back from her forehead. She knew she must look appalling. In the intense heat and humidity, her hair tended to break away from a smooth style and draw up into a mop of tight ringlets. Just then a horn sounded behind them.

"We seem to be blocking traffic," she said.

"Look," the young man proposed. "There's a restaurant about two blocks down this street. Let's get out of the way and out of this heat to exchange information. Shall we?"

"It's all right," he assured her, noting her hesitation. "And it will be cool," he promised.

Rhea started her car. He had noticed her discomfort as well as her hesitation at the neighborhood. He seemed harmless, nice even. The restaurant was a converted old house with checkered table cloths and hanging plants. And it was cool as he had promised. They chose a corner table by the window looking out upon a giant oak tree with a rope swing.

He told her that his name was Kevin Stacey, and while they waited for tall, cool drinks, he wrote down his driver's license number and his insurance agent, also, his address and phone number.

"I'm afraid my mind wasn't on my driving," he explained. "I guess I must have looked away and didn't see your brake lights until it was too late to stop. That's no excuse, I know, especially since I'm familiar with the neighborhood and should have remembered the stop sign. Perhaps you should see a doctor. You could have whiplash!"

"I'm sure I'm all right," Rhea replied, sipping her drink. "I don't think the impact was hard enough to do any damage."

They talked easily for a few moments, safe, impersonal subjects: Houston weather, traffic, restaurants. As he talked, Rhea noticed that he had an expression in his eyes which made him appear incredibly sad. There was something profoundly wrong with that, she thought. He was much too young. She found herself oddly possessed with an urge to put her arms around his shoulders and comfort him.

When they rose to go, Rhea accidently brushed against him in the cramped space of the corner. She was startled by the hardness of his body. He reached out to steady her and smiled. "I always seem to bump into you," he said, laughing, and the sadness in his eyes disappeared for the moment.

"My fault this time," she confessed.

His hand lingered on her arm, and she suddenly experienced an unanticipated shiver of desire coursing through her body. She turned away from him in acute embarrassment. He was only a boy. Shame seeped into her. Carter was the only man in her life that she had ever wanted in that way.

Quickly, she got out of the restaurant and into her car. She told herself that she would never see him again. The incident was better forgotten. She sighed as she headed home. She dreaded the thought of seeing anyone. Jill would be gone to work. Caroline would be locked in her room. If there was an ideal tenant, it would have to be Caroline. She had hardly seen her since the night they shared the champagne. Jacqui was the one she hated to face, but her car was not in the drive. A reprieve, she thought. She would get herself together before Jacqui returned.

"Hi, how did it go?"

Rhea was stunned to see Jacqui in front of the television set. She switched it off and faced Rhea. "Never mind," she said, "I can tell from your face."

Rhea burst into tears, "Oh Jacqui," she said in despair. "Sometimes, I don't think I even want to go on living. I don't suppose you can understand that.

"I can understand it," Jacqui replied softly.

"I'm so ashamed of myself, but I'm just not strong. I loved Carter so much. I depended on him for everything. I don't know why I'm bothering you. Forgive me. Go back to your program."

"It wasn't very interesting. Now tell me, what's really wrong?"

"It's everything. It's Carter. It's me. It's my financial situation. I can't find a job. I feel so useless, so worn out, so unnecessary. I don't want to go on living like this. I know you can't understand that."

"Stop saying I can't understand," she replied softly, and held out both her hands, palms extended, indicating visible scars along both wrists.

"I tried to kill myself," Jacqui said quietly.

"You slashed your wrists!" Rhea cried aghast.

"I was in love," Jacqui explained, "deeply and completely in love with a wonderful man. It was a love that comes once in a lifetime. Spence was twice my age, but he was tender and caring and intelligent and successful, everything I had ever imagined in a lover. But he was married when we met, and he went through a long, bitter divorce fight. Then one night just before we were to be married, he had a heart attack and died in my arms. Spence was my whole life. I could not imagine living without him. We had so many plans. I didn't know he was ill, but he had been aware of it for some time. He kept it from me."

"Oh, Jacqui, how awful."

"Yes, it was. I was completely destroyed by the loss, and I tried to kill myself. Sometime later, his lawyers gave me a letter Spence had written to me almost a year before he died. It was a beautiful, unselfish letter. He explained about his heart condition and why he had decided not to share it with me. He wanted to give me time, time free from worry, something he couldn't have. He said he wanted to live, but that if he didn't make it, he wanted me to live enough for both of us."

"He sounds like a beautiful person," Rhea said with tears glistening in her eyes.

"He was a beautiful person, and it was a beautiful letter, but I tore it up in a fit of anger."

"Anger?"

"Yes, I was furious with him. Furious with him for dying and furious with him for not sharing his illness with me."

Rhea shook her head sadly, not knowing what to say.

"It took me a year to forgive him for dying. The pain was so intense that I had to have someone to blame. My parents were dead, and my friends didn't really understand what I had lost. It didn't help at all to hear that I was young and that I would find someone else in time. I wasn't very rational, I'm afraid, especially, after Spence tried so hard to give me the most precious gift he could —time. And it was a perfect time. Now, in perspective, I'm not sure anyone has a right to ask for more than that. Do you remember a perfect time, Rhea?'

Rhea was silent, her thoughts whirling backward into time. She remembered the day she and Carter moved into this house. It seemed like only yesterday. They had been so happy.

"Yes," she said at last. "With Carter."

"Then remember it and release all the rest. Let it go. Anger and bitterness can eat at you, Rhea, until there's nothing left. You can have a new life, a new beginning. I know."

"That's easy for you to say. You're still young. I'm forty-two."

"Oh, Rhea," Jacqui said in exasperation. "Forty-two is—well, it's forty-two. That's all. It is not an acceptable excuse for anything."

"I wish I could believe that. You make me want to believe it. But how?"

"First you get up off your backside and do something. You look for a job. You start going out. You make new friends. You start going through the proper motions and, before you know it, you'll start to feel the appropriate emotions."

"I looked for a job, Jacqui. I really tried."

"You tried one day after you decided what you wanted. Then you got discouraged. All you learned today was that it isn't going to be easy, but you already knew that."

"I guess so."

"The first thing you have to do is to remember that the job you seek is seeking you. Follow your intuition."

"No job is seeking me. I'm fat and—"

"I know," Jacqui interrupted, "forty-two. You're not really fat, but in thirty days you could be slimmer. And I've already told you that forty-two is not an excuse for anything."

"I don't know where to start."

"Where you are right now. Let's go exercise. I have a rather neglected membership in a health club. We'll work out and then eat something green and healthy at the food bar. Do you have a leotard?"

"A leotard? Are you kidding? I wouldn't be seen in public in a leotard."

"Good grief! Shorts then."

"Wrong. I don't wear shorts in public."

"Rhea, you are trying my patience," Jacqui said sternly. "Go upstairs, put on anything you feel comfortable in. But, for God's sake, try to remember that you are forty-two and not eighty-two."

Dutifully, Rhea changed into a pair of dark stretch trousers and a big multi-print top. Jacqui called up to her that they would have to take Rhea's car since hers was being serviced.

"If you can stand it," Rhea said. "My air-conditioning isn't cooling very well."

Rhea found herself smiling as she brushed her hair. Somehow, it had not been such a bad day, after all. On the way home Jacqui insisted on stopping at a garage and having coolant added to the car.

When they returned home, Rhea was tired but relaxed, and she fell almost immediately into a deep, refreshing sleep.

It was Jacqui who lay in the darkness listening to the unfamiliar sounds of the old house. With more than a hundred years of history echoing through its rooms, it seemed to have a voice of its own in the dark of the night. Then in the distance, she heard the eerie wail of a siren. There had been a siren the night Spence died and two young paramedics who struggled in vain to save his life.

But that was long time ago, she reminded herself. She knew she could not go on remembering the ashen color of his face as he lay dying or the saliva foaming on his lips. She could not go on bleeding every time she heard an ambulance The pain had to stop.

She thought about the advice she had given Rhea earlier. Let go of all the bitterness and make a new beginning. Why couldn't she do that? If she could make herself go through the proper motions, she would begin to feel the appropriate emotions. It was easy to give advice to Rhea. But, somewhere beyond the emptiness, she wondered if there was anything left inside of her?

There had to be or she wouldn't hurt this way. She was still alive. Physician, heal thyself. It was time for her to start practicing what she preached..

She switched on the bedside lamp. Her room was enormous and opulent with high ceilings and a crystal chandelier. She loved it from the moment Rhea led her into it. The walls were painted a pale peach to harmonize with the tufted headboard and matching coverlet of peach print with splashes of spring green and pale coffee so delicate and lovely it might have been painted by Renoir. The floor was carpeted in a plush beige, and an antique salon set stood along one wall in front of the window. An eighteenth century Georgian mirror hung above a mahogany lowboy. Jacqui had filled the bookcases with books and bric a brac from her apartment.

An arrangement of silk flowers in a crystal bowl picked up the colors of the coverlet, and a large painting of a Paris street scene dominated the wall opposite her bed. It was the first thing she saw when she awoke each morning. It was a room in which she felt comfortable. Jacqui would change nothing.

She got out of bed and went to sit across the room with a magazine. While she thumbed idly through it, she thought of all the things she and Spence liked to do, try out new restaurants, dance, play tennis. She always beat him soundly, but he never seemed to mind. They loved to go to ball games, football in the Astrodome and basketball in the Summit.

Jacqui loved basketball. She and Spence seldom missed a pro game. It had been so much fun. It could still be fun. She rummaged through her papers until she found the renewal notice for season's tickets to the Houston Rockets. She made out a check and sealed it in the envelope. Tomorrow, she would call about theater tickets. How was that, old girl, she said smugly, for getting off your backside and doing something? Perhaps she would stop by the travel agency tomorrow and do something about taking that trip to Europe she and Spence had planned.

What was the sense in having Spence's money if she didn't enjoy it. She could tell that sleep would elude her for some time. She was too keyed up, almost as if she really were on the verge of something new. She closed the door quietly and went silently down the stairs, careful not to disturb Rhea.

She looked through Rhea's books, then turned on the television set. She found a marvelous old movie, Bette Davis at her best in Dark Victory. She loved old movies, and she settled herself among the cushions on the settee to give her full attention to the performance.

Just as the movie ended, Jacqui heard a car outside. Peeking through the draperies, she saw Jill standing by the side of a sleek, black Continental. There was a man with her, but Jacqui could not see his face clearly even with the illumination of the gaslight where they were standing. She watched him put his arms around Jill and draw her to him, pressing her body against his by holding her buttocks.

"Careful, little girl," Jacqui whispered. "You might find yourself in over your head."

Jacqui turned off the television set, extinguished the lamp, and went silently up to bed. She closed her door so that Jill would not know that she had been at the window watching.

CHAPTER NINE

Riker's Antique Gallery, just a block off Westheimer, was certainly not what Rhea had in mind when she envisioned herself working in an antique store. It could hardly be called a gallery, and even the word antiques was a misnomer. There were a few pieces of fine furniture, but hardly any that weren't reproductions. She did, however, uncover one good oak parquet table and some solid cherry Queen Anne chairs. There was a fine collection of depression glass, and she had found an interesting Connecticut horse weather vane among the junk.

But, since there was something of the scavenger as well as the artist in Rhea, she poked enthusiastically around the shop, cleaning and rearranging both the poor and the precious. Worth, she realized, was highly personal. It had more to do with one's private sense of beauty than cost.

Giles Riker, the owner of the store, grudgingly acknowledged the improved appearance of the place after Rhea had been there a few weeks, but he was niggardly with money even for cleaning supplies. He was, also, she discovered, not particularly knowledgeable about antiques. Most of the junk was overpriced and the oak table underpriced.

Still a job was a job, and she was grateful to be working, particularly since Riker spent so little time in the shop after her first few days, coming by only to scrutinize the sales slips and check out the cash register.

Even with the rents and her meager salary, Rhea still had to watch expenditures very, very carefully. She hated to think what would happen if an unexpected emergency arose, and she didn't dare let herself think about property taxes and insurance due in a few months. She would need a miracle to hold on to the place she loved so much. But she had been able to handle the huge electric bills so far, and that was an accomplishment.

Jill and Jacqui pitched in with the housework and mowing the lawn. All in all, it had not been such a bad summer. Even some good times, she remembered, and some ridiculous times like the night Jill and Jacqui went skinny dipping in the pool after midnight and had teased and taunted her until she joined them. She would have died of embarrassment if anyone had seen them. How could a plump, middle-aged housewife join in their silly capers? They were young; what was her excuse?

Then she reminded herself that she was no longer a housewife, but a saleslady in a rather shabby shop. Also, she wasn't that plump. She was losing weight, which she attributed to the combination of working so hard and a good diet and the walks she took while Jill and Jacqui jogged.

There were times, and that day was one of them, when she could have killed for a big, juicy hamburger and an order of French fries. Fortunately, she couldn't leave the shop, and the yogurt and fruit she kept in the old refrigerator in the back room seemed to be her only choice for lunch.

Jacqui had been merciless in dragging her off to the health club to exercise. But she was equally generous in her praise. "You're looking great, Rhea. I knew you could do it." And she caught herself looking in the mirror when no one was watching, sucking in her stomach and pulling back her shoulders. She started to take pride in the loose fit of her clothes, realizing that she was gradually beginning to like her life again except for the aching, empty space she would always hold for Carter. Carter—she had only spoken to him once in weeks. He had phoned early one morning just as she was leaving for the shop.

"How are you, Rhea?"

"I'm fine, Carter. And you?"

She knew he wanted to ask how she was managing, what she was doing for money. But he didn't. He didn't know about the job or the rented rooms, and she didn't tell him. They were excessively polite to one another. He seemed reluctant to end the casual conversation. He will come back, she told herself resolutely. It's just a matter of time.

Jacqui sometimes popped in for a few minutes on her way home from the university. Usually, she brought fruit juice or a diet drink, and her visits became welcome respites, especially on slow days of which there were many. Despite the lack of traffic in the store, Rhea was delighted to find that she could sell the merchandise. She was in her element. She honestly believed that a house should be designed to be a refuge from the outside world, as hers was, a thing of beauty to lift one's spirit. Beauty, however, didn't necessarily have to be expensive. She had proved that years ago when she and Carter first bought the old house, leaking roof and all.

Rhea loved driftwood and rocks and old photographs of people she would never know. And her pleasure was evident as she lovingly arranged simple things to create a magical effect from almost nothing. She brought roses from home to grace a chipped porcelain vase and colorful magazines and a basket of sea shells to enhance a bare table. She seemed to possess an uncanny knack for knowing when to let a customer browse and when to press for a sale.

It finally started raining about the middle of August and rained every day somewhere, either at the store or at home, heavy pockets of showers that left most of the city untouched. But the rains were cooling, and she knew that her electric bills would be lower. There was, by the end of the month, a subtle hint of change in the air, perhaps, an early fall, she thought. She would welcome the change.

Suddenly she laughed at the thought. She had never welcomed change. She had always been frightened of change even when she wanted it desperately. Like the night, for example, she had registered for classes at the university near her home.

She had wanted Jill to start school, but when Jacqui brought the schedule home, Jill had hedged. "Maybe later, Aunt Rhea." She was seeing a man repeatedly, and Rhea felt a little uneasy about that. He picked Jill up from work at the Aloha Room. Often it was dawn when she got home. But what could Rhea say? Jill was almost nineteen, and she had started making her own decisions when she left Arkansas.

Prodded by Jacqui, Rhea had registered for two night classes, accounting principles and small business management, even though she considered the expense of the tuition and books an extravagance. But, after working with Riker for a few weeks, she wanted her own store more than ever. As she closed the shop and prepared to leave for class, she was disappointed that Jacqui had not stopped by. She had come to depend on her for encouragement.

She had the distinct feeling of not belonging there as she pulled into the designated student parking. She had not been inside a classroom in twenty years, and she was scared. She tried to slip unnoticed in a seat in the back of the room.

"Mrs. Gregory?"

Astonished at hearing her name, she turned to look at the student in the row next to her. Kevin Stacey, the young man with the sad, serious eyes who had bumped into her car some weeks before.

"Are you taking this class?" he asked in surprise.

She nodded sheepishly, knowing he would think her foolish. She already knew she didn't belong there. The professor entered the room, introduced himself and called the roll from a computer printout. He stumbled over the pronunciation of her name, calling her Rheeah Gregory. She corrected him "Rhea as in ray, r-a-y," she spelled the letters.

"Ah," he said, making a notation on the roll, "a ray of sunlight."

Rhea flushed, knowing that he was making fun of her. She forced herself to listen as he lectured. "Civilization cannot exist without a system of record keeping. Business activities have been recorded on cave walls, on clay tablets, on papyrus, in books, and on computer chips. The earliest known business records date back to almost four thousand years before Christ, the payment of wages in ancient Babylonia, written on clay tablets.

"William the Conqueror compiled records in the eleventh century to establish the financial resources of the British Empire. Double entry bookkeeping as we know it today was begun in Italy in the fifteenth century by a Franciscan monk named Luca Pacioli, who, by the way, was a contemporary of Leonardo da Vinci. The basic elements of the double entry system of debit and credit, which comes from the Latin words, debere and credere, remain virtually unchanged."

Rhea was writing furiously when Kevin touched her hand and pointed to the textbook where he was underlining material with a yellow highlighter. All the information in her notes was in the first chapter of the accounting book. She felt even more foolish.

"I'm surprised to see you here," Kevin said when the class took a break. "You've lost weight, haven't you? You look terrific."

Rhea smiled, pleased that he had noticed. "I'm a little surprised to be here," she admitted. "However, I plan to open an antique store, and it seemed like a good idea. I went to college a long time ago and studied home economics and interior design. I do know antiques, but not very much about running a business."

"I know what you mean," he said. "I studied communications to be a photo-journalist. My father died recently and left me an industrial construction business that I know very little about. So I guess I'm here for the same reason you are. This seemed like a good place to start."

"I'm also taking a management class on Thursday night," Rhea said.

"I'm afraid this accounting is all I can manage."

"I hope I haven't bitten off more than I can chew," she said, laughing.

"I'm sure you haven't. But I'm just getting my feet wet in the construction business, and my mother isn't well. I've been very concerned about her since my father died."

"I'm sorry," Rhea said. "It seems as though you are going through a very difficult period."

"Yes, it has been difficult. The day I hit your car was probably the worst," he told her. "It was the day my father died."

He smiled down at her. "You were very kind to me that day."

He had the same clear blue eyes and golden tanned skin as Jill. And his blond hair was sun streaked in almost the same way. It occurred to her what a beautiful couple Kevin and Jill would make, although, it was obvious that he was older than Jill. She told him that her niece lived with her, and then she found herself confiding the heartache of her divorce to him as he listened sympathetically.

She walked slowly back to class with him and then turned her attention eagerly to the lecture. Assets equal liabilities plus capital. She underlined the equation in her book. Revenues increase capital. Expenses decrease capital.

Rhea knew that Carter was her only hope for capital to start her own business—a slim hope to be sure. She could not put up her house as collateral for a loan. It had, she knew, something to do with the homestead law in Texas. One could not lose a home except for failure to repay the money used to purchase it, and the lender would have no recourse if she were to default on the loan.

When Rhea arrived home from class, Caroline was just leaving for the hospital, Jill was working, and Jacqui had a frozen strawberry daiquiri waiting for her. "Sit down and tell me all about it," she said.

"It wasn't so bad," Rhea confessed. "In fact, it was interesting. And I ran into Kevin Stacey in the class. He's the young man who bumped the rear of my car one day when I was out job hunting. He's very nice, and he sort of took me in tow you might say."

"Good for you. I can tell it went well. Your eyes are shining."

"I am all keyed up," Rhea admitted. "I want to learn everything I can. Oh, Jacqui, I want my own antique shop so much."

"You'll have it," Jacqui said confidently.

"I wish I could be so sure."

"You will," Jacqui repeated. "Believe it."

Rhea slipped off her shoes and settled back on the settee to sip her drink. It really hit the spot. Just as she plucked the fresh strawberry off the top, the telephone rang.

"I'll get it," Jacqui volunteered. "Someone named Jimmy has been calling Jill all day, and she refused to talk to him. That's probably him again."

But Jacqui soon handed the phone to Rhea. "It's for you. Kevin Stacey."

Rhea took the phone perplexed. "I hope I'm not disturbing you," he said. "I just wanted to make sure you got home all right."

"Yes," she replied, averting Jacqui's questioning eyes, "I did. Thank you."

"Then I'll see you in class next week. Goodnight, Rhea."

"Goodnight, Kevin."

"What was that all about?" Jacqui asked.

"Oh, nothing really," Rhea lied, not looking at her. "I left a book in class, and he picked it up for me. Those calls for Jill," she said, changing the subject, "Did Jimmy say what he wanted?"

"No, only that he wanted to talk to her."

"Jimmy is the boy she left Arkansas with," Rhea explained. "When they ran out of money and his van was stolen, Jimmy went back home. My sister Ruth was beside herself when Jimmy came back without Jill. But Jill had found a job at the Aloha Room and had settled in here."

"Has Jill told you much about the guy she's seeing now?"

"No, not really. Only his name which I can't remember. Court somebody or the other. I'm afraid Jill is rather infatuated with him. He seems to throw around an awful lot of money. I guess I would feel much better about it if she brought him home to meet us. I know I sound like a mother hen."

"I caught a glimpse of them the other night," Jacqui said. "He's older, I think—much older than Jill, and she is such a little girl in so many ways. It's a little frightening how she grasps at living. It's almost as if she really believes there will be no tomorrow."

"Don't I know it! But what can I do? Jill isn't my daughter, and I could easily drive her away. She's making enough money now for her own apartment. She's very headstrong. I am worried about her."

"I'll talk to her," Jacqui promised. "Maybe she'll listen to me. She really needs to cool it a little with this Court character."

"Please do talk to her," Rhea begged. "I'm sure she'll listen to you. You have a marvelous ability to always say the right thing."

Jacqui laughed derisively. "Are you kidding? My mouth keeps me in trouble half the time. In case you haven't noticed, tact is not exactly my strong suit. And, as for always saying the right thing, I asked Lady Caroline to have lunch with me today, and she recoiled as if I had suggested we knock over the InterFirst Bank."

"That's strange. I find her reserved but friendly."

"She's hiding something," Jacqui said thoughtfully. "Her lips say one thing, but her eyes say another. How much do you know about her?"

"Not much really, except what she told me when she moved in, that she's a nurse and that she was recently widowed. I did check her employment. Maybe it's just grief. That does make one withdraw."

"No, I think it's more than that. I don't know why, but Caroline Kelly is scared. She almost opens up to you, and then she pulls back into her shell. Have you noticed that every time we all get together even for a casual encounter, a meal or coffee or whatever, that we don't see Caroline again for days? We frighten her somehow."

"You're right," Rhea said, "she does avoid us."

"Except for Jill. She trusts Jill. She opens up to her, but when you or I try to join them, she retreats to her room and shuts the door."

"You have such marvelous insight into people," Rhea said. "It's fascinating when you talk about people. I suppose it's your training. But it kind of scares me to think of what you say about me when I'm not around. You always seem to hit the nail squarely on the head."

"I don't talk about you, Rhea, when you're not around. At least not in any malicious way."

"That's not what I mean. I just think I might be afraid to know how you really see me."

"Well, I'll tell you anyway whether you want to hear it or not. I think you are very much like me."

"Oh, Jacqui, nothing could be further from the truth! You are so sure of yourself."

"It's true I have more confidence in myself than you, but that's a result of experiences and situations I've been thrust into. Yours is just beginning. From what you've told me, your life has been insulated. You let Carter take care of you too much. He protected you from a lot of the more unpleasant things in life, but he kept you from growing too."

"I think I'm just beginning to see that. But I'm growing now. And when Carter and I get back together—"

"Oh, Rhea!" Jacqui cried. "That may never happen. You have to let go of the past."

"I can't."

"You won't. When I said that you were very much like me, that's exactly what I meant. Neither of us can accept the idea that fate will deal us a winning hand again. We don't have to take another chance. You and I can both wallow in our fantasy of how wonderful it was. That way we don't have to risk a new relationship."

"You told me that your relationship with Spence was a once in a lifetime love."

"That's my point exactly. I have been using Spence as a security system, battening down all the hatches against a new involvement. Who knows what might have happen to me if I hadn't moved in here with you? The change made me face reality. I looked at you, Rhea, and it was like looking in a mirror. It's great to have good memories. But I just realized I can't dwell on them for the rest of my life. I've been avoiding reality. Spence is dead, and the last thing he would have wanted for me was to spend my life in perpetual mourning."

"I'm not mourning for Carter, he's still alive."

"At the moment, Rhea, he is as dead to you as Spence is to me."

"You're wrong, Jacqui," she answered with conviction. "Carter will come back to me. I can't face any other kind of future."

Jacqui picked up the empty glasses and took them to the dishwasher. "Goodnight, Rhea," she called as she went upstairs.

Rhea sighed and looked around the room. It needed attention—dusting and vacuuming. But somehow she didn't seem to care as much as she once would have. Then she too went up to bed, to lie in the darkness for a long time before she slept, thinking not of Carter, but of a tanned young man with sun streaked hair and deep blue eyes and a gentle, gentle smile.

CHAPTER TEN

September slipped into October as Rhea spent her days at the shop and her nights studying. She saw little of Jacqui who was making last minute revisions on her thesis and going to basketball games. A somewhat subdued Jill was seeing less of Court Randall whom Rhea still hadn't met. But, at least, now she knew his name. And none of them saw much of Caroline.

Rhea usually got out of bed early on Sunday morning to clean the house, but this morning she had overslept. It was already mid-morning, and she would have to hurry. Kevin Stacey had started dropping by the house on Sunday afternoon to study with her. She slipped into a pair of baggy pants—all of her pants were baggy now that she had lost twenty pounds—and pulled on a knit top. When she got downstairs, Jill was standing at the kitchen counter in a long T-shirt drinking a glass of orange juice.

"Jill, dear, didn't I give you a robe?" Rhea asked.

"Yes, you did. But I detest robes. They're so cumbersome."

"Honestly," Rhea complained as she filled the coffee pot with water. "I don't understand how someone as modest as Ruth could have a daughter as immodest as you."

"Actually, I'm not very much like my mother or my father. I must have been a foundling left on their doorstep."

"You weren't, believe me. I saw Ruth pregnant. She was as big as a house."

"You saw her! I always assumed she hid in a closet for nine months."

"What a thing to say!"

"My mother could never bring herself to say the word 'pregnant'. She never said the word 'sex' either. How could she do it if she couldn't even say it?"

"Say, what?" Jacqui asked, appearing at the door.

"Don't ask," Rhea advised.

"We were talking about mothers," Jill said. "Do you have one?"

"I did," Jacqui replied indignantly. "What do you think—somebody found me under a rock?"

"No, actually, I thought in a locker room," Jill said, laughing. "What else could explain your addiction to watching sweaty bodies run up and down a basketball court every chance you get?"

"But they're such gorgeous sweaty bodies," Jacqui protested.

"Enough of this nonsense," Rhea said. "I'm going out to cut my roses. Call me when the coffee's ready."

"If you can't take the heat, get out of the kitchen," Jill called after her.

"Don't be so hard on her," Jacqui admonished. "She's come a long way in the short time I've known her."

"She's still got a long way to go," Jill replied. "Did she tell you that Uncle Carter is the only man she ever slept with in her whole life?"

Jacqui was tempted to ask Jill how many men she had slept with but thought better of it. Instead, she said lightly, "When Rhea makes a commitment, she really makes a commitment."

"I don't mean to make loyalty sound like a vice," Jill replied. "Who knows where I would be if she hadn't taken me in? I love this old house. It's so great living here. You should see the place I grew up in. I just hate to see her waste the rest of her life. Uncle Carter came into the club about a week ago. I probably wouldn't have recognized him if he hadn't paid for his drinks with a credit card. I didn't tell her, but he was awfully surprised when I told him who I was and that I was living with Aunt Rhea. We talked for a while. He's really a nice person, and you wouldn't believe how handsome. But I definitely got the feeling that he isn't coming back. It's over for him, Jacqui, and sooner or later, she's going to have to face that."

"I suspected it, but I don't believe Rhea is as unhappy as you think. Look at her. She looks ten years younger. She loves working and going to school. She may discover that there's a whole world out there yet."

"Fat chance."

Rhea came through the back door with her arms full of roses. "Were you talking about me?" she asked. "I heard someone say fat."

"Fat doesn't apply to you any longer," Jacqui said quickly. "Remember the day you kept telling me you were fat and forty-two until I wanted to shake you?"

"And you said I could be slimmer if I wanted to and, Jacqui, you were right. All it took was months of starvation and absolute agony on the exercise machines."

"But it was worth it!" Jill exclaimed. "Just look how trim and gorgeous you are."

"Trim and gorgeous," Rhea repeated in a sing-song voice and began to waltz around the kitchen with the roses in her arms. Abruptly, she stopped.

"Can you believe this?" she gasped. "I'm as loony as you two."

"Not yet," Jacqui replied with a grin. "But maybe there's hope for you after all."

"You're right," Rhea agreed with a straight face. "And I know I'm not gorgeous yet, I have to lose another ten pounds. But I'm still forty-two. I haven't been able to do anything about that."

They all laughed. And, as Rhea put the roses in water, Jill and Jacqui served the coffee with warm croissants. Later Jacqui volunteered to clean and wax the kitchen floor while Rhea was scrubbing the downstairs bathroom. Jill went out to clean around the pool and mow the front lawn, and Caroline surprised them all by sweeping down the stairs in a long, ice blue caftan to dust and polish all the downstairs furniture.

In a few hours the charming old house was wearing its customary gleam with the rugs and carpets vacuumed, the lawn mowed and edged, the beds all made, and fresh towels in the clean bathrooms. Caroline went up to nap, Jill left with a friend to see a movie, and Jacqui was off to a bar-be-cue at a friend's house in West University.

Rhea showered and changed clothes four times trying to find something that fit well enough to wear. Sometime soon she would have make alterations to her wardrobe. It had seemed like a waste of time to do it until she finished losing weight. Thank goodness, she hadn't thrown away her clothes when she gained all that weight since she couldn't afford to buy anything new. At length she found a dress that she felt comfortable in, a burnt orange knit with a flared skirt and v-neck. She added gold jewelry and brushed her hair into soft swirls around her face.

Kevin arrived on schedule, but Rhea was surprised that he hadn't brought his accounting books. "I want you to take a drive with me," he said. "My father left me a house on Lake Conroe. I'm going to sell it, but I think I may have some valuable pieces of furniture. I need someone I trust to look at it. Perhaps, you could sell the furniture for me when you open your shop. Will you come?"

How could she refuse? "Of course, I will," she replied. She was excited by the prospect. Her own shop! It seemed closer to becoming a reality.

"I learned about this place through my father's lawyer," Kevin explained. "In fact, I learned a great deal about my father after he died. Not all of it pleasant."

"I'm sorry," she said. "It's the people we love the most who have the greatest potential to disappoint us."

"Rhea, sometimes I feel as if I never knew him—my own father!"

"I understand. Sometimes I feel that way about Carter, as if I never knew him, and yet I was married to him for twenty years."

He reached over and squeezed her hand for a moment. She smiled at him realizing that she had never had a man for a friend before. Carter was her husband, her lover—but not really ever her friend. Strangely, it had taken her all this time to become aware of the difference. It was a disturbing thought. But, when Carter returned this time, it would be different. She was sure.

They drove for more than an hour before they reached his house in a grove of trees on a bluff overlooking the water. It was a lovely old place—not large, but beautifully restored.

"It's a wonderful house, Kevin."

"Yes, it is. I didn't even know my dad had this place until he died," he said bitterly. "There was evidence he used it a great deal—and not just alone."

"Don't judge him too harshly. Maybe it fulfilled some kind of a need in him."

"I wouldn't expect that from you," he said startled.

"Oh," she said, sighing, "I've been thinking a great deal about my situation—why Carter really left me—about my life and marriage. Evidently, he needed something I couldn't give him."

"I can't imagine any man needing more than you could give

him," Kevin said. "At least he was honest enough to tell you. My dad went right on being married to my mother. He preferred to sneak around."

"What purpose would it have served if he had torn your mother's life apart? Perhaps, he chose the more difficult path. Have you thought about how your mother would have handled a divorce?"

"She couldn't have handled it. It would have killed her. She hasn't been in good health for years. I was only twelve when she had her first stroke."

"Do you think she ever suspected him?"

"I've thought about that. They say a woman can always tell. But I'm not sure she did. Dad always had this incredible amount of energy. Mother laughed and said that she could never keep up with him even when they were young together. There was always a vast area of his life that she never shared. We always supposed that he channeled all that energy solely into his business. But apparently he didn't."

The bitterness had edged back into his voice, and Rhea wondered if, in reality, Kevin had resented his father's freedom. Kevin had told her that he had gone to New York to work on the staff of a magazine when he graduated from college, but that his mother's health had deteriorated so badly that she had begged him to return.

Kevin's father traveled a great deal as an industrial contractor. Perhaps Kevin had not been entirely happy with the role of caretaker and confidant to his mother that his father's absence necessitated. Maybe he still felt trapped in a way he couldn't acknowledge even to himself. She studied him as he unlocked the door, opened draperies, and flipped on the air-conditioning to remove the stuffiness in the house.

Rhea went from room to room enchanted as a child. The house had been decorated by someone with exquisite taste. There was a massive fireplace in the living room flanked by Northhampton wingback chairs with claw and ball feet. The walls had been painted a spectacular shade of teal and set off with white glazed woodwork. The rooms were filled with a variety of decorative objects from all over the world, paintings, photographs, books, porcelain. She loved it. There wasn't much she would have changed, if anything.

"Why would you want to sell any of this?" Rhea exclaimed.

"It's beautiful, and it all belongs here. Kevin, you should keep it!"

"Oh, Rhea," he said, sighing in mock exasperation. "I can see that you aren't going to be very successful as a business woman. What are they teaching you in that management class? To talk yourself out of a commission?"

She laughed. "I guess I am pretty hopeless. But you said you wanted the opinion of someone you could trust. Yes, you do have some valuable antiques here and some very fine reproductions. I can't imagine why you want to sell everything."

"Because I don't feel right in this house. I feel like an intruder. If the truth were known, there's probably a lady somewhere who should have inherited this house instead of me."

"If your father hadn't wanted you to have it, he wouldn't have left it to you."

"It's almost as if he wanted me to know about the other side of his life—as if he were flaunting it. I know he was disappointed in me. He wanted me to be an industrial engineer—to be interested in the same things he was. But I couldn't. It's almost as if he were showing me that my mother and I didn't matter to him. He had something better."

"I'm sure that isn't true, Kevin. Maybe he thought that sometime you would need a place to get away from everything. Help me pull this armoire away from the wall so I can look at the back."

Rhea examined all the furniture carefully, listing it, and making notes. When she came to the master bedroom, she found one entire wall of photographs, some of them signed with a tiny Stacey in the right corner of the mat.

"Kevin," she exclaimed, "you took these!"

"Yes," he replied. "Another paradox of the mystery man who was my father. He violently opposed my choice of a profession. He never once acknowledged that I had done anything worthwhile in my work, and after his death, I find his love nest feathered with my photos. I wasn't even aware that he had them."

Rhea noticed that the bitterness had crept back into his voice. "Don't judge him too harshly, Kevin," she said gently. "He must have admired your work, and he must have cared about you, or all these photographs wouldn't be here."

"Then why didn't he ever tell me?"

"Perhaps, he did—in the only way he could."

"Did anyone ever tell you," he asked suddenly placing his

hands on her shoulder, "that you are a very wise and compassionate lady as well as a beautiful one."

Rhea didn't know what to say. Impulsively she kissed him lightly on the cheek but immediately regretted it as he pulled her close. She extricated herself and turned away from him, picking up her list of furnishings. "I need to research some of these pieces," she added quickly. "But I can give you an estimate of market value in a few days."

"Take all the time you need. I'm in no hurry. And I really appreciate your doing this, Rhea."

"Thank you for letting me see your house. I love old houses and looking at furniture. But I really think you should reconsider selling anything. In time you may feel differently about it."

"No," he said decisively. "I want to acquire my own things—furniture and art that suits my lifestyle and tastes. I want to live my own life, but before we go, I want to show you the lake. There is a wonderful view from the dock."

Rhea acquiesced. Years ago Carter had talked of buying lake property for weekend retreats. But there never seemed to be enough money. It all went into the house, and he had stopped talking about it. She wished she had enough money to buy this place for Carter. It would be perfect.

Kevin picked up a camera as they started out. She supposed it was second nature to him to want to photograph a lovely view. But when they came to the dock, it was evident that Kevin wanted to photograph her. She didn't know how to decline tactfully. She was suddenly shy, and she hoped he would tire of it soon. She leaned back against a tree at the water's edge.

"Wonderful," he said. "Turn your head a little more toward the lake. Super."

"My goodness, Kevin," she finally protested. "That's enough."

He didn't stop, however, until he had finished the whole role of film.

They were both silent on the way home. Rhea would have liked to regain the easy companionship they had enjoyed earlier, but she didn't know how. When they got back to her house, it was well past dark, and she wondered how the afternoon has passed so quickly. Jacqui was waiting for them downstairs.

"Someone called for you, Kevin," she said, "and left a message."

"Anya," Kevin replied knowingly.

"Yes, that's right. She said—"

"I know what she said," Kevin interrupted. "I'm needed home immediately."

"Something like that."

Kevin turned to Rhea. His look was one of patient resignation. "I have to go," he said almost wearily. "Anya is my mother's nurse. Goodnight, Rhea. I'll see you in class tomorrow night."

Rhea walked him to the door. "I hope it's nothing serious," she said.

"Probably not," he replied.

"What do you think of him?", she asked Jacqui later.

"I don't know—seems nice. Did you have a good afternoon?"

"Very good. I'm disappointed though that he had to leave before Jill got home. I wanted Kevin to meet her."

"Why?"

"Why? " Rhea repeated, puzzled. "I think they would be perfect for one another. Jill needs to meet some nice boys."

"Kevin isn't exactly a nice boy. He must be in his thirties. Besides, it doesn't matter. He only has eyes for you."

"Me? Don't be ridiculous. We're just friends—classmates. I'm years older than he is."

"That man," Jacqui said, "or boy or whatever you want to call him, has a terrific crush on you. It's written all over him. Open your eyes, Rhea."

"For your information, my eyes are open," Rhea said tartly and went up to her bedroom.

Jacqui had been home only a few minutes herself, and she followed Rhea up to bed. It had been a very good day for her too—surprisingly so. The atmosphere at an ordinary backyard bar-be-que with friends from college became electrified when a tall, tanned athletic man with silver hair and piercing blue eyes arrived. Jacqui's heart almost stopped.

For one marvelous, awful moment, she thought he was Spence. His eyes met hers and held them despite the fact that a very blond, very young girl was clinging tightly to his arm. Introductions were made. She was too stunned to really hear them, and, afterwards, all she could remember was that his name was Craig, and she had no recollection whatsoever of the girl's name.

Somehow the conversation turned to basketball. Someone

mentioned that Jacqui was a "sneaker freak." He liked basketball, too. They talked about the Houston Rockets and about draft choices and the team's prospects for the coming year. And Jacqui remembered that at some point the blond girl let go of his arm and drifted away bored. He hardly seemed to notice.

"Do you go often to Rocket games?" he asked her.

"Almost every home game," she replied. "My seat is in section 120, right behind the bench."

"Good," he said. "I'll see you there."

As Jacqui undressed and brushed her hair, she caught a glimpse of herself in the mirror. She was smiling. She couldn't remember how long it had been since she felt so good. "Idiot," she chided herself, "an attractive man pays you a little attention and you go off in orbit somewhere."

God, it had been such a little while since Spence died. And she didn't know anything about the man. Hardly his name. Craig, that was all. And he liked basketball. But he had those same mischievous, dancing eyes that Spence had, and that same roguish smile, and that same wonderful aliveness.

"Oh Spence!" She picked up a pillow and hugged it to her breast. "I'll never love anybody else. I swear it."

CHAPTER ELEVEN

Jacqui found herself waiting eagerly for the next home game. She left early, parked in the lower level of the garage and was waiting outside the Summit when they unlocked the doors. She went down to watch the teams practice, standing for a while behind each bench. There was no sign of Craig. By tip-off, she was so engrossed in the game that she forgot everything else. It was an exciting, close game—the crowd was enthusiastic, the officiating good. She loved it.

During halftime, she stood in line for a tall, cold beer and nachos sprinkled liberally with jalapenos. She looked for him, but he was not there. And when the game was over, Jacqui remained in her seat for a time, scanning the departing crowd. Still no sign of him. She sighed. It was just as well.

Then she moved down to the right front court section to listen to the visiting media conduct post-game interviews. The Rockets had lost; they only conducted post-game interviews when they won. No sense in rushing out, she thought, imagining the crowds in the outer lobby pushing for the escalator. No point in sitting in her car behind a line of other cars trying to leave the Summit garage. She scarcely heard what was being said in the interview.

Then there he was! Craig. He was inching his way toward her. His eyes were on her. He was alone, and he was smiling. She returned the smile.

"Hi, Jacqui," he said, easing himself into the empty seat beside her.

"Hi Craig."

"Greg," he corrected her. The interview was still going on, and when he leaned over close to talk to her, she caught the scent of him. It reminded her of deep woods and green mosses with a subtle hint of something exotic. An involuntary shiver of anticipation went through her. She liked being close to him.

"I missed the whole first half," he said. "I've been to Austin today and got back late. Then I was waylaid by a client on my way over to you. Did you enjoy the game even if we didn't win?"

"I always enjoy the game."

"Me, too, by golly. How would you like to go up to the top of the world and have a drink?"

"Where is the top of the world?" she asked and wondered why she bothered. She would have gone anywhere.

"You know, up there in the hotel—the one connected to the garage.

"In Stouffers? They call that the City Lights"

"I like the top of the world better. It feels like the top of the world to me. Well, how about it?"

"Why not?"

"Why not, indeed?"

"We had better hurry if we want a table," Jacqui suggested.

They walked out into the outer lobby, past the display cases where the Rocket paraphernalia, T-shirts, pennants, buttons, books, were being packed up. Empty cups and paper and cigarette butts littered the floor. The concession stands had been closed, and the rest rooms locked.

"It's all over but the crying," Jacqui said.

"Please don't cry," he responded. "I have a better idea. We'll drown our sorrows instead."

"Now there's a man after my own heart."

"That's what I'm after," he admitted. "Lucky for me, it's encased in such a beautiful body."

"I love your approach," she began, "but—"

"Oh no," he said, groaning, "don't tell me you want to see my departure. I humbly apologize. I'm abjectly sorry to have been so crude. I—"

"That will do," Jacqui interrupted. "Besides, I rather like your body too."

He stopped in surprise and looked at her. She was laughing.

"I have a feeling," he said, "that I'm not ever going to know when you are serious."

"I'll tell you," she promised, "when you need to know. Let's take the stairs instead of the elevator. I always take the stairs when I can. I've been led to believe that it's better for you."

"Oh, no," he pleaded. "The top of the world is twenty stories up."

"Relax, we'll take the glass elevator. It can't be that good for you."

They walked outside the Edloe Street entrance to the Summit, crossed the alley, walking through the upper level of the parking garage where green stripes painted on the support posts marked the entrance to Stouffer's Greenway Plaza Hotel.

"We'll never get a table," Greg grumbled, eyeing the crowd in front of the elevator.

"Stay close to me, and I'll show you how it's done."

When the elevator arrived, Jacqui squeezed herself in, refusing to be pushed from her spot in front of the elevator doors. Everyone else was maneuvering for a position in front of the glass panel at the back of the elevator.

"We're missing the view," Greg said as the elevator crawled slowly up the outside of the building, rising over the fountain in the square below.

"You can always look up," Jacqui pointed to the mirror on the ceiling of the elevator.

"And look at all the bald heads," a man standing close to her suggested ruefully. He possessed one. Jacqui looked at Greg's full, silver hair, his tanned, unlined face, his muscular build, his easy smile. She definitely liked the view.

The elevator arrived on the top floor. The doors opened, and Jacqui dashed off. When Greg caught up with her, she was at the front of the line waiting to be seated.

"That," she explained, "is called a fast break off the elevator."

"I was told you know everything about basketball. I'm beginning to believe you know everything about everything."

"Does that intimidate you?"

"It fascinates me."

They were seated at a table for two by the window.

"It's beautiful," Jacqui said, looking out at the myriad of city lights along the Southwest Freeway. "You were right. It is the top of the world."

"We should have something to celebrate."

"We didn't win," she reminded him.

"Correction. The Rockets didn't win. But I think we did. Do you like champagne?"

"I love champagne. Careful, Greg, I think you're going to dazzle me."

"I think," he said slowly, "that it takes rather a lot to dazzle you. Jacqui, are you married?"

"No, I'm not."

"I'm not either."

"I didn't ask."

"Why not?"

"I don't care. I'm not interested in marriage. Not now. Not ever."

"Once burned, twice shy?"

"No, actually, I've never been married."

"Then I don't understand. You're young, and you've never been married, yet you are totally opposed to it. I was married for twenty years. My wife was sweet and pretty, but I never loved her. Not really. Oh, I had been infatuated with her when we were in college, but I discovered that she was all surface—no depth. I woke up one morning and realized that my life was probably two thirds over. I'm forty-three years old, and I just couldn't face another twenty years of what we had. I know I hurt her. She fought the divorce to the bitter end. But I couldn't help it. I hated myself for what I was doing to her, but I had to get out. I needed something more than she could give me."

"You don't have to explain to me, Greg."

"I want to. I guess I just keep hoping I will run into somebody who understands. Everybody I know has written me off as the Bastard of the Year."

"I can't condemn you for getting out of a marriage that didn't make you happy, if you didn't divorce your kids, too."

"I didn't have any kids. If I had, I probably never would have made the final break. It was tough enough as it was."

The champagne arrived. Greg took a sip and pronounced it excellent.

"Just the thing to chase beer and nachos," Jacqui laughed.

"A woman after my own heart," he replied.

"Good thing it's encased in such a gorgeous body," she said. They both laughed and clicked their champagne glasses together.

"How did you get so interested in basketball?" he asked.

"It wasn't the way you think! I've always loved sports, playing and watching."

"How do you know what I think?"

"You are thinking," she said, "that I first got interested in a player—or a coach. But that wasn't it. I was always interested in sports. In fact, I was a physical education major in college. And I literally got dragged to my first pro game by a group of friends. I got totally caught up in it. The action was fast. It was exciting. You can easily recognize the players. They don't have all that protective gear that football players wear. I quickly got to the point where I knew individual players from their appearance and style without having to watch the numbers. I liked it so much the first time, I was eager to go again. And one of my friends took it upon himself to teach me all the finer points of the game—in a thoroughly condescending manner, of course, which I resented like hell. I mean it wasn't as if I were a rank amateur. I had played and coached girls basketball. But that didn't count for anything. So I decided that when the season was over I would know more than he knew.

"I checked out every book the library had on basketball. I started reading the sports pages in the newspapers. I memorized statistics. I went at it like I was studying for the most important exam in my life. I could name all the teams in the N.B.A., their histories, their coaches, their principal players, how each one was acquired. Before each game, I studied the statistics and the pictures of each player on the visiting team. Then I discovered that most people, outside the business itself, including the most fanatical of fans, had such a superficial knowledge of the sport that I had begun to sound like an authority."

"I like your style, lady," he said. "Let's dance. It will give me a legitimate reason to put my arms around you." They danced in the tiny space near the piano, talked and finished the bottle of champagne, then talked and danced again until the last call for drinks was past, and the bright lights came on, signaling that the club was closing.

Jacqui was reluctant for the evening to end. Apparently, Greg was, too, for he suggested breakfast. "I got to the game late, so my car is blocks away. I'll walk you to your car, then you can drive me to mine and follow me to the restaurant."

This time as the glass elevator descended slowly toward the blue-lighted fountain below, Jacqui stood at the glass panel and looked out. Greg stood behind her with his hands on her shoulders. She felt good in a way that she had not felt since Spence died.

Momentarily, the thought of him made her feel guilty. All evening long she had thought of Greg solely, not one thought of Spence.

"A penny for your thoughts," Greg offered.

"How dare you offer me such a paltry sum?" she demanded. "Do I look cheap?"

"Uh," he stuttered, sidestepping her question. "Can we negotiate."

"Of course, compromise is the American way."

"What did you have in mind?"

"Oh, let's see, how about a million dollars?"

"That's compatible with the way you look," he said smoothly. "And you know how to negotiate all right. But I'm afraid you're out of my league. Where's your car?"

"Right here. This little red job. How do you like riding with your knees up under your chin?"

"I would rather drive with my knees under my chin," he said, folding himself into the driver's seat as she moved awkwardly to the other side.

He drove out of the garage onto the service road, turned at Edloe and again on Richmond. He found his car easily, a sand-colored Cadillac. It was almost the only one in the garage.

He handed her his keys. "Follow me."

"Wouldn't it be simpler if you just told me where we are going?" she asked getting out of the car.

"Trust me."

Jacqui gave him a withering stare, standing stiffly beside his car.

He laughed, put her little red car in gear and shot up the ramp out of the parking garage. She had no alternative but to follow quickly. It was funny—really—she decided. Here she was behind the wheel of a brand new Cadillac; so new, in fact, she could smell the newness, following a man she hardly knew. Craig-Greg—whoever? She didn't know where they were headed. They had talked for hours, but she did not know where he lived, or what he did for a living.

She wonder how long it would take him to find her if she turned around, drove straight to Rhea's, parked his car in the drive, and went up to bed.

They were headed west on Richmond. He was driving fast but skillfully. She stayed close behind. Then he made a right turn, cutting over to Westheimer. As they continued past the Galleria, she noted that there were dozens of restaurants along the street, but most of them appeared to be closed. Then, abruptly, he made another right turn, past office buildings and apartments, onto a a tree-lined street to a row of townhouses with manicured lawns and softy-lighted courtyards. They had to be expensive so close to the Galleria.

"I should have known," Jacqui began as Greg parked and approached her.

"The kitchen," he said with a grin, "is always open."

"I don't cook," she replied sarcastically.

"Fortunately, I do. It's only one of my many talents."

He opened the door, and she allowed him to usher her into a small entry way made larger by mirrored walls. Lush green plants filled all the space except for a narrow walkway into the living room which was dominated by a baby grand piano.

"Another one of your talents?" she asked.

"A minor one," he replied.

Jacqui looked around the interesting room. Above the fireplace was a massive oil painting of a fog enshrouded suspension bridge that reflected shades of blue and grey from the decor of the room. The whole wall behind the piano was lined with bookcases and, in one sweeping glance, she scanned titles of literature and philosophy that she recognized. It was a room in which she could feel entirely comfortable. Soft music was playing on the stereo, and he asked her if she wanted a drink.

She shook her head. "You promised me breakfast," she reminded him.

"So I did," he said. "Is there anything in particular that you would like?"

"No, I always leave that to the cook's discretion."

"Good of you. Is there anything in particular that you would not like?"

"No," she replied. "I'm very easy to please—when it comes to breakfast," she added after a pause.

"I'm glad you said that," he said, laughing, as he placed thick slices of ham in a skillet. "For a moment I thought my ego was in for another shattering blow."

"Another? When was the first?"

"When you didn't even remember my name. You called me Craig, remember?"

"Sorry. Apparently, I didn't hear it correctly. But your ego appears in remarkable good condition to me. Who was the girl with you at the bar-be-que?"

"I don't remember. I only had eyes for you."

"Liar!"

He grinned that wonderful mischievous grin and continued breaking eggs into a bowl. In a matter of minutes, he served her a heaping plate of fluffy, scrambled eggs, thick slices of ham, and buttered toast.

"You really can cook," she acknowledged with mock seriousness. "I've been searching all my life for an attractive man who could cook."

"And I've been searching all my life for a beautiful woman who really understands sports. So where do we go from here?"

"We could go to San Francisco," she suggested.

"What made you say that?" he asked, suddenly serious.

"I don't know. Silliness, I guess. I've never been to San Francisco. Your painting in the living room, I suppose. Why?"

"Odd coincidence is all," he said. "I'm actually planning a trip to San Francisco. I know we're on the same wave length, beautiful lady, but I don't want you reading my thoughts."

"And why not?" she asked.

"Some of them are X-rated." he admitted, leaning over to kiss her and nibble on her ear.

Jacqui rose from the table. She felt strangely high—the champagne, she supposed. His arms encircled her and drew her close. She felt the pressure of his muscular body against hers. She felt desire building within her. He kissed her again, more urgently. Her arms went around his neck. She reached up to touch his silver hair. It was softer than she expected and curled around her finger. She found herself kissing him with the same urgency. Then he gently released her and led her to a loveseat near the piano where he sat down to play a familiar melody. She recognized it immediately. *As Time Goes By* from CasaBlanca.

"I love old movies," she told him, and he replied that he did, too.

But she was perplexed as he continued to play. Didn't he want to make love to her? Then it was he who picked up her thoughts.

"I want to make love to you," he said, "but that isn't all I want. I know this is the beginning of something special. You know that too, don't you?"

"Yes," she said softly.

He continued playing for a few minutes, and then came over to sit beside her. He took her hand and raised it to his lips, kissing her fingertips. "I want to know everything about you," he said.

"Just remember that you asked for it," she began. "I was born Jacquiline Wilder, twenty-eight years ago in Dallas. I'm in reasonably good health and very well-educated. I'll soon have a doctorate in psychology to prove it. I've just finished my dissertation. Are you sure you want to hear more?"

"Absolutely."

"My undergraduate work was in physical education with a minor in psychology. I taught and coached girls basketball for a couple of years. When I went to grad school to work on a master's, my advisers steered me into psychology because of my G.R.E. scores and my grade point average."

"What did you write your thesis on?"

"How women who were physically and sexually abused as children coped with the experience. I came to some conclusions about what factors contributed to their recovery or, conversely, lack of recovery."

"Will you let me read it sometime?"

"That could be arranged."

"Now what else significant about Jacquiline Wilder should I know?"

"I am an orphan, and since I am an only child, there is no protective relative to come after you with a shotgun."

"That's a relief."

"Currently, I'm living in a restored old mansion in Montrose that belongs to a marvelous lady by the name of Rhea Gregory."

His head jerked back abruptly. She saw the stunned look on his face. "You really don't know who I am," he said strangely.

"You're Greg," Jacqui said in puzzlement, pressing her face against his neck. "And you're wonderful," she murmured, "but you're right, I don't know your last name."

"Jacqui," he said, looking into her eyes with a stricken expression. "I'm Carter Gregory. Rhea is my ex-wife."

"Rhea is my best friend," Jacqui said in astonishment. "If I had known you were Carter Gregory, this would never have happened."

"Oh, I see," he said. "Now you're going to give me my Bastard Of The Year award."

"Oh, Carter," she cried. "It's not like that. It has nothing to do with you. I mean it's simply that you are Rhea's husband."

"Former husband. And the name is Greg. Only Rhea calls me Carter. She started it when we were in college."

"But she's still in love with you. She's convinced that you two will get back together again—that this divorce is only a temporary separation."

"That will never happen. I don't love Rhea; I'm not sure I ever did. She doesn't love me. She loves a way of life. Believe me, Jacqui, it's all over. I haven't felt the way I feel with you tonight in years. No, I take that back. I've never felt the way I feel with you."

She was shaking her head in protest. "I won't do this to Rhea. She's just beginning to get her head together. I can't. Forgive me, Carter—Greg—whoever the hell you are."

Jacqui was crying. She made no effort to hide her tears.

"I was wrong," Greg said sadly. "I do know when you're serious."

CHAPTER TWELVE

Jacqui spent most of the day in bed. How could she have been so stupid? she asked herself over and over again. To let it go so far without even knowing his name. But she would get over it in a few days. She would simply forget him. If she could give up Spence, she could give up anybody. All she needed was a little time.

Then she felt even more miserable when Rhea came home from work. Thinking Jacqui was ill, she brought up a bowl of chicken soup and a cup of tea on a silver tray with a perfect red rose in a little crystal vase. The sight of the rose brought tears to Jacqui's eyes and concern to Rhea's.

"Really, I'll be all right tomorrow," Jacqui assured her. And she was—if getting out of bed and dressing and going about her normal routine could be termed all right. She entrusted her completed thesis to a word processing service with an enormous sense of relief. She would submit it, defend it, and ultimately have her doctorate conferred. Dr. Jacquiline Wilder. Then what? She didn't know. The money Spence had left gave her many alternatives.

"Oh, Spence," she said over and over again, but her thoughts were not wholly on Spence who was dead but on Carter Gregory with his silver hair and boyish grin, who cooked and played piano and loved basketball. She wondered if he was hurting in the same way she was. No, of course not.

Late in the afternoon she stopped by a little bar not far from the university that many of her friends from school were known to frequent. She ordered a glass of white wine and nibbled on some cheese and crackers, but no one she knew showed up. It was just as well.

When she arrived home she was surprised to find Rhea's car in the drive. It was early for her to be home from work. Something must be wrong. Jacqui hurried inside. Rhea sat at the kitchen table literally attacking a huge plate of food, a china platter heaped with mounds of potato salad, baked beans, thick slices of ham and cheese, and big hunks of fresh bread.

"What are you doing?" Jacqui demanded. "What about your diet?"

"Who gives a damn? I'm tired of being hungry. I'm tired of exercising. I'm tired of everything. I'm even tired of being tired."

Jacqui could see that she was very close to tears. "Rhea, what happened?"

"Nothing happened, dammit. Nothing happened."

Suddenly she pushed the platter aside, put her head down and began to sob. Jacqui put her arms around Rhea's shoulders without saying anything, and let her cry for several minutes. Then she handed her a box of tissues.

"Now tell me what happened," she said firmly.

"That son-of-a-bitch Riker fired me."

"Fired you! For what?"

"There was a customer who came into the store from time to time. I sold her all the really good pieces Riker had. She bought an oak table with a parquet top and some other things."

"Go on."

"She came in today and mentioned that she was looking for a breakfront. We didn't have one, so I told her about the one I have here in the dining room, the mahogany breakfront secretaire bookcase from the late Chippendale period."

"That massive piece."

"Yes, it's ten by ten and two feet wide. It's beautiful, but I always thought it was too much for that room. And I'd like to replace it with something else. I offered to show it to her, and she said it sounded like just what she was looking for."

"What happened with Riker?"

"He made a scene. She left embarrassed. He told me that he wasn't paying me to sell antiques in competition with him, and that I could just go and sabotage someone else's business."

"Stop crying," Jacqui commanded. "It was time for you to

leave there anyway. Haven't you learned everything from Riker that you could?"

"I knew more than Riker the day I went to work for him."

"Which proves my point."

"But what am I going to do now?" she wailed.

"You'll never figure that out as long as you sit there weeping over that mountain of food. Where did all this come from anyway?"

"I stopped at the deli," Rhea said meekly. "Oh, Jacqui, what am I going to do? I needed the money I made there."

"Right now you are going to wrap up that food and put it away. It will feed all of us for a week. I'm going to ice down a bottle of wine. Then, we'll put on our bathing suits and go out to the pool. It's nice out there, and we may not have many days like this left. We won't even think about our problems tonight, and tomorrow they won't seem so bad. I promise you. Trust me."

"I've lost my job. I've lost my husband, and I'm probably going to lose this house," Rhea moaned. "And you tell me things won't look as bad tomorrow."

"There are other jobs, other men, and other houses, if it comes to that," Jacqui said quietly.

"You just don't understand, do you?"

"You're right—in a way, Rhea. I can't understand why this house is synonymous with life to you, and why you cling to the idea of a marriage that doesn't exist any longer. Despite that, I grant you the right to your feelings. I know that you can't understand how free I feel without possessions to tie me down. I don't have anything I couldn't dispose of in a day."

"I couldn't live like that," Rhea said flatly. "I need roots. I couldn't exist without this to hold on to."

"Who knows?" Jacqui said. "In time I may become more like you and you like me. Which wine would you prefer? There's a Gamay Beaujolais and a Pinot Noir."

"I don't care. You choose. You know how lousy I am at decision making."

After they had taken a leisurely dip in the small pool, Rhea lay back in a lounge chair sipping her glass of red wine. Jacqui was right. It wasn't even tomorrow, and she did feel better. Jacqui always made her feel better. If she were more like Jacqui, she thought, she would just go out and find a better job. Maybe she would. Kevin wanted her to sell his furniture for him. "I've half a mind to turn part of this house into a shop," she thought, and did not realize that she had spoken it aloud.

"What a perfect idea!" Jacqui exclaimed. "Why didn't we think of it sooner?"

"I could clear out Carter's study," Rhea said tentatively, "and the sitting room and the entry hall inside the front door. The shelves in the study would be perfect for small art objects. I could clean out the attic; I have a number of old pieces I could sell. Later I could turn the attic into a bargain room. I could start with Kevin's furniture. If only I had a few thousand dollars. Carter will just have to give it to me. He will just have to. I'll go to see him the first thing in the morning."

"You won't have to ask him, Rhea," Jacqui said quietly. "I'll lend you the money."

"You'll lend it to me!" It was more of an exclamation than a question.

"Yes, you must have wondered how I manage to live the way I do. I drive a new sports car, go to school, dress well, spend whatever I wish. You must have wondered about that."

"Yes," Rhea admitted. "I did."

"Spence was very well off financially. He left me a rather large sum of money when he died. I can afford it."

"Oh, Jacqui." Rhea's eyes were sparkling. "It would only be a loan. I know I can do it."

"I know you can, too," Jacqui said, and she sat by the pool finishing the wine long after Rhea had gone inside. It isn't guilt money, she told herself. She would have done it even if she had never met Carter Gregory. Rhea was her friend.

And, over the next few weeks, Jacqui knew her trust had not been misplaced. Rhea threw herself wholeheartedly into the business of opening an antique shop. A sign in the shape of an artist's palette went up in the front yard. RHEA ROBERTS GREGORY Antiques and Fine Furniture Objects d'Art Open Daily 10:00-6:00 (Except Sunday).

Rhea applied for a Texas sales tax resale certificate, a federal reporting number, had sales tickets and business cards printed. She spent a week in Dallas visiting wholesale showrooms and making purchases, small items that she knew would move quickly. From her attic she brought down a solid cherry Queen Anne table that had originally come with the house. An unusual brass lamp and silver candelabra were sent out to be electroplated. She worked eighteen-hour days, woke up refreshed and ready to begin again. Jacqui and Jill marvelled at her enthusiasm and energy.

Kevin seemed to be around almost every day, making himself useful in a thousand ways. He loaned Rhea a truck from his construction company each time she needed one and produced laborers to help her move furniture, all for which he would accept no compensation.

Rhea planned an open house to celebrate the opening of the shop. She telephoned all her friends and acquaintances, people she had avoided since her divorce, to invite them over on Sunday afternoon. Jacqui passed out invitations among the faculty and staff at the university. Jill pitched in to help enthusiastically, but Caroline was very disquieted by the idea of a shop in the house. She kept to her room more than ever and announced to Rhea that she was leaving at the end of the month. Rhea was too harried to pay much attention.

The open house was a huge success. Crowds of people attended. Rhea, beaming, conducted tours through the house pointing out the pieces for sale. Jacqui greeted people at the door, and Jill served tea and coffee from a gleaming silver service in the dining room. Near the end of the afternoon, a familiar sand colored Cadillac pulled up out front, and Jacqui's heart began to pound as Carter Gregory covered the distance to the front door in long, purposeful strides.

She decided quickly that the best strategy would be to pretend they had never met. "Welcome," she said as Jill looked on. "I'm Jacqui."

He took her proffered hand and held it rather longer than necessary before he turned to greet Jill.

"Carter," Rhea said effusively, seeing him at once. "How nice of you to come."

"Apparently, my invitation went astray," he said drily.

"I wanted to ask you," she said, "but I wasn't sure what you would think of my opening a shop in the house."

"I think it's a wonderful idea," he replied. "You should have thought of it years ago."

"It was our home then," she said reprovingly.

Jacqui walked away. She didn't want to hear anymore. Kevin was in one of the Northhampton chairs pretending to read a magazine, but Jacqui saw him watching Rhea and Carter. The boy was in love with her, Jacqui realized, and Rhea had no idea what she was doing to him. It really was a screwed up world, she thought, shaking her head.

"Come on, Kevin," she said to him. "Let's duck out to the kitchen and find ourselves a beer. Open houses are thirsty work."

He smiled gratefully and followed.

Jacqui went to bed early that night, almost as soon as the last guests departed, but Rhea, exuberant in her success, came in to perch on the loveseat with both feet tucked up under her.

"It went well, didn't it?" she asked for what seemed to Jacqui the hundredth time.

"Yes, Rhea, very well."

"Well, what do you think of Carter?"

"He's an extremely attractive man."

"Yes, he's even better looking now than when we were first married. Did you hear what he said to me—that I should have opened a shop years ago?"

"Yes, I heard."

"Some nerve! Especially, since he was the one who never wanted me to work in the first place."

"Maybe he was just thinking of you—that you might have been happier."

"Not a chance. He was just trying to assuage his guilt."

"Rhea, when are you going to release all that bitterness you feel toward Carter?"

"Never!" Rhea answered vehemently.

"Aunt Rhea, are you in there?" It was Jill at the door. "I think there's something wrong with Caroline," she said. "I can hear her in her room. She sounds funny."

Rhea and Jacqui both jumped up and followed Jill to the door of Caroline's room. "Caroline, are you all right?" Rhea called.

The only answer was something that sounded like a groan. Rhea tried the door. It was locked. She hurried back to her room and produced a key. They found Caroline on the bed doubled over in excruciating pain, grasping her enlarged stomach.

"Please call an ambulance," she whispered, "and get me to the hospital."

Rhea and Jill tried to comfort her while Jacqui called for an ambulance. There was blood on the back of her gown, and, although, the ambulance came in a matter of minutes, it seemed an eternity with Caroline in such pain. It was decided that Rhea would ride in the ambulance with Caroline. Jill would get dressed and follow in Rhea's car. And Jacqui, whose presence seemed to upset Caroline, would wait at home.

The ambulance had just pulled out of the drive with Caroline and Rhea when the phone rang. Jill had run back upstairs to dress, and Jacqui answered it.

"Hello, Jacqui," a deep, familiar voice said.

"Why are you calling me at this wholly unreasonable hour? What do you want?" she demanded.

"I want to see you."

"No." She was emphatic.

"Please. I have to see you again. Meet me somewhere. Anywhere."

"No." She was more emphatic.

"I won't give up," he said.

"Yes, you will—in time."

"Jacqui, please—"

"Goodnight, Greg."

She replaced the phone, and Jill appeared at the top of the stairs. Jacqui caught a strange, hostile expression on Jill's face, but she said nothing. She was getting paranoid. First Caroline and now Jill. What was wrong with her?

After Jill had gone, Jacqui was in a very restless mood as she waited for Rhea to call. She tried to read, then to watch television, but she was unable to concentrate. Suppose Jill had picked up the phone while Greg was talking to her. No, she would have heard that. Probably, she had just misread Jill's concern over Caroline. Jacqui nibbled on a cookie left over from the open house and made herself a cup of tea. It was much later when Rhea called.

"Caroline is resting now," she said. "If everything continues to be satisfactory, Jill and I will be home soon."

"What's wrong with Caroline?"

"You won't believe it," Rhea said incredulously. "Caroline is pregnant—very pregnant. They have the bleeding stopped, and she has been sedated."

"But Caroline's a nurse. How could she let this happen to her?"

"Apparently, she had some pain and spotting earlier, but she didn't want anyone to know about the baby yet, and she thought that if she could just get off her feet and get some rest, everything would be all right. It wasn't."

Jacqui remembered that every time she had seen Caroline lately she had been wearing the blue caftan or a full housecoat. And she had taken to wearing a loose coat over her uniform when going and coming from work when it certainly wasn't cold enough to warrant a coat.

"I wonder why she didn't tell us," Jacqui said, "or at least why she didn't tell you or Jill."

"I can't imagine," Rhea said. "Maybe she thought I wouldn't want a baby in the house. Who knows? Jill and I will be home soon."

Caroline Kelly having a baby, Jacqui mused. She wonder if there ever was a Mr. Kelly. Immediately, she felt guilty. What difference did it make? It was Caroline's business. Jacqui had known all along that she was hiding something, but she never dreamed that it was a baby. How little we ever really know one another, she thought as she went up to bed.

Jacqui fell into a deep sleep almost immediately and dreamed a confused dream in which she was looking for Spence and kept finding Carter Gregory. Rhea and Jill woke her when they returned, and she was surprised to find her face wet with tears.

CHAPTER THIRTEEN

In the middle of November a "blue norther," as the native Texans called it, blew in with a furious wind that scattered leaves across the lawn and dropped the temperature twenty degrees in an hour. It got colder all through the day, and Rhea called in a serviceman to clean and light the furnace. Caroline, who was just home from the hospital, was still spending most of her time in bed, and would continue to do so until the birth of the baby. There was no more talk of her leaving, and Rhea moved the small portable television set from her own bedroom to Caroline's. She rarely had time to watch it anyway.

Rhea had sold the breakfront in the dining room the first week she was open for eighteen hundred dollars. She was elated. She also sold the brass lamp that had been newly electroplated and several pieces of Kevin's furniture, including the wing back chairs. Many of her customers seemed as interested in touring the house as in shopping for antiques, and Rhea gladly accommodated them, taking care to avoid Caroline's room. The house was a perfect showcase for the kind of furniture she offered for sale. More often than not, she found people wanting to buy items that she had not planned to sell—like the porcelain goose.

But she couldn't part with it. In her mind the silly thing was almost alive, and selling it would be akin to selling a member of the family. She still talked to it from time to time—when nobody was around to hear.

She moved the rattan furniture from the sitting room to the top of the landing. That was one of the delightful advantages of old houses, there were so many places to tuck a seating group. Early residents never used the downstairs parlor except for company and special occasions. A disadvantage was the lack of closets. Early homes were taxed on the number of rooms, and closets counted as rooms. Some closets had been added over the years, and she and Carter added more. The space sliced from the huge bedrooms was hardly missed.

Rhea had been forced to engage a cleaning service to come in once a week. She simply couldn't keep up with the housework, running the shop, and going to school. She wasn't doing as well in her classes. She sometimes found herself copying Kevin's solutions to the accounting problems, rather than working them out for herself. Still, she was learning what she needed to know to keep a simple set of books, sufficient for the shop.

Carter called and asked to buy the leather topped desk from his former study.

"You can have it," she told him generously. "I originally bought it for you. I'm sorry I didn't let you have it earlier."

"I'll be glad to pay you for it, Rhea, if you'll put a value on it."

"Oh, no," she answered quickly. "I really want you to have it. You can take me to lunch some day, and we'll call it even."

"How about today?"

"Today would be lovely. Jill is here to mind the store."

Rhea hung up the phone and surveyed herself in the mirror. She was wearing a brown pantsuit that had just undergone alterations to fit her new slimmer figure, and she had on a simple ivory silk blouse. Before she left, she changed into a pair of pumps with higher heels and added the amber and gold necklace Carter had bought her on their first trip to the Caribbean.

He was waiting for her by the double doors just outside Nick's Fish Market when she emerged from the tunnel which led from the parking garage. Rhea thought wryly about all the changes that had taken place since that day in early summer when she had come down to Nick's from Carter's office after pleading with him for money. How different these last few months might have been if he had just written her a check for a few thousand dollars, which he could well afford. But he hadn't, and, as angry as she had been that day, she wasn't really sorry now. She had learned a great deal in these few short months, most of it about herself.

Carter ordered wine for them without consulting her. She

was surprised to be mildly annoyed even if it was the same wine she probably would have ordered for herself. And, when he suggested the trout, she told him firmly that she preferred the lobster salad.

"So, tell me, how are things going in the antique business?" he asked.

"Very good. You know me. I've always wanted to live in rooms that were filled with decorative objects and fine furniture. With the store, I can keep changing them all the time."

"I don't see how you manage to sell anything," he teased. "As I recall, you were always reluctant to get rid of anything. Is the attic still full?"

"Yes," she said, laughing. "I'm afraid it is. I'm using it for storage now, but I plan to turn it into a bargain room later. And I can sell antiques—very well, thank you."

"I hope you're keeping good records," he told her. "I can recommend an excellent tax man. You really should see him right away. You don't want to end the year with a big tax bill."

"I've already taken care of that," she said firmly. "I've been going to school, Carter, studying the management of a small business and accounting principles."

"Yes, I know. Jill told me."

"Jill?"

"Yes, I stop by the Aloha Room once in a while."

"She didn't tell me that she had seen you."

"She probably forgot. It's no big deal. However, it seems you've done more planning than I gave you credit for. How did you decide to open a shop in the house?"

"It was the only alternative I had," she told him. Then she recounted how it all came about—that she had been fired by Riker. She could laugh about it now. "Also," she explained, "I had an opportunity to sell a friend's furniture for him on commission. So I wasn't risking too much to begin with. The house is a perfect place for my business. Historically, the decoration of a home was to display wealth and status. In France and England, rooms were used as a setting for collections, butterflies and shells and minerals, objects from faraway places, to show visitors that the host was a gentlemen with a superior appreciation for the beautiful and the natural." She broke off with a little laugh. "You've heard all this before," she said.

"I must not have been listening," he said ruefully.

"I don't think either one of us was listening for a long time," she said thoughtfully.

"Rhea, I'm genuinely happy for you. I wish you all the success in the world in your business. I hope you grow to be the biggest antique dealer in Houston—in the state of Texas. You look better than you have in years. Are you wearing your hair differently?"

He hadn't looked at her in years, she thought. He doesn't remember the amber necklace. He didn't know she had lost thirty pounds. Kevin had noticed immediately. "You've lost weight," he had said. You look terrific. She didn't want Kevin to think she looked terrific. She wanted Carter to think so.

"No, same old hair," she said as their food arrived. Her salad was delicious—lobster resting on a bed of salad greens, garnished with tomato wedges and ripe olives and a tiny fluted lemon basket of caviar.

"And how is our little Jill adjusting to life in the big city?" Carter asked.

"Our little Jill isn't little anymore in case you haven't noticed. I worry about her, Carter. She's like a drunk at a wine tasting party. She never knows when to stop."

"She seems pretty level headed to me. Maybe you're worrying unnecessarily."

"Jacqui doesn't think so. She has tried to talk to Jill about burning the candle at both ends more than once."

"How did Jacqui come to move in with you?" he asked.

"She answered an advertisement I placed in the university newspaper. I liked her right away. We became good friends almost immediately."

"She seems so different from you," he mused.

"She vows that we are exactly alike. But, of course, it isn't true."

"Did Jacqui ever tell you why she never married?"

"Yes, she was deeply in love with an older man who died just before they were to be married. She talks a great deal about Spence. I don't think she will ever stop loving him. She even tried to kill herself when he died. She has scars along her wrists where she slashed herself with a razor."

"Yes, I noticed the scars," he said.

Rhea was in the elevator of the parking garage going up to her car when she began to wonder why Carter was so interested in Jacqui. He had only met her briefly at the open house. How did he know, she wondered, that she had never been married. Jill must have told him.

She had a slightly deflated feeling as she worked around the shop that afternoon rearranging furniture and pricing some new items. Carter had said all the right things. "I'm genuinely happy for you, Rhea." So why did she still have the feeling that he was looking past her—not really at her, not seeing her at all? She felt different. Why couldn't he see it? But he would see her, she vowed. He would look at her again with that special light in his eyes. She would work at it until he did.

Perhaps, she would give a dinner party. She would invite Carter and Jacqui and Jill, of course. Caroline wouldn't join them. She would seat Jill and Kevin together and ask Jacqui to bring one of the young men she played tennis with.

She would plan it for Sunday night when Jill wasn't working. That was good. It would give her all day to prepare the meal. She would fill the house with fresh flowers, prepare Carter's favorite foods. She would make a huge salad with romaine lettuce and hearts of palm. She was not sure about the meat—duck, perhaps. Some fresh asparagus. Also, a rich chocolate mousse and espresso. She was so engrossed in the planning that she didn't hear Caroline come down.

"I'm sorry," she said. "I didn't mean to startle you, Rhea."

"No problem. I was just about to make myself a cup of tea. Would you like one?"

"Yes, thank you."

Caroline sat down while Rhea went to put the kettle on. "I feel guilty," Caroline said when she returned, "having all of you wait on me. You've been wonderful to me."

"We're your friends," Rhea said simply.

"I don't know how I can ever repay you."

"Don't give it another thought."

"But I do think about it. I had planned to leave—to get my own apartment before the baby comes. Now that's impossible. And since I can't stand on my feet for any period of time, I can't go back to work at the hospital."

"Caroline, you can stay as long as you like. I'll do anything I can to help you. So will Jill and Jacqui. If you can't afford the rent, we'll work something out."

"Oh, no, Rhea, that isn't a problem."

When Rhea got up to make the tea, she saw tears in Caroline's eyes, but when she returned, the tears had been wiped away, and Caroline was her cool, composed self again.

Later a customer came in and, spying Rhea's ornate mahogany dining table and chairs, asked if they were for sale. Startled, Rhea made a quick, impulsive decision and said yes, tripling the price she had paid at an auction a few years back. The customer said she would have to think about that, but the following morning she was back, haggled only a little and arranged to have it delivered.

When they had gone, Rhea stood in the empty dining room. She had sold the massive breakfront secretaire some time before, and the room was almost empty except for the subtle shades of an oriental rug covering the bleached oak floor. Carter had wanted to carpet this room, but she wouldn't hear of it. The oriental rug had been a compromise, and he had grumbled about the cost of it for weeks.

Suddenly, she thought of the dinner party she had planned. What would she do for furniture? She would have to improvise. When Jacqui came home, she commandeered her to help move the old Queen Anne table into the dining room. Antique chairs, no two alike were gathered up from various parts of the house including the attic.

"It will have to do," Rhea said, "until I locate some Queen Anne chairs to match the table."

"I like it," Jacqui decided, "with all the different chairs. It's less rigid and more interesting—sort of like a person with many facets."

"You may be right," Rhea mused. "I think I like it too. It grows on you. If the chairs were all upholstered in the same fabric, I might like it even better. What do you think about a moss green tapestry?"

Jacqui looked around the room. The walls had been painted a pale, pale green. The rug had muted shades of green and brown, and a large oil painting picked up the same shades and added accent colors. "You're a genius at decorating, Rhea," she said. "You can make anything beautiful."

"Carter used to call me a scavenger," she replied.

"I think treasure hunter would be more appropriate."

"I like your choice of words better. Have you eaten yet?"

"No, I haven't."

"How does something Japanese sound to you? I cubed the beef this morning. A stir fry would take only a few minutes."

"Marvelous. May I help?"

"If you like. There are vegetables to be cut up. I picked up some shallots and fresh mushrooms at the market this morning."

"No doubt before I got out of bed." Jacqui said, groaning. "I don't see how you do it, Rhea. Even with the shop, you still have time for cooking and school and running this house."

"If you're doing something you love, it doesn't seem like work."

"That's true. I read a study somewhere that really successful people spend as much as eighty percent of their time doing things they enjoy. The key to success seems to be to find a job that you thoroughly enjoy. Most of us fall into the trap of making a living instead of living."

"Making a living is certainly an important part of living. I found out the hard way."

As Rhea heated oil in a wok she had placed over the burner, she showed Jacqui how to cut diagonal slices of celery. Then she started rice on the back burner. Jacqui watched as Rhea browned the cubed beef in the hot oil and added shallots, bean sprouts, celery, mushrooms, and water chestnuts. She took note of the seasonings and the soy sauce that was stirred into the meat and vegetables. As soon as the vegetables were crisp tender, Rhea removed the wok from the burner and served the meat and vegetables over a plate of steaming rice. It smelled so delicious that Caroline was enticed out of her room to join them.

"This is marvelous, Rhea," Jacqui exclaimed. "It looked so easy to make."

"It is easy."

"I seemed to have developed," Jacqui confessed, "a strange uncontrollable desire to learn to cook. Provided I don't recover sufficiently in a few days, where do you suggest I start to learn?"

"With a good cookbook and a well equipped kitchen," Rhea said, laughing. "Fortunately, I have both at your disposal. Seriously though, I think good cooking is a matter of timing as much as anything else—learning to make everything come together at the right time."

"I think there's probably a greater gem of wisdom in that than you realize," Jacqui said. "Timing is a very important element in our lives."

Timing, Caroline thought as she listed to their easy conversation. If she hadn't been sitting at that table by the window looking out at the city lights, feeling as if nothing in life was really worthwhile, at the precise moment that Rick Cortero walked in, all this might never have happened. He would never have said. "Why are you looking so sad, pretty lady?" There would have been no inane conversation, the meaningless things that people talk about in bars, no refilled drink glass, and no anguish and terror at having to flee from him.

"Opportunity lost comes not again," Rhea was quoting when Caroline picked up the conversation again.

"That's not true," Jacqui objected. "Each day is a new beginning *Each night I burn the records of the day; At sunrise every soul is born again.*"

"At sunrise every soul is born again," Caroline repeated. "How beautiful."

"I probably have the book of poetry it came from somewhere upstairs. I'll find it for you," Jacqui offered.

But after they finished, she volunteered to clean up the kitchen, and when she thought about the book, Caroline had already gone to bed. Jacqui showered and put on night clothes, but seeing the light under Rhea's door, she decided to tap lightly.

Rhea was sitting up in bed with her accounting book and working papers spread out around her as she called for Jacqui to come in.

"Burning the midnight oil, I see. I won't disturb you. I was just a little restless tonight."

"It's okay, Jacqui. I'm not getting anywhere with this. I'm going to have to call on Kevin for help. I couldn't have passed this course without him."

"Does Kevin date anyone, Rhea?"

"I don't know. I suppose, he's such a sweet, sensitive boy. I don't see why there aren't flocks of girls around him. He's evidently well off financially. His father left him a construction company and some other property. He drives a Corvette, and he has this lovely old house on Lake Conroe which he has up for sale at the moment. All the furniture I'm selling for him came from the house. He didn't have a good relationship with his father, apparently, and he seems to be something of a loner. I'm still hoping he and Jill will hit it off."

"I don't think there's much of a chance of that."

"You should date him, Jacqui," Rhea said suddenly. "He's a very interesting person and a fabulous photographer. I've seen some of his work—very dramatic, strong contrasts, and good composition."

"Sorry, Rhea. He is a nice person. I like him, but there aren't any sparks between us. We could be friends, nothing else. The chemistry just isn't right."

Rhea flushed, remembering the time Kevin bumped into her at the restaurant. Then she thought of the time he had embraced her at the house on the lake. She sighed. What was wrong with Jill and Jacqui? What did it take to excite girls these days?"

"I'm going to bed," Jacqui announced. "See you tomorrow."

"Goodnight," Rhea murmured and picked up the heavy accounting book to read. Abruptly, she put it down again and gathered up her papers. She was too tired for this tonight. In the morning, it might make sense.

She thought again about her lunch with Carter. He looked tired—probably working too hard and not eating properly. When they got back together, she would remedy that. She would insist they take a long, restful vacation, a second honeymoon—perhaps a month long cruise to the Mediterranean.

Then an alarming thought struck her. How could she leave her business for thirty days? She would have to start all over when she returned. Customers would forget all about her and take their business elsewhere. Then she had another equally alarming thought. How could she equate running an antique business with being Carter's wife? That was all she had ever wanted. With those puzzling thoughts circling in her mind, it was a long time before she slept.

CHAPTER FOURTEEN

Damn Carter Gregory! Jacqui kept asking herself why it had to happen just as she was getting her life back together after Spence. She had really looked forward to this basketball season. Well, she decided, he was not going to keep her from going to the game tonight. She wouldn't allow it. The Phoenix Suns were in town, and she really wanted to see the game.

She left early to get a parking place close to the ramp leading to the arena, then stopped by the lobby bar in the hotel which adjoined the parking garage to have a drink. Mostly, she wanted to kill time so that Greg would not be able to find her alone before the game started. She waited until just before tip-off before going to her seat. She need not have bothered. He was not there.

It turned out to be an exciting game; she was glad that she had come. The Rockets were a completely different team than the one she and Spence had cheered. There had been so many changes that there were few players Spence would have recognized.

Jacqui left her seat in the final few minutes and went up to stand at the top of the stairs. There was still no sign of Greg. At the final buzzer she rushed out into the lobby where crowds had already gathered and pushed in the direction of the stairs and escalator. She opted for the stairs and took them two at a time. She was among the first to leave after the game ended only to find her-self in a long line waiting to leave the parking garage—behind all those who had left early.

She knew it was cowardly not to want to face Carter Gregory. If she continued to go to the Summit, and she would, a meeting was inevitable. But if she could just postpone it, time would be on her side. In time she would forget him—forget the feel of his tanned, athletic body, the soft silver hair curling around her finger, the blue of his eyes, the warmth of his lips. Maybe she would forget, she thought dismally, perhaps in a hundred years—if she lived that long.

Sunday morning was quiet around the house. Jill had not come home until dawn and slept almost all day. Caroline was resting in her room as usual, and Rhea was dressing to go to an antique show at the convention center.

"Sure you won't change your mind and come with me?" Rhea called.

"No, I don't think so. I think I'll just be lazy today. There's a basketball game on cable I want to see."

"Okay, suit yourself. But let's go out to eat when I get back. Do you realize that it has been months since I've had a pizza?"

"You deserve a treat," Jacqui agreed. "I must say you have been persevering."

"I want to go somewhere and pig out on junk food. I feel like eating myself silly even if I have to starve all next week to make up for it."

"You've got it," Jacqui promised.

After Rhea had gone, she poured herself another cup of coffee and settled herself down in front of the television set to watch the game. Just as she was becoming engrossed, the phone rang.

"Jacqui, please don't hang up. Please listen."

She recognized the voice immediately. It was deep, resonant—the voice of an orator. She could imagine the mesmerizing effect it might have on a jury. She turned down the volume on the television set and gripped the phone with shaking hands. When she managed to answer, her voice was barely audible.

"I'm listening."

"We have to talk," he said.

It was a statement of fact that he expected her to accept. She did not say anything, and there was only the slightest pause as he continued.

"I'm at Intercontinental Airport," he said, "and I have two tickets on a flight leaving for San Francisco in one hour. Don't take time to pack, we'll buy everything you need when we get there. Park in the garage at Terminal C and meet me at the Western counter. Jacqui, I love you."

It was several seconds before she realized that he had hung up without giving her a chance to reply. She imagined him waiting at the counter for her—the way he looked when she had first seen him, the tall, tanned athletic body and the incongruity of his boyish grin and silver hair. In her mind she saw his searching blue eyes fill with disappointment when he realized that she was not coming.

Jacqui, I love you, he had said.

She flew up the stairs and pulled down a soft, small carry-on bag from the top of her closet. Quickly she threw in lingerie, make-up, a toothbrush, her portable hair dryer, and her curling iron. In a matching garment bag, she zipped up slender trousers and a matching silk blouse. Then she chose her favorite black crepe dress that curved in one narrow line down her torso making her feel tall and elegant. A pair of high heeled black pumps went into the side compartment of the bag. The whole thing took less than five minutes.

Almost as an after thought, she stuffed a luxurious cashmere and silk sweater into the bag. San Francisco in November—how cold would it be? She smoothed her hair, wishing that she had time to change. But the designer jeans and silk shirt would have to do. She grabbed a chic natural mink jacket Spence had given her just before he died. It seemed somehow appropriate.

She was speeding up Highway 59 North before the enormity of what she was doing hit her. If she walked into that terminal, she knew it would be the point of no return. She couldn't ever go back. She would be forever and irrevocably committed to Carter Gregory.

She exited at Jetero, turned left to cross under the freeway and paused at the stop light. She should turn again, she thought, get right back on the freeway and forget about him. But she didn't. She continued straight ahead, and by the time she had reached the parking garage at Terminal C, she had ceased to think at all—only to feel a deep, compelling sadness coupled with the first real joy she had known in more than a year.

Later when they were airborne and his hand caressingly covered hers, she looked at him and said thoughtfully, "If I'd thought about this, I wouldn't have come."

"I know," he answered. "But I promise you, you won't ever

be sorry."

The plane made a scheduled stop in Salt Lake City dropping down into a snow covered valley surrounded by breathtaking snow capped mountains.

"Have you been here before?" Jacqui asked.

He nodded. "I skied Snowbird one year. Do you ski? There are so many things I don't know about you."

"Yes, I ski. I had a roommate in college from Colorado. She invited me home for Christmas vacation and dragged me out on the slopes. When I saw the ski instructor, I fell in love, and I was hooked forever."

"You're joking," he said.

"No, I love to ski."

"That's not what I mean," he said.

"When were you here? Recently?"

"Three or four years ago."

"With Rhea?"

"No, Rhea doesn't ski. Did you know that when the Mormons came here, this beautiful valley was a desolate stretch of harsh land that nobody wanted? The civilization they carved out of it is truly amazing. You would enjoy the tour of Temple Square. I was here just before Christmas when the Square was decorated with Christmas lights. I went to the taping of the Mormon Tabernacle Choir's Christmas show. It was beautiful beyond words—the choir, a full orchestra, and the altar decorated with hundreds of Poinsettias. The acoustics in the Tabernacle are astounding. On the tour they demonstrate the dropping of a pin at the altar which you can hear from the back row of seats."

His face was alive with enthusiasm. She loved him, she realized. She really loved him.

"Penny for your thoughts," he offered.

"Are we going through that again?"

"Oh, I forgot. I can't afford it. Maybe I can intercept them with mental telepathy or something."

"Don't bother. I'll give them to you," she said softly. "I love you," she whispered, forming each word carefully with her lips.

"Oh, Jacqui," he said huskily, squeezing her hand.

The plane was taking on passengers, and soon they were airborne again. Jacqui sat with her head against the window looking out, drinking in the beauty of the landscape, acutely aware of the pressure of his leg against hers and his warm, strong hand imprisoning her trembling one.

"Where will we stay in San Francisco?"

"At the Hyatt on Union Square. You'll be able to see the bay from the upper floors, and it will be a good place for you while I work. There are fancier hotels, but I think you'll like it. I have to take a deposition. You will be within walking distance of Chinatown. Do you like Chinese food?"

"I love it."

"Good. And you can catch a double decker bus to Pier 39 or Fisherman's Wharf. You can shop in Ghiradelli Square. When I'm finished, I'll rent a car, and we'll drive over to Sausalito and up to the wine country. We'll take a bay cruise over to Marin County one night."

"It all sounds wonderful. Am I dreaming?"

"If you are, we're having the same dream. What did you tell Rhea when you left?"

"Oh my goodness!" Jacqui cried. "I didn't tell her anything. She was gone to an antique show. It was almost as if I were in a trance. I didn't even think of Rhea once. I know that sounds awful, but I didn't. I'll phone her when we get to San Francisco."

"And tell her what?"

"A lie, of course. I don't know. I'll think of something."

"She will have to know the truth sometime."

"I know. But I can't face that now. There is no point in destroying her until we, you and I both, know for sure that this is going to work for us."

"I'm sure now," he said. "And you're being overly dramatic. It won't destroy her. She must have considered the possibility that I would find someone else eventually. It wasn't a good marriage, Jacqui. Rhea and I had separate bedrooms for years."

"Please don't tell me anymore," she pleaded. "I don't want to think beyond today. Please don't force any decisions on me now. Can't we take this one step at a time?"

"Of course we can. The last thing I want to do is to pressure you. Just tell me again," he said softly, "that you love me."

She turned her face to rest in the crook of his neck. "I'll say it when we get to San Francisco," she promised, "as many times as you want to hear it."

"It's a deal."

They landed at the Oakland airport, and he arranged for a limousine to take them into San Francisco. Jacqui's conscience bothered her only a little as she called Rhea and repeated the lie she had carefully fabricated. An elderly aunt in El Paso had been stricken ill suddenly. Rhea wouldn't know that she had no elderly aunt. God knows, she didn't want to hurt Rhea, but she was in love with Carter Gregory, and today, she had passed the point of no return.

Greg noticed her silence on the way to the hotel. His arm, resting against the back of the seat, settled protectively around her shoulders. "These few days here," he promised, "are going to be the best of our lives up to now."

"I don't doubt it for a moment," she replied.

She turned to him, rubbed her cheek against his. He drew his arm tighter around her, and she revelled in his closeness. They were in another world; nobody existed but the two of them.

Jacqui couldn't believe this was really happening to her. She had never expected to love again—not like this. Why did it have to be Greg? She tucked the uncomfortable thought away and turned to look at Candlestick Park that Greg was pointing out on her right.

Darkness had settled comfortably around them by the time they reached the hotel. Jacqui stood in front of the windows of the room, looking at the city lights. Greg came up behind her, his hands resting on her shoulders.

"In the morning you'll be able to see the bay," he said. "That blinking light out there is Alcatraz."

"It's not used as a prison now, is it?" she asked.

"No. They finally decided it was too brutal and too inhumane. There is an excursion boat that goes over if you would like a closer look."

"No, thanks. I'm as close as I want to be. I only want to see pleasant, lovely things while I'm in San Francisco. I think there are enough to go around for the few days we are going to be here."

"Right you are, beautiful lady."

He turned her around to face him. "Now, what would you like to do first? We can go to Chinatown for dinner, or to Fisherman's Wharf for seafood. It's up to you."

Impulsively, she pulled his face down to hers and kissed him, unleashing all the pent up passion, loneliness, grief, and unhappiness she had held in check for so long. He responded by drawing her into his arms, their bodies pressed together, each savoring the glorious desire that had ignited when first they met.

"If it's up to me," she whispered, "I would rather make love to you."

"My love," he said huskily. "My beautiful love."

His strong, gentle hands began to caress her eager body as his lips moved over hers and down her throat, exploring, arousing. Slowly he undressed her. Neither of them spoke. There was no need for words.

Later she was surprised by the discreet knock on the door. Greg, wearing a blue velour robe that exactly matched the color of his eyes, went to receive a bottle of champagne iced down in a silver bucket.

"Dom Perignon," she said appreciatively. "That must have cost you a fortune."

"Whatever it costs, it was worth it—for the best day of my life," he said.

"It's the best day of my life, too."

"Then why are you looking so sad?"

"I thought of Rhea."

"Oh, Jacqui, when are you going to stop?"

"I'm sorry. I just can't help thinking of Rhea struggling to pay her electric bills, and you give me this—this trip, offer to buy me new clothes—Dom Perignon."

"Jacqui, Rhea chooses to struggle," he said angrily. "That house and that furniture are probably worth close to a million dollars. I don't have a million dollars and neither do you. If she chooses to cling to it and struggle, then it's her problem. We deserve this, you and I."

"I'm sorry," she said, encircling him with her arms. "I never thought of it that way. I suppose it is a prime piece of real estate—location and all. I only considered the fact that there are two things in this world that Rhea loves—that house and you. She's lost you. Somehow it doesn't seem fair for her to lose the house too."

"Jacqui, life isn't fair."

"I know that better than anybody, and I'm sorry, my love. I'm not being fair to you. This is our night, and I have no right to let anyone else intrude. I love you."

He handed her a glass of champagne. "To us," he said.

"To us," she repeated and reached for the hand he offered her. Together they went to stand by the window looking out at the lights below.

"When will you marry me?" he asked.

"When Rhea can accept it without hating us both."

"Do you think that day will ever come?"

"Yes, I do."

"Then you must believe in miracles."

"How could I not believe in miracles after today?"

"You have a point. Say it again."

"Say what, darling?"

"That you love me. You promised that when we got to San Francisco, you would say it as many times as I wanted to hear it."

"Haven't I?"

"Lady, you haven't even started."

CHAPTER FIFTEEN

Jill plucked the flowers from her hair and unwrapped the black sarong splashed with orchids that she had worn at the Aloha Room. She slipped out of her shoes and kneaded her tired feet on the cool tile floor of the lounge. It had been a long night; she felt drained, washed out.

Maybe she was coming down with something—or maybe it was just the inner turmoil of knowing about Jacqui and Uncle Carter and not being able to come to grips with the problem of telling Rhea. Should she tell Rhea? How could Jacqui do it? She knew how much Rhea wanted to put her marriage back together again. Jacqui pretended to be Rhea's friend—encouraging her, lending her money. And Jill knew the shop was successful at least partly because of Jacqui.

Now there was no doubt about what was going on between Jacqui and Carter. Jill knew she recognized his voice on the phone the night Caroline almost lost her baby, but in the following days, she almost convinced herself that she was mistaken. This couldn't be happening, she told herself over and over again.

It was happening, however. The day after Jacqui got back from her aunt's, Jill had seen them lunching at the Galleria. She and Carter couldn't take their eyes off one another. They hadn't even seen her with Court just across the room. But Jill had watched them all through lunch, laughing and touching hands. She wondered how they met. It had to be at Rhea's open house. How could Jacqui deliberately do this to Rhea? It almost made her sick to think about it. At least she wasn't hurting anybody by her relationship with Court Randall-unless it was herself. Court was the kind of man a woman could never be sure of. If only she could find a way to be sure of him.

Her preoccupation with Rhea and Jacqui had left her distracted the last time they were together.

"Earth to Jill."

"Oh, Court, I'm sorry," she apologized. "I was miles away. What were you saying?"

"I hope I was miles away with you—at least in your thoughts."

"You always are," she lied.

"Where would you like to go," he asked abruptly, "if money were no object?"

"I don't know. Hawaii, maybe. I never thought about it. I've really never been anywhere. One of the girls at the Club just got back from St. Thomas. She had a fabulous time. Maybe I'd like to go to the Caribbean. I'd like to go anywhere with you."

"That's what I like to hear. Do you have a passport?"

"Good heavens, no! I never needed one."

He pulled two hundred dollar bills from a wallet in the inside pocket of his coat. "As soon as you have a chance," he said, "go to the downtown post office and make application for a passport. This should cover the fee, including the photos you need. Do you have your birth certificate?"

"It's in Arkansas. But I can call my mother and have her send it to me."

"Do it as soon as possible. The passport will take several weeks."

Jill phoned her mother that same day. "I'm fine, Mama, really I am, but I need my birth certificate. Will you mail it to me? Will you do it today? Yes, Aunt Rhea is fine too. She has been wonderful to me. Yes, I miss you too."

It made her a little sad to hear her mother's voice. But she had stepped into a world her mother could not even dream of—a world whose focus was Court—handsome, rich, exciting. It was a world made up of luxurious hotel suites, expensive wines, gourmet dining, and business conducted over the telephone and in airport terminals. Jill knew that when he was in town, she was most often the woman at his side, and just the thought that he was waiting for her tonight banished all her tiredness.

It had been a busy night. She was glad to get out of the

sarong. She slipped into the pale blue wrap dress Rhea had given her. It was still her favorite even though she now had a closet full of new clothes—many of them gifts from Court. Just thinking about him pushed everything else from her mind. She left the club, took the elevator down to the ground floor and saw him standing just outside the glass doors—his black Continental parked at the curb. She seemed to float across the lobby to him. Court embraced Jill briefly and opened the car door for her. She slid across the seat and picked up an unopened bottle of wine lying there. Chateau Lafayette-Rothschild—one of his favorites. It was going to be a good night.

"Hungry?" he asked as they pulled away from the curb.

"No, not really," Jill answered truthfully. The excitement of seeing him had taken away her appetite. She moved closer to him on the seat.

"Well, I had a little something prepared for us, just in case," he said. "Maybe later?"

"Of course," she replied.

"Do you know how much I've missed you?" he asked, drawing her closer.

"I was beginning to think you had forgotten all about me."

"Not a chance, angel. I'm like a bad penny. I always turn up again."

"I'm awfully glad you did, Court."

"You'll get a chance to prove that later, Sunshine. Now tell me what you've been doing with yourself while I was away."

She chattered all the way to the hotel. He was easily amused by stories of what went on at the club during her working hours. He laughed easily, although, she was not always sure just what he was laughing at. It didn't matter. He called her his angel, and as long as she pleased him, she didn't care if he sometimes laughed at her.

A table had been set up in his suite. In the center were candles and the yellow roses Jill once told him that she loved. There were canapés and cheeses and ripe strawberries. Jill sampled a little sandwich that tasted of shrimp flavored with dill. It was delicious.

"This is lobster with artichokes," he said indicating the salad packed in ice to keep it chilled. "Try it."

"It's a feast!" Jill exclaimed delightedly.

"Still not hungry," he teased.

"You always know what I want even before I want it."

Later Jill lay contentedly against Court Randall's chest, savoring the exquisite after glow of their love making. He was a fantastic lover, she decided, virile and experienced. It wasn't fair, she knew, to compare him to Jimmy. Jimmy had really loved her—loved her still if his phone calls meant anything, but he would never have the elegant sophistication that Court had, and never in a million years would he be as wildly exciting.

It was wonderful to have Court back again even if their relationship seemed to lack any degree of permanence. It was his living out of hotels and his sudden disappearances for weeks on end that made her afraid that he would simply go one day, and she would never see him again.

He stirred, reaching for a wine glass and a cigarette. She pulled the damp, wrinkled sheet up over her naked body.

"Don't do that. I like to look at you."

It was a command—not a request, and she obeyed without question.

He took a long draw from the cigarette, put it down and turned to her. "A body like yours should be looked at."

Jill reached again for the sheet. "You're embarrassing me," she said and laughed uneasily.

He pushed the sheet away. "You will get used to being looked at, my lovely. I like to show off beautiful things that belong to me. If only I had a stable full like you, I could stay rich and never have to work again."

"A stable! That sounds like prostitution."

"Oldest profession in the world," he replied.

"I am not a whore," she declared, her blue eyes flashing suddenly with glints of cold steel. She reached abruptly for the blue dress. "You know I don't like it when you talk that way."

"Some women are turned on by the thought of being a high priced call girl."

"I'm not!"

"No, I can see that. Still the little girl from Arkansas," he taunted.

But as she tried to move away from him, he pushed her roughly down on the bed, and his searching mouth silenced the protest she was about to make. Soon she stopped struggling and accepted his probing tongue. He tasted of wine and cigarettes and a compelling strangeness that drew her, inexplicably, to him. As he kissed her, he ran his fingers gently through her tousled hair.

"You are so beautiful," he said softly. "I've known beautiful women, but none with your beautiful, golden hair, your gorgeous golden tan—your unbelievable eyes. You take the prize. You are easily the most beautiful woman I have ever known."

"And what is the prize?" she teased, thinking of the splendid gifts he always brought when he had been away.

"Don't you know?"

"Tell me."

"Court Randall, of course. I'm the prize. And you belong to me. You'll know one of these days what it really means to be my woman."

"Not prostitution?" she asked fearfully.

"No. No. I was only teasing you, angel. No other man will ever touch you. There will be no more Aloha Rooms. No more getting up in the middle of the night and going home to auntie."

"Court, that's not fair. You know we both agreed that as long as I have to live with my aunt, it's better if I don't make waves."

"Sure, sure," he said, reaching for the cigarette again.

"Please, Court."

"Just a minute, angel, when I'm finished with my cigarette," he smirked, raising one eyebrow. "Just can't get enough, can you?"

"That's not what I meant, and you know it."

"Maybe it runs in the family," he mused. "Your aunt is a good looking broad. I saw her one day when I picked you up. She's pretty sexy, actually. She looks like she might like to join us sometime—a menage a trois."

"What is that?"

"Three in bed for a good romp together."

"I think not. I don't want to talk about this!"

"What do you want to talk about?"

"I want to talk about you. Where have you been these past weeks?"

"Out of town."

"Out of town where?"

"New Orleans. Miami. Other places."

"What were you doing in those places?"

"Making money."

"How?"

"Now, Jill, my lovely, if I told you that, you would tell someone else, and soon so many people would know that I wouldn't be able to do it any more. Then I wouldn't be able to buy you trinkets like these."

Jill carefully opened the box he offered. "Oh, Court, it's beautiful!" she exclaimed, drawing out a gold bracelet with her name set in sparkling stones. "It's beautiful. They aren't real diamonds, are they?"

"Of course, they're real diamonds," he said in exasperation. "When I give you a gift, you never have to wonder if it's real. Here let me put it on for you."

"It's beautiful," she said again. "Thank you, Court."

"There. You're even more beautiful. One of these days I'm going to dress you in diamonds and nothing else and take you for a stroll along the beach in St. Tropez."

"You're teasing me again."

"I've never been more serious. And, by the way, they have nude resorts in Jamaica, if you still want to go to the Caribbean."

"You would really want me naked in front of other men?"

"I told you I like to show off beautiful things that belong to me. But they could only look—not touch. That privilege is reserved for only me."

"I would feel silly wearing diamonds and nothing else. I don't think I could do it."

"You'll get used to having men admire your beautiful body," he said reaching for the wine bottle and pouring himself the rest of the wine.

"None for me?" she asked provocatively.

"You get yours this way," he said, and slowly dribbled the warm red wine across her bare breasts.

She shivered with delight as he bent to lick the wine from first one taunt nipple and then the other, and she felt the fire deep within her began to smoulder anew.

"You're delicious," he murmured, "better than any wine," and she lay in exhilarating anticipation as he poured the remainder of the wine down her stomach. She shivered again as his warm tongue began the slow descent down her wet body until it ignited the fire between her legs.

As long as he could make her feel like this, Jill knew, she could forgive him anything, and she would follow him anywhere even to the nude beaches of St. Tropez and whatever else lay beyond.If he frightened her at times, she would just have to live with that.

CHAPTER SIXTEEN

Jacqui made a left turn onto Westheimer, creeping along with the Friday afternoon rush hour traffic on her way to Greg's place. The seat beside her was loaded with cartons from the Chinese restaurant—sweet and sour pork, shrimp in lobster sauce, won ton soup, egg rolls—all the things she knew Greg liked.

He had assured her that his failure to go to the office was nothing serious. "I'm just feeling a bit under the weather," he insisted over the phone. "It's what I get for trying to keep up with a young chick." She worried anyway.

"Hello, beautiful lady," he said with a kiss when she arrived. He was still in his pajamas and robe. "I've slept most of the day," he apologized. "I can't seem to get rested. Every time I move, it's as though I'm trying to crawl through a heavy ocean current."

"You may be coming down with the flu," she said. "I felt much the same way when I had it last." She pushed him gently down on the couch. "I'll make us some tea and bring the food in here."

"If I'm coming down with something," he warned, "you could catch it, you know."

She gave him a devilish grin. "It might be worth it. Then we would have a legitimate excuse for staying in bed all day together."

"Shameless hussy! What am I going to do with you?"

"Make an honest woman out of me."

"Name the day."

"You're too easy."

"Not true. I just know I've found the one perfect woman to share the rest of my life."

"Then just give me a little more time to tie up the loose ends of my life," she said seriously, resting her head on his shoulder. "But don't think for a moment, Carter Gregory, that I'm going to let you get away."

"I believe you, love. And it's a good thing I'm not trying to get away. I can hardly move."

"I'm worried about you, Greg."

"It can't be anything serious," he said. "I've never been sick a day in my life."

"Maybe you should have a check-up."

"I had one a few months ago. They gave me a clean bill of health."

"Do you think it could be stress?"

"I hardly think so. Things are going better for me now than they have in years. My law practice is great. I don't have to tell you what this relationship means to me. The wonderful thing is that you love me, too. It's like a dream you've waited for all your life suddenly coming true. Don't worry about me, Jacqui."

"Why don't you ask me not to breathe?"

"Why don't you serve dinner?"

"Why don't I? You sit right there. I'll bring it to you."

"There's some white wine in the fridge," he told her, "if you would like a glass before dinner."

"Will you have some?" she asked. "It might make you feel better."

"You make me feel better just by being here. But, yes, I'll have a glass, if you will join me."

Jacqui filled the kettle for tea and placed the food in the microwave ready to heat. Then she put out dishes and silver. She filled two wine glasses from the bottle of Chenin Blanc. Handing Greg a glass, she settled down on the couch next to him, planting a kiss on the side of his face.

"I'm sorry you don't feel well," she said.

"I'll have to try being sick more often," he teased. "I like having you make a fuss over me."

"You don't have to be sick to get my attention. I spend all my waking hours thinking about you."

"And why not? What else would you be thinking about?"

"Defending my thesis for one thing."

"You'll be brilliant."

"I'll get by. I doubt if I'll be brilliant. Then I suppose I had better do something about a job."

"Only if you want to."

"Oh, I want to. All those years in school seem so pointless otherwise. I think I need a career."

"What do you want? A faculty position?"

"Yes, I'll teach for a while and, perhaps, start a private practice in counseling. Eventually, I want to write a book. I started a novel once, but I lost interest in it and put it aside when Spence died. Spence was—."

"I know who Spence was, " he said quietly.

"How?"

"Rhea told me."

"Rhea? I don't understand."

"I took her to lunch one day. She didn't want to talk about you. I dragged it out of her. It wasn't her fault."

"When was this?"

"Just before we went to San Francisco."

"How did you explain your interest in me?"

"I didn't have to. It was right after her open house. I let her think that was our first meeting, and I was just curious about you. You still haven't told her, have you?"

"No, but I will. Things are going so well for her right now. She has had a couple of good decorating jobs. She made a terrific commission on one of them. That could turn out to be a very profitable sideline for her. She is really good at it, Greg."

"Yes, I suppose so. You loaned her money, didn't you?"

"How did you know?"

"I knew someone had. I figured it must be you. I'm surprised she didn't come to me."

"I talked her out of it. I offered her the money."

"Because of us?"

"I don't know. Partly, I guess. But mostly because she's my friend, and I believe in her."

"Jacqui, you don't owe Rhea anything because of me. Our marriage was over and finished long before I met you."

"Over for you, but not for her. Time has helped though. And she has a young man in love with her."

"You're joking!"

"No, you met him at the open house. Kevin Stacey."

"I remember him. You disappeared into the kitchen with him," Greg said.

"I gave him a beer and a shoulder to cry on."

Greg nestled his head on Jacqui's shoulder. "I must say," he said, "it's a very nice shoulder, indeed. Was he properly grateful?"

"He was properly miserable when you showed up."

"That's unbelievable!"

"Have you looked at Rhea lately? She has lost thirty pounds over the last few months. She signed up for two courses at the college. She started the shop and expanded into the decorating business. She seems to have unlimited energy these days. She really is a beautiful person."

"Isn't he awfully young?"

"Kevin? He's ten or twelve years younger than Rhea. I'm that much younger than you. What difference does it make?

"None, I guess. I'm surprised. Rhea was always so conventional. Somehow I just can't see her with this Kevin person."

"Does it bother you?"

"Don't be absurd. I'm glad she has somebody."

"Rhea is busy discovering that there is a whole world out there."

"Thanks to you."

"It would have happened sooner or later with or without me. You once said that Rhea was all surface—no depth. Nothing could be farther from the truth. You don't even know her."

"Perhaps you're right. I know I never loved her the way I love you."

"You married her, and you lived with her for twenty years."

"She is a very nurturing person; she makes life so comfortable for you."

"Don't I know it! The day after I came here that first time and found out who you were, I felt awful. I stayed in bed all day. I couldn't tell her why I was so miserable. So I let her think I was sick. She brought me up chicken soup on a tray."

"And tea and sympathy, no doubt," Greg laughed.

"Right, and a rose in a silver vase. Ready to eat now?" she asked.

He nodded, and she left him relaxing and went back to the

kitchen to steep the tea and to heat and serve the food.

They ate in a companionable silence. There would be many nights like this, Jacqui thought happily. Theirs would be a good marriage; their lifestyles were compatible. She could fit in comfortably right here with all his things, with very little adjustment. She could see herself rearranging his book shelves to make room for her books. There was that space on the wall opposite the piano that seemed to cry out for the seascape she kept wrapped in brown paper under her bed, because she couldn't find a spot in her room for it.

She would tell Rhea soon, she promised herself. Enough of this. She and Greg deserved to be together. She supposed it was naive to believe that she and Rhea could still be friends. She knew it wasn't likely to happen. But whatever did happen, Jacqui sighed, she didn't want Rhea to hate her.

"Why the sigh, darling?" Greg asked.

She laughed. "Just thinking of doing the dishes," she lied. "I told you the only domestic thing about me is that I live in a house."

She refused to let Rhea intrude any longer in their private moments. She had promised Greg she wouldn't in San Francisco, but she hadn't entirely kept her promise.

"Then you won't have to do dishes, now or ever," he declared as he began to stack the dishes and silver. "I'll do them tonight, and when we're married, we'll hire a housekeeper."

"No," Jacqui protested. "I was only kidding. You're not feeling well. Let me do that."

Greg, however, had already started for the kitchen with the wine glasses and tea cups balanced on the plates in one of his hands and the teapot in the other. Jacqui tried to take them from him.

"Sit, woman," he roared.

When Jacqui turned to obey in mock submission, she heard a shattering crash. Greg had dropped the plates, the cups and the wine glasses on the tile floor in front of the sink. He looked astonished.

"I started to set them down, and the muscles in my hand wouldn't cooperate," he said incredulously. "I don't know what happened."

"Oh Greg," Jacqui cried in dismay. "You should have let me

clean up."

"No problem," he said, laughing as he regained his composure. "It's all replaceable."

He refused to let her help sweep up, and later, he did seem to be feeling better. He even sat down at the piano and played for her. From a medley of love songs, she recognized among others Somewhere my Love and Some Enchanted Evening.

"Rhea never mentioned your music," she remarked.

"Oh, I gave it up years ago," he explained. "Too busy with one thing or another. It didn't seem important. After the divorce, I decided to go back to playing. It's one of the things I really enjoy; it relaxes me."

"It relaxes me too," she replied. "And, before I get any more relaxed, I think I had better go. You need to rest."

"Don't go," he pleaded. "I'll rest much better with you beside me. Stay, please Jacqui. We seem to have so little time together. San Francisco spoiled me. I want you with me all the time."

"I'll stay," she offered, "on one condition—that you promise to phone your doctor in the morning and make an appointment for a complete physical."

"I told you, I had a checkup a couple of months ago. I'm really okay."

Jacqui stood, gathering up her purse and coat. "Goodnight, Greg," she said pointedly.

"This is blackmail," he protested.

She put on her coat and started to button it.

"Haven't you heard of negotiation and compromise?" he asked.

"Haven't you ever heard of hardlining?" she asked taking her keys out of her purse.

"Are we negotiating a labor contract?"

"We aren't negotiating anything. Either you promise to phone your doctor in the morning, or I don't stay."

"My doctor doesn't work on Saturday."

"You're quibbling."

"All right, already," he conceded. "If I'm not feeling one hundred percent by Monday morning, I promise to phone my doctor. Word of honor."

Jacqui smiled and took off her coat. Greg pulled her close.

"You're a hard woman," he told her.

"I am not; you're a pushover."

"I am not," he protested. "Actually, I'm highly respected, even feared in some quarters."

"Let's go upstairs to bed."

"You talked me into it."

"See? You're a pushover."

Laughing, he kissed the top of her head and led her up the stairs.

CHAPTER SEVENTEEN

Jill slipped quietly up the back stairs with the package from the drug store under her arm. She didn't want Rhea to hear her and wonder why she was still home in the late afternoon when she should be reporting for work at the Aloha Club. She had called them from the drug store. It was no big deal. "I'm sick, and I can't come in tonight." They were used to it, she knew. Other girls called in sick periodically.

Court was out of town again. She had not heard from him in weeks. It didn't matter. This was her problem, and she couldn't have told him anyway. She was too afraid of losing him. He made it clear from the beginning that he wasn't about to be tied down. She knew he loved her, he often told her so. And he gave her fabulous gifts, clothes, jewelry, and wickedly beautiful lingerie. But he had said once that only stupid broads get themselves pregnant. He knew she had more class.

She hadn't been nauseated—only tired, but she couldn't remember when her last period was exactly. It had to be six or seven weeks, maybe more. She had never missed a period—never been late that she could remember.

Jill looked at the box. It said you could test as early as three days after a missed period. It promised the fastest results of any home pregnancy test—in a mere thirty minutes.

Mere! She knew that the next thirty minutes would be the longest in her life. Please, please, don't let this be. She repeated the words over and over. Don't let this be. A color change to blue would mean yes. No color for living, blue for dying.

"No," she said aloud, instantly ashamed. Not for dying. An unwanted pregnancy wasn't the end of the world. This wasn't the dark ages. She would just have to get rid of it. She had even heard that it was easy. No one would ever know. Well, almost no one. She considered telling Jacqui and asking for her help.

She walked over to the schoolboy desk beside the window and pulled out the drawer where the gold bracelet with her name in diamonds was wrapped in pale blue tissue paper. She unwrapped it and put it on her arm. It was beautiful, but it seemed cold against her bare skin. Would the knife be cold when it cut away that unwanted part of her and Court? Her hands were shaking as she took off the bracelet and tucked it back into the drawer out of sight.

Jill thought of Caroline struggling to carry her baby to full term, alone and pregnant. She was a nurse, but Jill could not turn to her for help. She would never understand.

But Jill was afraid not to tell someone. Court was out of the country. God only knew where. She had to tell someone. It would have to be Jacqui. She disliked the idea of asking Jacqui for help. She was still furious with her for seeing Uncle Carter almost under Rhea's nose. It was strange that she had stopped thinking of Rhea as her aunt, but that she still thought of Carter as her uncle.

She looked at the clock. A mere thirty minutes! A lifetime. With shaking hands, she drew out the colorstick. It was vivid blue.

Stunned Jill sat down on the side of the bed. This couldn't be happening. It couldn't be blue. Tears stung her eyes. It wasn't fair. She had forgotten to take the pill once—or was it twice? It wasn't fair. She wanted a baby, of course, someday. She looked at the colorstick again; it was unmistakably blue. Rhea would never understand. She was too old fashioned—just like Jill's mother. It wasn't right to upset Rhea. She could never understand in a million years that you couldn't say no to a man like Court, or that she hadn't wanted to.

Jill rapped lightly on Jacqui's door. "May I come in?"

"Sure, what's up?"

Jacqui was dressed in a red terry robe and was towel drying her hair.

"I'd like to talk to you."

"Sounds serious."

"Yes, it is."

Jacqui wound the towel around her head turban fashion and motioned for Jill to sit down.

"This isn't easy for me," Jill began.

"I can see that. Why don't you just come out with it?"

"All right. I'm in trouble, Jacqui, and I need your help. I have no one else."

"Of course, I'll help. If I can."

"You may not want to. There is something else we have to settle first."

"Go on."

"I know about you and Uncle Carter."

Jacqui sighed. "I thought you might."

"I heard you on the phone, and I saw you together in a restaurant in the Galleria."

"You didn't tell Rhea?"

"Not yet."

"Thank you for that at least," Jacqui said. "Will you let me explain?"

"Can you explain, Jacqui?"

Jacqui walked over to the window and looked down at the street below. "The last thing in the world I want to do is to hurt Rhea. Whatever else you believe about me, Jill, you must believe that."

Jill did not reply, and Jacqui came over to sit beside her.

"I met Greg—none of his friends call him Carter—some time ago. I honestly didn't know who he was until it was too late."

"I find that hard to believe."

"I know how it sounds, Jill. I never believed in all that some enchanted evening stuff myself. But, it honestly happened that way."

She did know that two people can meet unexpectedly, and that from the first time they looked into each other's eyes, nothing could ever be the same again. She remembered Court following her with his brooding eyes her first night in the Aloha Room.

"I love Greg," Jacqui said, "and he loves me. I didn't mean for it to happen. It just did."

"What are you going to do about it?" Jill asked.

"I'm going to marry Carter Gregory!"

"Even if it breaks Rhea's heart."

"Yes, Jill," Jacqui replied, reaching out to take her hand, "even if it breaks her heart."

"I don't know what to say."

"Why don't you just say how you feel?"

"That's just it, Jacqui. I'm confused about what I do feel. At first I was furious with you. I was going to tell Rhea, but I don't know how. I just wasn't sure she could handle it. I'm still not sure. She thinks the world of you."

"Your hands are as cold as ice," Jacqui said.

Jill pulled back and stood up. This time it was she who walked over to the window. There were cars out front, Rhea would be busy with customers.

"You asked me to help you," Jacqui remembered. "What is it, Jill? Why is it so difficult for you to talk about it?"

"I can understand loving someone so much that nothing else matters," she said softly, "someone that, maybe, you shouldn't love."

"Does this have anything to do with Court?"

"Yes, but it isn't his fault. It's mine. I forgot to take the pill a couple of times—"

"Oh, God, Jill! You're not—"

"Pregnant? Yes, I think so."

"Are you sure?"

"The stick turned blue."

"The what?"

"I bought a testing kit at the drug store. It was positive."

"I don't know how accurate those things are. Let's not jump to any conclusions until you've seen a doctor."

"Do I just pick one out of the phone book?"

"No, I'll call my gynecologist for you."

"Please, Jacqui, don't tell Rhea. She'll just freak out."

"I don't doubt it. Give me a minute to dress and do something with my hair."

"If I'm pregnant—" Jill began.

Jacqui stopped her. "Let's don't get carried away with ifs. Wait until you know for sure."

"The kit said it was 99 percent accurate."

"Then let's hope you're the one out of one hundred."

"Not very good odds," Jill said ruefully. "What will the doctor think—me not married and all? Will he—"

"He's a she, first of all," Jacqui interrupted. "And she is very professional. She won't pass judgement if that's what you are worried about,"

"There is something else you have to know," Jill said. "I'm going to have an abortion."

"Without telling Court?"

"I don't know where Court is. I haven't seen him for weeks. He may be out of the country. It doesn't matter. I wouldn't tell him."

"Oh, Jill!"

"I know what you're going to say. How could I have gotten myself into this mess?"

"No. That never occurred to me. I know exactly how you got yourself into this mess."

"Go ahead and say you told me so. You and Rhea both warned me."

"No, Jill, I just want to be sure that you know what you are doing—that you won't look back on this someday and regret it. Abortion isn't the only alternative, you know."

"Abortion is the only alternative for me. It's my body."

"You're right about that. And you are the only one who has the right to make that choice. I just want you to be absolutely sure."

Jill drew herself up, straightening her shoulders. "I am absolutely sure. But that doesn't mean," she said a little less confidently, "that I'm not absolutely terrified."

"I've heard that it isn't that bad," Jacqui said, "at least in the first couple of months."

"I'm no more than that. Will you come with me?"

"Sure, if you want me to."

"Oh, Jacqui, I do. Thank you. I'm sorry I was so angry with you. Somehow, I knew you would understand."

"It's okay," Jacqui said. "I've been pretty angry with myself. But I want to be the one to tell Rhea—at the right time and in my own way."

"I don't think there will ever be a right time," Jill replied, "or a right way."

Jacqui shrugged her shoulders in despair. "I have to try.

Rhea's friendship is important to me."

Jacqui dressed and dried her hair. Then she and Jill slipped quietly down the back stairs and left in her little red car.

CHAPTER EIGHTEEN

Rhea's eyes swept the house and lawn with a satisfied appraisal as she backed out of the driveway, careful to avoid Caroline's parked car. The sign in front, Rhea Roberts Gregory, never failed to astonish her. It was almost as if she expected to wake up and find it gone—her burgeoning young business only a pleasant dream. It was still there, however

It frightened her a little to think of how well things seemed to be going. She had to stop thinking that way. Jacqui had scolded her sharply for it only a day or so before she left to visit her sick aunt. "Let go of the idea," she had said, "that you don't deserve success, or that you don't deserve your good luck. Happiness and success are natural states. Every area of our lives is meant to work. Something is wrong if it doesn't—not the other way around. Believe in yourself, Rhea. Accept your good fortune as your right."

Rhea sighed. As much as she cared about Jacqui, she really didn't think that she would ever understand her. She had been so supportive, generous with her money and her time and her friendship, yet she had gone off on that trip without even a word, and there had been only that brief phone call while she was away. It was almost as if Jacqui were holding her at arm's length, and it was puzzling. Yet there seemed to be a new radiance about Jacqui when she returned. Rhea wondered if she had never noticed how really lovely Jacqui was.

She stopped for gasoline and checked to make certain that she still had the key to Kevin's lakehouse. She had sold most of his furniture and arranged for a truck to transport the remaining pieces. Jill had agreed to keep the shop open until she left for work, and Rhea planned to be back long before that.

It was a cold day—rather dreary with low hanging clouds. Not a day to particularly enjoy a drive out of the city. Rhea found herself thinking about Kevin—his sweetness, his gentleness. "He is a man, Rhea, not a boy," Jacqui had said, yet there was such a youthful innocence about him. She supposed that it was because he had been so long tied to his invalid mother. She remembered the first time they met—the day he bumped into her car. That awful sadness in his eyes. It was still there in an unguarded moment.

She was surprised to find Kevin's car at the lakehouse when she arrived. The moving truck was not there yet, but when she rang the bell, there was no answer. She knocked and called Kevin's name. Still, there was no responses. Cautiously, she used the key to open the door and called to him again. "Kevin, are you there?" She was greeted only by silence.

The cottage was almost empty. Several boxes stood in the living room along the wall opposite the fireplace. Kevin had used them to pack the linens and the dishes and kitchen supplies, intending, he told her, to give them to charity. The cottage that had been so charming on her last visit was bleak and forlorn. There was something sad about an empty, unwanted house. She heard the truck lumbering up the road to the cottage, and even after it was loaded and had departed, there was no sign of Kevin.

Helplessly, she looked around the cottage. She could not just leave. Suppose something had happened to him. Fear gripped her chest. She looked up and down the shore line, out across the cold, gray water. He had to be nearby. She started to walk in the direction of the boathouse. She would check to see if he had taken the boat out. The wind cut through her light coat. It was turning colder.

Then she saw him sitting alone on the dock by the boathouse. He made no move and did not turn around as she approached. She laid her hand on his shoulder. "Kevin?" He turned to her—surprise on his face.

"Rhea!" He scrambled to his feet, and the hand he gave her was as cold as ice. His eyes were swollen, and she was sure that he had been crying.

"Kevin, what are you doing here? Didn't you hear my car or the truck? We finished loading the rest of the furniture."

"No, I'm sorry. I didn't hear you."

She held on to his hand and propelled him in the direction of the cottage. "You're freezing." Rhea said. "What have you been doing out here for so long? The wind off the water is like ice. I hope it doesn't make you sick."

They were almost to the cottage when he told her. "Rhea, my mother died last night."

"Oh, Kevin, I'm so sorry."

"Anya found her this morning. Apparently, she died in her sleep."

"Anya? That's your mother's nurse?"

"Yes, she slept right in the room next to Mother's. She's cared for her for years. Anya didn't hear a thing during the night. She became alarmed this morning when she couldn't wake her and called me. It was too late. She was gone."

Rhea put her arms around him and drew him close. He started to cry with great shaking sobs. Finally, he pulled away from her.

"I should have expected it. She had been ill for such a long time. I knew it would happen. And I always hoped it would be like this. In her sleep—without any pain or fear. I think there were times when I wanted it to happen. She was such a burden to me—to herself, too. And she was so desperately unhappy after Dad died. But, my own mother, Rhea. I wanted her to die. What kind of a person am I?"

"Kevin, don't. Please don't torture yourself. I felt the same way when my mother died and so did my sister, Ruth. When our mother was critically ill, we thought anything would be better than seeing her suffer. But after she died, Ruth and I both felt the same way you do now. The guilt was almost unbearable. Come inside for a few minutes. You're very cold."

Rhea quickly located a soft blanket in one of the boxes of linens, and she draped it around his shoulders. Then with only a little trouble, she got a fire started in the fireplace.

"It doesn't matter, Kevin," she soothed, "at what age we lose our mothers, it's the most shattering experience we undergo. Only time will make it less painful. You'll see, it will help, my dear one."

"How long have you been here?" she asked, searching through

another box to find the coffee pot.

"I don't know. I don't even know why I came here. I walked along the shore for a long time. That's probably where I was when you drove up. I didn't even realize that it was cold. There is a bottle of brandy in one of those boxes. That one there, I think."

"Here it is," Rhea said, pouring a generous portion into a cup for him.

"Have some too, please. I need someone to talk to. I'm glad you happened to be here. I had forgotten all about the rest of the furniture."

To please him, she poured a second cup and settled down on the floor in front of the fire beside him. It seemed only natural to take his trembling hand.

"It's ironic," he said. "Only yesterday, I finished packing up all of Dad's things left here in the cottage. Now, I'll have to do the same thing for her. Oh, Rhea, must we all leave so many loose ends when we die Who will do it for me? There isn't any family left."

"Of course, there will be someone to do it for you. You'll have your own family someday. Someone who loves you. Tying up loose ends for someone you love is a form of mourning. You need that. You'll realize that someday. You have your whole life ahead of you now, Kevin. You're free to do all the things you wanted."

The blanket slipped from his shoulders. He had finished the brandy and he caressed her hand between both of his. He reached for the brandy bottle and refilled the cups. She didn't object. He seemed calmer.

"When I was in London," he mused, "working for the magazine, we used to drink tea laced with brandy. It was so bone-chilling cold that winter. But I guess, winter always is in England. It's a damp cold. I never want to go back in winter time."

"I thought you loved working for the magazine."

"I did. It was wonderful living in Europe. Cross the channel and you're in France. Take the train to Germany. The sense of history one feels. It's an entirely different kind of beauty. And, oh, Ireland. So beautiful. An idiot could take magnificent photographs there. Did you see the pictures I took of the eighteenth century residential buildings that border St. Stephen's Green in

Dublin? I took them after a rain. It rains a lot in Ireland. There is an old adage that Ireland is the cleanest place in the world because God washes it every day. I suppose that's what makes it so green. That and the mild climate. Did you notice the photographs I took of the River Liffey? It flows to the sea through the heart of the city. Dad had them on the wall of his bedroom."

"Yes, I saw them briefly. But, if you remember, you didn't want to talk about them that day."

"I was bitter, I remember. But you helped me, Rhea, to see my father from a different, more compassionate viewpoint. Just as you're helping me now."

He smiled at her, and his lips brushed hers. Rhea was surprised—not so much by the kiss as by the shock of desire building to flame hot in her own body. This was insane. Kevin was just a boy. Years younger than she. She felt ridiculous. His mother had just died. He needed comfort from a friend. Not this. His lips touched hers again. She pulled back, extricating herself from him.

"I'll find the coffee pot," she said quickly. Her hand was trembling as she opened a can of coffee and filled the pot with water, splashing the front of her blouse in the process. It was cold away from the fire. She breathed in the cold air and tried to clear her head. The brandy, she thought, and remembered that she had not eaten anything except a cup of yogurt in the early morning. She plugged in the coffee pot and returned silently to the living room.

Kevin was sprawled on the carpet in front of the fire, propped up on one elbow, sipping the cup of brandy and staring into the fire. He sensed her presence and spoke without turning around. "Come finish your brandy while the coffee perks."

"I really have to go, Kevin."

"I know," he replied. "But just stay a few minutes more. You can't leave without some coffee."

She sat down awkwardly, well away from him.

"Have you ever loved anyone but Carter?" he asked her abruptly.

She shook her head. "No, we dated all through college and were married right after graduation." She didn't tell him that Carter was the only one she had ever dated. She had been considered too serious and too studious in high school for anyone to be much interested in her.

"Did you know right away that you wanted to marry him?"

"No, not for a long time. It wasn't love at first sight for either one of us."

"I fell in love with you the first time I saw you."

"Kevin, please don't talk like that. We're friends. I want us to go on being friends."

"That day in the restaurant—the first time I touched you, I knew. You felt the electricity too. I saw it in your eyes."

"You were mistaken."

"No, and I'm not mistaken now. You feel the same way I do."

She shook her head in protest. "I'm sorry," she whispered, but with less certainty. He was close to her again, his intense blue eyes searching hers. He looked for the moment even younger than she knew him to be. This should be happening to Jill, she thought, remembering that Jill was the reason she first invited Kevin to the house. It was happening all wrong. Jill was interested in somebody named Court Randall, and Kevin was—what was Kevin interested in?

"Kevin," she began. "I'm years older than you. This is all wrong."

He took her hand again. "If it's all wrong," he asked, "why does it feel so right?"

She had no answer, and when he leaned over to kiss her again, she didn't draw away.

He took her face in both his hands, caressing it with his fingers. He kissed her forehead, her eyelids. "I need you. Life means nothing to me without you." Those were the same words she had spoken to Carter the awful day he asked her for a divorce. *I need you, Carter.* But there had been that distance between them that she couldn't bridge, that coldness she could not warm, and he had walked away.

There was no distance between her and Kevin, and he was warm. His lips moved down to her neck, and her arms slipped around him. Then his hands were on the buttons of her blouse, and it slid from her shoulders. As he gently touched her breasts, she was suddenly alive—wonderfully and completely alive—as she had not been in a long, long time.

Her clothes were off, and he looked at her naked body, his eyes so filled with love and longing that it took her breath away. She wanted desperately to be beautiful for him—to be younger.

"I knew you would be this lovely," he said softly, drawing the blanket around them. "I've dreamed about this moment for weeks."

She kissed him gently, passionately, pressing against his hard, lean body until there was no space between them. Her thoughts echoed his words. If it's wrong, why does it feel so right.

CHAPTER NINETEEN

Jacqui spotted her car easily in the hospital parking lot. That was one of the advantages of having a bright red car—sort of compensation for the fact that it was little and low and prone to hiding between Oldsmobiles and Buicks. She had visited Greg twice daily almost every day while he was in the hospital—once in the afternoon and again at night. She had missed only one day—the day she took Jill to the clinic.

Greg seemed fine this afternoon—really back to normal. In fact he had felt so much better that he hadn't wanted to have the last round of tests done. But apparently the doctor was concerned enough about his symptoms to insist.

Greg seemed to be sleeping a great deal, so he must have needed the rest. Probably, boredom had something to do with it, she decided. Greg was an unusually active man. The test results weren't all in yet, but he was impatient to get out and get back to work.

It had been a hectic week. Just when she was the most worried about Greg, she also had to worry about Jill. Sweet, troubled Jill. Brutally honest. "You may not want to help me; I know about you and Carter."

When Jacqui arrived home, she found Jill crawling reluctantly into a cab "Rhea's not here," she explained. "I'm worried about her. She left this morning to go out to Kevin's lakehouse to have some furniture picked up, and she hasn't come back. The truck returned and unloaded hours ago. I was supposed to keep the shop open until she gets back, but I can't. I just can't miss any more work. She should have been back long before now."

"I'll take over," Jacqui promised. "I'll check on Rhea, too. I'll get in touch with Kevin. Don't worry."

Jacqui unlocked the front door and looked around. It was strange that Rhea had not returned. She was nothing if not dependable and predictable. Jacqui sat down at the desk Rhea had planted in the entry way to greet customers and looked at Rhea's file of telephone numbers.

Rhea kept neat lists of everything. If only she were so organized. She found the list and ran her fingers down to the proper place. Kevin's business phone. Kevin's home phone. Kevin's lake cottage. The cottage number had been crossed out with the notation disconnected printed neatly above it.

She tried the business number first. "I'm sorry, Mr. Stacey is out of the office today." Jacqui tried the house. No answer there. Very strange. Someone should be there—a housekeeper or the nurse who looked after Kevin's mother. Jacqui redialed the number and let it ring several times again. Still no answer. Then she, too, began to worry. But, just as she picked up the phone again, she heard a car in the drive. Thankfully, it was Rhea. Jacqui met her at the door.

"Rhea, is something wrong?"

"No, nothing is wrong," she answered quickly. "Where is Jill?"

"Jill left for work. She waited for you as long as she could."

Rhea appeared confused, distracted. "Is it that late?" she asked in surprise.

"Yes, it's almost four. She was worried about you. So was I."

"Oh, I'm sorry. I should have phoned. I'm not thinking straight today. I simply forgot."

"Rhea, did something happen today?" Jacqui asked.

Rhea looked bewildered for a moment, and then she quickly replied. "Yes, something did happen. Kevin's mother died. I've been with him."

"I'm sorry. She's been ill for a long time, I understand."

"Yes, but it was still a shock to him."

"Death always is. Is there anything I can do?"

"No, I don't think so. I'll order flowers in the morning. But, yes, there is something you can do for me. I'm really exhausted, Jacqui. Would you mind locking up for me? I know it's early, but I need to go upstairs."

"I'll stay here a while longer—just in case someone stops by. Then, sure, I'll lock up."

"Thanks, Jacqui."

Jacqui watched Rhea climb the stairs. Her shoulders were stooped, her hair disheveled. She really has had a bad day, Jacqui thought. She stood up from the desk and walked into the study. The new pieces would be Kevin's, of course. But Rhea had quite a bit of inventory aside from his things.

The dining room had not been refurnished since Rhea sold the second set of dining room furniture—the Queen Anne table and chairs that didn't match. They had been snapped up almost as soon as Rhea got the chairs back from the upholsterer. Now the dining room was filled with odd pieces of furniture and a collection of depression glass. They had seldom used it, preferring the intimacy of the breakfast room just off the kitchen.

In fact, Rhea had items on display for sale in all the downstairs rooms with the exception of the kitchen. Sooner or later the whole downstairs of the big old house would be filled, and Rhea would be relegated to the second floor for living space.

This beautiful shop was a giant step for one who had internalized the idea that she was fat and incapable of taking care of herself and much too old to make a new start. Jacqui knew that for Rhea, marriage to Greg had been a fortress, and by the time the walls crumbled, she found it exceeding difficult to do anything alone.

Jacqui wondered if all women had that hidden core of self doubt that made so many of them choose the safe, the familiar, the known. She was so much like Rhea, she thought, after Spence died. She understood why Rhea felt so solitary, so disconnected. Freedom, when you hadn't planned on it, was frightening. When Spence died and left her the money, what did she decide to do? There were so many possibilities. But she chose to stay in school; it was safe and familiar. Her studies weren't challenging. They were just an endless series of chores that were nothing but obligations. There was no joy left in anything..

Jacqui sighed. Soon she would be gone, and Rhea would be on her own. She and Greg would be married, and she knew with certainty that Rhea would no longer seek her advice. No more designing advertising layouts on the kitchen table. No more shopping the competition. No more late night rap sessions, no more skinny dipping, no more wine and midnight philosophy.

Although she and Greg were friends as well as lovers, she would miss Rhea's companionship. And she was, also, concerned about the money she had loaned Rhea. She was not worried, of course, that Rhea wouldn't pay it back, but rather that she would feel compelled to do so sooner than it would be prudent. The money was tied up in inventory. Rhea needed working capital if the business was to survive.

There were no late customers. Jacqui phoned Jill at the club to let her know that Rhea had returned safe Later she took a phone message from a salesman that Rhea could answer the following day. At six she placed the closed sign on the door and locked up. She was tired, and there would be just enough time to take a nap before she went back to the hospital.

Rhea heard Jacqui go out later, grateful that she had been left undisturbed. She wanted to be alone. She just couldn't face anyone. Her wrinkled, water-soaked skin had finally returned to normal after the hour she spent bathing in hot, lilac scented water.

She slipped into an old pair of Carter's pajamas. They gave her comfort—almost as if his arms were around her. She looked undecided at the phone beside the bed. If only she dared call him. What could she say? Forgive me. Carter did not forgive easily. Her day with Kevin must forever remain her secret.

She tried to shut it out of her mind. She had embarked upon uncharted waters with Kevin, and she was frightened. How could she have dared? She needed to hear Carter's voice, safe and familiar. She dialed his number. She would hang up when he answered. She just wanted to hear his voice. The telephone rang again and again. There was no answer Not even an answering machine message. That was, indeed, strange.

She began to cry softly, knowing with a dreadful certainty that today she—not Carter—had betrayed whatever chance their relationship had. She was afraid that he would never be there for her again. She felt acutely alone and unprotected. She scurried down between the sheets and let the bitter, silent tears fall at will. Mercifully, at last she slept.

Rhea was not sure what awakened her, but she could hear water running in the hall bathroom. She glanced at the bedside clock—not yet nine. Probably, it was Jacqui. Or, it might be

Caroline. Jill wouldn't be back until much later.

Rhea's arm was tingling. When she tried to move her hand, red hot needles stabbed it. She massaged it to restore circulation and sat up on the side of the bed. A wave of dizziness flooded over her. Her heart began to pound. She found it difficult to breathe, and she was terrified.

She though she was having a heart attack. She eased herself back on the bed. It was several minutes before the pounding of her heart began to slow, and she was able to breathe normally. She sat up carefully on the side of the bed. Whatever it had been was over, but it left her shaken and depressed. What else could happen to her?

She fumbled for her robe and shippers, remembering that she had eaten nothing since early morning. Perhaps, the dizzying sickness was from lack of food. She went out into the hall. Caroline's door was open. It had been Caroline in the bathroom, she concluded.

Downstairs, Rhea felt better. She drank a glass of milk and searched the refrigerator for something to eat. It was poorly stocked. She had no time to shop lately. At last, she found a packaged of sliced ham.

Caroline, with her hair wrapped in a turban, was persuaded to come down and join her for ham and eggs. Just as they were finishing, Jacqui came in with a bag of chocolate eclairs she had picked up earlier, fresh from the bakery. They each had an eclair and a cup of tea.

"This is delicious," Caroline said. "I love chocolate."

"So do I," Jacqui replied. "It makes you feel so good. It produces the same sort of euphoria that being in love does."

"But being in love is less fattening," Rhea moaned.

"Not always," Caroline disagreed, patting her distended stomach.

They all laughed. It was totally out of character for Caroline. She seldom joined in their nonsense.

Suddenly, Rhea had a horrifying thought. What if she were pregnant? The doctors had never been able to find a reason why she could not conceive Carter's child. She had never been concerned with birth control; it was never necessary. What if by some cruel, inexplicable turn of fate she had conceived Kevin's baby?

There was no one she could turn to—to confide her fear.

Not even Jacqui, although Jacqui sometimes failed to come home for several nights in a row, and Rhea assumed there was a man somewhere who was responsible for that. Momentarily, she had an image of a tiny, blond replica of Kevin with enormous blue eyes reaching out to her.

"Rhea, is something wrong?" Jacqui asked.

Rhea snapped to attention. "No, why?"

"You looked so strange."

"I'm sorry. It's been a strange day."

Strange for me, too, Jacqui thought. Greg seemed distant tonight, almost as if he were pushing her away, and yet clinging to her at the same time.

He had become very upset when she told him about Jill's abortion.

"You had no right to keep it from Rhea," he accused. "She might have been able to talk Jill out of it. She would certainly have been against Jill getting an abortion."

"I shouldn't have told you," she said. "I had no idea that it would upset you so much."

"Jill is just a baby."

"Babies don't get pregnant."

Greg threw up his hands in helpless frustration.

"Besides," Jacqui said. "I didn't think anybody had the right to talk her out of it. It's her body, and it was her decision."

"So, we finally found a subject we disagree on," he said looking away.

"It was bound to happen sooner or later. We're both strong individuals."

"I suppose. But why didn't you tell Rhea? Don't you think she has a right to know?"

"Jill asked me not to. In her words, Rhea would probably freak out."

"It seems," he said with a quizzical lift of one eyebrow, "that I'm not the only one who tries to insulate Rhea from life's harsher realities."

"Yes, I did accuse you of that, didn't I? I wonder why Rhea seems so much more vulnerable than the rest of us. We all try to protect her."

Jacqui turned her attention back to the kitchen, offering to clear the table and load the dishwasher. But instead of going up to bed, Rhea began to clean and polish the new furniture, rearranging it and integrating it with her other stock to make everything more visually appealing. And when Jacqui went up to bed, she was still hard at work, dressed in the robe and slouchy pajamas.

Caroline went back to her room and took off the turban to dry her hair. She had trained herself not to look at the closet where the money was hidden behind the ceiling tiles. She hadn't used much of it, only a little to pay for the old car she had purchased. Her salary had been sufficient to pay Rhea and provide all the other necessities.

Now that she no longer had a job, her meager hoard of money was dwindling fast. Soon she would have to dip into Rick's money again. If only she could manage without it, she would gladly give it back to him. But how could she manage until the baby was born? And how would they survive until she was able to go back to nursing? Sometimes she was on the verge of telling someone—Rhea, perhaps—and begging for help. But unfortunately, begging was something she had never been able to do.

Caroline felt the child within her stir—a fluttering of life. She wondered if someday the baby would hate her as she had hated her own mother for the misery and the squalor and finally the desertion. I'll never leave you, she promised the baby. Never. And I'll give you something to make up for never knowing your father. She wasn't sure yet what that would be. Once she had thought it would be money. Now she knew it could never be. The dirty drug money must never touch her perfect, innocent child.

Caroline slid into bed and turned out the lamp. The baby moved again. If only she could go back in time, she thought. No Rick Cortero. But if that were possible, the precious burden she carried would not exist.

"I'll be everything you need," she promised, caressing her swollen stomach. "I'll love you, and somehow I'll create a beautiful life for you."

The room was dark, yet in her mind's eye, Caroline could see the beckoning field of bluebonnets depicted in the painting opposite her bed. She saw herself being propelled through that field knee deep in blue blossoms. A tiny hand was clinging to hers; she saw blond curls bobbing in the wind. And she distinctly heard a shrill, breathless voice, "Hurry Mommy, it's getting dark."

Caroline tightened her grip on the tiny hand and began to skip along with the child. She was happier and freer than she had ever been before.

CHAPTER TWENTY

Jacqui awakened to the sound of softly falling rain. She opened the draperies and looked down on the wet street. It was cold and dreary. Soon it would be Christmas. She had hated Christmas since Spence died. She supposed that she had been experiencing the Unmerry Christmas Syndrome. All the symptoms were there, depression, a heightened sense of futility, an absence of hope, unreasonable resentment of other people's happiness.

This year it would be different. This year she had Greg. Rhea had already began to put up decorations. It was hard not to get into the holiday spirit. All she had to do was think of Greg, wonderful, laughing, roguish Greg—who was everything she had ever wanted and more.

Regretfully, they hadn't spent much time together. Greg had been in the hospital for ten days—all the time assuring her that there was nothing to worry about. But the day he was released, he phoned her from the airport saying that something had come up unexpectedly and that he had to go to Dallas for a day or two. He said he would call her, but he didn't. She was disappointed that he hadn't asked her to go. Days passed, and she did not hear from him.

Enough was enough. She called his office. "I'm sorry, Miss Wilder. Mr. Gregory is still out of town. No, he didn't give me a number where he could be reached. When he checks in, I'll be happy to tell him you called."

Jacqui waited all day, but there was no phone call from Greg. Where was he? She couldn't shake the nagging feeling that all was not well. Something was going on. Greg was avoiding her. After weeks of seeing him every day, it was confusing to have him unavailable to her. Some important case, she supposed. He probably thought that she would read him the riot act for going back to work so soon. And, without doubt, she would have.

Surely Greg had time for a phone call. He was not an inconsiderate man. That made it all the more puzzling. She had even driven by his place a couple of time. The garage doors were closed, the draperies drawn.

Late in the afternoon she went to the university to meet with her adviser and to return some books to the library. With nowhere else to go, she found herself driving out by the Galleria, looking at the restaurants along Westheimer, trying to decide where to eat. But instead of stopping at one, she drove to Greg's place.

A young boy was pushing a grocery store shopping cart laden with newspapers down the street. He stopped at Greg's sidewalk and, expertly taking aim, threw a paper to land just outside Greg's front door. She had seen the paper boy before. Maybe it was the last time she had driven by—yesterday or the day before. But, there were no stacked up papers outside Greg's door. Perhaps, someone was collecting them for him while he was out of town or, perhaps, he wasn't out of town at all. It was very strange, the feeling she suddenly had.

She parked and went up to the door. There was no response when she rang the bell. She kept on ringing it. Somehow she knew that Greg was just inside that door. "I know you're there, Greg," she said, knocking on the door. "Let me in!"

There was no answer, but she kept ringing the bell for a long time. "I won't go away," she said determinedly. "I know you are in there. Let me in." She kept knocking and ringing the bell. "Why are you doing this to me?" she asked the closed door, certain that she heard a movement inside.

"Please Greg."

The door opened slowly. He looked awful. Much worse than the morning she checked him into the hospital. There were dark circles under his eyes. He looked as if he had not slept in days. She wondered briefly if he might be drinking. The crazy idea that Greg might have an alcohol problem raced through her mind as she searched for a rational explanation. That was ridiculous. She knew him better than that.

"Why, Greg?" she asked as the door closed behind her.

He didn't take her in his arms; he walked away. She followed him to the dining alcove.

"Please sit down." He gestured to a chair on the opposite side of the table from him. "I have to talk to you."

"Greg, you're scaring me."

"Oh, my love," he said, reaching for her hand. "I don't want to scare you or hurt you. That's why I didn't want to see you just now. I wanted more than anything in the world to make you happy—as happy as you've made me. Jacqui, do you know how happy you made me the day you decided to go to San Francisco with me?"

"You've made me just as happy," she said in bewilderment, "and you'll go on making me happy. I love you."

"No." He shook his head sadly. "We don't have a future now. You see, I'm ill. Really ill." He let go of her hand.

Jacqui felt a rush of sudden fear.

"I have multiple sclerosis."

"I know that's very serious," she said, "but, I guess I'm not really sure what it means."

"It means," he replied in a flat tone, "a permanent numbness in my left hand and foot. It means extreme fatigue. When I'm having an attack, it means falling down, dropping things, trying to talk with my tongue tied in knots, seeing double images when I try to read."

"Oh, Greg," she said in dismay. "What causes it?"

"Nobody knows for sure. They suspect that it's a slow virus that can be dormant in the body for a long time before it shows any symptoms."

"Are they sure?"

"Unfortunately, yes. There was a definite diagnosis. They did a spinal tap and detected abnormal antibodies."

"What is the prognosis?" she asked, unable to believe that they were calmly discussing his illness as through it were a news story happening to someone else. Spence had chosen not to discuss his heart condition with her. She had a momentary vivid image of Spence dying in her arms. This could not be happening to her. It wasn't fair. Not Greg, too. She took his hand, but he didn't respond to her touch.

"There is no effective treatment except a balanced diet to

keep weight down and megadoses of vitamin C to help prevent bladder infections. They can't make a prognosis until they see how the disease progresses during the next five years. I will be given steroids to reduce the symptoms during an acute attack. Some patients suffer a series of attacks occurring several months apart or several years apart with long remissions in between. That seems to be the most I can hope for."

Jacqui took both his hands. "There is hope," she said fervently. "You'll go into remission. I know you will. We'll have some good years, Greg."

"Jacqui, we can't. Don't you see? I could become totally dependent."

"Whatever happens, happens. We'll handle it," she said with conviction.

"You don't understand. You're too young—too alive to be saddled with this. You have your whole life ahead of you. The doctor warned that I could become paralyzed by allowing myself to become too tired. There might be a loss of control or sensation in the bladder or the bowels or the genitals. Speech can even be affected. Don't you understand? I love you too much to do that to you."

"You have no right to shut me out!" she cried suddenly. "I love you, Greg. You can't spare me anything just because you send me away. I'll suffer just as much—probably more. Spence did this to me. But I won't let you. You have no right. I won't let you! Do you hear? You said yourself there can be long periods of remission—several years."

He didn't seem to hear her. "Do you know what the worst part would be?" he asked. "I could be totally dependent, but there is rarely ever any mental impairment. I would see you and know what I had done to you. I love you, Jacqui. God knows I love you. And to continue seeing you even as a friend would only make me want you all the more. It has to be over between us. Don't you see? I'd give anything to spare you this pain."

"You don't remember that afternoon on the airplane going to San Francisco, do you Greg?"

"Of course, I remember. I remember every minute we spent together."

"You promised me I wouldn't ever be sorry."

"For God's sake, Jacqui! Do you think I wanted this to happen?"

"You wanted me to love you, to commit myself to you. And I did."

"I'm sorry," he whispered, "so very sorry. I never wanted to hurt you."

She could see tears in his eyes. When they slid down his cheeks, she wiped them away with her fingertips.

"I won't leave you, Greg. You don't have to marry me. But I won't leave willingly. I'll be here until you forcibly have me ejected. And if that happens, I won't go far. And I won't stop loving you and trying to see you and begging you to let me back into your life. You'll never be free of me as long as I live."

He started to shake then—his whole body became racked with uncontrollable sobs. Jacqui wrapped her arms around him and held him without saying anything.

Later she led him to bed and wordlessly helped him undress. She slid into bed beside him, holding him, comforting him with her body, but she did not try to talk. There was nothing more to be said. She knew he didn't sleep, nor did she. And she heard him crying intermittently through the night.

Finally, just before dawn, he put his arms around her and drew her closer. "Promise me, Jacqui," he begged, "that you won't ever stay with me out of pity or a sense of duty. I couldn't stand that."

"I promise," she said truthfully.

And when he slipped into a deep, exhausted sleep, she knew that he had at last come to terms with his illness. Tomorrow would be better.

CHAPTER TWENTY-ONE

Rhea came down from the attic with another box of Christmas decorations. She had always enjoyed decorating the house for Christmas and was, inevitably, reluctant to pack the decorations away when the holidays were over. Some of her happiest memories in this house were associated with Christmas. Carter always gave her extravagant presents. Like the year he went skiing in Utah and didn't get home until late Christmas Eve. That was the year he gave her a diamond bracelet.

Sometimes it was hard to believe that things would ever be the same again. She had made so many mistakes. In her more defensive moments she laid all the blame on Carter. He had taken care of everything. No wonder she didn't know how to manage on her own. The twenty thousand dollars she received in the divorce settlement, along with the house, furniture, and her car, was gone before she knew it. Sometimes she wondered where she'd gotten the courage to start a business. She had bungled everything else in her life so badly. Even her relationship with Kevin.

Oh, God, she thought miserably. How did she get herself into this? All she wanted was friendship, a little warmth, a little indication that she still mattered to someone. How did it go so far? She had never thought of herself as a sensual person, but Kevin was right. There was a sexual excitement when they met. And Rhea wondered what that said about her. She didn't even know him then. There was no candlelight and roses. He was years younger than she.

Maybe it would serve Carter right if he knew about Kevin. Oh,

God, no! Carter must never know. He would never be able to for-give her for something like that.

Rhea picked up Santa Claus in a fur trimmed velvet suit and straightened his whiskers. Familiar things gave her a sense of comfort. Somehow everything would work out in spite of her doubts and fears, and, yes, even her weakness.

She avoided Kevin after his mother's funeral. Probably, she would have to deal with it sooner or later, but she hated con-frontations. She and Carter never quarreled. She knew that time had a way of resolving most things. If she would just not see Kevin for a while, perhaps, the problem would work itself out. He would see how impossible their relationship was.

Rhea put the Santa down to answer the phone.

"Rhea, it's Kevin. Let's have lunch today."

"No, Kevin, I'm sorry. I can't. Jill and Jacqui are both out. I have nobody to mind the shop."

"Then I'll pick up something and bring it over there."

"No. I don't think that's a good idea."

"What's not a good idea? Lunch or my coming over?"

"Kevin, please don't make this difficult for me. Please don't misunderstand, but I think it's probably better if we don't see each other for a while."

"Better for who? You can't mean that. I have to see you."

"Please, Kevin. What happened between us—well, it should-n't have happened. I'm very sorry for the grief you're going through, and I wanted to comfort you. I care about you, but I don't take sex lightly."

"I didn't think for a moment that you did. Neither do I."

"I can't talk about this now. Someone might overhear—a customer."

"We have to talk sometime."

"Kevin, please. What is the point?"

"The point is," he said slowly, "I love you, and you might not know it yet, but you love me. At least I think you do. I'll see you when the shop closes."

"No, I can't."

"Yes," he said abruptly, and she realized that he had hung up.

When the phone rang again, she answered it with dread. She knew she couldn't hide from him forever, but the voice she heard was Jacqui's.

"Rhea, will you have lunch with me?"

"Gee, Jacqui. I would like to, but Jill isn't here. I don't know. There's no one to keep the shop open."

"It's important."

"Well, I suppose I could just close for an hour. Where are you?"

Her question went unanswered, but Jacqui arranged to meet her at a small neighborhood Italian restaurant not far from the house. Actually, Rhea knew it well. It was the one where she and Kevin had stopped on the day he bumped into her car. And they had gone there several times after class in the last few weeks.

Jacqui was already seated when she arrived. She was at a table by the window, and as she looked out, she seemed far away, almost unapproachable. She had finished one drink—there was an empty glass on the table. As the waiter took away the empty glass, it was replaced with a fresh drink, and Jacqui downed it. Rhea had never seen her drink that way. She was puzzled.

Rhea sipped her glass of red wine and tried to make conversation.

"This is the house wine," she said. "It's very inexpensive, but it's good. You should try it."

"Do you know what multiple sclerosis is?" Jacqui asked abruptly.

"A disabling disease," Rhea replied. "I don't know much beyond that."

"I didn't either. It's a disease that attacks the central nervous system and destroys the covering that surrounds the nerves. Let me tell you about it. The most common symptoms are weakness, numbness, and sensations of heat or cold in the legs or arms. Usually, there is difficulty walking and diminished bladder control. Dramatic swings from depression to euphoria are common. There may be a series of attacks several years apart. The disease in its worst form may be totally disabling."

"How awful. I'm almost afraid to ask, but why are you telling me this?"

"Because the man I love has multiple sclerosis!"

"The man you love!" Rhea exclaimed. "Oh, Jacqui, how awful for you. Especially after Spence. Do I know him?"

"Yes, you do. Spontaneous remissions are common in most cases during the first five years. I couldn't bear it if I didn't keep reminding myself of that. At the present, there is no cure. But many patients improve if they believe something is going to help them, a special doctor, religion, or even therapy of one kind or another. I've made up my mind to be what he believes in. I must tell you, Rhea. I'm going to be married."

"I don't know what to say. Married? Isn't this sudden? Are you sure you know what you are doing?"

"Very sure. That's why I didn't tell you until now. Your friendship means a great deal to me."

"I don't understand."

"You will. Just let me talk."

Rhea looked at Jacqui quizzically as she spoke of a chance meeting with a warm, vibrant, exciting man and of the instant rapport between them—so dramatic, they didn't even exchange last names.

"It was as if we had always known each other," Jacqui explained. "If I believed in reincarnation, and I'm not sure I don't, I would say that we had been together in a former life.

"The feelings that developed between us," she continued, "can't be explained. I don't believe in fate. Life is a result of the choices we make—not fate. But I didn't choose to hurt you, Rhea, and neither did Greg."

"Greg?" Rhea whispered in shocked surprise. She felt as if the breath was being squeezed from her lungs.

"My Greg?" she gasped finally. "Carter?"

Jacqui nodded. "I never heard you speak of him as Greg, so I didn't make the connection when we met. By the time I found out, I honestly tried to back out of the relationship. I know you won't believe that."

"How could you?" Rhea breathed in cold fury. "How could you do this to me?"

"The last thing I wanted to do was to hurt you, Rhea."

"How could you? You knew how much Carter means to me."

Rhea's voice had risen. People in the restaurant were beginning to stare.

"You don't love Carter," she accused. "You're just trying to make up for Spence."

"That's not true, Rhea. Please let me explain."

"You have explained quite enough. Leave—now."

Rhea's voice was a dull, flat monotone. "Just leave now."

With a gesture of helplessness, Jacqui rose. Rhea watched her walk away. She reached for the wine glass, trying to cool the white hot pain searing inside her.

"Jacqui and Carter," she said incredulously.

She hailed a passing waiter and ordered another glass of wine. Jacqui and Carter. She felt a stab of guilt. All her pain had been for her own loss and none for Carter. The reality of his illness had paled in comparison to her own loss—to know that he was never coming back—that all her plans for their future were in vain. Carter ill? Unbelievable. He never had a sick day. It couldn't be true. Once in a while he had suffered from a pulled muscle or twisted ankle, mostly from athletic pursuits. Never susceptible to infections, Carter was the healthiest person she knew. It couldn't be true. Jacqui was making it up to overshadow her ultimate act of treachery. It couldn't be true. She refused to believe it.

Rhea frantically searched the menu in front of her. What looked good? Everything. She loved Italian food. Veal Parmesan. Fettucini. Linguini with squid. Yes, that all looked good. A salad drenched in garlic and oil—hot bread. Bread sticks. Lots of bread sticks. She began to nibble on a bread stick before the salad arrived.

She would talk to Carter. It was all a mistake. For better or worse. In sickness and health. She should have been the one to take care of him. Why he had chosen Jacqui? Jacqui, who was tall and slender and self-assured and articulate. Jacqui, who had vowed never to marry anyone after Spence. Jacqui, who was stimulating and fun. Jacqui, who was warm and loyal and caring.

The bitch! The horrible bitch! How could she do this? It was the ultimate betrayal.

Rhea's food arrived. She ordered another glass of red wine and methodically began to eat. It was delicious. Veal with just the right amount of tenderness, smothered in marinara sauce and cheese. She took a large bite of warm bread and became aware that someone was standing over her table. Kevin!

He sat down without saying anything.

"I was hungry," Rhea said defensively as he looked at the food.

He didn't answer her, and he waved the approaching waiter away. "Nothing for me, thanks."

"You wanted to have lunch," she reminded him. When he didn't reply, she asked, "How did you know where to find me?"

"Jacqui called me."

"Jacqui! What did she tell you? The bitch!"

"Nothing, except that you could use a friend," he said quietly. "I hope I still qualify."

Rhea could feel the tears sliding out of her eyes. Kevin made no move to touch her.

"Do you still want all of this food?" he asked.

"Yes—no. I don't know. I always eat when I'm upset."

"Yes, I know. Let's get out of here."

She let him take care of the check and put her coat around her shoulders. Later she did not remember handing him her car keys, but they were in her car, and he was in the driver's seat. She sat staring ahead, unseeing until the car rolled to a stop. It was not her house.

"My house," he said, answering her unspoken question.

"The shop," she protested. "I have to get back."

"Okay— but not for a while. Let's get something warm to drink."

Somehow it seemed as if they were replaying the scene at his lake cottage, the day his mother died. But it wouldn't end the same way, she promised herself silently.

The house was depressing. The structure was as large—more imposing, perhaps, than her own. But, it was dark and cheerless. Even when Kevin poked at the fire in the fireplace, it still seemed cold. It had none of the charm of the cottage; everything seemed old and faded, unloved, and uncared for even thought it had a magnificent staircase and huge chandelier.

"I could make this beautiful for you," she said, raising her arm in a sweeping gesture.

"I know you could," he replied.

Then he silently handed her a cup of tea. She took it and chose a chair well away from him. She felt uncomfortable with the silence, yet reluctant to tell him about Jacqui and Carter or about Carter's illness. He couldn't possibly understand. No one could.

"I was approached this morning," he told her, "by a group of long time employees of my Dad's. It seems they want to get together and buy the construction company."

"How do you feel about that?" she asked.

"Obviously, I'm not cut out to run it. I've tried, but I don't want to. I thought of selling it when Dad died, but I felt I owed the people something who had worked there all those years. It's been profitable—even with the recession. This seems to be the right thing to do. I've already made up my mind to take whatever they offer."

"What will you do then?" she asked.

"I don't know for sure. Take a long trip perhaps, reevaluate my life in terms of all the changes that have taken place."

He took the empty cup from her hand. "I know what I want," he said. "But life seldom lets us have what we want easily."

She did not reply.

"Aren't you going to ask me what that is?" he asked.

Rhea walked over to the window. "No," she answered. "You think you want me, and I could give you a thousand reasons why that wouldn't work, and you wouldn't believe any of them."

"I've told you before that you're a very wise woman."

No, she thought, not wise, just experienced. She had already been where he was now. She had been given a thousand reasons why she couldn't have Carter, and she still refuse to believe any of them.

He was standing behind her, she realized, with his hands on her shoulders. How easy it would be to turn to him. The slightest gesture in his direction, and she would be in his arms. She could say to Carter that she didn't care. Take Jacqui! She had someone younger, richer, and a better lover—someone who loved her. She knew now he never had.

Quickly, she moved away. She couldn't do that to Kevin. Most of all, though, she couldn't do it to herself. Someday she would be able to forgive Carter. In her truly honest moments, she realized that there had been an emptiness in their marriage. She had always believed it to be because they had no children. Now, she wasn't so sure.

"I really have to go," she said. "Thank you for coming to my rescue. And, by the way, you still qualify as a friend—maybe the only one I have left."

"Do you want to talk about your problem with Jacqui?" he asked.

"No, not now at any rate. I suppose I need time to put things in perspective."

"Whatever it is, you and she will work it out," he predicted.

Rhea smiled at him, but inwardly, she knew they never would. She could never forgive Jacqui. That much she knew for certain.

CHAPTER TWENTY-TWO

Rhea was up before dawn despite the fact that she had hardly slept at all. Most of the night, it seemed, she searched for answers. What had she done wrong? What could she have done differently? She should have lost the weight sooner—paid more attention to her appearance. But would it really have mattered? She remembered the day downtown at lunch when she had wanted Carter to notice, and he hadn't. It was already too late. He had asked about Jacqui.

A surge of anger swept over her. Jacqui! She wondered if Jacqui would come personally to retrieve her things from the house, or, like Carter, would she send movers? Rhea hoped it would be movers. She never wanted to see Jacqui again.

Rhea moved about the house quietly so that she would not disturb Caroline or Jill. And, as soon as it was barely light outside, she took a small brush and a can of white paint and went out to her sign in the front yard. With careful, determined strokes, she blotted out the word Gregory. Now the sign read Rhea Roberts. She stood back and looked at it with satisfaction.

She had signed her name Rhea Roberts Gregory for so many years, it was going to be difficult to drop the word Gregory. But drop it she would. Later she phoned Ben Howard who had once been an associate of Carter's and their good friend.

After exchanging pleasantries, she asked, "What do I have to do to be able to use my maiden name again? I want to drop Gregory and go back to Roberts."

"Once a woman has used her husband's name in the State of

Texas," he told her, "it becomes necessary to apply to the District Court to return her maiden name. The request is routinely granted. We just have to show that you're not making the change to escape from creditors."

"That is certainly not the reason," Rhea assured him. Then she took a deep breath. "Carter is getting married again. And, since I now have a business of my own, I want it to be associated with my name, not Carter's."

"I understand. I'll file the necessary papers," he promised.

"Thanks, Ben."

"And, by the way, it's been much too long since we've seen you, Rhea. We're having some people over Saturday night. Why don't I get Liz to give you a call? Both of us would love to see you."

"I'm really very busy with my business," she said hesitantly.

"Too busy for old friends?"

"No, of course not."

Rhea had last seen Liz Howard at her open house. She was almost sorry that she had called Ben. Liz would waste no time in spreading the word that Carter was getting married again. She supposed it didn't matter. She seldom saw any of the old crowd except when someone dropped into the shop. They had long ago stopped inviting her to social functions. Probably it was her own fault. People stopped issuing invitations when they were never accepted.

What did it matter? Nothing mattered except the fact that she had lost Carter. She should have been the one to care for him. In sickness and in health, she had promised. Even in sickness, Carter had pushed her away, preferring someone else.

Try as she would, Rhea could not imagine Carter ill. She tried to remember exactly what Jacqui had said to her. Difficulty in walking, weakness, loss of bladder control. No, not Carter! Not Carter.

Rhea was sitting at the desk in the entry way just inside the front door with her face in her hands when the first customer of the day walked in. She forced herself to smile, remembering the old Chinese proverb, A man without a smiling face must not open a shop. The customer looked familiar, but it took her a while to associate a name with the face.

"Come right in. May I show you something, or would you like

to browse?" Rhea asked.

"Yes, I think I would just like to browse. This is a lovely place you have here."

"Thank you very much. Feel free to look in all the downstairs rooms. Let me know when I can help you."

Rhea turned back to the desk, and the telephone rang. It was Liz Howard. She had certainly wasted no time.

"You must come Saturday night," Liz said, and Rhea imagined her bubbling over with curiosity. "Everyone is dying to see you."

Everyone is dying to see how she was reacting to Carter's remarriage, Rhea thought. Well, she just might show them. Maybe she would go to the damned party after all.

Finally Liz worked up to the question Rhea knew she called expressly to ask. "Ben tells me that Carter is getting married again. To anyone we know?"

"No, I don't think so. She's a graduate student."

"Isn't she a little young for Carter—I mean—a graduate student?"

"No, not really. Anyway, I don't believe that age really matters in a relationship."

Rhea was appalled to hear herself defending Carter. What a ridiculous thing to say—that age didn't matter. She just couldn't stomach the thought of Carter and herself being the prime subjects of Liz Howard's gossip.

That wasn't fair, she thought, instantly contrite. Ben and Liz Howard had been their friends, Carter's and hers, for twenty years. Of course, Liz was interested. How could she not be?

"I really will try to come," Rhea promised. "I will come. But I have to go now, Liz. I have a customer, I'll call you later in the week."

Rhea found the customer in the living room looking at a miniature Conestoga wagon with six carved horses and a driver. It was very old and had graced Rhea's mantle for several years. She had bought it at an auction in very bad condition, but an artisan in San Antonio restored it for her—even replacing the cloth on the wagon to look like the original. Even though that had probably lessened its value as an antique, it was certainly more decorative. She had not considered selling it before.

"Are you looking for a Christmas gift?" Rhea asked.

"Not exactly. My husband has just moved into a new office; he's been made Vice President of his company. I'm looking for something for his new office. Liz Howard told me about your shop."

Rhea sized up the customer quickly—attractive, designer suit, snakeskin shoes and matching bag. She looked familiar.

"Haven't we met?" she asked. " I'm Rhea Gregory—that is, I used to be Rhea Gregory. I'm Rhea Roberts now."

"Yes, I'm Laura Massie. We served on a committee together two or three years ago. Liz Howard is a close friend of mine."

"I remember now," Rhea exclaimed, "a charity ball."

"Yes, we've missed your help. You were wonderful, I recall, with food and decorations."

"I miss the volunteer work I used to do, but I've been very busy with the shop and all."

"I can imagine. Is this wagon for sale?"

From this moment on, Rhea decided, everything in this house was for sale. She was an antique dealer, and she would replace everything she sold with something of equal or greater value.

"Yes," Rhea replied. "This dates back before the turn of the century. It's hand carved, of course. This would be wonderful in an office—on a credenza, perhaps. Does your husband like Western art?"

"Yes, he does. You remember Sam, of course."

Rhea did indeed remember Sam Massie, a giant of a man with an attractive full head of gray hair and a booming voice.

"Yes, and I'm sure he would like this. It's a wonderful piece, quite unique. You won't find another on the market quite like it. It's priced at twelve hundred dollars."

Laura Massie raised a quizzical eyebrow.

"If you would like something more contemporary," Rhea added, "I have a bronze bust of Will Rogers in the other room."

"No, I like this. I just hadn't planned on spending quite that much."

"It's wonderful that Sam has been named a Vice President," Rhea smiled. "I'm sure he deserves it."

"Are you certain that this really dates back to the turn of the century?"

"Quite sure. I can furnish you a certificate of authenticity."

"Would you take a thousand dollars for it?"

"No, I'm sorry, Laura, I can't. It's worth more than twelve hundred. But I would be glad to show you something less expensive."

"You drive a hard bargain, Rhea. Will you take a check and will you deliver it to Sam's office?"

"Yes, to both questions," Rhea replied happily.

Later when Laura Massie had gone, she sat alone fingering the check. One more treasure gone. How long would it be before everything she cared about was gone? It didn't hurt as much as it should have. Perhaps she was beyond hurting.

She realized that she could no longer afford to ignore the people who had once been her friends. She hardly knew Laura, but she knew many of the same people Laura knew. In fact, Laura and Liz were close friends. It was time she got back into the swing of things. She would go to Liz's party. Her friends could well afford the kind of furniture and art she dealt in. She would use all her contacts. Networking, her management teacher called it. She would renew all her old acquaintances, starting with Ben and Liz Howard. And, if she should happen to run into Carter and Jacqui, she would smile and pretend it didn't matter, and, if she died a little inside, who would know?

Jill came down earlier than usual, gave Rhea a hug, and asked about the mail.

"It hasn't come yet, dear," Rhea replied. "Are you expecting something?"

"Sort of. I think I'll cook breakfast for us. I know you haven't eaten. What would you like?"

"Thank you, Jill, but I'm just not very hungry. You go ahead. Perhaps I'll have a cup of coffee with you."

Jill spied the check Rhea had put down on the desk top. "Wow! Twelve hundred dollars. You're rich. What did you sell so early in the morning."

"A piece of art. The Conestoga wagon and carved horses on the mantle. I'm going to deliver it today."

"But you loved that. I didn't know you wanted to sell it."

"I just decided on the spur of the moment. I really couldn't afford not to sell it—or anything else for that matter—the way things are now."

"With Jacqui gone?" Jill asked softly. "Will you rent her room?"

"Yes, I suppose—as soon as she moves her things."

"Rhea, I'm really sorry. I wish there was something I could do."

"I know, Jill. You mustn't worry about me. I really will be all right."

"Oh, I know that. I just wish I could make it easier for you now."

"Do you realize that you sound exactly like Jacqui?"

"Do I really? I think I learned a lot from her. I know you hate her right now."

"You can't possibly know how I feel about Jacqui. I'm not even sure how I feel just yet. I'm still in shock. I don't even know what I feel."

"I'm not helping, am I?"

"Yes, you are, Jill—more than you know. Now, why don't you get your breakfast while I find a packing box. The coffee is already made, and I'll be with you in a few minutes."

"Super."

Rhea carefully packed the carved horses and wagon. Soon she would have her own distinctive wrapping paper with her own logo on it, she thought. Something very elegant that immediately identified the Rhea Roberts shop. Why was she worrying about paper and boxes now? What possible difference could it make in the whole scheme of things? But it was her work that seemed to be keeping her sane—if, indeed, she was sane. She seemed to be standing to one side, watching herself, as if this weren't happening to her at all.

She thought she should be feeling something more—not wondering what she did feel. Carter was never coming back—he might even be dying—and she was wondering what she was going to wear to Liz Howard's party. She had half a mind to take some of this money and buy herself a new dress. She knew it was simply a defense mechanism, She was thinking of all those things that mattered not in the least to avoid thinking of Carter and Jacqui.

Rhea checked to make sure that the buzzer on the front door was working so that she would know if a customer came in and went through the arched stained glass doors to join Jill in the breakfast room. She allowed herself to be coaxed into eating a slice of melon and a piece of whole wheat toast, and Jill did not mention Jacqui again.

"I must do something nice for you as soon as the shop becomes really prosperous," Rhea said when Jill volunteered to key an eye on things for her while she made the delivery to Sam Massie's office and deposited Laura's check.

"You have already done something nice for me, Rhea," Jill reminded her. "You took me in off the streets when I had no place else to go."

"You certainly paid your own way," Rhea answered.

"Neither of us knew that I was going to be able to do that when you let me move in."

"I wish I could have done more. I wish you didn't have to work at that club."

"It's really not so bad. Most of the time, it's kind of fun. You know it's only temporary. I don't intend to be a cocktail waitress for the rest of my life."

"I should hope not."

Later after Rhea had run her errands, she stopped at a small dress shop in a strip mall not far from her house—attracted by the holiday dresses in the window. But, once inside the store, she bypassed the sequins and glitter and chose to try on a rich nut-meg rayon matte jersey that caught her eye. She surveyed herself in the mirror, fingering the luxurious fabric that shaped to envelop her body in softness but left just the right amount to the imagi-nation. The dress was made for her.

"You look wonderful in that," the salesgirl said. "You have the perfect figure for it. It's wonderful with your coloring."

Wonderful was overstating things a bit, Rhea decided, but she did like the dress. It would definitely show off the weight she had lost—if she did go to Liz Howard's party. Her amber jewelry would be wonderful with it. Dear God, now she was doing it! Nothing was wonderful—nor would it ever be again. Carter had torn her apart for the second time, and she was afraid that she could never put the remnants of herself together again.

She looked at her watch. Would she ever get through the day? She had to stop thinking about it. She handed the salesgirl a business card.

"I have an antique shop," she said. "Come by and browse some time soon."

When Rhea got home, she could hear voices. Jill was show-ing a customer around the shop. Rhea was shocked when they come out of the study, and she discovered that the voice belonged to Giles Riker, her former employer.

"What are you doing here?" she demanded.

"Just checking out the competition," he drawled.

"My shop is hardly competition for the junk you peddle," she retorted.

"Rhea!" Jill exclaimed in surprise. She had never known Rhea to be rude to anybody.

"It's all right, Missy," he grinned. "I'll say you've done all right for yourself, Gregory. This is some place. I've got another one now—makes four in all."

"Am I supposed to be impressed?"

"Now, don't get all riled up. I have a proposition for you. I've come across some furniture that would bring a whole lot more in a place like this than from my stores. We might work out a deal."

"I'm not interested in any kind of a deal with you now or ever," Rhea said evenly. "I would appreciate it if you would leave."

She saw Jill looking at her in astonishment. She didn't know, Rhea realized, how deeply hurt she had been by Riker's firing—particularly the way it was accomplished. Well, she had showed him.

Riker turned to leave, but at the door, he delivered one last parting shot. "Well, I always felt you were more of a housekeeper than a businesswoman—always cleaning and polishing."

"Oh, the nerve of that bastard," Rhea fumed.

"I'm sorry. I didn't know who he was," Jill apologized.

"Of course, not. How could you? I'm sorry I was gone so long. Anything else happen?"

"The mail came. There was a package for you. It's right there on your desk."

"A package!" Rhea exclaimed. "I wasn't expecting anything."

She examined the package. It was, indeed, addressed to her, but there was no return address.

"What do you suppose it could be?"

"Why don't you open it and find out?" Jill said, laughing.

"Good idea. Why didn't I think of that?"

Rhea cut the tape on one end of the box and drew out a large padded envelope. Carefully, she extracted a framed portrait. It was several seconds before she realized who the woman with the shinning eyes and mystical expression was. It was she—

leaning against a tree with the lake in the background. Kevin had taken it weeks ago, and she had forgotten how he photographed her the first time she visited his cottage until she begged for mercy.

"It's you!" Jill exclaimed.

"Yes, Kevin took it."

"I love it. You look so beautiful—and so happy—as if you didn't have a care in the world."

"That particular day, I didn't," Rhea remembered. It was the only portrait of herself she had ever liked. All the others seemed posed and artificial. She had known that Kevin was good when she first looked at his work.

"But why did he mail it to you instead of bringing it in person?" Jill asked.

"Because," Rhea replied. "I asked him to stay away for a while."

"Because he's in love with you?"

"Jacqui told you that," Rhea accused.

"Nobody told me. I was born in a little town in Arkansas, Rhea, but it wasn't yesterday."

"It was almost yesterday," Rhea said, laughing. "Twenty years went by so fast. Do you realize that in another twenty years, I'll be sixty-two and Kevin won't even be fifty?"

"Rhea, haven't you ever lived just for the moment?"

"Oh, Jill, that's exactly what I'm doing now. Moment by moment is how I'm getting through today."

"Then why are you worried about how old you'll be in twenty years?"

"Out of the mouths of babes," Rhea conceded.

"Well, this babe has some advice for you, oh ancient one. Why don't you call Kevin and ask him to come by for a late lunch so you can thank him properly and take back all that nonsense about not wanting to see him?"

"Don't you see, as much as I would like to, I can't do that?"

"Why not?"

"Because it isn't fair to him. We can never be more than friends."

"Have you told Kevin that?"

"Yes, of course, I have."

"It seems to me than that you are not being very friendly."

"It hurts too much to hope and have those hopes shattered again and again."

"Are we talking about you and Kevin or about you and Uncle Carter?"

"Isn't it the same thing?"

"I don't think so. You can't keep him from hoping. And if you told him you could only be friends, then don't you think he should at least have the option of accepting or rejecting that friendship?"

"I never thought of it that way. I wish we could go on being friends. I really do."

"Then do something about it."

"If you were me, what would you advise for this late lunch? The cupboard is bare."

"If I were you, Rhea, I would send my niece Jill to the deli for some cold seafood salad and warm bread and cheese and fruit and a marvelous bottle of chilled wine. She could be back in a flash."

"Do you think my niece Jill could be persuaded to do that for me?"

"I think she could, and I, also, think she could be persuaded to wait on customers so you wouldn't be interrupted during your late lunch."

"Why are you so good to me?"

"Because, my goose of an aunt, I like you."

"Goose of an aunt," Rhea said indignantly. "You haven't called me aunt in months."

"That's because," Jill explained, "most of the time, I feel we are the same age."

"And the rest of the time?"

"I feel years older."

"How did I know you were going to say that? I really shouldn't spend money on expensive deli food. I bought myself a new dress today."

"Good for you, you deserve it."

"True—but can I afford it?"

"Sure you can. Better days are coming. You sold the wagon this morning. That's a good omen."

"I wish I could believe that. But, at any rate, I'm going to take a chance and call Kevin. If he agrees to come, will you go to the deli?"

"Right away."

Rhea picked up the phone and dialed Kevin's number. "Goose of an aunt," she muttered as she waited for him to answer.

CHAPTER TWENTY-THREE

Rhea threaded an amber earring through the lobe of her ear and attached the gold back. She had misgivings about going to Liz Howard's party. How could she be sure the night would not turn into another disaster? Especially since she had asked Kevin to be her escort. He had been pathetically eager to oblige. She had promised herself that she would tread very carefully with Kevin after the long talk they had at lunch a few days ago.

Asking him to the party, she acknowledged, was really an act of cowardice. She just couldn't face Liz and Ben and all the others alone, although these people had once been her close friends. She couldn't discard them now; she hadn't any others.

All of a sudden she felt incredibly weary. It would be so easy to take off her clothes, turn out the lights, and climb back into bed. She longed to do it, but the die had been cast. Liz was expecting her and Kevin. He would be here any minute.

She took one last look at herself in the long mirror, dismayed at the dress that seemed so flattering in the shop. It was too revealing, she decided. It would just be one more thing to ignite the gossip. She was almost to the point of changing.

She had to stop being so indecisive—so fearful of making mistakes. "You're stronger than you think," Kevin had said. But he didn't really know her, she thought He saw an idealized version of the older woman, wise, experienced, self assured. If only she were really like that. "Believe you are, and you will be," Jacqui had said time and time again. "It's the self-fulfilling prophecy, Rhea, and it really does work."

Baloney! Rhea thought. If she were strong, why did she have so much trouble telling Kevin that Carter and Jacqui were going to be married. Finally she had just blurted it out over lunch, sort of like serving him the wine and seafood salad, next course—my heartbreak. Here, try this, Kevin!

"Jacqui and Carter!" he repeated incredulously. "When?"

"I don't know. Right away, I think. She has moved in with him. But there's more. Carter has a very serious illness—multiple sclerosis."

"Rhea, I'm sorry. I don't know what to say. When did you find out?"

"A few days ago. Jacqui told me in the restaurant the day you came to my rescue. She's been seeing Carter for months. Swears she didn't know who he was when she fell in love with him. But she just found out about his illness. She has some kind of a martyr complex, you know."

"That doesn't sound like Jacqui to me."

"There are things about her that you don't know. Her fiance died of a heart attack a little over a year ago. He had been ill for some time, but she didn't know, and he literally died in her arms. She can't forgive herself, and she is trying to make up for failing Spence with Carter."

"Jacqui has always seemed pretty straight forward to me," Kevin said gently. "She was concerned about you when she called me to come to the restaurant. I wish I had known then why you were so upset."

"I just couldn't talk about it. I had to come to terms with Carter's illness and Jacqui's betrayal first."

"And have you?"

"No. At first I hated Jacqui, and, then, I felt an overwhelming sense of loss."

"And now?"

"And now, I'm just numb. I don't honestly feel anything at all. I don't think anything could touch me."

"So where does that leave us?"

"I don't know, Kevin. I just don't know. I seem to be paralyzed emotionally. I feel so anchorless."

"Considering the shock you've had, I think that's to be expected."

"I'm afraid, Kevin. I don't seem to be able to think beyond

today. I know I can't run a business that way. And I have to make this work now. I don't have any other choice."

"You'll do it, Rhea. Everything will work out in time."

"I don't know," Rhea continued. "I owe Jacqui money. There is no way I can pay her back right now and continue to operate."

"Surely, she doesn't expect you to. But, if it comes to that, I can help you, Rhea."

"You're very sweet to offer, but I feel guilty enough for letting you fall in love with me. I can't take money from you."

"You didn't let me fall in love with you. I don't recall asking your permission. I want to help you in any way I can."

"Then just be my friend, Kevin, and don't ask more of me than I can give you."

"I'm sorry if I've been doing that. I am your friend."

Yes, Rhea thought, he really was.. She know she should end the relationship for his sake. It wasn't fair to him. But she couldn't. She needed him too much. She hoped someday he would be able to forgive her.

She straightened up the dressing table and went downstairs to wait for him. She certainly didn't feel very festive—not at all in the mood for a Christmas party.

The house was abnormally quiet. Caroline, who was feeling better, had gone out earlier and Jill was working as usual on Saturday night. Rhea turned on the outside Christmas lights and started for the kitchen to mix herself a drink. Clipped to the refrigerator with a decorative magnet was a note in Jill's handwriting. Why would Jill be leaving her a note?"

> Dear Rhea, I know you won't approve, so I'm taking the easy way out. Court has asked me to fly to Jamaica with him. I know how upset you are, and I don't want to add to your problems. But, please try to understand. Court and I love each other. Don't worry about me. I'll be back in a few days. Love Jill

Rhea was stunned. This couldn't be happening. How could Jill do this? She had been so sweet and solicitous the last few days. How could she? What would Ruth say?

When she opened the door to Kevin, the first thing he said was, "What's wrong, Rhea?"

"It's Jill. She's gone off to Jamaica with Court Randall."

"They've eloped?" he asked in surprise.

"No, no! At least I don't think so. She didn't even tell me. She left for work this afternoon as usual without saying anything. A few minutes ago, I found this."

Rhea handed him the note. Quietly, he read it and handed it back to her.

"It doesn't look as if you can do anything about it," he said at last.

"She's my responsibility. What will Ruth say? She's depending on me to look after Jill."

"Jill took responsibility for herself when she left Arkansas. What can your sister say? She doesn't seem to have any more luck than you in influencing Jill."

"Then why do I feel like there was something more I should have done?"

He put his arms around her and drew her close. She made no protest.

"Because," he said, "you care so much about people. You're open and honest, and people aren't always open and honest with you."

"She said not to worry, but how can I help it? The man is twice her age."

"I wouldn't worry so much about that as who he is and where his money comes from. If she loves him, the age doesn't matter."

"That's exactly what Jill said to me the day I invited you to lunch. She asked me if I had ever just lived for the moment."

"You weren't talking about her," he said. "You were talking about us."

"How did you know?"

"Because, you have this hang up about age. Rhea, if I don't care that you're older, why should you?"

She extricated herself from his arms. "I don't have a good answer to that," she admitted.

"Is the party still on?" he asked.

She sighed. "I don't see why not. As you pointed out, Jill is already gone, and there doesn't seem to be anything I can do about it."

"Good girl. By the way, did I tell you that you look terrific. New dress?"

Rhea was pleased. Kevin always noticed anything new or different. She assumed it was his photographer's eye for detail. The drive was pleasant, the night clear, but not too cold. They talked easily. Kevin was thinking of dropping out of the accounting class.

"You can't," she protested. "There's only one more week of classes and then the final,"

"I'm selling the business. There doesn't seem to be any point to continuing. I don't like it It's just not my cup of tea."

"What will you do? Go back to photography?"

"I suppose, eventually. I still have a few loose ends to tie up from my mother's estate."

"I think you should finish the course and take the exam. It can't hurt. Besides, who's going to help me study if you quit? I don't think I can make it without you."

"I wish you weren't talking about a stupid accounting course," he said suddenly.

"Oh, Kevin, I'm sorry."

"No, I'm sorry. I promised no pressure. Now, where is this party, did you say—off Memorial Drive?"

"Yes, Liz and Ben have a new condo overlooking Buffalo Bayou."

"There's been an effort to clean up Buffalo Bayou," he said.

"Yes, I've read about it. Liz said Ben invested a bundle in their place so the area around it must be nice."

"I used to canoe on Buffalo Bayou. I raced once in the Reeking Regatta."

"Reeking Regatta?"

"That's what they called it—for obvious reasons."

"There's so much I don't know about you, Kevin."

"You met me at a bad time in my life, " he said, "coping with my dad's death, taking over a business I hated, then losing my mother."

"Yes, the thing I remember most about you was the sadness—the pain in your eyes the first time we met."

"And you recognized a kindred spirit," he said.

"Maybe. I was job hunting that day, unsuccessfully, I might add. But I went to work for Riker a few days later. Oh, did I tell you, he came into my shop this week?"

"No, some nerve, huh?"

"I threw him out."

"That must have given you a great deal of satisfaction."

"Yes, at the time, it did. However, I've been thinking about it since. He wanted to offer me some kind of a deal to sell furniture for him. I refused to even listen."

"That's your prerogative, I would say, after the way he treated you."

"He did treat me badly, but the point is that I really can't afford not to listen to him."

"I don't like the idea of your doing business with a man like that."

"I'll be careful, and I'll probably have Ben Howard look over any agreement I make with him. Let's see, I think we should be getting close. Take a left here. There are two highrise buildings together. That looks like it. Make another left at the light."

Rhea had forgotten how lavishly Liz entertained. A few people turned out to be a crowd. There was a bar set up just inside the door, and a three piece combo played jazz in one end of the spacious living room. Liz, dressed in red sequins, greeted them warmly, and Ben pressed drinks into their hands.

As it turned out, there were even people there Kevin knew— the lawyer who was handling his mother's estate for one. Rhea's friends seemed genuinely pleased to see her. Soon she was telling them about her antique shop and decorating business.

"What made you decide to open a business in your lovely home?" Liz asked.

"Years ago," Rhea answered, "when we decided to buy the old house—it was, well, just an old house—something we could afford to buy on our limited budget and fix up in our spare time. But it totally absorbed me. It took all my energy and time and money. Every muscle and bone in my body ached as I worked to restore it. I fell in love with it; it became almost human. So, after my divorce, I decided that the only way I could afford to keep it was to turn it into something I could make money with. "It was the only way I could hold on to it," Rhea said truthfully.

"But you always loved old furniture," Liz said. "In fact, I remember your telling me years ago that antiques, unlike new furniture, would always be worth more than you paid for them. I found that very good advice."

"True," Rhea agreed, "but antiques don't always add up to be blue chip investments. So I encourage people to buy what they like rather than what they think is going to go up in value."

"How do you know when you buy antiques that you're not being cheated?" a young woman who had been introduced as Liz's neighbor asked.

"First of all you find a reputable dealer," Rhea answered. "Good dealers don't have to exaggerate to make a sale. In fact, no sale is worth their integrity. Also, you should learn something about antiques. If you can distinguish one kind of wood from another, you can tell something about where a piece was made— whether it's English or American and in what period it was made. But, style doesn't always indicate age or date of manufacture. Wide boards usually suggest an early piece.

"For example, you can tell whether boards were cut with a straight saw or a circular saw. Plywood wasn't invented until about 1900, so if the back is all in one piece, you usually have a reproduction. But, that's okay, as long as you know it's a reproduction. If it has lasted for a long time, then you know it will probably never go out of style."

"You sound very knowledgeable," the young woman said. "I would like to see your shop, but I think I would be intimidated by a decorator."

"You shouldn't be. I think every woman is a decorator at heart. I can't imagine anyone willing to turn their house carte blanche over to a decorator. I think of myself as an adviser. I can save you time and energy and money by locating sources for you, but the final decision should be yours. Your home should reflect you and your personality. I also function as a buying agent. There are lines of fine furniture sold to the trade only. A private customer can't purchase them, and they aren't sold in retail outlets."

"Do you teach classes in antique collecting?" someone asked.

"She could," Kevin said. During the conversation, he had come to stand with his hands on her shoulders. "She has an ideal place, and she certainly has the knowledge."

Rhea smiled. Perhaps she would think about that. She was surprised at how well Kevin seemed to fit in with her friends. She had always thought of him as a loner, and it was strange to see the gregarious side of him. He danced with all the ladies, and once she saw him performing a cha cha with Liz, and both of them were laughing outrageously.

Later Liz asked, "Where did you find him, Rhea? He is an absolute doll—and all that Stacey money, too. You really are a sly one."

"Oh, we just bumped into one another," Rhea countered with a laugh.

But, as the evening wore on, she was even more puzzled about Kevin. Money? She hadn't known about the Stacey money. The boy with the pain in his eyes had emerged as a handsome, outgoing, smiling stranger. It made his feelings for her all the harder to explain. He was right, maybe she didn't really know him.

"I had a good time, Rhea," Kevin said on the way home. "I hope you did too."

"I did. It's just that I couldn't help worrying about Jill," she confessed. "I know virtually nothing about this Court Randall. I've never even met him."

She leaned her head back against the seat and closed her eyes. She would stop thinking about Jill. The evening hadn't worked out too badly. It was easier than she had supposed it would be. Actually, it was fun. Why had she been so afraid that it would turn into a disaster?

But when she arrived home, Rhea found that the night had turned into a disaster after all, but this time, it wasn't her fault.

CHAPTER TWENTY-FOUR

The street where Rhea lived, it seemed to Jacqui, exuded a quiet elegance. She remembered the first time she saw the stately old homes and towering oaks, wondering if she had come to the right place. It was difficult to imagine that only blocks away, massage parlors and porno shops and topless bars flourished amid shabby old mansions fallen into disrepair.

The house looked the same, yet in some way she could not fathom—different. Perhaps, she suspected, the difference was only in herself. This would probably be the last time she was ever there. Packing shouldn't take too long. She had wanted to come alone, but Greg insisted on driving her. It had taken some persuasion, however, to get him to agree to go to his office for a couple of hours until all her things were ready to be moved.

"I don't see why you won't let me help you, Jacqui," he protested. " I really feel fine."

"I know," she replied. "It isn't that. This is something I have to do alone. I don't have much—some books, a painting, and my clothes. I don't form attachments to things, you know. But I just want to say goodbye. This was an important part of my life."

"How can you say goodbye? Rhea is out for the evening. Jill will be at work. You and Caroline were never friends."

"I don't know. Maybe I just need to say goodbye to the house."

"For someone who doesn't form attachments to things," he observed, "that doesn't make much sense."

"Look, Mr. Lawyer. Will you please take your infuriating logic down to your law office and give me a little space here?"

"Lady, you've got it. But I'll be back!"

"I'm counting on it," she said, laughing, as she got out of the car.

Jacqui started up the walk and noticed Rhea's altered sign. The Gregory was missing. It had been painted out leaving a slightly lopsided effect. Rhea was probably feeling a little lopsided right now, she thought, inserting her key in the lock, As the door opened, she turned to wave to Greg and watched him pull away. She locked the door behind her and looked around.

The house was quiet. Caroline, probably, was the only one home and was, no doubt, shut up in her room. It was just as well. Jacqui had never been able to break through that ice.

Jacqui wondered what the man in Caroline's life had been like. She never talked about him at all. Who could have guessed a few months ago when they were all drinking champagne together that it would come to this? She and Greg—quietly married in a judge's office, Caroline pregnant, and Jill growing up too fast and unwisely involved with some character Jacqui didn't even know. Rhea had pressed Jill to meet him, but Jill had always been evasive, vaguely promising sometime soon.

Jacqui wondered where Rhea was. *I'll be out for the evening,* she had said icily.

Maybe she was lucky to be getting out of there. Maybe Caroline eventually turns everything to ice. No, that wasn't fair. She was to blame for what happened to her friendship with Rhea, and Jacqui knew, that in all probability, Rhea would never forgive her—couldn't forgive her. To hope for anything else was totally unrealistic. "You see, my love," she said to an invisible Greg, "I can be quite logical."

Jacqui walked silently up the stairs pausing to look at the porcelain goose beside the wicker settee. Its unwavering stare was as disdainful as ever. Rhea confessed once that she talked to the goose. *It keeps me humble,* she had said, laughing.

Stop it, old girl, Jacqui cautioned herself, or you'll be talking to the goose. There were too many memories in this house. Pack, she reminded herself. That's what she had come to do. Everything was exactly as she had left it except for a stack of boxes in the corner Evidently Rhea couldn't wait to be rid of her. Thank you, Rhea. Thank you very much. It would save her the effort. Coming here alone was not a good idea. The house was too quiet, almost a malevolent silence. Rhea and Jill were both out, and, perhaps, Caroline was, too. Jacqui felt like an intruder.

When all the boxes were filled, the bed was still stacked with items to be packed. Where did it all come from? It seemed to have multiplied. She needed two more boxes, maybe three. Darn! The attic stairs had to be pulled down after all.

Passing quietly by Caroline's closed door, she was startled to hear voices. It must be the television. A menacing masculine voice demanded loudly, "Where is it?"

Jacqui carefully climbed the stairs and turned on the light. The attic was a sort of mini museum. Rhea was the most organized person in the world. She could charge admission to this place. A large stack of boxes in assorted sizes, folded flat for storage, stood against one wall. As Jacqui bent down to pull out the size she wanted, a horrific scream came from the room below, Caroline's room!

"No, don't!" a terrified voice begged. "No. No."

Jacqui stood motionless. Caroline screamed again, and there were two earsplitting shots.

Dashing down the unsteady stairs that had sprung up a few inches from the floor, Jacqui reached the bottom step, and it settled on the floor with a sharp thud. She raced past Caroline's door, desperately trying to reach her old room.

Caroline's door opened, and as Jacqui turned, she saw a man step into the hallway holding a gun. Their eyes met for a split second before she dived through the open doorway, falling to her knees as another shot shattered glass behind her.

"He's trying to kill me," she gasped in horror as the heavy, solid oak door was slammed and bolted. With an overwhelming sense of relief she heard him running down the stairs. She dialed 911 on her cell phone that had been in her bag on the bed. She peered out the window just in time to see a dark figure run across the street and disappear into the shrubbery at the corner house.

"Send help quickly," she pleaded, surprised at the calmness of her voice as she explained her plight. Only her rapid breathing revealed her terror. Torn between fear and a conviction that she must help Caroline, she cautiously unbolted the door while still talking to the emergency operator. The thought that there might have been more than one intruder made her hesitate. She listened intently, but there was no sound outside the door.

"Caroline," she called tentatively. "Caroline, are you all right?"

There was no sound from Caroline's open door.

The operator had told her to stay in her room with the door locked until a patrol car arrived, but Jacqui inched her way along the hall with the phone still in her hand. The porcelain goose lay in shattered pieces. She suppressed the impulse to scoop them up and try to fit them back together.

Caroline was lying on the floor between the bed and the wall. The room was in shambles—drawers pulled out with the contents spilled on the carpet. The front of Caroline's blue caftan was soaked with blood. Jacqui dropped to her knees.

"Caroline," she implored. "Can you hear me?"

Caroline's eyes fluttered, then opened wide and fixed on Jacqui with a glassy stare. Jacqui put down the phone, gently raised Caroline's head, and cradled her arm beneath it.

"Jacqui," Caroline whispered, "I'm so sorry."

"Who did this Caroline? Did you know the man?"

Caroline appeared not to hear.

"I was afraid," she said brokenly, "of the wrong person. Forgive me, Jacqui."

"Just try to hang on," Jacqui pleaded. "Help is on the way."

Caroline's eyes had closed, and the intervals between her shallow breaths seemed to be longer and longer.

Just like Spence, Jacqui thought. Oh, please, no!. Not like Spence, please. She eased Caroline's head down again and drew back her arm. "Where is that ambulance?" she almost screamed into the phone. "Why haven't the police arrived?"

"They are on their way," the operator said. "Please try to remain calm. You will hear them any moment now."

Almost immediately, Jacqui heard the siren. Two patrolmen rushed in through the front door that the intruder had left wide open. She explained how the man had fled across the street as they knelt beside Carolina and felt for a pulse. She had stopped breathing.

As one of the policemen began to administer mouth to mouth resuscitation, his partner cautiously went out to cross the street, gun in hand. The paramedics arrived and began to work on Caroline. She's going to die, Jacqui thought as she took Caroline's hand. There was no response.Caroline was far away in a field of bluebonnets. A tiny hand clung to hers. "Hurry Mommy," a shrill little voice urged, "it's getting dark." Caroline scooped the child up in her arms, savoring her sweetness She smelled of wild flowers and peppermint candy. Soft, warm arms wound their way around Caroline's neck and a sleepy head rested against her shoulder. "I love you, Mommy," a sleepy voice whispered in her ear. Caroline hugged the child as total darkness overwhelmed them, and then, the dream was over.

Jacqui squeezed Caroline's hand. "Caroline," she said softly. "My prayers are with you."

"She's still alive," the paramedic said, "but she's unconsciousness. I don't think she can hear you, but you never know. We've done everything we can for her here, so we're going to transport her now."

The knot of dread in Jacqui's chest tightened as she telephoned Greg to tell him that she would ride to the hospital in the ambulance with Caroline. As much as she believed that death was only a transition to another plane of living, her heart was breaking as she climbed into the front seat with the driver and began to pray.

CHAPTER TWENTY-FIVE

Rhea stared at her house in shock. All the lights were on, and the yard had been cordoned off with a bright yellow band. Police Investigation in Progress. Do Not Cross. Patrol cars blocked her driveway. A familiar figure emerged from the doorway and met them at the curb.

"Carter!"

"Rhea, something terrible has happened," he said. "Caroline has been shot."

Kevin's arm tightened around Rhea's shoulders protectively. Without it, she would have fallen. She stared at Carter in disbelief.

"Caroline," she repeated incredulously. Only hours before Caroline had gone out—to the drugstore, Rhea remembered. "How? Where?"

She looked again at the yellow band. Police Investigation in Progress. Police Line. Do Not Cross.

"Not here," she cried. "Carter! Not here—not in my house."

"I'm afraid so," he replied. "I've been trying to locate you for hours."

Rhea caught the reproof in his voice. She glanced at Kevin, but his face was impassive. He looked so youthful compared to Carter, his blond sun-streaked hair a stark contrast to Carter's silver.

"We've been to a Christmas party," she explained, "at Liz Howard's."

"I called everyone I could think of," he said curtly. "I didn't know you were still friendly with Liz. I didn't think of her."

"Why don't you tell us exactly what happened," Kevin suggested evenly, "and what you're doing here?"

"Jacqui was here when it happened. Of course, she called me right away."

Rhea turned to Kevin. "I forgot to mention it, but Jacqui called this morning and asked to come over for her things. Where is Jacqui, Carter? Is she all right?"

"Yes, thankfully, she is. She was badly shaken, but she insisted on going to the hospital with Caroline."

This could not be happening, Rhea told herself. This was all part of a grotesque nightmare. But it wouldn't end. She was questioned at length by detectives, but she could tell them nothing that Jacqui had not already told them. Rhea knew very little about Caroline's background—nothing about her family. She simply had assumed there was no family. Caroline received no mail. She seldom talked on the telephone, and, if she had any friends, Rhea did not know them.

"Do you have any idea," the detective asked, "why she is using the name Caroline Kelly. The name on her driver's license is Caroline Kelly Cortero."

"No," Rhea said in surprise. "I've been using my maiden name, Rhea Roberts, while my attorney Ben Howard petitions the court to restore my name. I'm divorced, and I don't want to be confused with the present Mrs. Gregory. Caroline told me that she was a widow. I can't imagine why she wouldn't use her husband's name."

A few minutes later, Jacqui phoned from the hospital. "It's so awful, Rhea. I don't think Caroline is going to make it."

"No," Rhea protested. "That can't be true. What about the baby?"

"I guess that means," Jacqui said after a long hesitation, "the poor baby won't make it either."

"No, that can't be true," Rhea kept saying over and over. "It can't be true."

"Rhea, did you know that Caroline had a brother in Louisiana?"

"No, she never mentioned any family."

"Apparently, she listed him as next of kin on her employment forms at the hospital. They called him. He's en route. May

I please speak to Greg now?"

"He isn't here. He left for the hospital a few minutes ago. The police are still here. A forensic team has just arrived. I'll see you at the hospital just as soon as I can get away."

"You're not alone, are you Rhea? Greg couldn't find Jill."

"No, I'm not alone. Kevin is with me."

"Good. Rhea, Caroline said something very strange to me."

"She was conscious when you found her?" Rhea asked.

"Yes, and she begged me to forgive her."

"To forgive her? For what?"

"I have no idea."

"Maybe she was confused and thought you were someone else."

"No, she called me Jacqui and asked me to forgive her—more than once."

"That's very strange. I don't know why."

"And, if Caroline dies," Jacqui said, "I may never know."

Kevin pressed a cup of coffee into her hand. "I gather that was Jacqui," he said.

"Yes, it was." Rhea took a sip of the coffee. It was laced with brandy.

Wordlessly, she put it down on the table. It brought back a flood of unwanted memories—a cold, bleak day, a bottle of brandy, a pot of coffee, a warm fire, trembling hands, and searching lips. She tried to put the memories away.

"Jacqui thinks Caroline is going to die." she said.

Kevin put his arms around her. This time he was the strong one—she in need of comfort. She had to stop this before it went any farther.

"Kevin, I must get to the hospital."

"I'll speak to the detectives. We have to let them know where we'll be. Then I'll drive you."

"You don't have to," she protested.

"I want to."

"You didn't drink your coffee," he said.

"It was too hot," she lied.

"It's cool by now. Why don't you take it with you?"

"Perhaps I'd better," she said capitulating. "It has turned out to be an awfully long night."

"There isn't much of it left—the night I mean."

"Carter told me," Rhea remembered, "that Jacqui swears she locked the front door when she came. She thought no one was home, and she felt a little apprehensive about being alone in the house for some reason."

"The detectives couldn't find any signs of forcible entry. It's possible Caroline let her assailant in."

"That's crazy," Rhea said. "Caroline was a very cautious person."

"Is a cautious person," Kevin said gently.

"Oh no, I'm talking about her as if she were dead."

"It's just the strain, Rhea. As you said, it has turned out to be a very long night. Let's go."

She sipped the coffee as Kevin headed for the Medical Center.

"Jacqui once said," she remembered, "that Caroline was hiding something. She thought Caroline was afraid—scared of close friendships for some reason."

"Maybe tonight was the reason," Kevin said. "What do you think?"

"I just think Caroline is a very private person. But she never seemed to like Jacqui very much. It was Jill she really warmed up to. If only Jill were here."

"Do you think robbery was the motive? Caroline's room had been torn apart."

"No, I don't. Nothing else in the house seems to have been touched. Nothing is missing as far as I can determine. It must have been someone Caroline knew—someone she let into the house. She must have had something that person wanted. Otherwise, it just doesn't make sense."

"Unless she can tell us, we won't ever know."

"She has to recover, Kevin."

Jacqui met them in the lobby. Rhea knew before she spoke what the words would be.

"Caroline is dead," she said sadly. "At least, she's brain dead. They still have her connected to the life support systems to keep the baby alive. But there isn't any hope for her. They told me just a few minutes ago."

Rhea began to sob. Kevin led her to a nearby chair. "I'm so sorry," he said. "I realize I don't know her very well."

"Nobody knew her well," Jacqui said. "God knows, we all tried."

"We didn't try hard enough," Rhea maintained stubbornly. "Is there any hope to save the baby?"

"The doctors are going to discuss taking the baby by caesarean section when Caroline's brother arrives."

"When will that be?"

"Some time later today. He said he would leave immediately. He hasn't seen Caroline in over two years. He didn't even know where she was until he got the call."

"Poor Caroline," Rhea said shaking her head. "Do you think they would let me see her?"

"Are you sure you want to?" Kevin asked.

"Yes, I do. I cared about her. She was sweet and pathetically grateful for the few small things I was able to do for her when I found out about the baby."

"I know you cared about her," Jacqui said. "You did everything for her you could. But she said something very strange to me after she was shot. She begged me to forgive her. She called me by name. I'm sorry, Jacqui, please forgive me. Do you have any idea what she meant?"

"No, I can't imagine. You never quarreled?"

"No. In fact, I hadn't even seen Caroline since the night we all had the chocolate eclairs."

"Where is Carter?" Rhea asked suddenly.

"I persuaded him to go home in a taxi," Jacqui explained. "It isn't good for him to get overtired. I was afraid that he had too much excitement for one night."

"How is he, Jacqui, really?" Rhea asked.

"Tired a great deal of the time, but otherwise okay. He has curtailed his workload and watches his diet. And I know he's concerned about you, Rhea, how Caroline's death will affect you."

Rhea glanced quickly at Kevin and suppressed the urge to reply sarcastically that everyone was aware of just how concerned Carter was about her welfare. This was not the time nor the place. With an effort, she put aside her personal feelings.

"I want to see Caroline," she said doggedly.

Later she wished she had not insisted. Caroline looked so small and vulnerable. What was it about hospitals that dwarfed a person—took away one's identity? Caroline had ceased to exist even though she still breathed in rhythm to a machine.

Rhea started to reach for Caroline's hand, but drew back without touching her. Caroline had retreated too far within that cool silence she had drawn around her. Jacqui was right; they had all tried to reach her, but she wouldn't or, perhaps, couldn't or had simply been too afraid, to let them in.

Rhea wondered what choices brought Caroline to this place and time. She was beginning to believe, like Jacqui, that there was no such thing as fate—only cause and effect, and one's previous choices determined events as they happened.

Rhea left her name and number and a message for Caroline's brother at the nurses' station. She took the elevator to the parking garage with Jacqui and Kevin.

"I feel as if I'm abandoning her," Rhea said, "although I don't see how our staying will help."

"I know," Jacqui replied. "I feel helpless, too."

"Both of you did everything you could for her," Kevin told them.

"Thanks, Kev," Jacqui smiled weakly. "Keep telling us both that. I know I'm going to need to hear it for a while."

Kevin insisted on walking Jacqui to her car.

"Goodnight," he said. "Drive carefully."

"I will. Kevin, you aren't thinking of letting her stay in that house alone?"

"No way," he replied.

"It wouldn't look right," Rhea said after Jacqui had driven away, "for you to stay with me."

"Murder doesn't look right. Until we find out who murdered Caroline and why, you are not going to stay in that house alone. Period!"

As they drove along in silence, Rhea found herself leaning closer to Kevin. He took her still shaking hand and raised it to his lips. She did not trust herself to say anything, but didn't pull away. It was almost dawn by the time they reached the house. Forensics had finished; the tape identifying the crime scene was gone. But the image of it was etched so indelibly in Rhea's mind, she was sure she would see it every time she looked at her beloved house.

All the lights were on, including the outside light that illuminated her sign. In fact, lights were on all up and down the block. The quiet, serene neighborhood had been violated. For the first time ever, Rhea was reluctant to enter the stately old mansion that had been her haven for so many years. Her eyes filled with tears.

The police had left. Rhea wanted to believe that they had never been there. Even when the detectives were questioning her at the hospital, she had somehow half believed that it wasn't real. Everything would be all right in the morning. But it was morning and the nightmare was still going on.

"I'm afraid to go in," she whispered.

"You don't have to, Rhea."

"I have to sometime. It might as well be now."

"You stay here. I'll check everything out."

"No, I'm coming with you. It's my house."

Suddenly, she felt an unreasonable anger at Carter. If there had not been a divorce, she wouldn't have taken strangers into her house. This terrible thing would never have happened.

"Rhea, are you okay?" Kevin asked gently.

"No," she sighed, "I'm not, and I don't think I ever will be again."

CHAPTER TWENTY-SIX

The first pang of uneasiness came as Jill stepped out of the cab in the driveway. The house looked all closed up. That was strange for the middle of the week. She put down her bags in the entrance hall.

"Rhea, where are you?" she called. "I'm back."

There was only one small light on above the desk just inside the front door. The house was absolutely quiet.

Jill bounded upstairs. "Anybody home?" she called again. "Rhea? Caroline?"

She knocked softly on Rhea's door, calling her name. When there was no answer, Jill opened the door and called again. The room was undisturbed as always, bed made, closet doors closed, nothing out of place. She tried Caroline's door. No response. Tentatively, she opened the door. The room had been stripped, the bed showed a bare mattress. Even the carpet was gone from the floor.

"What on earth is going on?"

Jill closed the door quickly. It was obvious—Caroline had gone. Why? What had happened in the short time she had been away. Her own room was just the way she had left it—basically clean, but sort of messy. But somehow things just didn't feel right, and she went uneasily down the stairs. Maybe somebody had left her a note.

They often left notes for one another on the refrigerator door secured by a decorative magnet. She had left Rhea a note telling her that she was going away for a few days with Court.

A note was there. *Call Jacqui as soon as you get home.*

Something had happened to Rhea! Frantically Jill dialed Jacqui's number from the wall phone in the kitchen.

"Jacqui, it's Jill."

"Something happened while you were away, Jill."

"It's Rhea, isn't it? Something happened to Rhea?"

"No, Jill, it isn't Rhea. Rhea is fine. It was Caroline."

"Caroline! She lost the baby."

"Worse, Jill," Jacqui said gently. "Caroline was murdered."

"What? Caroline was what?"

"Somebody shot her. Caroline was murdered."

"I don't believe it," Jill cried, knowing with a terrible certainty that it was true. There was the feel of death in the house. A chill. A silence. She remembered it from when Granny died. Granny had died in her sleep when Jill was barely thirteen years old.

"Rhea and Kevin are in Louisiana for the funeral. Come stay with me until Rhea gets back."

"She can't be dead. She can't be. She was going to have a baby. Oh, Jacqui, it's so awful."

"Jill, are you listening to me. The baby is alive—barely. A tiny, tiny girl, but Caroline's gone. You don't want to stay there alone. Rhea's car is in the garage. The keys are in the desk drawer."

"Where was she murdered, Jacqui, where?"

"Jill, you aren't listening to me. I'm coming to get you. I'm leaving right now. Stay there until I get there."

"No, I can't," Jill cried. " I'm too scared. She was murdered here, wasn't she? In this house? I can feel it."

"Just wait for me, I'll be there as soon as I can."

"No, no. I can't stay here. I'll come to you."

"Are you sure you can drive? Jill, you must calm down."

"I'm okay. I can make it."

Jill found the keys in the top drawer of the desk. Her hand was shaking so hard she could hardly get the key in the ignition.

She would be all right as soon as she got out of there. But as she watched the overhead garage slowly close, she remembered her bags inside the front door. She had nothing with her but the clothes on her back. It didn't matter. She would borrow something from Jacqui. Wild horses couldn't drag her back inside that house.

The rush hour traffic on Westheimer was horrendous. It

would take her an hour to get to Jacqui's, she was sure. She tried not to think about poor Caroline. Instead she thought about Court, handsome, exciting Court.. She thought about beautiful, blue water and white sand beaches and gentle island breezes. She thought about the tenderness in Court's voice. He had been the Court she loved—the one who was real. There was none of the secretiveness she hated, nor the unexpected business meetings.

Court had explained that the lavish, isolated villa overlooking a stretch of pristine beach they were enjoying belonged to his business partner who was in South America. He talked for the first time of his import-export business and how he planned to expand.

It had been a week she would never forget. She remembered the smallest detail—like the morning she awoke in the strange bedroom. Filmy curtains swayed against an open window. She knew immediately that it was not her room, and she could not remember where she was. Then she heard the unaccustomed sound of the surf, and there was a rush of sudden joy almost akin to pain as she felt the pressure of Court's thigh against hers. She propped herself up on one elbow and looked at his sleeping face in the near-dawn light. He was, she thought, incredibly handsome. She wanted to tell him how much she loved him. As if he sensed that, he stirred and opened his eyes.

"What's the matter, Sunshine?" he asked. "Can't you sleep?"

"I just don't want to," she replied. "I'm having such a glorious time, I don't want to waste a minute. Sleeping seems like a waste. Thank you, Court, for bringing me here. I'll never forget this time as long as I live."

"Jill, baby," he said, pulling her closer and laughing. "You know what I like most about you?"

"With me, you don't need an alarm clock?" she teased.

"Not exactly," he conceded. "But I like the way you get a tremendous kick out of everything. I don't know how to describe it, but you have such a spark within you. When I look at you, I think of sunshine—or wildfire."

"And you like playing with fire," she laughed.

"Maybe I do. Especially since the last woman in my life was like ice."

"Was or is?" Jill probed. "I really know so little about you, Court."

"Was," he assured her. "Definitely in the past. You won't

ever have to worry about anyone else. Didn't I tell you last night that you were the only woman in my life?"

"Yes, but I've been warned not to put too much faith in pillow talk."

"Don't go cynical on me, Sunshine. Your innocence is another thing I like about you."

"I'm glad you like me, Court."

He cupped her face in his hands and touched her lips with a slow, gentle kiss.

"I love you, Jill," he said slowly. "But I need to know if you love me in the same way."

"Oh, Court, I do. I do," she said passionately.

"The last woman in my life betrayed me," he told her. "I never thought I would be able to trust any woman again. But you're different. I can trust you, absolutely. Can't I, my love?"

"I would give my life for you."

"I believe you would, angel. Will you marry me and live wherever my business takes me even though you might not be able to see your family for some time?"

"Yes, yes." She threw her arms around him, delirious with happiness. It was the moment she had dreamed about since the first time she met him and yet hardly dared to hope would ever happen.

"We can have it all," he promised. "We'll see the world together. If you have any reservations, tell me now."

"No. No, reservations. It's just that Rhea needs me right now."

"I need you, sweetheart. You have to make a choice."

"I love you, Court, and I believe that love is the only thing in life that really matters. I'll go with you anywhere."

"I knew I could count on you. And I have something for you. I planned to give you this on our last night here, but I want you to have it now."

From a drawer in the nightstand, he took out a tiny velvet covered ring box and opened it for her. Jill's eyes widened in surprise and delight as he slipped the largest diamond she had ever seen on her trembling fingers.

"Well, what do you think of pillow talk now, Sunshine?" he asked.

Jill looked down at the ring on her finger. If it were not for the ring, she could easily believe, driving down Westheimer in Rhea's car, that she had dreamed the whole thing.

She had left Court in Miami to fly back to Houston. He had wanted to be married in Miami, and she almost gave in. But when she pleaded to tell her mother and her aunt in advance and be married in her aunt's house, he had finally, reluctantly agreed.

"I just don't want to share our special day with a bunch of strangers," he explained. "I just want you and me."

But, she pointed out, there had to be witnesses. There would only be her Aunt Rhea and one other person, her friend Caroline.

It was really true. She was going to marry Court Randall. All her dreams had come true. Court loved her. She had planned all the way from the airport how she would tell them—Rhea and Caroline. Now she could never tell Caroline. Poor, poor Caroline.

Jill wondered if it was wrong to be so happy when Caroline was dead. And what about the poor little baby girl? Never to know her mother or her father. Who would love her and care for her? She wished she could be the one to do it, but Court didn't want a child—even their own child. We have too many things to do and a whole world to see. A kid would only slow us down, Sunshine, he had said when she brought up the subject of a family.

She knew she had to stop thinking about Caroline's baby. Someone would take care of her. It just wouldn't be her. She had other things to think about. Endless days of happiness with Court.

Jacqui met her at the door, and they embraced without speaking. Jill felt very strange. She thought she should be crying, but no tears came. She didn't understand why. She seemed to be caught up in a whirlwind where nothing made any sense.

"I should have been there," Jill said at length. "I should have been there."

"No, Jill. There wasn't anything you could have done for Caroline. You would have been working Saturday night. I was there, and I couldn't help her."

"You were there when it happened?"

"Yes, but I was up in the attic getting boxes. I had been packing the last of my things. Greg dropped me off and went downtown to his office. Rhea was out for the evening. I thought she had gone out just to avoid me, but she and Kevin had been to a party."

"You were in the attic? Then you didn't see the person who did it?"

"Oh, I saw him. He even took a shot at me. I will never, never forget that face as long as I live. There was something about his eyes—so hard and evil. No, I'll never forget him."

"Jacqui, how awful!"

"Yes, it was awful. Caroline was still alive when the paramedics arrived. She even spoke to me. They delivered the baby three days later by caesarean section. She is so tiny, it doesn't seem possible that she could survive. But there was no hope for Caroline."

"I just can't believe all of this."

"Of course you can't. I know it is a terrible, terrible shock to you. You were closer to Caroline than any of us. Did you know she had a brother?"

"No. I don't know anything about her really. But she was a good person. She didn't deserve this."

"Come on, Jill, let's have a cup of tea. You've had quite a shock. Your hands are still shaking."

"I think I could use something stronger than tea."

"So could I. How about a glass of sherry? Or would you rather have something else?"

"Sherry would be fine. How is Rhea taking this?"

"Better than you would expect. Kevin had hardly left her side."

They were sipping sherry at the kitchen table when Greg arrived.

"Uncle Carter," Jill exclaimed and grinned sheepishly. "I guess I can't stop thinking of you as my uncle."

"I hope you'll always think of me as family. Just because Rhea and I aren't still married doesn't mean that I care about you less. Hey, what's that on your finger, young lady?"

Jill beamed and held out her hand. "Court asked me to marry him."

"And you said yes," Jacqui prompted.

"I said yes," Jill replied, beaming.

"Wow, what a rock!" Greg said. "When do we get to meet the guy who has stolen your heart, little girl?"

"Not stolen, Uncle Carter, freely given. And soon, I hope. I know you'll like him."

"When is the wedding?" Jacqui asked.

"Soon," Jill replied. "Nothing fancy. Neither of us wants to wait."

"Not too soon, I hope," Greg said, frowning. "Baby, are you sure you know what you're doing? What do you think Rhea is going to say—or your mother, for that matter?"

"When they see how happy this makes me," Jill said, "I hope both of them will be pleased."

"What if they aren't?" Jacqui asked.

"Not everybody was exactly thrilled when the two of you got married," Jill said defiantly.

"Touché," Jacqui replied. "Greg, my love, I think she is telling us to butt out. And she has every right. Shall we put a bottle of champagne on ice and think up something festive to have for dinner?"

Jill hugged her.

"Uh oh," Jacqui remembered, "you don't like champagne."

"I remember the first time I tried it. That was the night we were together for the first time—you and Rhea and Caroline and me. We were all so hopeful that night."

"I guess," Jacqui said, "that nothing turned out quite the way any of us expected."

"Would you mind," Jill asked, "if I just went up to bed. I'm not hungry, and all of a sudden, I'm very, very tired."

"Of course, we wouldn't," Jacqui replied. "We understand. I'll go up and help you get settled."

"Thanks. Goodnight, Uncle Carter."

"Goodnight, little Jill."

Chapter Twenty-Seven

The drive back to Houston from Louisiana after Caroline's funeral was exhausting. The whole week had been exhausting. Rhea had never felt quite so drained, so emotionally depleted in all her life. As Kevin drove, she rested her head against the seat with her eyes closed. She couldn't sleep, but she could avoid his concerned questions about her welfare.

The closer they got to home, the more anxious Rhea became. She wanted to be home; the shop had been closed for a week, and she certainly could not afford that with Christmas so near. Yet even though she longed to be home, she knew that she had lost her sense of safety there. She had always believed that the beloved home would protect her. If she could just hang on to it, eventually, everything would turn out all right. That illusion had been irretrievably shattered.

She tried to focus on memories of an earlier, happier time. Like the day she moved to Montrose soon after her marriage when being with Carter was fun and exciting. It was fascinating to research the area and to discover that it had been named for a seaport resort town in Eastern Scotland, and that in 1911, the developer had built himself a mansion with terra cotta accents for $60,000 which was, to say the least, an impressive sum in those days.

The streets of Montrose were paved when few streets in Houston were, and the area was landscaped with broad esplanades. The residential subdivision became one of Houston's most fashionable neighborhoods and continued to be so for many years.

After World War II, Rhea found out, the area began to decline. Suburban growth in Houston mushroomed, and the old brick and clapboard houses in Montrose were not much in demand. Parts of the economically depressed area became seedy, and low rents in the 1960's beckoned dropouts and radicals. Property values plunged.

Rhea and Carter moved to Montrose because of the low rent and because of its proximity to Carter's downtown law practice. They first lived upstairs in a fairly well maintained old house that had been converted to apartments. The house they eventually bought at Rhea's insistence with a small legacy from Carter's mother had been on the market for more than a year without any serious prospect of a buyer.

Rhea had made a practice of driving by everyday and dreaming that the house would be hers. She refused to consider any other alternative, and, finally, the out-of-state owners to whom it had passed upon the death of its elderly, lone occupant, accepted Carter's meager offer.

"It was a fabulous buy," Rhea was prone to exclaim for years. But Carter maintained that its value was in the land not the structure. "We'll see these old houses go one day," he said, "to make room for denser development. When that happens, we'll be on easy street." Rhea refused to speak to him for the rest of the night.

The house was classified as Georgian Revival. Rhea knew that the Georgian style was applied to a wide variety of houses which followed formal rules of architecture having their origins in ancient Rome. She was entranced with the elaborate doorway framed with classical moldings, She loved the Corinthian pilasters topped with three openings, the central one arched and wider than the flanking ones.

The main staircase was the dominant element of the interior, rising from a spacious entrance hall that separated twin parlors, each with a fireplace and carved oak chimney pieces. Rhea's neighbor had once related the story, passed down in her family, of how the impulsive, spoiled young son of the original owner had once ridden his horse up the stairs to the horror of his mother, earning himself a sound thrashing from his father, who was not amused.

The restoration and the furnishing of the house had become,

for Rhea, a labor of love. She had seen a lot of changes in the area. In the seventies, there had been an influx of gays, but contrary to her fears, the gay segment contributed to the restoration and revitalization of the area. The Middle East oil crisis forced many people to take a new look at the adjacency of Montrose to downtown. Europeans, new to Houston, were drawn to Montrose, because it reminded them of the old country.

Rhea found herself a leading voice in neighborhood organizations advocating that as Montrose improved and property values rose, the undesirable businesses would be forced out. She loved Montrose. Its uniqueness was apparent in The High School for the Performing and Visual Arts, The Consulate for the People's Republic of China, The Contemporary Arts Museum, The University of St. Thomas, Rothko Chapel, and Courtland Place— a private street with eighteen historic homes.

It was an area where Lyndon Johnson, once lived and taught school, where Howard Hughes grew up, and where Clark Gable once took acting lessons. To live in Montrose with its three quarters of a century of history, Rhea believed, was to live with one's roots in the past when life was simpler and values less complicated.

"I can't live anywhere else," she said aloud.

"What did you say?" Kevin asked.

"Oh, nothing," she sighed. "I guess I was just thinking out loud. It really doesn't matter."

"I think it does matter. You were thinking of your home."

Yes," she admitted. "I suppose I was. Nobody understands how I feel about my home. Jacqui couldn't, and I don't think Carter really ever did."

"I think I understand," he said softly, "but I'm not sure you would agree. That house seems to be the only stable, permanent thing in your life. I have an idea that you never really felt that you belonged anywhere before. It was your own place that you created, and because so much of yourself went into it, I'm not completely sure that you know where Rhea stops and the house begins."

She didn't answer, and finally, it was he who broke the long silence that followed.

"Have I upset you?" he asked.

"No—well yes. Maybe you have. You sound exactly like Jacqui. With the two of you around, I'll never need a psychiatrist.

Think of the money I'll save. How can you think that you see me so clearly, when I don't seem to be anything but hollow and empty? If I feel anything right now, it's a tangle of conflicting emotions. Yes, I do love that house. But something happened to it. It has been changing so subtly I didn't even notice at first. It started when Carter left and it picked up momentum when Jacqui betrayed me. And now with poor Caroline murdered and her tiny baby clinging to life by a thread, I almost hate that house. At this moment I think I do."

"But maybe it isn't the house that has changed."

"Oh, I haven't changed," she said. "I wish I could change. Everything changes except me. I'm still the sweet, colorless, bland Rhea I've always been. Kevin, I don't have the courage to be anything else."

"Sweet, yes. Bland, no. I love your sweetness. I wish you could see yourself as I see you."

Rhea began to cry. She couldn't stop the choking sobs. Kevin braked and pulled to the shoulder of the road. He took her gently in his arms. "Rhea, darling, don't do this to yourself."

She realized desperately that she could not go home that day. She just couldn't. With Caroline's funeral, she had endured all that she could face for one day. She looked at Kevin and knew that she needed him. She needed him to hold her—to caress her—to be there for her. How else could she stave off the awful terror of ultimate aloneness? She needed to feel his skin touching hers—reassuring her that she was not a valueless, unlovable person. Maybe she would be sorry tomorrow, but she needed him tonight.

"Do we have to go back tonight?" she asked suddenly.

"We can do anything you like," he replied.

"Do you think that we could find a nice hotel?" she began tentatively, watching his quizzical eyebrow shoot up. "We could have a quiet dinner," she continued, "and just be alone together before I have to go back and face tomorrow."

"If that's what you want."

"It's what I want," she said without hesitation.

But as she waited in the car while he registered, she wasn't sure at all. The sense of standing outside herself and watching was with her again. There were consequences to wrong choices, she knew. And she understood that she was using him as a sort of psychological quick fix for her pain. Where had she heard those words—"psychological quick fix"? She remembered. Jacqui, of course.

Caroline's death had released an avalanche of despair, and Rhea was afraid that nothing would ever be truly right again. The rage and anger she had harbored against Carter and Jacqui seemed to have rushed out of her—leaving her deflated, and she teetered on the brink of collapse without it. She needed that anger; she drew strength from it. It was replaced with a panicky feeling—the terror of being totally alone. It had been almost impossible to give up the deeply held belief that Carter, in spite of everything, would rescue her when she needed rescuing. He hadn't.

Rhea had listened to Jacqui all these months, trying to take responsibility for her own existence, knowing that Jacqui was all the things she wasn't—beautiful, intelligent, confident. Rhea had found her unsought freedom overwhelming. It was too big a challenge, changing an entire way of being—a total life structure. Everything that had gone before in forty-two years of living just couldn't be cast aside.

Yet here she was—waiting for a man she didn't love to check into a strange hotel. "I'm sorry, Kevin," she whispered, "you deserve better than this."

She knew that she was trading sex for the relief of loneliness. She had never believed that she was the kind of woman who could do that. It seemed to confirm the fact that she was, indeed, weak and useless. But when Kevin returned with the room key, there was such obvious pleasure and anticipation on his face that she thought, perhaps, he was getting a fair return after all. Most men would think so, she rationalized.

His arms went around her almost as soon as they were in the room. "I can't believe this is happening," he said. "You fought it for so long."

"I'm not sure I'm doing the right thing," she replied.

"It's right, you'll see," he insisted.

He kissed her gently, tenderly. But unlike the day in the lakehouse, her body felt no answering response. Despite that, she did not resist, and it was he who pulled away from her.

"Shall we eat here in the hotel?" he asked, "or would you like to look for another restaurant?"

"The hotel is fine," she replied. "But do you mind if we wait a bit. I feel so grimy. I think I would like a shower and a change of clothes before we go."

"Good idea," he agreed. "You go ahead. I'll get some ice and find us something to drink before dinner."

Rhea turned on the water and began to remove her clothes. She tried not to think, adjusting the temperature as hot as she could stand. She stepped into the tub, drew the shower curtain, and raised the lever to start the shower. As the water cascaded over her tired body, she felt the tension lessen.

She could almost forget why they were here—what had happened to bring her to this point in time. The vague fear of everything and of nothing seemed to wash away. She lost all track of time, letting the water caress her, tenderly touching her naked skin. Then the curtain parted, and Kevin stepped into the shower with her. His sinewy, athletic body caressed her in the steamy enclosure as the water streamed over the two of them, pressing together as one.

Deliberately, he turned off the water and dried her body with a soft, white towel. His lips found her neck and then her breasts and, when he carried her to the bed, Rhea found that her impassioned desire matched his.

Later as they lay entangled in the damp sheets, Kevin lifted her hand to his lips. "I wish this night could last forever," he said.

"Kevin," she implored, "what do you see in me?"

"I see a beautiful, wise lady—who still retains enough fragility and vulnerability to tempt any man."

"But I'm so much older than you."

"Only in years. You're not the first woman in my life. I'm in an awkward position. I've discovered that I'm too old for Barbie dolls, but I'm not ready for the new woman. You have grace and sensuality that appealed to me the first time we met. Remember that day I bumped into your car?"

"How could I forget?"

"There was an electricity between us even then. Don't deny you felt it."

"Yes, I felt it."

"But you're still hung up on this age thing. Rhea, do you ever feel when we're together that I'm lacking in experience in some way? Is that what this age thing means to you?"

"Oh, no, its not that. You've had experiences I haven't had.

I sometimes feel that way with Jill. I know that I spent almost half my life waiting for Carter—waiting for him to give me something that I was lacking. Now, I'm just waiting. When I think of the future—I don't think I have any."

"You have a future, Rhea. We both do. We have a future together. The waiting is over."

He drew her closer, and for a little while she could almost believe him.

CHAPTER TWENTY-EIGHT

Despite brisk traffic in the shop the week before Christmas, sales were slow. How many of the people who came were merely curiosity seekers, Rhea could only guess. She cringed every time she thought about how many times her beautiful house with the sign in front had been flashed across the television screen since Caroline's death.

"I'm afraid," she told Kevin, "that people will always think of it as the place where the nurse was murdered."

"You'll be surprised," he said, "at how quickly people in this town forget."

She didn't think so, but she knew he was trying to make her feel better. Having him in the there in the house did make her feel better. She had wondered how in the world she would explain it to Jill, but she, too, seemed relieved to have Kevin there. Rhea had put his things in Carter's room. She supposed that she would always think of it as Carter's room, and if Jill remembered that there was a connecting door into Rhea's room, she never mentioned. it.

Kevin had installed a new security system, changed all the locks, and added more outside lights. When Rhea questioned the cost, he brushed away her protests.

"Think of it as a Christmas present," he said.

"I don't want to think about Christmas," she repled. "I wish I could wake up tomorrow and it would be over. The tree would be gone, all the decorations packed away. If I hear another Christmas carol, I think I'm going to scream."

"Let's skip Christmas!" Kevin said suddenly. "Let's go away. You know you won't make any big antique sales in the next few days. We'll find a warm beach and pretend it's summertime."

"You know we can't," she said wistfully. "it truly sounds inviting, but—"

"But nothing! Why can't we?" he demanded. "Let's call a travel agency."

"What about the baby? What about Jill? We can't just leave."

"We can't do anything for Caroline's baby. When she's able to leave the hospital, Caroline's brother will take her back to Louisiana. We may never see her again, and Jill is a grown woman about to be married. She can stay with one of her friends or with Jacqui. She did before."

"No, Kevin. It's out of the question," she insisted, and she was grateful when the bell on the front door signaled the arrival of customers.

She wished she could say yes, she found herself thinking later. She really wished she could. But what was she thinking? This was all so unreal. When was she going to wake up from this nightmare? Jacqui and Carter married. Caroline dead. Her poor little baby being nurtured in an incubator instead of her mother's arms. Jill, almost a baby herself, engaged to a man nobody knows. Kevin's clothes hanging in Carter's closet. Kevin's body next to hers while she slept.

Kevin had gone out when Jill, who always slept late even though she was no longer working at the club, came downstairs.

"Do you think they will ever find out who killed Caroline?" she asked.

"I don't honestly know," Rhea replied. "I don't think they have anything to go on. She lied to us about her husband being dead. They haven't been able to find him. Maybe he's the key. We weren't much help, I'm afraid. We knew so little about her."

"I would sleep a lot better if we knew who did it and why. I'm glad we have the new locks, but I don't mind telling you that I'm afraid. Aren't you afraid, Rhea? You seem so calm."

"I don't have any other alternative. I have to go on with my life. Let's face it, Kevin can't stay here forever. Logically, I don't think I'm in any danger. Caroline was killed, apparently, by someone she knew—by someone she let into the house. Jacqui heard them arguing. But, unfortunately, I'm not always logical, and, yes, there are times when I'm afraid."

Jill poured herself a glass of orange juice and came back to where Rhea was working on her ledger.

"Rhea," she asked tentatively, "would you mind very much if I went home for Christmas? I've been thinking a lot about my mother and, since I'm getting married as soon as Court gets back, I think I would like to spend Christmas at home."

"Of course, I wouldn't mind," Rhea answered. "Ruth will be so pleased."

"I wouldn't leave you," Jill said, "if you didn't have Kevin."

"Oh, Jill, you'll be leaving me soon anyway. I'm not your responsibility. Go home for Christmas."

Jill put her arms around Rhea. "I care about you," she said. "When I was a little girl, I thought you were the most beautiful lady in the whole world. I thought this house was a castle. When I was mad at my mother, I would lock myself in my room and pretend you were my real mother—that she had somehow stolen me away from you. I used to dream that you would find out and bring me here to live."

"Jill, all children have those fantasies of being someone else's child."

"But my dreams came true. I did come here to live, and I feel closer to you than I've ever felt to my mother. I guess I feel a little guilty about that. Maybe that's why I want to go home for Christmas."

"Whatever your reasons, Ruth is your mother. You should go home. Maybe she can talk you out of this crazy marriage."

"Not a chance," Jill laughed. "She'll try, I know. But she won't have any more success than you. Be happy for me, Rhea."

"Jill," Rhea said with dismay. "Of course, I want you to be happy. You know I do. You're just so young."

"I know what I want. I love Court, and I want the life he promised to give me. You know what you want too, but you're afraid to risk it."

"I don't know what you're talking about."

"I'm talking about Kevin."

"My friendship with Kevin isn't something I want to discuss," Rhea said stiffly.

"Oh," Jill quipped. "You even sound like my mother. It's all right for you to give me advice, but I'm not allowed to talk to you about Kevin. Has he asked you to marry him?"

"I promise," Rhea said, sighing, "not to voice any more objection to your marriage, at least not until you get back from Arkansas."

"Cross your heart," Jill prompted.

"Don't push your luck, kid," Rhea warned. "How about some breakfast?"

"Great, I'm starved."

"I have a favor to ask of you. Will you watch the shop for me for a while this afternoon?"

"Sure. How long will you be gone?"

"I don't know. A couple of hours at the most. I'm going to see Riker."

"That jerk you used to work for? Why?"

"I'm going to bite my tongue and apologize for throwing him out and find out if he is still interested in having me handle his antiques."

"I think you should stay away from him," Jill declared flatly.

"I can't afford to. If he has come across some good items, maybe we can make a deal. I won't have any of his junk though. And, if you're worried about being here alone, Kevin should be back soon."

"Okay, I'll do it."

A cold winter rain settled a gray, dismal pall to match Rhea's mood over Riker's old, dilapidated warehouse. She expected the meeting with him to be difficult and distasteful, but once she had swallowed her pride and apologized, he was surprisingly civil. And when she inspected the furniture stacked carelessly in the dusty warehouse, she found it just as good as he had promised. Many pieces needed only a good cleaning and minor repairs.

Rhea immediately began to think of clients she would call and the advertisements she would place. She felt her spirits lift even more as she and Riker came to an agreement with only a little haggling over her commission. And he hardly objected at all when she insisted on having her lawyer, Ben Howard, draw up a formal contract for their signatures.

Driving home, she was surprised at the enthusiasm she was able to generate over the new project. Maybe she would send photographs of choice pieces to interior decorators around the state. She could picture herself successfully selling all of Riker's furniture in a reasonably short period. Also, he had hinted that he might be acquiring other pieces if he could put together another deal.

For the first time since she started her business Rhea really believed that she was going to be okay. Her commission would keep her going, pay the real estate taxes at the end of January, and, perhaps, be enough to repay part of the loan to Jacqui.

She knew that she would have to live frugally. She would no longer have the rent from Jacqui and from poor Caroline. Soon Jill, too, would be gone. She decided not to rent the rooms again. Nothing had turned out the way she expected. She had invested too much emotional energy into her friendships with all of them, and, it seemed, received so little in return. Caroline couldn't be blamed, of course, but she was still very, very angry with Jacqui and Carter. The two of them had knowingly hurt her. She was also having trouble with her feelings about Jill. She had no reason to feel such foreboding when she thought of the upcoming wedding. But it was there nonetheless.

She resolved to be very careful from now on with her feelings; she would extend her friendship sparingly. She would concentrate on the business, expanding her income in as many ways as she could think of. Perhaps, she would start teaching a class on antiques in her home, limited to a small group, of course. She would fill all her waking hours with work. It would be enough. It had to be.

Jill left for Arkansas the next day. Kevin drove her to the airport while Rhea met with Riker in Ben Howard's office to sign the contract. Then she went home to make room for the first load of Riker's furniture.

She emptied the downstairs rooms of all her personal items and carried them upstairs. Prices went on paintings and china that she had expected never to part with. Whereas she had tried to fit things for sale in around her personal possessions, she now regarded the downstairs space as wholly a shop and no longer living space. But she would be careful not to move in too much furniture at once. She felt that she had been successful by showing her inventory to its best advantage in the natural setting of the spacious rooms in the lovely old house.

Someone had told her once that to be a good antique dealer, one could not love antiques. It was just simply too hard to part with them. Maybe he was right, she thought. But, remembering how much pleasure finding the right furniture and decorating the beloved house had given her, she found a great deal of satisfaction in helping others to do the same.

She had to get Riker's furniture out of that awful warehouse as soon as possible before the dust and temperature changes wreaked havoc with the finishes. From the musty smell of the place it probably leaked too. Some of it would go in the garage until she had a chance to clean, appraise, and catalogue it.

Kevin was gone longer than she expected. Probably, the traffic, she decided. She could hardly wait for him to get back to help her rearrange to make more space. But, when he did arrive, the last thing on his mind was moving furniture. He pushed a handful of travel brochures at her.

"With Jill gone, you don't have an excuses to refuse a holiday. Please say yes, Rhea. We deserve a vacation."

"But I can't," she protested, turning a deaf ear to the pleading in his voice. "I have so much to do."

She told him about her ideas for Riker's furniture, eagerness creeping into her voice. "I have to move as much of the furniture as I can fit in here," she said. "And I have to figure out how I'm going to promote it and sell it. I still have my final exams to make up. When am I going to study?"

"Just don't say no," he pleaded, "until you hear me out."

"I can't go away," she stubbornly resisted. "I don't have the time."

"Will you listen to me?"

"Yes, as long as you understand that I can't go away."

"I understand that you think you can't go away. But will you sit down for a few minutes with me and hear me out?"

"Of course, I will."

Rhea poured two cups of coffee and reluctantly sat down with him where she could keep an eye on the front door in case a customer came in. She wanted to be up working, but she forced herself to smile at him and take a sip of her coffee.

"I've been thinking," he said, "with all the bad publicity the house attracted with the murder investigation, we needed something to counter that."

"I don't know of anything that we could do," Rhea replied. "You yourself said that people would forget in time, remember?"

"Yes, but I thought of something a little more positive."

"What?" she asked, interested at once.

"A guy I went to college with at the University of Houston is a producer for a television show. A local show. It's called Texas Morning Talk. Are you familiar with it?"

"Sure, it's interesting. I don't watch television much anymore, but I've seen it. I like it."

"Well, they are going to have another very interesting segment in a few weeks. It's about a remarkable lady in Montrose who turned her beautiful old mansion into an antique showplace."

"Oh Kevin," she cried, spilling her coffee. "You don't mean."

"Careful there," he said, taking the cup from her hands. "You are going to be featured in an upcoming show."

"As a favor to you," she cried.

"No, not as a favor. I pitched the idea to them and they liked it. Otherwise, they wouldn't do it."

"Oh, Kevin, what will I say?"

"Don't worry about that. You will simply show the host of the show around the house, talking about the things you care passionately about, antiques and this house. Your face will light up like it always does when you show someone through the house, and you will be beautiful and charming, and people will flock here to see you and your antiques. You won't even notice the camera, I promise you."

"Money can't buy that kind of publicity. It sounds too good to be true."

"It is true," he said. "And you're long overdue for some good luck."

She threw her arms around him. "I can't believe it," she said excitedly. "How can I thank you?"

"By going away with me over the holidays."

"But, Kevin," she said in dismay. "I have so much to do."

"We'll do it together when we get back," he said firmly. "I'll find somebody to move the furniture as soon as we get back. I'll be your slave to command. I'll do anything to help you."

"Where would you like to go," she asked smiling.

"Wherever you want to go. How about Hawaii?"

"Too far away. Too long a plane ride."

"The Bahamas, Virgin Islands, Acapulco?"

"You decide," she said happily.

"Where haven't you been with Carter?" he asked suddenly, and Rhea was puzzled by the expression in his eyes.

"What does it matter?" she asked. "I haven't been anywhere with anyone in a long, long time. Just a break in the routine would be nice, I suppose. We don't have to go far, you know. Christmas is the worst of all possible times to travel, congestion at the airports, unpredictable weather, delays, impossible crowds."

"You don't really want to go anywhere, do you?" he asked.

He was watching her intently, and she sensed the deep disappointment he was trying to hide. He had been so good to her, and she had given him so little in return. She decided to go away with him, not because she really wanted to, but she felt she owed that much.

"Yes," she said, forcing a wide smile. "I definitely want to go. But I want you to choose the place and make all the arrangements. Surprise me. All I want is a grand hotel with a spectacular view—something magnificent like a harbor, or a mountainside or dazzling lights. I don't care where. I want three or four long, lazy days with no clocks, no telephones, no customers—a five star restaurant, of course, and an open agenda to do whatever we feel like doing at the moment. My problems will all disappear, and I will come back with a new perspective for the new year."

"Do you really mean it?"

"Of course, I mean it. It may take a miracle to get a reservation at this late date, but I'll settle for whatever you can find."

"Rhea, you should never have to settle for anything less than the best. Coming up," he promised, "one miracle!"

CHAPTER TWENTY-NINE

Jacqui popped the cork on the last bottle of champagne from the California vineyards she and Greg had brought back from San Francisco. It was a memory she would always treasure— walking hand in hand with him through the winery surrounded by the aura of new found love, tasting the various wines and knowing that their delicious heady sensation had little to do with the wines they had sampled.

She remembered crying when they left, and Greg laughed and kissed her and promised they would come back again whenever and as often as she liked. It seemed to her now such a long time ago. Sometimes it was hard for her to accept the reality of their marriage, but the reality of his illness she would not accept. There was no such thing as an incurable illness, she told herself, and Greg was getting better every day.

"A kiss for your thoughts," Greg said as she stood motionless holding the champagne bottle.

"I was thinking of California," she said, and it was partly true. They rarely discussed his health, and tonight she was determined to let nothing spoil their Christmas Eve celebration. "It seems like such a long time ago," she said truthfully.

"It was," he replied, "in terms of all the things that have happened to us since then."

Jacqui filled two glasses and carefully handed him one, making certain he had it firmly in his grasp before she let go. Suddenly, she realized that she was doing what she said she wouldn't do, acknowledge the reality of his illness. She knew that prayer was answered before it was uttered. So where was her faith?

"Jacqui, you're a million miles away tonight," he protested. "Where are you, lady? I want to be there, too."

"You are," she said, snuggling down beside him on the sofa. "You always are."

The small white flocked Christmas tree was trimmed with blue satin ornaments. Blue feathery peacocks and miniature blue lights mingled with shimmering blue icicles. The coffee table in front of them held a snow white azalea in full bloom dressed with silver foil and a blue velvet ribbon.

Jacqui had a fire going in the fireplace, and she had turned on the Christmas lights as he rested after their late lunch downtown. He fell asleep easily these days, she noticed, but he looked rested now and contented. She wondered if life could be better than this.

The room was bathed in candlelight and the glow of the fire. There was a fondue for later with fruit and bits of French bread to be dipped in the warm Swiss cheese. One of Greg's clients had given him a delicious rum cake which would be perfect with espresso.

They agreed to give each other inexpensive, fun presents. She delighted him with an espresso maker and an alarm clock in the shape of a basketball that could be thrown across the room when the alarm sounded. He gave her a sheer, sexy nightgown and a cookbook. Her lack of cooking skill had been a joke between them since the beginning of their relationship.

"How about a refill, love?" he asked, indicating her empty champagne glass.

"Sure," she replied, "but first I have one more gift for you. She slipped a thin, narrow box into his hand.

"What is this?" he demanded. "It wasn't under the tree."

"It was a last minute impulse gift," she admitted. "I know we agreed no expensive presents but—"

"You mean you didn't stick to your end of the bargain. We did agree, Jacqui."

"Open it before you get angry with me, will you?"

Without smiling, he pulled off the paper she had wrapped so carefully, exposing a satin lined box containing a handcrafted Swiss watch in white gold with an elegant black face.

As she watched him, he sat holding the watch in his hands without speaking. Slowly he turned it over and read the inscription engraved on the back. Always, Jacqui.

"Don't you like it?" she asked tentatively.

"Well, of course, I like it," he said crossly. "But it's obvious that I'm married to a woman I can't trust. We did have an agreement. Why did you do it?"

"Well, you see," she began lamely, "this little, fat man in a red suit stuck a gun in my back."

"Seriously, Jacqui," he demanded. "How do you think this makes me feel?"

"I hoped it would make you feel great. How does it make you feel?"

She saw the little smile playing around his mouth before he spoke.

"Great," he said laughing, "because now you can't get mad at me became I didn't stick to the agreement either."

He handed her a package pulled from beneath the sofa pillows.

"You scoundrel," she shrieked. "How could you do that to me? I thought you were really mad at me."

"Mad for you, darling," he said, planting a kiss that almost missed the side of her face.

Playfully, she pushed him away. "Let me open my present. Then I'll decide how to get even with you, you unprincipled rogue, you shameless rascal, you good-for-nothing scalawag, you—"

"Stop! Time out! Open your present."

Jacqui carefully slipped off the satin bow and removed the paper without tearing it. Then she smoothed it and folded it before she opened the box.

"I see you ran into the same little, fat man in the red suit," she said.

"No, not at all. I was in the jewelry store, and they were playing Jingle Bells, and I guess I got too close to the display counter. The darn thing jumped right into my hand."

"Yes," she said drily, "you have to watch those display counters when you hear Jingle Bells."

Strangely enough the box was the same size as the one she had handed him. A watch, she thought incredulously. He had bought her a watch, too!

It was the most beautiful watch she had ever seen. Diamonds circled the face which was also set with diamonds at each hour point. The band was fashioned from strands of gold rope.

"It must have cost a fortune," she exclaimed. "You didn't have to do this. How did you find out I was giving you a watch? Who told you?"

"Nobody told me," he protested. "Who could have told me. Who did you tell?"

"I didn't tell anybody," she declared. "Wait a minute. The jeweler told you. That's how you knew."

"Sorry, but you're wrong. Anyway, the watches are from different jewelry stores."

"I can't believe that we both gave each other watches after we agreed not to exchange expensive presents, and it was just sheer coincidence."

"Wait a minute. I know how we can settle this," he said. "When did you buy my watch?"

"Three days ago."

"That settles it," he exclaimed. "I bought yours a week ago. My worst fear is realized. Remember the night we met after the ball game when I told you that I believed you could pick up my thoughts. Now I know you can. How will I ever be able to keep anything from you?"

"It is strange," she mused. "They say that couples who live together become more alike as the years go by, so much so that they even begin to look alike."

"If that's true, my love, we won't be able to tell where I end and you begin."

"I like that idea."

"Then come over here and show me how much you like it," he suggested.

"Just a minute, you don't get off the hook that easily. If I could really read your thoughts, you wouldn't have been able to put me on like that."

"What was it you called me—unprincipled, good-for-nothing, rascal, scoundrel, scalawag?"

"You left out rogue."

"So I did."

"I'm thinking up some exquisite torture for you," she declared.

She took his face in her hands and gave him a long, lingering kiss.

"Such exquisite torture I could endure forever." He returned her long, slow kiss before he asked suddenly, "Jacqui, are you happy? Really happy?"

"I'm happier than I ever thought possible," she said solemnly. "I wish Caroline hadn't died. I wish Jill would decide not to marry Court Randall. I wish Rhea weren't so desperately unhappy."

"Why don't you wish for peace in the Middle East and a cure for AIDS?"

"I do," she said. "But I am happy, and I don't feel guilty because negative conditions exist. I love you, Greg, more than I can ever tell you. I have this inner awareness that we are perfect together. I expect this perfection to last forever."

"Nothing lasts forever," he said sadly. "And you are right about us being perfect together. I wish it hadn't taken us so long to find each other. But I don't think it matters if we have a year or thirty years. It won't be enough time."

No, she thought. As much as she believed that death was only a transition to another plane of existence, she was still fearful of losing him. She couldn't seem to help it.

"We're wasting the bubbly," Greg said.

"We can't have that. From now on, we are not going to waste a single drop," she replied, and they both knew she was not speaking of champagne.

"Merry Christmas, darling," she said touching her glass to his.

"Merry Christmas, my love."

Later she served the fondue, and they had espresso together and sampled the rum cake. They listened to music and watched the flickering fire burn down to glowing embers.

"This is the best day of my life," Greg sighed contentedly.

"You always say that," she reminded him.

"When did I say that?"

"Over a bottle of champagne, as I recall, in San Francisco."

"You're right. I do remember. I said nothing was too good for the best day of my life. But I guess I'm going to have to stop saying that. I don't think it can get any better than this."

"Wrong again! It's midnight, and we're about to start another day. We're going upstairs. You still have to experience that exquisite torture I promised you."

"You've just made me an offer I can't refuse."

They made love, tenderly, passionately, until they lay in each other's arms satiated and totally content. Jacqui was almost asleep when she heard him whisper in her ear.

"I love it when you prove me wrong, beautiful lady."

CHAPTER THIRTY

January was filled with cold, damp, depressing days, and it seemed to Jill that since it rained almost every other day, hard, drenching rains, that she would, undoubtedly, wake up one morning and find everything covered with fuzzy, green mold, including herself.

People were beginning to make jokes about the sun whenever it put in a rare appearance. What is that funny yellow thing in the sky? The sunny days that Jill had shared with Court in the Caribbean seemed long ago. She was glad that she had the magnificent diamond on her finger. It was proof that she did not dream those days.

Court was gone again. She wasn't really sure where. He phoned her often, but he was vague about his destination, and she had learned that to question him too closely was to incur his displeasure.

Jill loved Court Randall completely, but she would not admit to anyone but herself that she did not trust him completely. There were too many blank spaces in their relationship—spaces where she dared not venture.

Perhaps that was the reason she kept on building up her secret cache of money even after she left her job at the Aloha Room. Court was very generous with cash. Sometimes it almost took her breath away, and he had promised that she would never have to worry about money again. But she did worry. She took the cash he gave her, and after paying Rhea for room and board, she squirreled away the rest in a saving account.

Court didn't seem to notice very much what she wore. And nobody else did either. She was well aware that she could turn heads in the simplest little dress or a pair of faded jeans. Jill didn't understand why. When she looked in the mirror, she saw nothing spectacular. She didn't know what all the fuss was about. But she had lived since she was twelve with the growing awareness that to other people, her looks were something special. She half expected whatever it was to disappear when she left Arkansas, but to her surprise, it didn't.

Jill's trousseau, so far, consisted entirely of clothes bought at sales and fashion outlets—she carefully spurned the ones who cut out labels—and at resale shops. Most of her elegant evening clothes came from a resale shop in River Oaks where Houston's wealthy lived in beautiful old mansions with manicured lawns.

Court would be furious with her if he knew, but Jill couldn't forget landing alone in downtown Houston with only a hundred dollar bill in her shoe and nothing else but the clothes on her back. She was rather proud of the way she could take a knock-off from the bargain basement, adorn it with the expensive jewelry Court got such a kick out of giving her, and mingle with his wealthy friends. She knew one thing for sure, she never intended to be poor again.

And she was sure she wanted to marry Court. She could make herself dizzy with excitement just thinking about his dark, sensual good looks and his hard, lean body. Even if she wasn't sure where the marriage was headed, travel was exciting. Money was exciting. Court wanted no children or family around and seemed to care little for friends or a permanent home. When she would see her mother again was anybody's guess—not to mention Jacqui and Rhea.

"Do you really like your life?" she asked Jacqui as they lunched in the Galleria Atrium amid potted palms and sunlight, "I mean, being married and all."

"I love being married to Greg," Jacqui said. "Yes, I do like my life, although it's different from anything I ever imagined for myself. But, that question, dear one, sounds like pre-wedding jitters to me. Have you and Court set a date?"

"Sometime next month."

"Wow, that soon! Any second thoughts?"

"No, not in the way you mean," Jill sighed. "I just wish we

were doing it in a different way."

"The wedding, you mean?"

"Yeah, we're getting married at the courthouse by a Justice of the Peace. Court doesn't want any fuss."

"I thought you wanted to be married in Rhea's house," Jacqui protested.

"There isn't even room to live in Rhea's house anymore. You should see it now. She moved in a whole warehouse full of antiques."

"A whole warehouse?" Jacqui asked skeptically.

"You got it. A whole warehouse. Rhea's business is going great. I'm glad. It makes me less guilty about leaving."

"How does she feel about me? She seemed to put her hostility on hold when Caroline died. Has she softened any?"

"I'm afraid not. I think she's still furious. But she doesn't have much time to dwell on it. She works sixteen to eighteen hours every day."

"How does Kevin feel about that?"

"Who knows? He still follows her around like a puppy, grateful for being in her presence. She did go to Mexico with him for Christmas. He seems restless a lot of the time, sort of at loose ends."

"Is he working at his photography at all?"

"Some, I guess. He took pictures of me one day and, Jacqui, you wouldn't believe how they turned out. He made me look like a professional model. He even did my makeup for me, and I guess I really hammed it up, 'cause you wouldn't believe how I look in the pictures."

"Of, course, I believe it."

"Kevin says the camera loves me," Jill laughed. "I'm a natural."

"Have you ever considered modeling?"

"No, of course not. I really hate being photographed. Besides, Court wouldn't hear of it. He won't let me work once we're married. He made me quit the Aloha Room as soon as we got engaged. He's giving me money to live on."

"Funny," Jacqui laughed, "I have the opposite problem. Greg is threatening to kick me out of the house if I don't start trying to find a job."

"You're joking."

"No, I'm serious. Not that he would kick me out of the house, of course, but he really does want me to find a job. He thinks my doctorate is going to waste, and he keeps calling me Dr. Wilder-Gregory around the house to remind me."

"Isn't it, going to waste, I mean?"

"I suppose. But, honestly, I'm content right now just taking care of Greg."

"He is feeling all right, isn't he?"

"Yes, he has a cold, but otherwise he's fine. He takes it easy when he doesn't feel well. He didn't go into the office today."

"I'll stop by when he feels better," Jill promised.

"He's very unhappy with you, you know, for not letting us meet Court."

"I really tried, Jacqui, it just hasn't worked out. Court is gone so much of the time, and when he is in town, he wants us to be alone."

"I know the feeling," Jacqui laughed. "But somehow you are going to have to manage it."

"I will. I promise. How about going shopping with me this afternoon? I'm in the market for a wedding dress."

"Oh, Jill, I can't. I promised Greg that I would go downtown to his office and pick up some papers for him. I left him napping, but I don't want to be gone too long."

"Sure, I understand."

"You will let me know," Jacqui said, rising, "when you have a firm date for the wedding. I'll be there to lend you moral support, wherever it is."

Jill smiled and watched Jacqui leave, without telling her that she would not be invited to the wedding. Court had forbidden her to allow anyone but Rhea and Kevin to see them married.

CHAPTER THIRTY-ONE

The day of Jill's wedding arrived with bright sunshine and pleasant warm weather. Rhea insisted on preparing brunch for Jill and Court since they planned to leave directly for the airport following the two o'clock ceremony.

Rhea closed the shop for the day. She felt she really couldn't afford to do it. With Jill gone, she knew that she would have to hire someone at least part-time. A student, perhaps. As long as she had decorating jobs, she couldn't be tied to the shop all day every day.

But Jill was the closest to a daughter that she would ever have. And although she disapproved of the way Jill was getting married, she tried to make it as festive as possible. She moved a small drop leaf table into the living room and covered it with a fine old lace cloth. She arranged elegant flowers and candles amid her best china and crystal. The polished gleam on the silver was Kevin's contribution.

There should have been a proper wedding and reception, Rhea thought, but if Jill had any regrets, they were not evident today. She was dressed in an ivory raw silk suit with a cornflower blue blouse that exactly matched the blue of her eyes. She was radiantly happy, and Rhea noticed, pleased, that Court's eyes followed her every move.

Rhea had to admit that she was charmed by the man. He was as handsome as a movie star, and it was apparent that he adored Jill. All the misgivings she had harbored for so long about his suitability for Jill melted away, and Rhea and Kevin raised their glasses to toast the couple.

Court announced that the wedding would not take place downtown at the courthouse as they had all supposed. "We're going to Pasadena," he told them. "It's still in Harris County, and they have a small courthouse annex there. There won't be a parking problem. Everything is arranged, and it won't take more than a few minutes. And then you," he said cupping Jill's face, "will be mine forever and ever."

"As long as we're married," Jill said, "I don't care where it takes place. What time do we have to leave?"

"We should leave a little after one. That will give us plenty of time."

"Will you excuse me?" Jill asked. "I need to go upstairs for a moment."

Court followed her to the foot of the stairs, and his eyes followed her all the way up the landing. She turned and blew him a kiss and mouthed the words, "I love you."

Rhea and Kevin, watching from the living room, smiled at one another. Court came back to join them.

"If there is ever to be a more beautiful woman in the world, nature had not yet created her," he said.

He smiled at Rhea sheepishly. "I guess I sound like a bridegroom."

"It's allowed," Rhea replied.

Upstairs, Jill applied fresh lipstick and fussed with a wayward strand of hair. She felt so guilty about not asking Jacqui to the wedding. Jacqui was her friend. She had turned to Jacqui for help when she dared not trust anybody else. And that help had been freely given.

Court didn't want anybody but Rhea and Kevin at the wedding. He had met them. He hadn't met Jacqui. She should have insisted. How could he refuse? What would he do if she called Jacqui right now? Refuse to go through with the ceremony when she arrived. That certainly wasn't likely to happen..

On that impulse she went into her room and reached for the phone. Jacqui answered on the first ring.

"I know this is short notice," Jill explained, "but I'm getting married this afternoon at two o'clock in the Pasadena courthouse. If you leave right now, you can just make it."

Jacqui was full of protests as well as surprise. "Why didn't you let me know sooner? I'm not dressed. Jill, I can't possibly be there by two o'clock."

"Yes, you can. Come as you are. It doesn't matter. It's very casual. Please Jacqui, I want you there."

"I'll try, Jill, I'll try, but I don't understand why you didn't let me know sooner. I don't even know where the Pasadena court-house is."

"I don't have time to explain. Just come, Jacqui. You can find it. Ask directions when you get to Pasadena. Please."

She'll be there, Jill thought happily, but she wouldn't tell anybody. She would just let it be a surprise to them. Rhea would-n't be thrilled either. But, after all, it was her wedding.

Rhea brought out a cake she had ordered for the occasion. It was topped with wedding bells tied with a blue icing bow with the names Jill and Court in flowery letters.

Jill was delighted, and she pulled Court's hand over hers as they cut the first piece and fed a bite to each other.

Court seemed restless. Several times he went to the window and looked out. Nervous, Rhea thought. Well why not? Wasn't everybody nervous just before their wedding?

While Court loaded Jill's luggage in the car, Rhea took Jill up to her room.

"Something old, something new, something borrowed, some-thing blue," Rhea reminded her.

"Well, my suit is new, and my blouse is blue," Jill laughed.

"So, we work on old and borrowed," Rhea said. She opened her jewelry box and drew out an antique gold locket on a fragile gold chain. "This is old; it belonged to my mother, your grand-mother. She gave it to me before I got married. I'm sure it would please her to know I'm giving it to you to wear at your wed-ding."

She hoped it brought Jill more luck than it had brought her, Rhea thought, but she did not say it aloud. She had been remem-bering her own wedding all day. After all these years she could still remember exactly how she felt. It was, she acknowledged, the hap-piest day of her life. How could the marriage have turned out the way it did?

"Thank you, Rhea. I'll take very good care of it. Now that takes care of everything but borrowed."

"Let's see, Jill. What can I lend you?"

"Lend me a handkerchief just in case I start to cry."

"Silly, you're not supposed to cry at your own wedding. I'll lend you a handkerchief, but you leave the crying to me."

"I think I'm going to cry right now," Jill said, wrapping her arms around Rhea.

"Don't you dare," Rhea said, giving her a hug and pushing her out to arm's length. "Court just said that you were the most beautiful woman in the world. We can't have him seeing you with red eyes and tear stained cheeks, can we?"

"Rhea, are you sure you're going to be all right?"

"Of course, I'm going to be all right. You are not to worry about me. I'm fine."

"We had better be going, Sunshine," Court said to Jill when they came downstairs. "We wouldn't want to be late to our own wedding."

"We'll see you there," he said to Kevin. "You know how to get there. Highway 225 to Richey Street."

"I think so," Kevin said. "We'll follow you."

Jill sat next to Court. All her dreams were really coming true. There was not a doubt in her mind that the love between them would last forever.

CHAPTER THIRTY-TWO

Jacqui sped down the South Loop past the Astrodome on the left and Astroworld on the right. It was already after one-thirty. She would never make the courthouse in time. She shouldn't have taken so much time to dress, but she could hardly attend any kind of a wedding, formal or not, in a pair of jeans and a faded college sweatshirt. She had been vacuuming the bedroom when Jill phoned.

Greg was in court, so there was no possibility of reaching him. Jacqui knew that he would be disappointed. He was very fond of Jill.

What had happened, she wondered, to account for the rush? Mercifully, the traffic was light. She made good time, but she could not be sure it was good enough. She changed into the right lane to follow Highway 225 as the Loop curved north. She passed the oil tanks and an industrial plant belching gray steam into the air. She was familiar with the area. She had taken a course one summer at the junior college in Pasadena.

She exited on Richey Street and pulled into the service station on the corner to ask for directions. She was headed wrong on Richey Street, so she turned around in the driveway and crossed over the freeway. A turn at the next light put her on the street where the courthouse was located. She had no trouble finding a sparking space. She locked her car and ran into the building. It was just a few minutes past two.

Without too much trouble, she found the courtroom where the wedding was already in progress. Jill and her groom were standing in front of the judge, and Kevin and Rhea were standing behind them.

"For richer or poorer, in sickness and in health," the judge was saying.

Jacqui hesitated at the door, hoping to slip in quietly without being noticed. Jill, however, saw her and flashed her a brilliant, welcoming smile. The man standing beside her turned and looked Jacqui squarely in the face.

Jacqui stared into the hard, sinister eyes. Eyes that were forever etched into her memory! She was thrust abruptly back in time to the night of Caroline's murder when she had first looked into those cold, evil eyes.

A look of recognition passed between Jacqui and the startled man standing at Jill's side. Then he bolted for the door where Jacqui stood in shock. He gave her a violent shove that pushed her to the floor. "Goddammed fucking bitch," he hissed as he rushed past her. She looked up into the startled eyes of the judge and began screaming. Rhea had her arms protectively around Jill whose stunned face was drained of color.

Kevin came immediately to Jacqui's aid. "He killed Caroline!" she cried. "That man is Caroline's murderer.

"Are you sure?" Kevin prodded her.

"Liar!" Jill screamed, finding her voice at last. "That's Court. He never killed anybody. You're crazy."

Rhea led Jill to a seat with her arms still around her shoulders.

Kevin lifted Jacqui to the feet, and the judge beckoned them into his private office.

"I am absolutely positive that the man who ran from the courtroom is the same man who murdered Caroline Kelly," Jacqui said breathlessly. "He recognized me, too."

"There is some reason he dashed out of her in the middle of his wedding," the judge said. "Highly irregular, I must say."

Police were summoned. A deputy sheriff was in the building, and Pasadena City Police were there within minutes. Kevin went back to the courtroom where he had left Rhea and Jill.

Jill was sitting beside Rhea, staring straight ahead without saying anything.

"There must be some mistake," Rhea said as Kevin sat down beside her.

"I don't think so," Kevin replied. "Jacqui positively identified

Court Randall as the man who ran out of Caroline's room the night she was murdered with a gun in his hand and took a shot at her."

"It isn't true," Jill cried. "It isn't true! Court was with me the night Caroline was killed. We spent the night at a hotel out by the airport and left on an early morning flight for Miami where we caught a plane to Jamaica. It isn't true. He couldn't have killed her, he was with me."

"Then, why did he run?" Rhea asked gently. As angry as she was with Jacqui, she knew that Jacqui would never make such an accusation lightly.

"I don't know, Aunt Rhea."

"You poor, poor baby," Rhea soothed. "Find out if we can take her home, Kevin. She's had such an awful shock. She can't tell them any more."

But they were not allowed to leave. Jill was questioned extensively about Court Randall. It surprised Rhea and Kevin that she seemed to know so little about the man she was planning to marry. Court was a man with no permanent address, a man who lived out of hotels, drove a rental car. Jill only knew that he was an importer—or was it an exporter, but she knew virtually nothing about his business. She gave them the names of some of his acquaintances that she had met in the course of their courtship. She described the villa where they had vacationed in Jamaica, and she gave them directions from the nearest town.

However, she still insisted that Jacqui had accused the wrong man. Court had been with her the night Caroline died. An awful mistake had been made. Jacqui must be made to see that.

"He'll come back," Jill told them stubbornly, "and explain everything. I know it."

When they go back to the house, she went straight to her room and closed the door.

"I wish I could help her," Rhea said, "but I don't know how."

"You can't help her," Kevin said. "Nobody can. Until she finds out for sure, she can't even begin to deal with the situation."

Rhea put away the candles and the lace tablecloth and transferred the flowers to a vase in the entry hall. Kevin checked the locks on all the doors and windows and made sure the alarm was turned on.

"You don't think he'll come back here, do you?" Rhea asked.

"Yes, I do. If he loves Jill, and it's evident that he does, I think he'll come back for her."

"If he had anything to do with Caroline's murder, I think he would be afraid to come back. If he does, we have to notify the authorities, don't you think?"

"We don't have any other choice," Kevin said. "We won't take any chances."

Rhea left the closed sign on the front door and busied herself cleaning and rearranging furniture. Kevin went upstairs to work in the darkroom he had created in one of Rhea's upstairs bathrooms.

Rhea remembered the sense of foreboding she had not been able to shake. She was thoroughly confused—Jacqui insisting that Court Randall was the man who shot poor Caroline and Jill insisting that he had been with her. She didn't know what to believe.

Later she prepared a light supper, but when she knocked softly on Jill's door, there was no answer.

"I wonder if she's okay," Rhea said.

"Do you think I should go in and check on her?" she asked Kevin.

"I wouldn't. Let's give her a little more time," he suggested. "I heard her moving around in her room earlier. Maybe she's sleeping now. I doubt if she's hungry, Rhea. Let's give her some space. She'll come down when she's ready. I can't imagine her wanting to face anyone after what she's been through today."

Rhea agreed with him, but just as she and Kevin sat down to eat, the bell on the front door sounded.

"I'll get it," Kevin said, jumping up, but she followed him into the entry way. To her amazement, he opened the door to Jacqui and Carter.

"We've just come from the police department," Carter said. "We wanted to tell you what happened before they did. Where is Jill?"

"Upstairs in her room, sleeping, I think."

"Poor baby. The detectives are going to want to question her again. I think I should be there. The man she knew as Court Randall has been under surveillance by the DEA."

"The man she knew as Court Randall," Kevin repeated. "Does that mean he wasn't Court Randall?"

"His name is Rick Cortero; he was married to Caroline Kelly. The DEA has been after him for some time. He rented a plane after he fled today, and the Coast Guard reported receiving a mayday shortly after he took off. Fisherman in the gulf saw a plane go down. They assume he was on it."

A gasp from the top of the stairs made them all turn to look at Jill, standing on the landing above, holding on to the railing to keep from falling.

Jacqui reached her first, and Jill crumpled into her arms.

"I'm so sorry," Jacqui soothed. "We're all so sorry."

"I can't believe it," Jill sobbed. "I loved him so."

They helped her into her room, but she couldn't stop crying, and, at length, Rhea had to summon her own doctor to come and give Jill a sedative.

Rhea put the untouched supper away as Kevin walked Jacqui and Carter out to their car. Then she took the leftover wedding cake and washed it down the garbage disposal.

CHAPTER THIRTY-THREE

The week following Jill's disastrous wedding, Jacqui tried to telephone her and was told by a polite but distant Rhea that Jill had gone home to Arkansas. It was mid-week before Jacqui was able to reach her at her mother's place.

Jacqui was surprised by the calmness in Jill voice and her apparent resolve when she said, "I really am going to be all right, Jacqui."

It was difficult to believe that this was the same hysterical girl who had wept so piteously that her life was over.

"I shouldn't have come home," Jill said. "I love my mother, but I really can't talk to her anymore. I really can't talk to anybody about Court right now."

"I understand."

"But there is something you can do for me, Jacqui."

"All you have to do is ask. You know that if I can, I will."

"My luggage was in the trunk of the rental car. Almost everything I own is in that luggage. Will you check with the police to see if it's been found and get it for me. There were five bags—blue leather with my initials. I have to get them back."

"I'll see if Greg can take care of it. I'll call him right away. And I'll call you back as soon as I find out anything at all."

"I'll probably be back in Houston early next week," Jill said. "I'm not a little girl any longer, and running home to my mother was not the thing to do. I know that I've got to figure out what I'm going to do with the rest of my life. This isn't a very good place to do that. Once I got here, I remembered all the reasons

I left in the first place."

"I'm sure you'll work it out."

"Thanks for saying that and for not giving me advice. Everyone else—my mother, Jimmy, Rhea, Kevin—seem to know exactly what I should do. They all agree that I should just forget Court. I'm supposed to feel lucky I didn't marry him."

Sarcasm had crept into her voice.

"Jimmy wants us to get back together. Mother wants me to stay here—go back to work at the Dairy Queen, I suppose. Rhea and Kevin both think I should start to college. Rhea already picked up catalogues from The University of St. Thomas and The University of Houston. The crazy thing is that I don't know what I want, but I know what I don't want. I don't want any of those things. There has to be something else."

"There is something else. Something that's right for you. When Spence died, I didn't think things would ever be right for me again. You just have to know that life goes on, and what you make of it depends on the choices you make."

"I just can't forget Court and be grateful I didn't marry him regardless of what he did."

"I know that. But there is something that bothers me, Jill. You said that Court was with you the night that Caroline was killed."

"He was with me, Jacqui, I didn't lie. It was the night before we left for Jamaica. We spent the night at the hotel near the Airport. But he did go out for a while. I was napping. I don't know how long he was gone. He could have slipped back to the house and murdered Caroline. And there's something else. Caroline might not have let him in. I lost my house key once, and it turned out later he had inadvertently put it in his pocket—or so he said. But I just couldn't believe he would do such an awful thing."

"Of course, you couldn't. I wish I could give you a hug."

"I feel as if you had."

"Hold that thought," Jacqui said. "I'll see you next week."

Jacqui phoned Greg who promised to look into the matter of the luggage.

"How did she sound?" he asked.

"Calm, thoughtful, and completely in control of herself. Determined not to let anyone pressure her into something she doesn't want to do."

"Good for her. And I'm glad she is coming back to Houston. Rhea will take care of her."

"I gather," Jacqui said, "that Rhea is part of the problem. She wants Jill to start to college as soon as a new term starts."

"Sounds like a good idea to me. Jill is so young. She can put this behind her. What else is she going to do? Be a cocktail waitress until she meets someone equally as bad as Court Randall or Rick Cortero or whoever he was."

"I hope not, but then I don't think she is going to ask my advice, love, nor yours either."

"Probably not," he said sighing. "Little does she know what she's missing—expert that I am in finding the perfect mate."

"I won't argue with that."

"Jacqui," he asked, suddenly serious. "Do you ever think we are the only two people in this whole insane world who are truly happy?"

"Sometimes, it seems that way, doesn't it. How do you suppose we got so lucky?"

"Was it luck, beautiful lady, or was it destiny?"

"We should not be having this conversation over the telephone."

"Why not?"

"Because it sounds like pillow talk."

"What's wrong with pillow talk?"

"Nothing is wrong with pillow talk—on a pillow."

"I get the message. I'll be home early."

"Promises, promises," she laughed.

But he did get home early.

"Did you find out anything about Jill's luggage?" she asked him at once.

"Yes, it was in the rental car. They went through it, of course, but I managed to get it released. I have it in the trunk. I'll drop it off at Rhea's on the way to work in the morning."

"That sounds like a good idea. I'll call Jill later and put her mind at ease."

"She really sounded okay on the phone?" he asked.

"Yes, she did. It's as though she has accepted it and knows that life goes on."

"God, how did she ever get mixed up with that one? I looked at his rap sheet. He's been in and out of jail a dozen times."

"Do you suppose that Caroline was trying to tell me that she knew Court was involved with Jill? I distinctly remember her saying that she was afraid of the wrong person."

"It would explain things, wouldn't it?"

"Caroline distrusted me for some reason. Maybe that's what she meant when she asked me to forgive her."

"I guess we'll never know."

"I know one thing," Jacqui said, "I'll never forget the sight of him."

"You can't imagine how I feel every time I think about you in that house with him that night. It was a miracle he didn't shoot you."

"He must have been a pretty lousy shot or else he needed glasses. Apparently, he couldn't tell me from a goose."

"Jacqui, it isn't funny," he said. She went into his arms, and they closed around her.

"I don't think I could live without you," he said pressing her so closely that it almost took her breath away.

"I know I couldn't live without you," she replied.

"Don't say that!" he said sharply, pushing her out to arms length. "Don't even think it."

"It's true."

"It isn't true. What if I don't beat this dammed thing? Jacqui, I could die or become disabled."

"I won't even consider the possibility."

He drew her hand up to his lips and kissed the scars on her wrists.

"Promise me," he said, pulling her close again, "that if something happens to me—hell, I could get killed on the freeway. You know that. Promise me that you will go on living."

He's thinking of Spence, she thought astonished. He had never asked her about the scars on her wrists, and she had never told him about Spence. That could only mean that someone else had—Rhea.

"You have no right to try to exact that kind of a promise," she said, turning her face away.

"I had no right to fall in love with you," he said. "You didn't want me to, but I wouldn't take no for an answer. I had no right to marry you, but I did."

"Because I wouldn't take no for an answer."

"Perhaps. But, all the time I was trying to push you away, I was praying that you wouldn't go. I had spent so much of my life just settling. Settling for a marriage that didn't really work—at least it didn't work for me, and I don't see how it could have worked for Rhea. We never had a common purpose. We were just two people sharing a house and talking about nothing that mattered. For years I tolerated it, putting up with things I didn't want—and not only in my marriage, but in my partnership with Ben Howard as well.

"We were both a great deal more successful after the partnership broke up. When I finally worked up the nerve to tell Ben that I wanted to go out on my own, I found out that he had been trying to tell me the same thing for months. What if I hadn't risked it all? I would have never found you, and life with you is—promise you won't laugh?"

"I won't laugh."

"Being with you is like a celebration of life."

"I'm not laughing. It sounds beautiful to me. A celebration of life. It's exactly the way I feel."

"Promise me then, that if something happens to me, you won't ever be content to just settle—that you will commit yourself to living fully."

"I am committed to living fully," she said quietly, and she suppressed the urge to add, with you, my love. They were going to be together for always. Nothing could come between them.

CHAPTER THIRTY-FOUR

Rhea could not remember a time in her life when she had been busier than the days following Christmas. The television crew was due the end of the week to tape, and she wanted the house to look its best. She cleaned, polished, and rearranged, all in between waiting on customers and trying on every garment in her wardrobe to find something suitable and flattering to wear in front of the camera.

To her surprise Jill phoned that she would be flying back the following day. Rhea wasn't sure that Jill's coming back to Houston so soon was a good idea, but then she certainly understood her wanting to get on with her life. She was determined, however, to dissuade Jill from returning to her old job at the Aloha Room, but Rhea seemed to have so little time or energy to cope with anything but the upcoming taping for the television show.

Kevin had left early, promising to be back soon to help her move furniture and hang the bluebonnet painting that Caroline had loved back in the library. She decided to sell the painting along with the Jenny Lind bed from Caroline's room, and she planned to use the salon set and the Georgian mirror from Jacqui's room in an apartment that she was decorating for a friend of Liz Howard.

She was thinking about turning the upstairs into an apartment for herself when she had the time and money. Moving the kitchen would be expensive, the rest fairly simple. The shop had already taken over all the space downstairs, the living room, the dining room, library, and foyer, as well as her sitting room that overlooked the rose garden. Even the double garage was so full right now that she couldn't get her car inside. She had to find a place for all of it.

Carter, unexpectedly, dropped off Jill's luggage just after Kevin had gone and insisted on carrying it all upstairs to her room.

"You look tired," she noticed as he walked to the door.

"I'm okay," he replied. "I just have this damned cold that I can't seem to shake."

Rhea, however, wasn't sure that it was just a cold. He didn't look good. It wasn't something she could put her finger on, certainly, it wasn't that he looked older, yet something was amiss. He was still an incredibly handsome man, and Rhea couldn't explain why watching him walk slowly back to his car filled her with so much uneasiness.

Kevin picked Jill up at the airport the following day. The three of them had a late supper in the kitchen, and Rhea apologized for not unpacking Jill's bags.

"I really meant to put everything away for you," she said, "but every time I thought I had a few minutes to do it, someone came into the shop."

"I'm glad you didn't," Jill said. "I might as well tell you now as later. I'm not staying."

"Not staying?" Rhea echoed. "What do you mean?"

"I'm going to New York," Jill said quietly. "I'm leaving in a few days."

"But you just got back," Rhea protested. "Who's going with you? Surely you aren't going alone."

"Yes," she said slowly. "I am. And it isn't just a trip; it's permanent. I'm moving to New York."

"How can you move to New York? What will you live on? How can you be sure you'll find a job right away. New York is horribly expensive. You won't be able to afford a place to live even if you can find one."

"Why don't you tell us what you have in mind?" Kevin interrupted Rhea's barrage of admonitions.

"First of all," Jill explained. "I have some money. Not a lot, but enough to see me through for a while even if I don't find a job right away. Yes, I know how horribly expensive New York is. I have my engagement ring and some other jewelry that I plan to sell."

"I have decided to try my hand at modeling," she said simply. "New York is the top modeling market."

"Good for you," Kevin exclaimed.

"Don't encourage her," Rhea snapped. "This is insane."

"Please don't think I don't appreciate everything you've done for me, Rhea. I do. But, I'm going to do this. Maybe Kevin planted the idea when he took those pictures of me. Maybe I've wanted to do this for a long time. I just know that I have to try. I know that used jewelry brings very little, considering what it originally cost, but I don't want it. I'm going to sell it all."

"You'll have to sell it in Houston before you go to New York," Rhea said. "If you're really serious, I know someone who might help you and won't rip you off in the process."

"Super," Jill exclaimed.

"This doesn't mean that I approve of your going," Rhea said unhappily. "It just means that I will help you sell the jewelry. What are we talking about besides the ring?"

Jill bounded up the stairs and returned with a small leather case. She spread several items out on the table where her plate had been, the engagement ring, the bracelet with her name in diamonds, a number of gold chains, a watch with the face set in diamonds and sapphires, a pair of diamond earrings, a wide gold bracelet, and a crouching tiger pin with a jeweled collar.

"Court gave you all of this!" Rhea gasped.

"All of it," Jill conceded.

"Paid for with drug money, no doubt," Rhea said disapprovingly.

"Paid for—at any rate," Jill said. "And I'm not giving it back. So, will you help me sell it?"

"We'll have it appraised, first of all," Rhea replied. "Put it away, Jill. It makes me nervous having all that in the house."

"You have lovely jewelry," Jill reminded her.

"True, but I keep most of it in a safety deposit box," she answered, "and take it out when I want to wear it. You can't be too careful these days."

"Do the police know you have all this jewelry?" Rhea asked, at length. "Isn't there a law that lets them confiscate anything paid for with drug money."

"I certainly didn't tell them," Jill retorted.

"Was this in your luggage?" Rhea asked.

"I was wearing the ring, the two bracelets, and the earrings. The rest was in the luggage along with some inexpensive costume stuff. So, I guess if they found it, they didn't realize its value."

Kevin, who had quietly finished his dinner as they talked about the jewelry, excused himself and went upstairs.

A few minutes later he was back. "I just spoke to a friend of mine, a photographer I used work with in England. He lives in Greenwich Village now, and he promised to do what he could to help you get settled and find work. I told him how wonderfully photogenic you were, and he said that if you were half as gorgeous as I claimed, he would be delighted."

"Thanks, Kev," she said. "You see, Rhea, it will work out."

"Oh, God," Rhea sighed. "I hope so. I hope you'll be all right. Your mother is never going to forgive me."

"You and my mother both are going to have to realize that I'm not a little girl, and I have to live my own life in my own way."

"It's only because we care so much about you. And don't you forget that!"

"I know. And I'll never forget it," she laughed. "Not even when I'm rich and famous."

"Jill," Rhea said seriously. "Do you know how many young girls go to New York every year full of hopes and dreams and never see them come true?"

"Do you know how many people," she retorted, "never dream, and if they do, never do anything to make their dreams come true except wish and hope and wait? How many people are there like my mother who just hold on—surviving in any way they can and miss living and never know why? I'm not going to be like that. I'm different. I'm going to make it. Just wait and see."

"Nobody can argue with that kind of determination," Kevin applauded. "Go get 'em, tiger."

Jill blew him a kiss and smiled, and Rhea marvelled at how really beautiful she was. She looked like a magazine cover with the light from the overhead lamp playing around her golden hair and her cornflower eyes shining with anticipation. It was almost as if Court Randall never existed.Rhea resisted the temptation to remind her that a short while ago, she was determined to marry Court and live happily ever after. The thought that, perhaps, she had never really loved the man, but loved, instead, the things that she thought he would give her bothered Rhea.

She, too, loved the life Carter gave her, she thought, but she really loved him. And, unfortunately, she would probably go on loving him as long as she lived despite the fact that he was now married to Jacqui.

As soon as the table had been cleared and the dishwasher loaded, Rhea went upstairs to soak in lilac scented water and think about her own future.

Carter gone, Jacqui gone, and now Jill gone. How much more would she have to give up? How much more was there?

CHAPTER THIRTY-FIVE

Jacqui lay in the semi-darkness, listening to Greg's labored breathing, punctuated with bouts of coughing. She raised up on one elbow to look at him, but he did not waken fully and turned over on his side away from her. He had suffered with this cold for more than three weeks now, and it was getting worse instead of better in spite of two visits to the doctor.

Jill had lunch with them the day before, but he had been too ill to enjoy it, even thought they knew it would be the last time they saw her before she left for New York. Jacqui had applauded her decision to go; Greg had opposed it. She smiled to herself wondering if, when they had kids, it would be this way. One parent too liberal, one too strict. One who thought that to love was to protect, and one who thought that to love was to free.

But they would work it out, she and Greg. They always came to an agreement eventually. She snuggled up to his back, but he began to cough again.

"I'm sorry, love," he said hoarsely. "I know I'm disturbing you."

She hugged him. "You aren't disturbing me. Do I sound disturbed?"

"I know I'm keeping you awake. You should move into the other room for a few days."

"Not a chance. It will take more than a little cold to get rid of me," she teased.

"I'm afraid," he said ruefully, "that it's more than a little cold. My chest really aches. That damned antibiotic's not strong enough. Call the doctor, will you, as soon as the office opens, and tell him to send me something stronger?"

"I'll call right now."

"It won't do any good; all you'll get is an answering service. He won't return the call until morning."

"Then I'll drive you to the emergency room."

"Maybe you'd better."

Fear stabbed at Jacqui. Greg, who usually valiantly fought going to the doctor, had given in too readily. She was out of bed in a flash. When she suggested that he just wear his robe and pajamas, he insisted on getting dressed, but then he was so weak that she had to help him.

The young doctor who examined him ordered chest x-rays, a throat culture, and blood work. Privately, he told Jacqui that Greg's blood pressure was dangerously elevated. Greg's personal physician was summoned, and hospitalization was recommended.

He has pneumonia, she was told. And, when they put him in intensive care, she knew that he was very, very ill. She waited at the hospital all that day and through the night, and only left briefly the next day to shower and change her clothes.

Part of the time, he was perfectly lucid asking her to phone his secretary with instructions and part of the time he hallucinated, talking to people he only imagined and seeing images on a blank wall.

On the third day he rallied and was able to drink liquids and eat soft food. Jacqui was so relieved. She ate a complete meal herself for the first time since his hospitalization.

"You've been here all this time, haven't you?" he asked her. She nodded.

"Tonight, you are going home," he said firmly.

When she started to protest, he put his finger against her lips. "I'll rest better," he said, "knowing that you are asleep in your own bed, my love."

"Our bed," she corrected him. "And I won't rest until you're back with me."

"Jacqui, I love you so much," he said huskily, and she noticed that his eyes had filled with tears.

"I love you too," she said puzzled. "Is there something wrong?"

"No darling, everything is right. You go now, and take care, my love."

He blew her a kiss as she left him, and she remembered the warmth of his smile all the way home. It was the last thing she thought about before falling into an exhausted sleep.

Sometime later, the ringing phone aroused her immediately. "Mrs. Gregory. Please come to the hospital right away."

An agonizing fear squeezed the breath from her, and even while she was affirming that he was going to survive, she knew with an awful certainty that when she arrived at the hospital, her beloved Greg would be forever lost to her in this lifetime.

CHAPTER THIRTY-SIX

Jill boarded the plane for New York with very little luggage. Rhea had promised to ship the rest of her clothes as soon as she was settled. How different this flight was from the one before when she had returned from Miami with Court's magnificent diamond on her finger. Who would have believed such a short time ago that he would be dead and the diamond in a jeweler's vault waiting to be sold?

She looked down at her ringless fingers. She had not yet been able to sort out her feelings about Court. It wasn't easy. She didn't quite know what she should feel. Maybe that was what made it so difficult.

She had spent all that time with him, but he never revealed very much about himself. She knew, of course, that his choices were always completely self-serving, but he was handsome, charming, intelligent, and very sexy. To have murdered Caroline and put his own child's life in such jeopardy, he had to be entirely lacking in normal emotions. Jacqui had helped her to see that.

But she dreamed of him—often. In her dreams, he was always loving and generous. He explained to her that it was all a mistake. He wasn't dead, and they were still going to have a wonderful life together. In her dreams she wondered why she had thought he was dead. It was somebody else in the airplane that went down in the water. Everything was going to be all right.

Those dreams confused her more than ever. She didn't tell Jacqui about the dreams.

She refused lunch when it was served although it looked

appealing, ham and cheese on a croissant with salad and fruit. From now on, she had to be careful, the camera added pounds.

The plane arrived nearly on time, but Jill could not find the photographer who had promised to meet her. However, Kevin had prepared her for that eventuality.

"His name is Cole Warren," Kevin had said, "and, unfortunately, he wakes up in a new world every day. But, don't worry, it's part of his charm. He may even forget what day you're arriving. He left me stranded in London once, and didn't show up for two days.

"If he isn't there, have him paged. If that doesn't work, and you can't get him on the phone, take the train to Penn Station and catch a cab. The cab won't charge much more than seven or eight dollars to take you to the Village."

"I think I can manage that," she said lightly.

This isn't exactly getting off to a great start, Jill thought, when Cole failed to answer the page. When she phoned his apartment, a recorded message informed her that Cole, baby, couldn't come to the phone and demanded with all the finesse of a gangster that she leave a message at the tone or she would be hunted down and shot. She hung up without leaving a message.

She managed to get to Penn Station without any difficulty and hailed a cab. Cole lived across the street from New York University right in the heart of the Village, and Jill was captivated by the neighborhood. She chatted with the taxi driver. He loved her southern accent. When they arrived at the address she had given him, he drove off wishing her good luck.

"I'm looking for Cole Warren," she told the doorman.

"Your name?" asked.

"Tell him Jill from Texas."

The man spoke into the intercom and then laughed.

"He says you can't be. You're not due until tomorrow."

"Sorry," Jill said with a rueful face. "I'm here today."

He pointed her in the direction of the elevator. "Third floor, first door on the right."

When the elevator doors opened on the third floor, she was greeted by a bearded young man in ragged jeans with a deep voice that bore a remarkable resemblance to the one on the recorder that threatened to have her shot.

"You're Kevin's friend," he gasped.

"I'm Kevin's friend," she agreed, and he took the bags from her.

"You're not due until tomorrow," he said, ushering her into the apartment. "See, I even wrote it down on my calendar. Kevin's friend—Wednesday, the 21st."

"This is Wednesday, the 21st."

"Are you sure?" he demanded.

"Afraid so."

"Then I screwed up again. Kevin baby won't like it. But let's forget about him. You're everything he said you were and more, Goldilocks. You do have a name besides Kevin's friend?"

"Jill."

"Jill who came tumbling down?"

"No," she said laughing. "Actually, it was a very smooth landing."

"You're quick," he said. "I like that. What do you do when you're not fetching pails of water."

"Actually, I'm not much into nursery rhymes these day."

"What are you into?"

"Modeling."

"Modeling? Are you any good?"

"You tell me," she said, and with sure, deft fingers she undid the buttons of her plain, little dress, slipped her arms out of it and let it fall around her feet. Standing before the astonished Cole in a figure hugging French cut teddy, she turned from side to side demanding, "Well, what do you think?"

"I think," he said, ungrammatically, taking a deep breath, "that, baby, if you ain't got it, nobody don't need it."

Jill laughed, pulled her dress into place, slipped her arms back in it, and fastened the buttons.

"Do you have a portfolio?"

"Yes, right here."

He began to leaf through the pictures she produced from her bag.

"So old Kev took these," he said. "Not too bad. I could do better, of course."

"He said you would say that."

"And is Kev the Jack in your life, my Jill?"

"No, Kevin is just a friend. Actually, he's involved with my aunt."

"Involved? How involved?"

"Living together."

"That's involved. Surprises me, too. How's the old girl taking it? His mother?"

"She died some time ago."

"That figures. Why don't you stow your gear in the bedroom and freshen up if you like? We'll go to dinner and see a little of the Village."

"Great."

Jill showered and changed into a tiny neon green slip of a dress. She applied fresh makeup and fluffed up her hair. The results elicited an appreciative whistle from Cole.

"I'm going to show you where to get the best Italian food in the whole Village," he promised. "And then we're going to talk about your future."

"I love Italian food. Kevin promised that you would help me find an apartment."

"That I will, but later, my pet. You can stay here as long as you want. You can have the bedroom, I'll take the loft. And, Jill, I will be as much of a gentlemen as you want me to be."

"Thanks, I really appreciate that. Kevin said that under all the bullshit, there was a really nice guy."

"Oh, he did, did he? Well—I guess he's right. If you're looking for a nice guy right now, I'm your man. It's just as well. Anything less, and Kevin promised to break my neck."

CHAPTER THIRTY-SEVEN

It was late afternoon when Ben Howard called Rhea to tell her that Carter had died of a heart attack the previous night. Kevin tried his best to comfort her, but she was inconsolable. His attempts to reach Jill were in vain; he kept getting an irritating message on Cole's recorder and although he left an urgent message for Jill to call back, she didn't.

"She's never around when we need her," Rhea said bitterly between tears. "We couldn't find her when Caroline died."

"She didn't know Carter was in the hospital. Nobody expected him to die. Even Jacqui had gone home," Ben said.

"He died all alone," Rhea sobbed. "Somebody should have been with him. Jacqui never should have left him."

"Do you honestly think she would have if she had any doubt whatsoever that he wouldn't live through the night?"

"I should have been there," she insisted.

"You didn't even know he was in the hospital."

"I should have been told. Dammit! I should have been told. I had a right to know."

"Your estrangement from Jacqui was your choice, Rhea," Kevin said bluntly.

She didn't answer, but she looked at him with such pain in her tear swollen eyes that he was immediately sorry. He tried to put his arms around her, but she moved away.

"I think we should pay a condolence call on Jacqui," he said carefully.

She shrugged her shoulders, but did not answer.

"Will you come with me?" he urged.

"No!" she replied sharply. "No, I won't. Go if you must. We aren't joined at the hip, you know."

"I'm well aware of that."

"You know how I feel about Jacqui!"

"Yes, but I thought under the circumstances, you might—"

"How can I be sorry for her?" she demanded. "I'll never forgive her. I won't go to her house, but I'm going to the funeral. I know she won't want me, but I'm going."

"I'll come with you."

"No!" she said emphatically. "Why would you want to go? You barely knew Carter."

"I know you," he said. "I know how you're hurting. And I know Jacqui. I know what this loss means to both of you."

"You can't possibly know what this loss means to me," she cried and fled, in tears, to her room, leaving him staring up the stairs after her.

Later when he knocked lightly on her door, she didn't answer. After a while, she heard him go out. She hardly slept at all, but then she hadn't expected to, and when he came in very late and slipped in beside her, she didn't open her eyes or move at all. She knew she should apologize to him, but the pain she couldn't share with him kept her drawn up within herself.

It wasn't his fault, and she didn't understand why she was so unreasonably angry with him, but everything he said irritated her. She didn't want him to hold her; she wanted to be left alone to deal with her grief in her own way. For the first time, she regretted his moving into the house. She hated her own weakness for allowing it in the days following Caroline's death. If only she hadn't been so frightened by the murder. If only she had handled things differently.

Rhea left the closed sign on the front door all the next day. She went to the funeral home to see her beloved Carter one last time, slipping out of the house without telling Kevin that she was leaving. She wept openly at the casket, not caring that others who had come to pay their respects, Ben and Liz Howard among them, were watching her intently.

True to her word, Rhea insisted on going to the service alone, and Kevin did not press her. She sat in the back of the chapel and did not make eye contact with anyone who might want to speak to her. It occurred to her how few friends she and Carter had in common these last several years. There were many people there that she did not know at all.

The chapel was filled with flowers even though Kevin had told Rhea, Jacqui requested donations to a charity in lieu of flowers. It was a strange service, the minister was unfamiliar to Rhea—a friend of Jacqui's, no doubt. He spoke again and again of death merely being a transition to another plane of living, assuring the mourners that Greg was now expressing in another consciousness.

When it was over, Rhea sat for a long time paying no attention to the people filing out. Ben and Liz stopped to squeeze her hand and offer her, in hushed tones, a ride to the cemetery with them. She refused.

She knew it was over, but she was reluctant to leave. It was final. She would never see Carter again. He would never come back to her. Somewhere deep within the core of her, beyond reason, she had harbored that faint glimmer of hope. All things were possible if you believed enough. And she had believed.

She felt a sense of betrayal permeate her incredible sadness. Life had betrayed her. It was really nothing more than an endurance test; you endured as much pain as you could, and then you died—alone. She would never expect anything else.

As Rhea slowly left the chapel, she encountered Jacqui standing with a group of people by the side of the black limousine that would transport her to the burial. Their eyes met for a moment. Jacqui, dry-eyed and composed, took a step toward Rhea who burst into tears and rushed past her. Rhea did not look back until she reached her car.

Jacqui had stolen her place. She should be riding in that limousine; it was her rightful place. She was Carter's widow. Jacqui was the interloper.

She watched until they were out of sight, tears still streaming down her face. She did not follow, but turned in the opposite direction. She had endured as much as she could for one day.

Kevin was waiting for her when she returned home. Wordlessly, he handed her a tall, cool drink. Mercifully, he did not press her to talk, and when she took the glass upstairs, he didn't follow.

The rest of the week passed with agonizing slowness for Rhea, even though she threw herself into a frenzy of work, not stopping until well after midnight when she fell finally into an exhausted sleep.

Even the appearance of the television crew didn't seem to matter now. She had expected to be petrified with stage fright, but she moved easily through the house with the camera following and answered all questions with no signs of nervousness. It just didn't matter. Nothing mattered.

In the days that followed, she rebuffed all Kevin's attempts to comfort her.

"What have I done, Rhea?" he asked in bewilderment.

"You haven't done anything, Kevin. I have to deal with this grief in my own way," she said. "You're a wonderful, caring person, but—"

"But I'm not Carter!"

"I wasn't going to say that," she said in a shocked voice.

"No, of course, you weren't. You're much too kind. You know, Rhea, I thought that in time you would come to accept the fact that Carter and Jacqui were married, and that there wasn't anything that you could do about it. But, now that he's dead, I can see that it won't ever happen. I'm not sure that it will ever be over for you. You just can't give it up. And, you know, the sad thing is that I believe you really love me."

"I don't know what to say."

"Don't say anything. There isn't anything you can say. I'll have all my stuff cleared out by tomorrow."

He gave her a long, searching look, and then turned abruptly and left.

Rhea sat down on the bottom stair and began to cry. Much later, she still didn't know if she was crying for Carter who had died and left her, or for Kevin whom she had just driven away.

CHAPTER THIRTY-EIGHT

Jacqui poked her fork at the plate of scrambled eggs on the table in front of her. As hard as she tried she could not force herself to eat more than a few bites. It was too easy to remember the first time she had eaten in this kitchen—breakfast in the small hours of the morning with Greg. The room was empty without him. Her life was empty without him. It had been ten days. Ten days since her life had ended with his.

She kept going over the memory of the phone call in the middle of the night. "Mrs. Gregory, please come to the hospital right away." And even though she had raced through the dark night, Greg had already slipped away from her. Gone, in fact, when the phone call had been received.

Thoughtfully, she looked down at her scarred wrists. The evidence, she once believed, of how much she loved Spence in that irrecoverable past so long ago. She could hardly remember his face. Somehow, his beloved image had diffused into the mists of time. Would the same thing happen to her memory of Greg? No, it was not possible. The scars she bore as evidence of her love for him were invisible, but they were no less real than the marks on her wrists.

Greg would be a part of her—always—as long as she lived. But how long would that be? She looked again at the scars. Don't go there, she warned herself, don't even think about it.

The tears slid easily from her eyes. How could she not think about it? she asked herself. It would be so easy.

No. No. No. She needed help. Somebody had to help her.

She knew Rhea couldn't help her. Rhea was hurting as badly as she. Jacqui mentally went down her list of friends one by one. Nobody could help her. She had experienced this before. There was no one then to help her—until David. David Harper, her old friend and metaphysics teacher. He had helped her then.

She left the table abruptly, knocking over a chair. She left it lying there in her haste to find her address book with David's number. Her hands shook as she dialed the number.

"David, this is Jacqui Wilder. I need to talk to you as soon as possible. Could you possibly fit me into your schedule this morning?"

"Of course, Jacqui" he replied. "Why don't you come right away?"

"Thank you. I'm leaving now, and I should be there in half an hour."

She was wearing faded jeans and a loose, bulky sweater, but she didn't bother to change. Quickly, she ran a brush through her hair and drew it back with a clip. The least important thing in the world to her was the way she looked. She grabbed her bag and left through the back door, leaving the table untouched.

She had told David that she was Jacqui Wilder. Had she forgotten already that her name was Gregory? No, she hadn't forgotten. David would not recognize Jacquiline Gregory. She couldn't ever go back to being Jacqui Wilder. She was forever changed.

"Hello, Jacqui, my old friend," David greeted her warmly.

"I'm glad you remember me, David," she said.

"It's been a long time, but the heart always remembers those who have touched it in a special way."

"I've missed you," she told him. "And I desperately need help. I feel as through my life has lost all meaning."

"You felt that way once before," he reminded her gently.

"I feel it a thousand times more acutely. I've just lost my husband, my soul mate, and I can't accept his dying. I can't let go, David. I'm not sure I can go on living without him. Nothing means anything. I can't even envision a life without him. I don't want a life without him."

"How is it different this time, Jacqui? You've known great sorrow before."

"I'm confused. I have questions, but I can't bear the answers. I want to die, too. I long for it."

"Have you thought about what happens to the soul when a person takes his own life?"

"Yes, I know that if I take my own life, I won't have fulfilled my soul's purpose. I'm afraid that I will have to live this pain all over again in some other existence. Yet the desire to escape from this life is so strong, I'm not sure how much longer I can fight it."

"So, you came to me," he said, covering her hands with his. "You want me to impart some wisdom to you that will help you to understand this painful, bewildering experience and give you the courage to live?"

"You helped me once before. I had no one else to help me then. And, again, I find myself without anywhere else to turn."

Jacqui looked down at his wrinkled, old hands covering hers. Old hands with distended blue veins. Wise hands, she thought. Loving hands. She desperately needed his wisdom, his peace, his love. "Give me something, David, I'm hopelessly lost, and I don't think I can ever find my way back."

"Let us speak our word," he said softly, bowing his head and closing his eyes.

Jacqui clung to his warm, strong hands.

"Father, Mother, God," he began in a voice that was soft and sonorous. "Jacqui and I are together in our thoughts on the slope of a grassy hill. We smell the freshness of morning as we listen to the stirring of a new spring day. We feel the gentle breeze on our faces. We are warmed by the sun. We hear birds singing, and somewhere down below us, a pure, clear spring wells up from the earth, and water joyfully winds it way around the base of the hill. We see the beauty of the universe, and know that God is all there is. We see the beauty of the universe, and we feel, deep in the innermost parts of ourselves, the serenity of being one with all creation.

"We are part of the hills and the breeze and the sun and the pure water. They are part of us. We are part of God for we know that God is within us. We are individualized expressions of God, and we have a purpose just as the water has a purpose and the sun has a purpose.

"We must follow the path of that purpose as the water follows its path along the foothills. Our purpose is to express life, and we revel in that purpose, knowing that there are many paths upon which the soul may journey.

"Our tears are the washing of our sorrow into the universe to be absorbed into the soft morning. We are sorrowing because a cherished soul has chosen to leave—a soul whose purpose in life has been accomplished. A beloved soul has made a transition to another plane of living. We hold tightly to the memory of where a great love has led us, and that is good. Our sorrow is not for the soul making his transition, but for ourselves in our confusion. We know that nothing in the universe is ever lost, and that what appears as loss today is only a change.

"Jacqui knows that love is never lost. She carries deep within herself the warmth of being loved, the sense of safety from being loved. She lets go now of her sorrow as she lets go of her tears. The warmth of love and the sense of safety are hers forever, because she knows love and has only to remember the spring morning and the grassy hill and the blue sky to feel a sense of peace in the days to come.

"We thank you, God. We release and let go, and so it is."

Jacqui opened her eyes. They were filled with tears.

"Don't be afraid to cry," David urged. "I have no wisdom to give you, my dear one, but you have everything you need within yourself. I can only remind you of what you already know. Now tell me, Jacqui, what troubles you so."

"If I accept the reality of Greg's dying, then I must accept the fact that his death was his own choosing. How can I do that? If I believe that each one of us has a purpose, then I must believe that having accomplished his purpose, he chose to make his transition. His soul chose to die. But I can't accept the fact that he chose to leave me. We were perfect together. We both knew it."

"Was it a sudden death?"

"I didn't expect it. Greg was hospitalized, but I thought he was improving, and I went home to rest."

"And now you feel guilty. If you had been there, you think, perhaps, it wouldn't have happened?"

"I'll never know, will I?"

"Dear Jacqui, I think you know the answer to that. You said the words yourself. The soul chooses its time to die—when its purpose has been accomplished. Would you take that choice away from him? Would you accept the responsibility for making that choice for him? Would you, in actuality, take that choice away from him?"

"Oh, David, I don't know! I don't know. I loved him so."

"You love him still; love is never lost."

"David, why wasn't my faith enough to keep him alive? I was so sure that if I refused to accept the reality of his illness, then it couldn't exist. I was so certain that if I never considered the possibility of his dying, then it couldn't happen. That's what faith is all about. Why didn't it work for me?"

"You tried to take the responsibility for someone else's destiny. As much as you love him, you have no right to do that. Did the two of you ever talk about the possibility of his dying?"

"Yes, in the beginning when he first learned the extent of his illness, he tried to send me away. He married me reluctantly, not because he didn't love me, but because he wanted to spare me his pain. Once I refused to take no for an answer, we never spoke of it again. He did tell me—Christmas, it was—that it didn't matter how much time we had together, it wouldn't be enough. Oh, David, there was so much left unsaid between us."

"Was there, Jacqui? Think about it, my dear. Did you not tell him how much you loved him, and that his illness didn't in anyway diminish that love, but in fact made it stronger?"

"Of course, I told him that."

"Did he not tell you how much he loved you?"

"Yes, he did, time and time again, beautifully, passionately. He was romantic and funny and wonderful."

"What was it you left unsaid? What would you say to him if he were right here with us at this moment?"

"That I love him, and I miss him, and that our time together was the best part of my life. He used to say that to me a lot, *today is the best day of my life.*"

"Then you must hold on to those thoughts. I believe that somehow across time and space, he will hear you in whatever essence of life he is now expressing."

"Sometimes, I feel him so close to me that I turn to speak to him, and then I realize that he isn't really there. And I can't bear it."

"Do you not want to feel his closeness?"

"Yes, I do. I guess I do," Jacqui said covering her face with her hands.

"Now," David urged, "tell me what it is you think you can't face?"

"How did you know exactly what I was thinking?"

"Because, you have repeatedly covered your face with your hands as you talked to me," he said simply.

"You're a better psychologist than I," she said wryly. "I can't face going home alone. I can't bear the thought of sleeping in our bed alone. There are so many things I have to do—loose ends to tie-up. I have to dispose of his clothing, sort out his papers, close his office. I don't know how I can face doing that. It seems so final. But I know it has to be done."

"Then don't do it. Why must you? Love and nurture yourself, Jacqui. Let someone else—someone who isn't emotionally involved, pack your husband's things and give them to someone who needs them. Is there not someone who will do these things for you?"

"I don't know. My cleaning lady, perhaps."

"And your husband's office?"

"His former law partner, I think."

"There, you see, you are free. Don't chain yourself to those aspects of living that reduce your life to merely going through the motions. Allow yourself to feel what you feel, of course, don't bury your feelings, but love and support yourself."

"Wouldn't that be running away?"

"Running away? Didn't we say that there are many paths on which the soul may journey. Why must you choose the one that brings you the most pain?"

"I don't have to go back," she said, incredulously. "I just won't do it. I won't go back. Oh, David, how can I ever thank you?"

"Don't thank me. All I did was remind you of what you already know. At the center of you, there is perfect harmony, perfect peace. If you listen to your innermost self, you can't make a mistake. You have personal and immediate access to all the power there is in the universe. We are all struggling toward our ultimate good. But you have what the French call joie de vivre— the joy of living. Everyone who knows you recognizes that. Remember who you are. You are constantly unfolding, letting life happen. Don't hold back. You never have. People are drawn to you. They love being in your presence. I love being in your presence. Don't take that away from us. Remember that your good will come to you. Nothing can keep it away."

"I didn't realize until now," she said, "how much I've missed seeing you and studying with you."

"Come again soon, Jacqui. I'm always available for you."

"I'll remember that. Thank you, David."

She thought about all the things that he had said as she drove west on the Katy Freeway. You are free, love and nurture yourself.

Suddenly, she remembered the last words Greg had spoken to her. "Take care, my love." He had been trying to say the same thing.

She did not go back to the house, leaving her bed unmade and her breakfast dishes on the table. With no particular destination in mind, she simply drove west. "I can't make a mistake," she repeated over and over, "if I listen to my innermost self."

With credit cards and a checkbook, she would buy whatever she needed. How much could that be? A toothbrush, a T-shirt to sleep in, clean underwear, and a spare pair of jeans. How little one really needed.

She remembered telling Rhea once that she didn't have anything that couldn't be disposed of in a day. "I couldn't live that way," Rhea had said. "I need roots and stability." But both of them had needed the same man. Poor Rhea, Jacqui thought. Maybe now she can let go and love Kevin.

Tomorrow Jacqui would call her cleaning lady with instructions to clean the house, empty the refrigerator, pack Greg's clothes and arrange to have them picked up by Goodwill. She would call Ben Howard about the office. There must be a will somewhere. Ben, she was sure, would know about that.

Perhaps, she decided, she would go back in a few weeks. But, then again, perhaps, she wouldn't.

CHAPTER THIRTY-NINE

Depressed and miserable, Rhea was frozen in the pain of the present moment. She knew she had no choice except to get on with her life, although she found it utterly inconceivable that she would ever be happy again. The only thing that helped at all was serving customers in the shop. She could forget everything but showing her beloved antiques or designing rooms for people who loved beautiful things.

Watching herself on television, when the program finally aired weeks after the taping, Rhea was surprised and pleased to see how well she had done. She sounded knowledgeable and confident. The house was beautiful. It prompted her to run an ad in the neighborhood weekly offering a class in antiques. Twelve people signed up.

Rhea was with a customer when Ben Howard phoned and asked her to come by his office to discuss Carter's will. Surprised and very curious, she made an appointment for later in the day and went back to her customer.

Acknowledging that she simply must hire someone to help her in the business, she hung a closed sign on the door and went to see Ben. She was surprised that Jacqui was not there, but Ben explained that she was in California and had retained him to settle all of Carter's affairs.

Carter, Ben told her, had named her as the beneficiary of a two hundred and fifty thousand insurance policy.

Rhea was speechless.

"Why me?" she managed at last, "and not Jacqui?"

"She inherited the townhouse and all of the personal property as well as a couple of smaller insurance policies."

"Does she know? Jacqui, I mean, about this?"

"Yes, she knows. She didn't seem surprised. I'm sure she understands that Carter felt an obligation to you."

"Well, Jacqui will benefit in any case," Rhea said. "Now I can pay her back the money she loaned me to open my business. What is she doing in California?"

"Living in L.A. and working in a clinic. She left Houston right after Carter died."

"Is she okay?"

"As far as I know. She sounded okay the several times I spoke to her on the phone."

"Well, it isn't as if she were married to him for years and years. I had an idea that she would bounce back rather quickly. If I send you a bank draft for the money I owe her when I get the insurance, will you see that she gets it?"

"Sure, but I can give you her address."

"No, I'd rather that you send it to her."

Rhea simply could not let go of her animosity toward Jacqui. The money Carter left proved that he still cared for her. But she would forgo it in a minute if she could have him alive again—even married to Jacqui.

Liz Howard showed up at the shop the next day at noon and practically dragged Rhea to lunch.

"But I'll have to close," Rhea protested. "I can't afford to close."

"You must get away from this place now and then," Liz lectured her sternly. "When you and Carter divorced, you hibernated for months and months. I am not going to let you do that this time."

"I am not hibernating," Rhea insisted. "I'm really not. I have been thinking of hiring someone to help out. I just haven't gotten around to it yet. When I have a decorating job, I have to close, and I know I lose business. I used to be able to count on Jill until late afternoon. Now I just have to put up a closed sign and hope customers will come back later."

"Why don't I help you?" Liz exclaimed. "I could come in part-time, either mornings or afternoons. I would love it, Rhea. You wouldn't have to pay me."

"Are you sure you want to?" Rhea asked hesitantly.

"I'm sure! I'm sure! It would give me something to do. I've been a little bored with myself lately. I should have started my own business years ago. I admire you, Rhea. Working here would be fun."

"Think it over, Liz. And if you want to try it for a while to see how you like it, we'll see how it goes. Of course, I would pay you. Not much, I'm afraid, but—"

"Oh, the money doesn't matter in the least. I'm excited. When should I start?"

"Whenever you like. The sooner the better."

"How about tomorrow morning."

"Wonderful!"

Rhea was relieved, not that she expected Liz to stick with it, but it was the answer to her problem for the moment. She could trust Liz, and maybe Liz would enjoy it for a while.

They used to have fun together, shopping, lunching—when Carter and Ben first started their law practice. Neither of them had any money back then, but they enjoyed playing bridge and grilling steaks when they could afford them, and the four of them had taken their first cruise together. It seemed like such a long time ago. It had been actually.

After lunch Rhea returned to the shop and worked the rest of the afternoon. She started making a list of inventory, showing the location and description of each piece, the asking price, and the lowest price she could accept.

It was nearly nine when she finally went upstairs with a glass of iced tea and a hastily prepared salad. She was exhausted, but she felt better about things in general. The money helped, of course. Money always helps. But it had been a long, long day.

She dumped her favorite lilac oil into the tub and ran a deep, hot bath. She took a fresh gown from the amoire and looked for her robe. Darn! It was downstairs in the dryer. There had to be another one somewhere. She went into the adjoining room.

Kevin had used this closet, and there was the empty space where his clothes had hung. Pushed to one end, she found the robe she was looking for, but when she took it from the hanger, she saw a sweater of Kevin's hanging in back of it.

A forgotten sweater. Blue—almost the color of his eyes. She reached out to touch it. Tears overwhelmed her. She drew the sweater against her face and inhaled his lingering scent.

She went to the phone and dialed his number. The recording told her the number had been disconnected.

She had lost him. What was wrong with her? She loved him but she had driven him away. She was so incredibly stupid. All she had to do was to reach out to him and he would always have been there for her And now she had lost him.

She sat down on the side of the bed and began to sob. This time there was no doubt who she was crying for.

CHAPTER FORTY

Days turned into weeks, spring into summer, and summer into fall. Rhea found Liz a god-send. She was wonderful with customers, more aggressive than Rhea. If there were no customers in the shop, she spent her time on the phone cajoling friends and acquaintances to drop by. Gradually, her half days expanded to full days and, miraculously, Rhea was able to afford her salary and even give her a small raise.

Although she said the money wasn't important, Liz was delighted.

When the house next door went on the market, Rhea didn't think too much about it except to hope that the new occupants, whoever they were, would be reasonably pleasant and not pose any problems for her business. Parking on the street was sometimes a problem and had brought complaints from neighbors in the past. Three months later, when the house was still unsold, Rhea called the realtor handling the listing.

It started as an act of curiosity more than anything else, but she thought the price quite reasonable and wondered why the house had not sold. Later, she was not sure when the idea of buying the house took root, but the prospect of extra storage and added parking was certainly appealing.

She could open the tea room she had thought about. Then, sternly, she chided herself for even thinking of such a thing. She was all alone; there was no one to back her up if she faltered. No Carter to come to her rescue. No Jacqui to lend her money.

Still the idea of expanding and opening a tea room adjacent

to her antique business filled her with an excitement she had not felt since she first opened the business. On an impulse, she phoned the realtor and made an offer far below the asking price. She knew it wouldn't be accepted, but a counter offer was made, and it was far below what she expected.

"So now, what do I do?" she wondered aloud to Liz. "Even if I could find a banker willing to lend me the money, I might fail and lose everything."

"How could you fail?" Liz asked excitedly. "There's no way you could lose. The house has the same immense staircase, and we could put the restaurant on the second floor. We could take out all the walls, leaving only the necessary supports and decorate around them. I can see it now—intimate, little tables and plants— lots of plants and paintings."

"We could fill the downstairs with items for sale, big interesting pieces and little things locked in beautiful cabinets. Customers could browse while waiting for a table. You could keep all the expensive, really good stuff over here. I can see it now, Rhea, it would have just the right ambiance, don't you think?"

"I think," Rhea objected, "that you are forgetting who's the decorator around here."

"Oh, every woman's a decorator at heart, and I have a million ideas," Liz said. "You'd have the job of making them work. What do you say? Am I crazy or what?"

"Yes, you are. And so am I, or I wouldn't be considering it. I just don't know if I can swing it financially. A new restaurant would take a while to get off the ground."

"Maybe you wouldn't have to," Liz said thoughtfully. "What if you had a partner? If I bought the house next door, we could connect it to yours with a walkway. I would be in charge of the restaurant."

"What do you know about running a restaurant?"

"I've eaten in a million of them."

"Running one is not the same thing."

"What did you know about selling antiques when you opened this place?"

"I studied interior design in college. I've collected antiques for twenty years. I know antiques."

"So I know food. I studied business in college. and, what I don't know, I'll learn. There is a hotel and restaurant management school right here at the University of Houston. I'll study. I'll hire a consultant. I can do it. I know I can."

"This is too big a step to take on the spur of the moment, Liz. Talk it over with Ben. See what he has to say before you decide."

"I will, of course. But it doesn't matter what he says. It's what I want to do."

"You haven't worked in twenty years."

"Where did you get that idea?! I've worked every day for twenty years. I've cooked and cleaned and shopped, ran a household, raised a son, raised money for charities, and a thousand other things."

"I didn't mean that. What if Ben objects?"

"Then I'll sue him for divorce and take half of everything he's got. And, believe me, it's plenty."

"You're kidding."

"Only a little," Liz said laughing.

The weeks that followed were chaotic. Rhea found herself, alternately, tingling from head to toe with excitement and the next moment shaking in her shoes.

The partnership agreement with Liz was drawn up and executed. Liz closed on the house and started renovations. As her stress level increased, Rhea began to have misgivings about the partnership. She was losing control. When she tried to talk seriously to Liz about her fears, Liz laughed the whole matter away.

"Of course, you're losing some control," she agreed. "That's what happens when you take a partner. Don't you think its remarkable, we haven't even had a serious disagreement yet."

"But everything seems so chaotic!"

"Creation comes out of chaos, is surrounded by chaos, and will end in chaos," Liz mused. "Somebody said that, but I can't remember who. We're creating something here, Rhea."

"Then why do I feel as if I'm not coping well?"

"Because, dear Rhea, you're a perfectionist. You think you have to be perfect in every way. Stop being so hard on yourself."

"God, you sound like Jacqui!"

"The woman Carter married."

"None other. There was a time when she was my best friend. She had a Ph.D. in psychology, you know. I think she practiced a lot on me, and she was always right."

"Where is she now?"

"In California, according to Ben."

"Good riddance, I say," Liz proclaimed. "She is the last thing you and I should be talking about. Believe me, Rhea, the day will come when all the carpenters and plumbers and painters will be gone, and we have a thousand things to do before the world beats a path to our door."

"I hope the world beats a path to our door, but I'm afraid we're moving too fast. We agreed to a tea room—lunch only. And you're already talking about expanding that into a full service restaurant."

"I know. I know," Liz agreed. "but I really am heeding your advice. Keep it simple, stupid."

"I never called you stupid."

"Maybe you should. Rhea, don't you ever get tired of being such a perfect lady? Not that I don't think you are a very elegant lady. You're so polished and you have your own distinctive style."

Tears rushed to Rhea's eyes.

"I didn't mean to make you cry," Liz apologized. "I'm sorry Rhea. In my own stupid way, I was giving you a compliment."

"I cry a lot," Rhea confessed. "Usually when I'm alone. Sometimes, I don't even know what I'm crying about. It's just that what you said reminded me of someone."

"Jacqui again?"

"No. Not Jacqui. Although Jacqui helped immensely to improve my self esteem when she was here."

Rhea couldn't admit to Liz that her thoughts had been for a young man with intense blue eyes who held her close and called her a beautiful, wise lady.

"I know it's none of my business," Liz said, "and you can smack me if you want, but have you ever thought about seeing a psychiatrist?"

"Yes, I've thought about it," Rhea admitted. "My own doctor recommended it. He thinks I had a panic attack some months ago probably brought on by stress."

"I was in analysis for two years," Liz confessed.

"You? You always seem so in control."

"Something happened to me that I couldn't cope with. Ben's affair."

"Ben had an affair?" Rhea asked incredulously. "When?"

"About the time Ben and Carter broke up their partnership.

Along about the time Carter asked you for a divorce."

"I'm stunned."

"So was I. I even thought about killing myself. Maybe I would have except for my son. Unlike Carter, Ben didn't want a divorce. He was strictly a *have your cake and eat it too* man. I told myself that I was staying in the marriage for the sake of my child, but that was a lie. He was in high school at the time, and I was staying in the marriage for me. I wanted all the things Ben's success could buy. At least Ben had the decency to feel guilty. That's one of the reasons I knew he would never object to buying me this restaurant."

"I guess things are never what they seem," Rhea said. "I would have bet money that you and Ben were one of the happiest couples I know."

"But, Rhea, we are. The marriage survived. Partly, I think, because I did go into analysis."

"Is Ben faithful to you now?"

"I guess so. Either that or he's more adept at hiding his infidelity. So you see, Rhea, I need this project. I want to make a success of this restaurant more than I ever wanted anything in my life. I desperately need it."

"In that case," Rhea replied, "you and I had better knuckle down and get some work done. We have to come up with a name and a logo. What's your best guess for an opening date?"

"December 1."

"Can we do it by then?"

"Absolutely."

When Liz left for the day, Rhea entered the day's receipts in her simple set of books. Her business was showing a profit now, and the restaurant was bound to increase traffic in the antique store. But, with Liz devoting so much of her time to the renovations, Rhea was right back where she started without sufficient help in the shop. She needed an assistant. Someone to learn the business, help with customers, and perhaps, take over the bookkeeping.

Rhea put down her pen and sighed. Maybe she should start seeing a psychiatrist. At least now she could afford it. Perhaps a competent analyst could help her to understand why she clung so desperately to a man who no longer loved her and drove away the one who did.

After she went to bed, Rhea's thought kept drifting back to Jacqui. Where was she living? How was she coping with her widowhood? Somehow, she couldn't imagine Jacqui not competently taking care of all the necessities, not being surrounded by a circle of admiring people, never collecting a backpack of anxieties that would sooner or later topple her.

She had been such a fool, Rhea realized, to believe that Jacqui, or anyone else for that matter, could lead her by the hand. She wondered if there would ever be a time in Jacqui's life when she needed someone to lead her by the hand. Probably not.

CHAPTER FORTY-ONE

The energy of Greenwich Village filled Jill with fascination. She was astonished to find the streets full of strolling people in the wee hours of the morning, going in and out of shops and examining the wares of street vendors. Cole had advised her to get to know the city, acclimate herself to New York before she made the rounds of the modeling agencies. It seemed like a good idea, and she was enjoying every moment.

A taxi from Cole's apartment to midtown Manhattan cost seven dollars, and Jill discovered Fifth Avenue on her first excursion. Loving Saks and Bergdorf Goodman and Lord and Taylor and the Trump Tower, she studied their displays for hours, and tried on expensive, elegant clothes. The shops along Madison Avenue and Macy's on 34th Street were her next target.

Jill wandered in and out of the art galleries in Soho. Looking at furs in the Soho Emporium, she found a full length red fox that seemed to have been designed just for her. "I'll be back for you," she whispered softly to the coat as she turned first one way and then the other to view herself in the three-way mirror. "Promise me you won't find another home before I can afford you."

An elegant salon on Madison Avenue created a chic new hair style that left most of the length intact while giving her a more sophisticated look. Cole was pleased with the results and snapped picture after picture as Jill moved around the room, imitating poses she had studied in the fashion magazines. "You're a natural, girl," he said approvingly. "Every move you make is spontaneous and photogenic!"

She hoped an agent would think so because she had worked to overcome her initial dislike of being photographed. Cole had warned her about agencies. "Stay away from the ones that primarily operate modeling schools. Some of them promise a lot more than they deliver. You don't need an expensive portfolio. You already have enough pictures. Just be careful to read everything before you sign on the dotted line. The good agencies will provide everything you need without asking you to put up any money."

Jill was anxious to get started, but Cole told her to relax and let him set up some appointments for her. And, while she was discovering New York, she also discovered that Cole had a serious girlfriend. A girlfriend, it turned out, who was not too thrilled to have Jill sharing Cole's apartment and friendship. Melissa Simon was a marketing executive with a cosmetics manufacturing and distributing company. Her job involved a great deal of traveling. At first, Jill made an effort to develop a friendship with her, trying her best to assure Melissa that she had no intention of causing trouble between her and Cole, but she could see that Melissa wasn't buying it. She told Cole that she planned to find a place of her own.

He asked her bluntly how much money she had.

"About ten thousand," Jill answered truthfully. "But Rhea is selling some jewelry for me."

"New York can gobble up ten grand before you turn around twice," he told her. "I think that what you need is a job-job."

"A job-job?"

"Yes, my dear. That's what it is known as in the business. Something to pay the bills while you pursue your great calling."

"Did you have a job-job when you first came to New York?"

"Certainly. I worked as a waiter, and then I got a night job in a photography lab. Do you have any idea how much a place like this rents for?"

"No, not really."

"I was paying two thousand a month for a place in this same building before I bought this apartment."

"Wow! I guess I had better start looking for a job-job."

Cole laughed. "What do you have in mind, Jill? I don't think there's much demand for fetching pails of water in New York City."

"There's always a demand," she replied, "for fetching scotch and soda, especially if you happen to have great legs. I was a cocktail waitress in a hotel bar in Houston and I made a fetching sum of money, thank you very much."

"Why do I get the feeling," he said smiling, "that under all that childlike innocence and vulnerability that you project so well with those incredible blue eyes, that you are about as helpless as a saber-toothed tiger."

"You're very perceptive. Not many people see that side of me," she said thoughtfully. Then she playfully imitated a cat exposing its claws and jabbed at him with long, blood red fingernails. "Get in my way, and I'll scratch your eyes out," she threatened in jest.

"Whoa! I'm convinced," he assured her with a light kiss, "I'll be saying I knew her when—"

Jill slipped out of the apartment the next morning without waking Cole and caught the bus into Manhattan. She had intended to start looking for a job in the plush downtown hotels, but she decided to postpone it for another day when she overhead a couple of tourists planning to go to The Metropolitan Museum of Art. She sort of tagged along behind them.

She spent the entire day in the museum, entranced. She discovered the gold nude statue of Diana in the Courtyard of the American wing. Maybe I'll change my name to Diana, she mused. Jill Turner just doesn't cut it in New York. Diana Turner? No, that didn't sound right either.

Late in the afternoon she took the bus to Times Square and stood in line for a half price ticket to a Broadway play. Remembering her conversation with Cole about finances, she opted for a fast food restaurant near the Palace Theater. And, when the curtain went up, Jill fell in love—totally and completely with the Broadway stage.

Afterward, she climbed into a cab to go back to Greenwich Village and turned to look at the marquis. Someday, she promised herself, her name would be up there in lights. It was more than a dream, it was a vision. And, somewhere in the deep recesses of her soul, she knew it was destined to be.

Court Randall had been a stepping stone. He had opened up the world to her, but he was gone now, and modeling would be the next stepping stone.

So it came as no surprise to her the next morning when Cole told her that he had succeeded in getting her an appointment with a top agent. Bernie Goldstone was leaving his agency and going out on his own.

Cole had given her a lot of advice for her first meeting with Bernie. She ignored it, preferring to go with her own instincts. Almost immediately, she could tell that he liked her.

"I think I can work with you, Jill," he said. "But you must be willing to put yourself completely in my hands. Anything I say goes, and I mean anything," he said. "Are you willing to do that?"

"I'm willing to do whatever it takes," Jill replied determinedly. "Whatever it takes!"

"Good girl! Now, the first thing I want you to do is lose ten pounds."

"I can do that."

"Good. Now about Cole. Exactly what is your relationship to him?"

"Friend," she answered.

"Boyfriend?"

"No, just a friend who happens to be a boy."

"Good, I don't want any distractions. You're going to have to work very hard, and you have to be free for auditions."

"I'm free."

Jill walked out of Bernie Goldstone's office hardly touching the floor. The next few weeks went by in a whirl of activity. Jill was a natural mimic, and she learned fast.

Bernie agreed that she needed a new name. It came, however, almost by accident. "What's your middle name?" he asked.

"Roberts," she replies. "Jill Roberts Turner. Roberts was my mother's maiden name."

"It won't do. Any nicknames?"

"Not, really," she said, "but someone used to call me Sunshine."

"Sunshine. That suits you. Sunny," he mused. "Sunny Turner. Sunny Roberts. We'll have to think about that."

The next day he left a message for her on Cole's recorder asking for Sunny from Houston. She continued to be Sunny from Houston for a while until one morning, he called and asked for Sunny Houston. Sunny Houston, she became. It felt natural—as natural as if she had only pretending to be Jill Turner.

Sunny Houston's first big break came not from Bernie, although he negotiated the deal, but from Melissa Simon, Cole's girlfriend from the cosmetics company who recommended her to the advertising agency handling their campaign for a new line of cosmetics called Yellow Rose aimed at the college market. Sunny's young, clean, innocent look and golden hair turned out to be just what they were looking for. Magazine layouts led to a television commercial, and Sunny Houston took a giant step into the big time and a giant step out of Cole Warren's life when she was able to move into an apartment with another model.

The only cloud on her horizon appeared when she learned that Uncle Carter had died while she was learning to ski in Vermont with her new roommate. It was the weekend she had so much fun and met a dashing young congressman from New York who wasted no time in calling and inviting her out for dinner.

She tried repeatedly to call Jacqui, getting no answer at first and then a message that her phone had been disconnected. Rhea told her that Jacqui had left Houston, and nobody seemed to know where she had gone after California.

After the television commercial Sunny Houston found herself in much demand, and, in little more than a year, her face was on the cover of three magazines. On the first one, she was holding a perfect yellow rose. There were public appearances on behalf of Yellow Rose Cosmetics, and she was busier than she had ever been before.

She was mentioned in the newspapers as the stunning blond model being seen around town with Congressman Chase Williams. Later, when she became known as the Yellow Rose, to her delight, she was recognized everywhere even without the congressman. But Sunny Houston wanted to be more than a pretty face around town: she wanted to be an actress. The Broadway stage had been calling her name since the day she first ventured to the theater. Somehow, someway, she would make it happen.

Studying with a voice coach from the university was the first step. Her goal was to learn to speak without a southern accent.

"Don't try to lose it altogether," Chase had advised. "It's part of your charm."

But, as she studied and talked incessantly into a recorder for feedback, she knew that she was succeeding. Nothing could stop her now.

CHAPTER FORTY-TWO

The placid darkness that Jacqui found cool and comforting seeped into morning as the miles on the interstate clicked away. The thought of a new beginning brought her no sense of anticipation, only a dreaded knowing that nothing really would be different. She knew she should be used to new beginnings by now. It seemed as if her whole life had been filled with them, yet there was no place she could say she belonged. And invariably, the time always came to push on to another place.

Now Arizona was another place. She wasn't sure why she had chosen Arizona. It was plain that she hadn't belonged in California. But, in fairness, wandering from place to place with her few clothes in the trunk of the car, pouring out her rage and despair into a journal that she never planned to let anyone see, was really all she could remember of those days following Greg's death. Periodically, she told herself that there was probably a book somewhere in that journal among all the garbage, but in her more rational moments, she knew it was filled with nothing but gibberish. *A tale told by an idiot signifying nothing.*

"Life sucks," she said, her tone vicious and almost instantaneously, a red warning light appeared on the dashboard.

What now? When would she ever learn? She surrounded herself with nothing but negativity, knowing all the while that nothing positive could happen to her in such a state of mind.

Greg had been dead for almost a year, and the rage would not go away. She was a psychologist, for God's sake. Dr. Jacquiline Wilder-Gregory. She knew about the stages of grief. She was a

Religious Scientist. She knew that her thoughts created her reality.

And David had told her many months ago in Houston that there were many paths on which the soul could journey. How was it then that she always seemed to choose the wrong one?

Maybe she belonged in Arizona. She loved canyons and deserts and horseback riding and skiing in the mountains. What if she didn't like Arizona people? she thought suddenly. It's a long way from Texas. That was utter stupidity. People were people.

What if she couldn't find a suitable place to live? Of course, she could find a suitable place to live. She had money to buy a condo overlooking a golf course or a quaint adobe house or anything else she liked. What was suitable anyway? She once thought Rhea's house was suitable. She could have saved them both a lot of grief if she had stayed in her unsuitable apartment. She would have met Greg at any rate. They were soul mates, and they would have gone on searching until they found one another. But she could have loved him without guilt if she had never known Rhea.

Guilt was a new emotion for her. She had never felt much guilt before in her life. It was bewildering that she should experience it now. David had told her the last time she called him that guilt was a totally useless emotion. Guilt, he had said, was anger that you believed you did not have a right to feel.

"Don't be angry with yourself, Jacqui. You are a good person. You don't have it in you to deliberately hurt anyone. If you must be angry, be angry with your friend Rhea for not making an effort to understand you, and then forgive her. Give up the anger, Jacqui."

Maybe she would go into analysis again, she thought, when she got settled. It had been a part of her curriculum when she was studying for her Ph.D. She kept reminding herself that she had put her life back together again after losing Spence. Why couldn't she do it again?

Perhaps she wouldn't go into analysis. She wondered if she could ever be totally honest with another person. She refused to justify her feelings about Greg and about Rhea. She told herself that she didn't need another person to give her permission to be angry, to be hurt, to be afraid of the future. She gave herself permission.

The warning light on the dash went out. Perhaps that was a positive sign. "I will be positive," she said aloud. "This is new and exciting. I am alive. Every day will be filled with something different—something remarkable." Dr. Wilder-Gregory has just embarked on a new adventure. All kinds of wonderful things awaited. A new life, a new apartment, a new job, skiing, museums, galleries, historic places, theater, restaurants, tennis, professional sports—basketball and baseball spring training. "Keep going, Jacqui," she said wryly, "eventually, you might be able to convince yourself that you can stand this new adventure."

The garage where she left her car to be checked was within walking distance of a small cafe overlooking the park. Jacqui ordered a light breakfast and picked up the sports section of the local newspaper abandoned in the booth behind her.

After too many cups of coffee and a vow to give it up entirely, she wandered out of the cafe and crossed the street to the park. It was empty at that time of the morning, and she made her way to a curved concrete bench overlooking a small pond with a fountain in the center, spewing up an umbrella of water. Jacqui watched the early morning sun turn the widening ripples from the fountain into sparklers. It was lovely and tranquil.

She was wearing her running shoes and a pair of purple stirrup pants with a purple wind breaker she had picked up a few weeks before at a discount store. Her paper and pen lay beside her in a portfolio decorated with graceful white swans bathed in purple shadows.

Everything matched, she mused. Everything seemed to belong, except her. She had developed a habit of grinding her teeth until her jaws ached, and she realized that she was doing it now. She stood up, relaxing her jaws, stretching her neck, and rotating her head.

The tranquility was shattered by two boisterous youngsters bouncing a basketball on their way to the basketball hoop on the top of the hill by the tennis courts and swimming pool.

Jacqui trudged along behind them hoping to pass some time watching them shoot baskets. When she got to the top of the hill, the boys had been joined by a tall young man in tennis shorts. She watched him moving agilely under the goal. He was an athlete; it was evident in the way he moved. And it was evident, too, that he was aware she was watching him. He shot a turn around jumper, and then as the ball passed cleanly through the net, he shot her a glance to make sure that she was still watching.

Without warning, she was suddenly angry again. Angry that she and Greg would never play a little one on one, or compete at tennis, or ski together. She felt cheated, and she resented this tall stranger with his strong, tan legs and muscular shoulders.

He played with the boys a few more minutes and then came over to join her.

"Hi, I'm Jon," he said flashing her a wide smile.

"Hello," she replied without smiling. "I'm Wilder."

"That's an unusual name," he said.

"I'm an unusual girl," she shot back, not sure why she didn't tell him her first name. But she was unreasonably angry without understanding why he had become the object of that anger.

"Well, unusual girl," he asked, "do you play tennis? It appears my date is not going to show. I have an extra racket."

"I play a little," she said, inexplicably glad that he had been stood up.

"Let's hit a few balls," he suggested.

Jacqui watched him waiting for her to serve, both hands on the racket, crouched over in the proper stance, confident almost to the point of arrogance.

The rage within her surged again. She released the ball upward and struck at it with all her pent-up fury. The surprise on his face as he scrambled to return the ball pleased her.

They played hard and fast, and he began to look at her with a new respect. The arrogance was gone. He was struggling. Jacqui was all over the court, playing with almost demonic speed and energy. Suddenly, it seemed to her that winning was crucial. Rebuffing his attempts at conversation, she beat him three straight sets. They were both drenched in sweat when a blue convertible pulled up to the courts and a leggy blond in a tennis dress got out of the car.

"My tennis date," he explained ruefully.

Jacqui shrugged her shoulders and put on her wind breaker. "It's been fun," she said nonchalantly and offered him a smug smile.

"I'll bet," he replied. "You will give me a rematch to try to salvage my wounded pride."

"Sorry," she replied. "I won't be around long enough. As

soon as I get my car out of the repair shop, I'll be on my way."

"On your way to where?" he asked.

"I wish I knew," she answered softly, and left him standing at the edge of the court where his date approached him and immediately entwined her arm around his.

Jacqui walked back in the direction of the pond. The wind carried the sound of their voices to her.

"Who is she?" the girl asked.

"Someone who just showed up," Jon replied. "Sort of weird really, but a hell of a tennis player."

Jacqui laughed, and the sound of it startled her. She couldn't remember the last time she had been genuinely amused. She sat down on the bench and opened her journal. But, at some point, she found herself deep in meditation. She had turned without conscious thought to the One and Only Power in the universe, coming without effort to a realization of her oneness with God. "I let go," she whispered softly, "of the anger, the guilt, and the self-pity, knowing that there is no power in the universe that can free me except myself."

She knew in that instant that her healing and restoration had begun. And, suddenly, she felt the essence of Greg so strongly that she was surprised when she turned slightly and found only her bag and portfolio lying on the bench beside her.

CHAPTER FORTY-THREE

Jacqui knew the moment she saw the low, rustic house, clinging to the canyon wall, that it was meant to be hers. She felt an instant affinity with the stark beauty of wood and rock and native plants. She was sold even before she stepped out the double doors leading to the redwood deck and saw the breathtaking panoramic view of the mountains in the distance.

In this house with its polished wood floors and spacious windows, she knew somehow, that if she were ever to put her shattered life together again, it would be there. The purchase took a good chunk of her cash, including the loan repayment she had received from Rhea by way of her attorney, Ben Howard.

She thought momentarily of Rhea and wished fleetingly that she could tell her about the new house. She was beginning to understand how Rhea felt about the house in Montrose. A home could truly become a part of you.

Jacqui furnished it sparingly to preserve the air of spaciousness. She commissioned a few good pieces of custom made furniture, designed to go with her Navajo rugs and Indian pottery. A pair of colorful, carved wooden Kachina dolls, for which she had paid a small fortune, graced the mantle. She had found them in a Hopi village where she had gone to watch the ceremonial masked dancers perform to insure health, happiness, and harmony in the universe.

She had bought baskets made of rabbit brush and sumac and dried yucca fibers. The house felt right. There was little to remind her of her former life. Greg's piano, his painting of San Francisco, and her seascape were all that remained from the condo in Houston. The condo had not sold, but it was leased, and she could count on the monthly rent.

More than three months had passed since the morning she had poured out her rage on the tennis court and so soundly defeated the arrogant young man who happened to be in her way. She had hoped that she might run into him again to make amends, but she never had, although, she went often to the little park with the pond and the tennis courts.

Jacqui went out frequently, exploring, shopping, trying new restaurants. Gradually, she began to lose the feeling of standing outside herself, watching. She met her neighbors, and she went to the university and introduced herself to the Chair of the Psychology Department. There was the possibility of an adjunct faculty position in the fall, teaching a couple of introductory courses.

In the meantime, she decided to look seriously for a job. She volunteered one day a week at a free clinic counseling adults who had been abused as children. Through her connections there, she picked up several private patients whom she agreed to treat on a sliding scale fee.

She went out to the newsstand early one Sunday morning to pick up the weekend papers. Startled, she saw Jill's image on the cover of a magazine. Jacqui was stunned! Jill was absolutely beautiful, holding a perfect yellow rose. She had an amazing fresh, young innocence that was at the same time provocative. Jill on the cover of a magazine!

Quickly, Jacqui turned to the inside cover to look at the credits. It wasn't Jill. It was somebody named Sunny Houston. What are you doing with Jill's smile, Sunny, whoever, you are? What are you doing with her slender, graceful hands and long red fingernails?

"Hi, unusual girl. Wilder, isn't it? The tennis whiz. I'm Jonathan Cory, remember me?"

"Hi, yourself. Of course, I remember you. It is Wilder," she said. "Jacqui Wilder. Actually, It's Jacqui Wilder Gregory. But I'm not really a tennis whiz."

"You could have fooled me."

"I just took you by surprise. Next time, you'll be prepared."

"I'm glad to know there will be a next time. If I remember

right, you were just passing through."

"I thought so too, but it's a long story."

"I have plenty of time. How about coffee? Or breakfast? I know a place down the block that serves a mean Mexican omelette."

"Sounds great," Jacqui said. She paid for her newspapers and the magazine with the cover girl who so resembled Jill and walked easily with Jonathan to the restaurant nearby.

"So," he said, when they were seated with steaming mugs of coffee in front of them, "what made you decide to stay in our fair city?"

"Well, perhaps, it isn't such a long story after all. I was at loose ends," she said. "This was the place I decided to stop running. I bought a house, started to work again, and before I knew it, I had a life."

"Good for you," he said earnestly.

"Hi Dr. Cory," a young boy greeted Jonathan in passing.

"Hi Bobby. How's it going?"

"Dr. Cory?" Jacqui asked, raising an eyebrow.

"Education," he explained. "I'm in school administration."

"I have a doctorate too," she laughed. "In psychology."

"So that's how you psyched me out on the court," he said ruefully. "I was hoping for a moment that it was in physical education. I desperately need a girl's basketball coach."

"Then, Dr. Cory, this might just be your lucky day. I have an undergraduate degree in physical education. I taught for three years in Texas before I went to graduate school."

"But I thought you said you had a job."

"I volunteer at a clinic, and I have a few private patients. I could still work that in around coaching."

"You're serious!"

"I'm perfectly serious. I'm a good coach, and coaching would be good for me right now."

"A physical education major," he mused. "That explains why you're so good at tennis."

"I'm good at basketball too. Wanna play a little one on one?"

"I don't think my ego could take it."

"But I wouldn't have the same incentive to win," she laughed. "I'm not angry with you now."

"Angry with me? Why were you angry with me?"

"For living."

"Well, excuse me!"

"I have," she said, smiling sweetly. "I'm a fierce competitor, but beyond that, I had just lost my husband. Nothing was going right for me. I hated the world that day. And there you were—so alive, so fit, showing off on the basketball court. I remember being very, very angry, and I poured out my rage on the tennis court."

"I'm sorry. It must have been rough for you."

"It was," she admitted, "but I'm much better now."

"I'm glad. I was afraid that I was never going to see you again. And that bothered me a great deal."

"It bothered me too," she said honestly. "I didn't know your last name or where to find you again."

He handed her a business card. She was surprised to see that he was Superintendent of Schools. He looked so young.

"Can you be in my office in the morning?" he asked. "That is, if you're really serious about wanting to coach."

"I'm serious," she assured him.

The waitress appeared with their food.

"Look how much we've accomplished before breakfast," Jonathan quipped. "Imagine what we could do with a whole day?"

Jacqui laughed. It felt good. Then she remembered that she and Greg had become acquainted over breakfast—after a basketball game. It has happening to her all over again. She felt alive. Jon was attractive and a good conversationalist.

She found herself relaxing into the present moment. She felt a strong sense of having turned a corner in the right direction. Later, at home, she didn't try to analyze what she was feeling for Jonathan. David, her old teacher, had reminded her that when one door closes, another always opens. It had taken her more than a year to find the open door.

She leafed through the magazine with Jill's image on the cover. Just maybe, she thought, She would call somebody and ask about Jill. Not Rhea, of course, who didn't want anything to do with her. But perhaps Ben Howard. He should know where Jill was, or he could find out.

The good feeling stayed with her all day. She stood on her deck at dusk and embraced the evening. She was alive, albeit forever changed. "I'm Dr. Jacquiline Wilder Gregory, Ph.D." She said the words aloud again, knowing they were now deeply ingrained in her subjective mind.

Grief was no longer her dominant emotion. She felt protected, loved, less vulnerable, less fragile. She could coach basketball and counsel broken people. She was, again, in charge of her own destiny.

Greg had been her dream—unexpected, joy and pain co-mingled. Now she would find another dream. Perhaps his name was Jonathan. And this was another new beginning.

CHAPTER FORTY-FOUR

The opening of the restaurant and Jill's first big success in New York coincided and did much to banish the dark, devastating future Rhea had envisioned for herself when Carter died. She also took Liz's advice and began to see a therapist to work on her anxiety and lack of self-esteem.

Thoughts of Carter still brought incredible sadness and pain. But as time went by, she thought of him less often. She could at long last accept the fact that he was lost to her. Kevin was another matter. The pain was just as deep, deeper perhaps than when he left her. She had done everything humanly possible to prevent Carter's leaving her and nothing to prevent Kevin's going. She deserved the pain and loneliness. It was her own fault, she could see that now.

She tried to contact him, but his telephone had been disconnected. She was able to track down his mother's nurse, Anya, who told her that the house had been sold, and Kevin was in Europe working for a magazine.

Part of Rhea wanted to wish him well in his endeavor to resume the career his mother's illness had forced him to relinquish. But part of her longed desperately to have things the way they once were—to have him need her again. In those moments she would have given anything to have him back, developing his photographs in her bathroom, bringing her coffee in bed, snapping her picture at the most inopportune times, loving her, and almost convincing her that she deserved to be loved.

Late in the afternoon of one particularly hectic day, Ben

Howard appeared as Liz was closing the restaurant. They summoned Rhea to come over and have a drink with them. She left the shop in the care of the girl she had just hired and joined them.

In the course of the conversation, Ben casually mentioned that he had received a letter from Jacqui.

"What did she want?" Liz asked.

"Mainly to thank me for handling Carter's affairs. And to thank me for arranging to have his piano shipped to her."

"Carter had a piano?" Liz asked all the questions Rhea wanted to ask, and she was grateful she didn't have to.

"He hadn't played in years," Rhea murmured.

"Where did you send it?" Liz asked.

"To Arizona," Ben replied. "It seems that Jacqui bought herself a house. Up in the hills—sounds fantastic."

Rhea remembered that Jacqui once said that she didn't have anything that couldn't be disposed of in a day. Now she had bought a house. Rhea thought of her own home, which seemed less of a home every day. The business had spread to every part of it, except for the bedroom and bath she occupied on the second floor along with the kitchen she had moved to Caroline's old bedroom. Every other room was either used for showing merchandise or storage.

"Is Jacqui working?" Liz asked.

"She said she had a part-time job coaching basketball," Ben replied, "and she mentioned something about counseling private patients and a support group for widows."

"She could hardly consider herself an authority on widows," Liz snorted. "What were they married, a few months at the most?"

"They were married," Rhea said quietly.

"I think of you as Carter's widow," Liz said.

"I do too," Rhea replied. "Don't you think it's time I stopped?"

"Of course, I do. And I know just the person I'm going to invite to our Christmas party and introduce to you."

"Cut it out, Liz," Ben warned. "If Rhea wants a man, she's perfectly capable of finding one without your help."

"Pooh, that's what friends are for," Liz said, laughing, "to help you whether you realize you need help or not. Gosh, look at the time, I have to get to the bank. Will you lock up for me, Rhea?"

Rhea nodded.

"I'll see you at home, Ben," Liz flung the words to him as she raced out the door.

Rhea picked up the empty glasses, rinsed them at the bar, and put them away. Just as she finished, she turned and Ben was standing behind her. His hands were on her shoulders.

"Long day?" he asked softly as he began to massage her tired back.

"Thank you," she said as he expertly kneaded her tender shoulder and neck muscles. "That feels wonderful."

"How does this feel?" he asked as his hands reached around and cupped her breast.

Rhea vigorously pushed him away. "Stop that!" she demanded.

"Or what?" he asked with a mocking little smile. "You'll tell Liz?"

"No," she replied in cold fury, looking him straight in the eye, "or I'll break your Goddammed arm!"

He drew back, shock registering on his face, as though she had slapped him.

"Rhea, don't be like that. We've been friends a long time. I just want to give you what you need."

"I need your friendship, Ben, and nothing else. Go home and give Liz what she needs, a loving, faithful husband."

Ben flushed. Angrily he turned, heading for the door. She heard him burn rubber getting out of the driveway.

Later when Rhea told her therapist about the incident, she was asked," How do you feel about the way you handled it?"

"I'm surprised. It didn't feel like me. It felt like another person—the way Jacqui or Jill or Liz would have handled it. Not me."

"Why is that?"

"I suppose, I've always been afraid of hurting other people—even when they've just hurt me."

"Do you think you deserved to be treated like that by a man who had been your friend for more than twenty years."

"No, I didn't deserve it. I think that's way it made me so angry."

"Good for you. Will you tell Liz?"

"No."

"Why not?"

"Liz already knows about his infidelity. She and I are partners. We have a great relationship, and we have a good business arrangement. I don't want to complicate that relationship."

"What if he tries it again?"

"Then I'll deal with it!"

"Good for you. How did you feel when Ben mentioned his conversation with Jacqui?"

"Curious, I think."

"No longer angry?"

"The underlying anger is still there. Sometimes I think I've gotten past it. But I haven't really."

"Do you think you can ever be friends again?"

"No."

"Why not, Rhea?"

"It's just too complicated. I doubt that she wants it any more than I do. She's put down roots in Arizona. I don't ever expect to see her again. I hope she puts her life back together. I really do. She just isn't a part of my life any longer."

But Rhea couldn't stop thinking about Jacqui—or Jill, or even Caroline. She remembered the night they had all shared the champagne when Jacqui first moved into the house.

To this marvelous house, Jacqui had toasted, and to you for letting us share it.

They were all so hopeful that night, she, Jacqui, Jill, and Caroline. Now Caroline was dead; Jacqui was two thousand miles away toasting a new home. Only Jill had managed to make her dreams come true.

"Enjoy it, girl," she whispered as she thought of Jill's radiant smile. Caroline never even got to hold her baby, and Jacqui and she both had to settle for second best. Neither of them had gotten what they wanted. And both of them would have to live with that for the rest of their lives.

But as time went by, Rhea began to believe that the second best that she had settled for wasn't so bad after all. Her business totally absorbed her, and she realized that if she wasn't totally happy, she wasn't unhappy either. She found renewing old acquaintances easier with her new found confidence, and she even began to date again, a widowed lawyer she had met at one of Liz's parties.

Their relationship didn't have the passion she had been so

afraid of with Kevin, but they frequently dined together and enjoyed the same friends. It was, she suspected, as much she had a right to expect at this period in her life.

CHAPTER FORTY-FIVE

NEW YORK CITY

THE WEDDING

Sunny left the boutique after the final fitting on her wedding gown. It was the most beautiful dress she had ever seen. And it clung to her trim figure like a second skin. It should. She had literally been sewn into it.

The exquisite dress was every girl's dream of a romantic gown, fashioned from pure silk and Venetian lace. Tiny back buttons led to a bow bustle and a magnificent flowing chapel-length train, dotted with hand sewn pearls. There was a matching headpiece with a waterfall veil and hand-sculpted silk roses. A pair of silk shoes with rose accents on the toe completed the ensemble.

She would be wearing a pearl and diamond necklace with coordinated earrings that had been in her groom's family for generations. When her future mother-in-law had offered it, Sunny knew that she had been accepted into the staid old family that traced its roots back to English nobility.

She had wanted Jacqui to be her matron of honor, but it had been difficult enough just getting her to agree to come to New York for the wedding. She had chosen instead her future sister-in-law which pleased Chase's family.

The bridesmaids were all friends that she had made in New

York in her modeling days. Her little sister would be a junior bridesmaid. They would be wearing pale yellow—little sleeveless dresses with petaled skirts in back and embroidered lace hats. She had given them Victorian chokers with matching earrings to be worn with their dresses. They would be carrying yellow roses.

Yellow roses would be everywhere—in her own bouquet with Casablanca lilies, on the immense wedding cake that would serve two hundred guests, and in the lavish floral arrangements.

It was the happiest time of her life. Nothing could compare with this. She knew the meaning of the word bliss. What more could she ever have wanted, a wonderful career—a shooting star, the newspapers called Sunny Houston—and an impending marriage to a handsome, wealthy congressman, Chase Williams.

Little Jill Turner had disappeared; she didn't exist any more She rarely thought of Court Randall or Rick Cortero or whatever his name really had been. It was a secret buried deep within her. A secret that disappeared with Jill Turner. There was no need for Chase to know. She would protect him at all costs.

She hailed a cab to meet Chase for lunch. As she settled into the seat for the short ride, she had a nagging little pang of uneasiness that had been with her for the last few weeks. Maybe it was pre-wedding jitters, but it seemed to be more than that. She looked around as she had been doing often lately—at the people in the cars beside her and the car behind her. She had the eerie feeling she was being watched.

She was used to being watched. It came with the territory. She had been a successful model—what the tabloids called a super model, and now she was starring in a Broadway show. She had become acclimated to being looked at with adulation. But this was different. She thought about the famous people who had been stalked and threatened or worse. No threats had come, but the uneasiness would not go away.

Rhea was arriving in a few days and Jacqui would soon follow. Her mother and little sister would fly up the day before the wedding. Maybe then the apprehension would go away. But just to make sure she had taken precautions to protect herself. She had programmed 911 into her cell phone, which she was never without, knowing that the police could be summoned with the touch of one button. She even practiced finding it in the dark.

Chase was waiting for her in the bar of the restaurant, surrounded as always by a group of people. She immediately felt better. Chase made her feel safe and protected in a way Court never had. If there wasn't the same grand passion, well, she didn't need it. She had been lucky enough to have a truly good man fall in love with her, and the fact that he was successful and wealthy and came from a prominent family was icing on the cake.

The waiter led them to their favorite secluded table, and she explained that she planned to put Jacqui and Rhea together in her Fifth Avenue apartment while she stayed with his mother in her Long Island home. "It's all arranged," she said.

"They haven't spoken in five years, and you're putting them up in the same apartment?" he asked skeptically.

"It's the only way I can think of to get them speaking again."

"What makes you think it will work?"

"They'll make it work if I get out of the way. They used to be best friends."

"Until one of them snagged the other's husband."

"Ex," she corrected him. "Ex husband."

"And you think they're ready to kiss and make up?"

"Yes. I know Jacqui wants to, and I really think Rhea does, too. She asked about Jacqui when she came up the last time to finalize the wedding plans."

"What if you're wrong, Sunny? What if there's a terrible row? It could backfire and spoil the wedding."

"Not a chance!"

"What makes you so sure?"

"They're both too nice. Neither of them would do anything to spoil my wedding day. They love me."

"Well, I love you, too, my beautiful one. And I hope you're right."

"Trust me."

"That's supposed to be my line. But what about your mother and sister? Won't they expect to stay in your apartment?"

"I've reserved a suite for them on Broadway—right next to the Palace Theater. They'll love it. They're from a little town in Arkansas, remember. I even have tickets for them to see the show at the Palace the night before the wedding. The bright lights of Broadway will dazzle them."

"Like it once dazzled you," he teased.

"What do you mean, once? It still does. Seeing my name on

the marquis is the most exciting thing that ever happened to me."

"Aw shucks, I thought I was the most exciting thing that ever happened to you."

"You are the best thing that ever happened to me," she smiled.

"But, not the most exciting?"

"Darling Chase, you have made me totally and completely happy for the first time in my life."

"I'll settle for that. Now tell me who else is coming to the wedding that I should know about."

"Cole Warren and his wife, Melissa. He's the photographer who helped me get started when I first came to New York."

"The one you lived with?"

"It was a purely platonic relationship."

"It's hard to imagine anyone living with you and having a purely platonic relationship, Sunshine."

"Don't call me that!" she said more sharply than she meant.

He looked surprised.

"I don't like to be called Sunshine," she explained. "My name is Sunny."

"Okay, okay," he replied. "Sorry."

"Oh, I almost forgot to tell you. Kevin is flying in from London for the wedding."

"And Kevin is?" he asked.

"Kevin is one of my best friends. He was once involved with my aunt, Rhea. But they went their separate ways, and neither would ever talk about it. So I don't know what happened. Rhea doesn't know he's coming."

"Sunny, did anyone ever tell you that your life is like a soap opera. All these complicated relationships. Is this what our life is going to be like?"

"I promise you, it will never be dull," she laughed.

"That I can believe," he said, taking her hand.

CHAPTER FORTY-SIX

Rhea stared at the papers in front of her almost as if she were staring at a serpent about to strike. It was an offer to buy the antique business and the restaurant, including the real estate. It was an offer to buy her whole way of life—not just buildings and a thriving enterprise—but her very existence.

Liz was in favor of accepting the offer—probably more than she had let on, Rhea suspected. "But it's up to you, Rhea. You're the one who started all this. And it's your home."

"But," Liz reminded her, "we'd both be set for life. We may never get another offer like this."

If it could just be anyone but Giles Riker, her old nemesis. The humiliation of his firing her more than five years ago was a still painful memory, even though she had been forced by circumstances to do business with him over the years. She had to admit that he had a genius for locating and buying antiques. But he had neither the personality nor the aptitude for sales. And Rhea still often found treasures among his trash that he failed to recognize. What would happen to her lovely business in his grubby hands?

She shuddered at the thought of him tracking across her oriental rugs in dirty boots. The man was a pig! A pig with the Midas touch, all right. He had money to back up his annoying mouth. If he hadn't, someone would have closed it for him, permanently, by now.

He wanted her house, her business, and Liz's restaurant. He didn't know the first thing about the clientele she and Liz served.

She knew without conceit that she and Liz were largely responsible for the success they enjoyed. It was not only the long hours and incredibly hard work both had contributed, but their creativity and the way they complemented one another.

Liz, the risk taker, took them to heights Rhea wouldn't have dreamed, and cautious Rhea kept them on firm financial ground. What started out as The Victorian Tea Room, serving lunch and catering mostly to women, quickly became The Victoria, a full service restaurant. Rhea was able to hire full time sales help and a bookkeeper for the shop and restaurant. As her decorating business soared, she hired a full time decorator. They were successful beyond her wildest dreams.

In Giles Riker's hands, if the business survived, it would be vastly different. Rhea was not sure that she could endure that.

"Take the offer to New York with you," Liz had advised. "After the wedding, spend a few days by yourself. Do some shopping, see a play, visit the museums. Then decide. Away from all this, you'll be more objective. Whatever your decision, I'll be with you one hundred percent."

Rhea tucked the papers back into her briefcase and pushed it under the seat in front of her. She had taken Liz's advice and was on her way to New York for the wedding. A wedding she had planned down to the last detail—with the help of a wedding consultant, of course. She had been in New York on three separate occasions and her telephone bills had been enormous. It was going to be the wedding every girl dreams of and few actually experience. A wedding fit for a princess.

Beautiful, exuberant Jill was the daughter Rhea never had. She still couldn't get used to calling her Sunny. To Rhea she would always be Jill—sweet, little Jill. Her sister Ruth certainly wasn't up to the task of planning a wedding of this magnitude. And she had been glad to defer to Rhea. Jill was, of course, much too busy with her new show.

Rhea ordered a martini and settled back to enjoy the flight. She looked forward to the festivities. She had met a number of Jill's friends over the past few years, her agent and models and actresses mostly. She adored Chase. If she could have chosen a prospective husband for Jill, it would have been Chase. And she liked his family, especially his mother. Her sister Ruth and Jill's little sister would arrive in a couple of days, but they were to stay at a hotel, which seemed a little strange.

Jill had confided at the last minute that Jacqui would be at the wedding. Rhea tried to work up some of the old animosity she had felt for so long, but it was hard. To her surprise, it just didn't seem to be there anymore. She supposed that five years was too long a time to maintain a grudge. Time had diffused the sharp edges of her grief. Carter was gone and had been for a long, long time. Somewhere along the way, she suddenly realized, she had let go. She had a new life now.

Reluctantly, she admitted to herself that she hardly ever though of Carter and their time together. When she thought of Jill's wedding, she found it difficult to harbor discordant thoughts. She supposed a wedding brought out the best in everyone. In her, at any rate.

Jacqui's betrayal seemed so long ago. She never thought she could get over those feelings of rage and pain, but Rhea hadn't thought about her in ages. She wished she didn't have to see her, but it really didn't matter very much.

It was going to be a wonderful and exciting few days. Everything would go according to clockwork, even though, the intimate little wedding that Jill and Chase had originally planned had grown to more than two hundred people. There would be a welcoming party for out-of-town guests on Thursday night that included a sunset cruise.

The bridesmaids' luncheon was on Friday, and a fabulous restaurant which featured a dining terrace overlooking a mountain waterfall had been chosen for the rehearsal dinner that night. All of the out of town guests had been invited to the rehearsal dinner.

The wedding was set for four o'clock Saturday afternoon and would be followed by a twilight supper with a jazz combo. Dancing would follow with an orchestra featuring the big band sounds of the forties and fifties. The bride and groom would be off to a local hotel for the night, but would reappear at a Sunday morning brunch hosted by the groom's parents at their Long Island home.

Then Jill and Chase would be off on a Caribbean honeymoon. Rhea sighed. Everything was falling neatly into place. She had planned it to the last detail.

Jill met Rhea at the airport. She was wearing big, dark sunglasses and her golden hair was all tucked up beneath a floppy sun hat. She had on jeans and sneakers and she could have been any young girl instead of the celebrity she had become.

She embraced Rhea with enthusiasm and talked a mile a minute as they waited for her luggage. "I feel like a celebrity myself," Rhea laughed as Jill ushered her to the curb where a limo was waiting.

"I rented it," Jill explained on the way to the apartment, "with the driver for the rest of the week. I knew there would be a million things to do before the wedding. I though it would just make things much easier." She didn't add that it made her feel safe from a danger she couldn't identify. She relaxed knowing, that with Rhea here and Jacqui to arrive later in the day and her mother and sister, also on their way the following day, that she would not be alone again. And, after the wedding, she would be Mrs. Chase Williams. Nothing could threaten her or frighten her again.

CHAPTER FORTY-SEVEN

Jacqui rang the bell and stood awkwardly outside the door of Jill's spacious, chic apartment, looking a bit uncertain as Rhea opened the door.

"I didn't expect to see you here," Jacqui said at length. "When I arrived, there was a message for me to take a cab to this address. I thought Jill would be here. The doorman was expecting me. He let me come right up."

After a short pause, she asked, "How are you Rhea?"

"I'm fine," Rhea replied. "I wasn't exactly expecting you either. But I might have guessed. Jill has been acting strangely all morning. I have an idea that she planned this. For you and me to be here alone for a while. Come in, Jacqui."

"I could always go to a hotel."

"No, don't do that, it's okay. I'm sure we can manage for a few hours until Jill gets back. She had some last minute errands to run."

Rhea noticed that Jacqui was thinner, her high cheekbones more prominent. The long, straight hair she had worn so often pulled back with silk flowers had been cut and permed into short ringlets. She had a healthy tan and she looked no older, perhaps even younger.

Jacqui sensed more than saw the change in Rhea. Outwardly, she looked much the same. Maybe it was the nervous energy that had characterized Rhea in the old days that was missing. She seemed so much more confident now, with an air of self assurance that hadn't been evident before.

"Jill will make such a lovely bride," Rhea said at length.

Good choice, Rhea, Jacqui thought. Jill was a good, safe subject while they were still feeling each other out.

"Yes," Jacqui agreed. "It's easy to understand why Jill has been so successful. She was always absolutely gorgeous, and yet she still had that sweet, child-like innocence in spite of all the things that happened to her."

"Yes, that's true. Why don't I make us a cup of tea?" Rhea offered.

"Good idea, I'll just put my bags in the bedroom."

She hung up her garment bag that contained the emerald green silk faille suit with the long skirt and matching shoes she planned to wear to the wedding. Then she dropped her suitcase on the floor beside the bed. It was a lovely room, monochromatic, decorated all in shades of blue. Rhea had something to do with this, she thought It looked like her touch.

There were so many things she wanted to say to Rhea, but she didn't dare. Something told her to tread lightly—to give both of them a little time.

They finished the tea, and Rhea showed her around the apartment. The balcony had a fantastic view of the New York City skyline. A gentle summer rain had washed the park below and enshrouded the buildings in low hung clouds.

"I hope the weather clears for the wedding," she said. Another safe subject.

"Yes," Rhea agreed. "The forecast is for showers ending late tonight."

There was a long silence as they stood on the balcony, but it was not an awkward silence. At last Rhea spoke.

"Is this your first trip to New York?" she asked.

"No," Jacqui replied. "I was here with Spence several times when we were together. He came here often on business. I did a lot of shopping while he worked. We went to ball games and to the theater together. I loved it, but I never thought that I would want to live here."

"Nor would I," Rhea said. "Jill loves it, though."

"Who wouldn't if you were the toast of the town? How did she get interested in the theater?"

"She said that she went to her first play right after she got here and knew immediately that she wanted to see her name in lights.

She studied acting and worked with a voice coach, and then, I suppose, it was just a combination of knowing the right people and phenomenal good luck."

"And incredible talent that, apparently, nobody knew she had," Jacqui added.

"That too," Rhea agreed, laughing.

Jacqui unpacked, showered and rested for a while before Sunny returned.

Sunny looked so pleased not to see them at each other's throats that Jacqui wanted to laugh.

"I've made dinner reservations for the three of us," she said happily. "Chase and a couple of friends may join us back here for a late nightcap, but the evening belongs to us. We have so much to catch up on. It'll be just like old times."

It was difficult for Jacqui and Rhea not to catch Sunny's enthusiasm. She dressed for dinner in a bright red silk dress with buttons down the front, adorned with simple gold jewelry. Her long hair was caught up in the back and long tendrils spiraled around her face. Her bright red lipstick matched the polish on her long fingernails. Jacqui changed to a white linen pantsuit, and Rhea appeared trim and chic in a purple and green printed sheath with a long sheer jacket.

When the limo arrived, Sunny told them that they were going to a country inn north of the city for dinner. "You'll like it," she told them. "It's very private, and we won't be bothered by autograph seekers."

"Does that bother you?" Jacqui asked.

"At first, I thought I'd never get tired of it. It was so exciting to be recognized and sought after. But, yes, there are times when it bothers me. Like tonight, when I just want to enjoy a quiet evening with my two best friends."

Once they were settled in, Sunny produced a chilled bottle of champagne and glasses.

"Just like old times," she chattered happily.

"Only there were four of us," Rhea remembered.

"I wish Caroline could be here," Sunny said sadly. "I wanted her little girl to be in the wedding, but she isn't strong. She had such a rocky start in life and, apparently, although she is doing well now, they felt that the trip might be too much for her."

"I saw her several months ago," Rhea said. "She's precious,

but very fragile.""It seems like such a long, time ago," Jacqui mused, sipping her champagne. "I remember the night we all had the champagne just after I moved in, but you, young lady, didn't even like it."

"It is a taste I reluctantly acquired," Sunny laughed, refilling her glass. Then she regaled them with tales of backstage gossip from her show. She was taking a month long hiatus and would return as soon as she was back from the honeymoon.

Time passed quickly. Sunny looked at her watch. They should have arrived by now. She looked out the darkened windows of the limo. There was nothing that she could recognize. The old familiar fear was with her again. They were travelling down a deserted, tree-lined narrow road. Where were they? She knocked on the glass that separated them from the driver. He didn't respond.

Sunny leaned forward and knocked again. On the seat beside him was a bottle of wine. Chateau Lafite-Rothschild!. A shiver of fear infiltrated her body. It couldn't be. Court Randall was dead.

The car braked and pulled off the road forcing its way down a faintly discernable pathway. The night was very dark.

"What's happening?" Rhea said, sensing Sunny's panic.

"We have a flat," the driver said. "I had to get off the road, or we might have been hit. It will only take a few minutes to change the tire, and we'll be on our way again."

"Where are we?" Sunny demanded.

"We're almost there," he answered politely. "I apologize. Just make yourselves comfortable, and we'll be on our way soon."

Sunny, Jacqui, and Rhea exchanged puzzled glances.

Sunny searched frantically for her bag, but the door was opened suddenly, and she was pulled out of the car before she had a chance to retrieve it from the floor. When she regained her balance she was in the arms of a stranger with cold, hard eyes, with a gun at her head.

"Get out of the car," he ordered Jacqui and Rhea, "or I'll blow her head off."

Panic rose in Rhea's throat. For seconds she was frozen, unable to move. Jacqui prodded her gently. "Do what he says."

Jacqui looked into the eyes of the man holding Sunny. Court Randall! She would never forget those evil eyes as long as she lived. The face was different. Something about the nose—the cheekbones. The hair was lighter but it was Randall. An altered Randall to be sure, only the hard, evil eyes were the same.

He herded them through the woods to a clearing with the gun at Sunny's head. Rhea and Jacqui hardly dared breathe. Finally, he released Sunny and handed her two lengths of rope.

"Tie them to the tree," he directed.

"This isn't about them," Sunny said evenly. "This is about you and me, Court. Leave them out of it. Take me with you, if you must, but let them go."

"If you don't tie them, I'll shoot them here and now," he threatened. "And, if you don't do a good job, I'll kill them."

Sunny obeyed, trying first Jacqui then Rhea. "It will be okay," she promised them desperately. "Somehow it will be okay."

Holding the gun on Sunny, he checked the ropes to be certain that Jacqui and Rhea were securely tied. As he drew near Jacqui, he learned over and hissed in her ear. "I'll be back, bitch, to kill you. Think about it and get ready for it."

He grabbed Sunny roughly by the arm and pushed her back in the direction of the car. Rhea and Jacqui struggled to free themselves, but the ropes only cut deeper into their wrists. The night was dark and silent, except for a gently falling rain. It mingled with their tears as they both waited, trembling, for their abductor to come back.

Time passed. A half hour. An hour. Who could tell? Then three sharp, staccato shots punctuated the still night. Fear stabbed Jacqui's heart. Rhea began to sob wildly.

Just like Caroline, Jacqui thought with horror. He's killed her. She took a deep breath and wrestled with the ropes on her wrists. The more she struggled, the more they cut into the tender flesh where the scars of her suicide attempt many years ago were still visible.

Is this the way life ends? she asked herself. In the woods with the rain pouring down and her hands tied behind her back? Had she fulfilled her life's purpose? She had a strong conviction that she had not.

Rhea's sobs subsided. She told herself sternly to stop sniveling. If her life was over, it was over. She had had twenty years of marriage to a handsome, successful man, and had lived most of those years in her dream house. She started a business, all alone, on a shoestring, and it had grown and prospered. She had grown and prospered in the past five years. Her only regret was Kevin.

She had been lucky enough to love again and have a wonderful, sensitive man love her. But she had clung to the dream of a man who didn't want her and drove away the man who did. If only she could start all over. Oh Kevin! She loved him so much, and he would never know.

"I know that God is all there is," Jacqui affirmed aloud. "And I know that I am a part of all creation. The God in me is in all things and in all people. God is pure spirit, therefore, I am spirit. God is creative intelligence, therefore I am creative intelligence. God is perfect love, therefore, I am perfect love. Nothing can happen to me that is not for my highest good. And what is true of me is also true for Rhea and Jill. It is even true for Rick Cortero. I give thanks that it is so, and I let go and release my word into law. And so it is."

When Jacqui had finished speaking, Rhea did not say anything, and there was no sound except for the gentle summer rain falling through the trees all around them and their frightened, shallow breathing as they waited.

CHAPTER FORTY-EIGHT

"Well, Sunshine," Cortero said as he and Sunny neared the parked limo, "or should I call you Sunny? It's been a long time."

She did not answer. The fear that erupted when she first saw the bottle of wine threatened to overwhelm her, but she knew that she must keep her head. She was the only chance Jacqui and Rhea had.

"They told me you were dead," she said softly.

"You knew I'd come back," he said defiantly, "and I did, but you had left. It took me a while to find you. And even longer to figure out how I was going to deal with you."

"The way you dealt with Caroline."

"That cunt left me and stole a hundred thousand dollars of my money. She deserved what she got. I never found the money. You've been living pretty high on the hog. Maybe you found my money after the bitch died."

"I don't know what you're talking about. I came to New York and started modeling. I took dancing and acting lessons until I got a part in a play, and now I'm in a hit show. I don't need your money. If I had your hundred thousand dollars, I would gladly give it back to you. I'll give you a hundred thousand dollars if you'll just let us go."

He laughed derisively. "You think I need your money, you silly bitch. You're going to give me something all right"

Abruptly, he pulled her to him, pressing his lean, hard body into hers. His searching lips found hers, and he kissed her brutally.

Her thoughts went back in time to when he used to fill her

with ecstasy. He kissed her again, slowly, more gently. But there was no answering response. Only revulsion. She tried to push him away.

With a derisive laugh, he suddenly caught the front of her dress at the neck, and with one powerful yank, he tore the buttons loose, exposing her breasts in a provocative red lace bra.

He reached out to cup one of her breasts. She twisted out of his reach. He was enraged, and he pushed her roughly backward until she was opposite the open door of the limousine. Then shoved her into the back seat. He took a swaggering step toward her as he unzipped his pants and forced his engorged penis closer to her.

"If I remember right, you gave the best head of all my women," he said.

Jill felt the vomit rising in her throat. He came closer, ripping what was left of her dress from her body As he struggled with the rest of her clothing, she was able to free her right hand. She grappled wildly for her bag on the floor, and when she managed to pry it open, her probing hand closed around the cell phone. She turned it on, pushing what she hoped was the button where she had programmed 911. In her panic she couldn't be sure. She reached again for the phone, but he caught her hand and forced it around his penis.

"I have very definite plans for you," Court said to her. "When I'm finished with you, I'm going to tie you to a tree near your friend Jacqui. Then I'm going to shoot her and your aunt while you watch, my pet. After that I'm going to leave you tied there. You'll be naked and helpless. How long do you think it will take you to die of starvation and exposure? Days? Weeks? We're miles away from the nearest house. This isn't the time of year for hunters to be roaming the woods. Nobody will find you, at least for a long time. When they do, you won't draw any applause. The stage lights have gone out. This is your last curtain call, Sunshine."

"How could you do this to me, Court? I loved you; I was going to marry you."

"Oh, you really loved me, didn't you. You wasted no time getting out of Houston. You knew I would come back for you. You even told the feds about my island villa, and it hasn't been safe for me to go back there since.

"I didn't know it was your villa. You told me it was your

business partner's. I would never have done anything to harm you. I loved you, Court."

"Stop calling me Court. You know by now my name is Rick. Rick Cortero."

"You'll never get away with killing us," she said desperately.

"Au contraire. I killed one bitch and got away with it. What's three more?"

The rain had stopped abruptly, and Sunny saw the moon trying to break out of the clouds. She began to struggle savagely. She had to stop him. She had to.

Suddenly, Court saw the lighted face of her cell phone "What the hell is this?"

He grabbed the phone. Sunny scrambled out of the back seat, pretending to reach for it, but he laughed derisively, holding the phone for a moment high over her head before he flung it violently away into the brush.

Sunny realized this was her only chance to save herself. If she couldn't do that, Jacqui and Rhea were doomed. She was strong, she knew, from her grueling schedule at the theater and her mornings in the gym to maintain physical fitness for her demanding role. But she knew that even a physically fit woman was no match for a man's strength. All she had on her side was the element of surprise. She went for his eyes first, digging into soft flesh with her long fingernails while he was still distracted with throwing the phone. He screamed in pain, and she caught his hand with the gun in both of hers, struggling in vain to take it away. He fired two shots, but they went completely astray, hitting the trees around them. Court forced the gun lower. Sunny felt the cold metal between them. With a might effort, she forced it away from her as blood streamed down his face from the wound her fingernails had inflicted in his eye.

It seemed as if the whole scene was played out in slow motion. And, when the gun went off a third time, Sunny wasn't sure who had been hit until she saw the look of shock and impending death on the face of the man who was trying to kill her. With a curse on his lips, he crumpled to the ground.

She leaned against the back of the limo. She had been crazy to have ever loved Court Randall, or Rick Cortero, or whatever his name was. He was evil, and in her heart, she always knew it. Would it ever have come to this if she had walked away from him when she first had misgivings about the business he was in? Would Caroline still be alive? Or, did he already know where to find her?

She glanced at the man on the ground. He had not moved. She was sure that he was dead. But nothing in the world would have induced her to touch him. She pulled her under garments into place. The red silk dress that had been so festive earlier hung in shreds covering very little of her body now stained with his blood. She wondered if she would ever feel clean again.

Torn between wanting to rush to free Jacqui and Rhea and knowing she had to call for help, Sunny frantically searched in the brush until she found the cell phone, praying that it would still work. It had to. It just had to! Mercifully, the face lit up. Unsure of what to do, she called Chase and, miraculously, he answered. She told him briefly what had happened. "I don't know what to do," she cried. "I don't even know where we are."

"Oh, my God, Sunny, he could have killed you all," Chase said in horror. "Call the state police. I'll call them, too. Then get in the car and drive to the main road. I'll find you. Do you think you were close to the inn?"

"I think so, but I'm not sure."

"Just hang in there until we find you. You have great courage, Sunny. I'm very proud of you. Stay calm, and I promise you everything will be all right. I love you."

Sunny called the state police and asked for help. They agreed that she would be much easier to find if she drove the limo to the main highway. With the phone in her hand and the line still open, she rushed toward the clearing.

CHAPTER FORTY-NINE

In the hushed silence that followed Jacqui's prayer, neither she nor Rhea dared speak. The rain had stopped, but they were already soaked to the skin. It seemed an eternity since they had heard the shots.

At last a figure burst into the clearing. Jacqui felt her knees go weak with relief.

It was Sunny.

They both beseeched her with questions She put the phone on the ground at the edge of the clearing and ran over to them. "It's okay," she said softly. "Don't be afraid."

She worked at the ropes on Jacqui's hands, tightened by her struggling, until they reluctantly gave way. Then, she untied Rhea.

"Is he gone?" Rhea asked.

"Yes," she replied. "He's gone."

But Jacqui knew from the strangeness in her voice that Rick Cortero had not simply left. She put her arms around Sunny who was trembling and found her hands were as cold as ice. Jacqui took off her blazer and placed it around her shoulders. Even thought it was wet, it was better than the torn dress.

"What happened?" Jacqui asked her gently.

"We struggled over the gun," Sunny said dully. "It went off, and he was killed."

"Those were the shots we heard," Jacqui said softly. "We thought he had killed you."

"Oh, my God," Rhea cried. "You poor, poor baby."

"Are you sure he's dead?" Jacqui asked.

"Yes, he's dead. I think he might have been following me. I'm been afraid for days without understanding why."

"Why didn't you tell somebody?"

"Chase would have thought I was imagining it. Who would have believed me? I never saw anyone—I only felt the hair on the back of my neck stand up at times, but I never saw anyone. I couldn't tell anybody. I thought Court was dead, and I never told Chase about him."

"Well, he'll have to be told now," Jacqui said.

"He's already been told," Sunny said. "I called him first. He's getting in touch with the state police. He promised to help find me."

"What are we going to do?" Rhea wailed.

"We're going back to the car and drive out to the main road so they can find us," Sunny said."Don't be afraid. The worst is over."

When they cautiously reached the spot where Cortero's body lay, Jacqui felt for a pulse at his wrist and then his neck. There was none. She said nothing; her expression confirming the fact that he was dead for Sunny and Rhea.

Cortero's face was covered with blood, and the gun was still in his hand. Jacqui had prayed for a resolution that would be for his highest good as well as theirs. Perhaps she thought, he had reached the point in life where death was his only alternative. From her perspective, his was a wasted life, but who could see into the mind of God? She prayed that his tortured soul had found peace at last.

Sunny was on the phone again, informing the dispatcher that she had freed her companions, and they were with her as she was driving to the main road.

CHAPTER FIFTY

Jacqui and Rhea waited for Jill to come back to the apartment. They had both given their statements and been released. An aide of the congressman drove them home. They had not seen Sunny since they arrived at the police station, but they were assured that she was fine, and that Chase would drive her home when the police were finished. They both discarded their wet clothes, showered, dressed, and dried their hair.

Jacqui poured them each a large, stiff drink. Rhea gulped hers down and poured another. As they waited for Sunny, who was gone for almost two hours, Rhea and Jacqui had little to say to one another. Finally, they came to stand on the balcony overlooking the city lights.

"I thought nothing could spoil this wedding," Rhea said at last. "We planned it down to the last detail."

"How could any of us know that Cortero was still alive?"

"He really would have killed us all, wouldn't he?"

"Yes, I'm afraid he would have."

"Do you really think that Jill was aware of Cortero's involvement in drugs."

"At the very least she had misgivings about him," Jacqui said. "But she chose to marry him anyway. Not everyone sees things in absolute black and white the way you do, Rhea."

"I'm afraid that you can't say that about me," she replied. "When I remodeled the upstairs of the house to make an apartment for myself, the workmen found a bag hidden in the ceiling of Caroline's closet."

"A bag. What was in it?"

"Money. Almost a hundred thousand dollars."

"What did you do with it."

"I kept it."

"No, you wouldn't do that."

"I did. I put it in a safety deposit box. Then I opened a savings account for Caroline's baby. I'm been depositing small sums frequently ever since. When she's old enough to go to college, it will all be there for her."

"So that was what Rick Cortero was looking for the night he killed Caroline."

"Probably. I made up my mind that the government was not going to take the money that rightfully belonged to the baby. Caroline had paid too high a price for it."

"Good for you, Rhea. I'm proud of you. It was the right thing to do."

"So you see, I don't always see things in black and white. I could never convince myself that it was wrong."

"I have something for you," Jacqui said suddenly, trying to take Rhea's mind off the horror of the night. She emerged from the bedroom with a large white box tied with a red satin bow.

"For me?" Rhea said in surprise. "I assumed that was a wedding present."

Jacqui watched her face expectantly as she pulled off the bow and carefully pried open the box.

"My goose!" Rhea squealed in delight.

"As close as I could find," Jacqui said. "The moment I saw it, I knew I had to buy it. It isn't the same, of course."

"Nothing is the same," Rhea said ruefully. "I'm not the same either. Thank you, Jacqui, I love it, and I have just the place for it. Jill used to call me her goose of an aunt. Affectionately, of course."

"Of course."

"I am a goose, I guess."

"I think we both are," Jacqui said. "We had such an extraordinary friendship, and we let it get away. I know it was my fault."

"Jacqui," Rhea asked suddenly. "Would you do it all over again? I mean knowing how it would all turn out, would you?"

"I won't lie to you. Yes, I would do it all over again."

"In a way, I'm glad," Rhea replied. "After all the pain—for

both of us-I don't want to believe that you have any regrets."

"You're unbelievable, Rhea. No—I have no regrets. I needed Greg in my life. You accused me once, I remember, of using Greg to replace Spence—to make up for Spence I think you said."

"I'm sorry, Jacqui, it's all in the past."

"I need to say this, Rhea. In a way, Greg did make up for Spence. In fact, he made up for every rotten thing that ever happened in my whole life. After all this time, I still miss him intensely, but the raw edges of my grief eventually healed. I just got on with my life."

"I guess I did too," Rhea replied. "I can't say, however, that I don't have regrets."

"Kevin?" Jacqui asked.

"He left me you know."

"I'm sorry it didn't work out. I hoped it would."

"The truth is I drove him away. I couldn't let go of Carter until it was too late. Kevin really loved me, Jacqui."

"Everyone could see that but you."

"I told you I was a goose. He was gone before I realized that just because I loved him differently than Carter that I didn't love him any less deeply."

"Is there anyone in your life now?"

"No, not really. I've dated a little. Liz keeps fixing me up. You?"

"There has been. My boss, actually, Jonathan Cory But he has a job offer in California. He's there now. I think he'll take the job. He wants me to go with him, but I won't. He helped me so much when I first moved to Arizona, and I do care about him, but the relationship hasn't been good for some time now. The end is in sight. I'm sad but, in a way, relieved."

"I'm sorry it didn't work out for you. Did Jill tell you that Liz and I have had an offer to sell the business?"

"No, I'm surprised. I can't imagine your wanting to sell. That house seems like such a part of you. Will you take it?"

"I don't know. I just don't know. With wise investing I'd be financially secure for the rest of my life if we sell, but it's my whole life. The offer includes the property, but the contract has a clause that I can't start another antique business or even work in the field for five years. One of the things I had planned to do in New York after the wedding is try to sort out my feelings and come to a decision."

"I just can't see you parting with the house. Have you thought of anything else you would like to do—if you decide to sell. Being financially secure certainly gives you options."

"I've thought about starting another business. I've had so much fun with Jill's wedding, I've thought about a bridal shop and wedding consulting business. There are so many wonderful old houses in Montrose that would provide a wonderful setting. And people know me from my decorating and antiques."

"Sounds wonderful."

"Something in me gets excited at the prospect of buying another place and starting out fresh with all I've learned, and then something else tells me I've absolutely taken leave of my senses."

"That sounds like the old Rhea."

"I haven't changed much." She managed a small laugh. "I still agonize over decisions."

They heard a noise at the door, and Sunny slipped into the apartment. Her hair was plastered to her head in long, tight ringlets and she was still wearing Jacqui's blazer, yet she was beautiful, wholesome and fresh and incredibly appealing, belying the horror of the night.

"Chase is with me," she said. "He's parking the car. Tell him I'm getting dressed. I'll only be a few moments." She poured herself a glass of vodka and started for the bathroom. At the door, she turned.

"I'm so sorry I got the two of you into this," she said.

"It wasn't your fault," Rhea replied.

"I had misgivings," Sunny continued, "about the business Court was in—almost from the beginning. But I'm making both of you a promise. I will never be involved with anyone or anything that I even remotely suspect is illegal again. I'll never even drive over the speed limit."

"We'll hold you to that, young lady." Rhea said wryly as Sunny closed the door.

When Chase arrived, Rhea offered him a drink, which he gratefully accepted, but conversation between them was awkward. None of them seemed to know what to say.

Sunny was out of the bathroom in just a few minutes with perfectly coiffed hair and impeccable makeup, dressed in a stunning hot pink pantsuit trimmed with gold studs.

"It's a wig," she explained as Jacqui and Rhea stared in disbelief.

"It looks exactly like your hair," Rhea exclaimed.

"That's the point, dear aunt," Sunny laughed.

"Isn't she phenomenal?" Chase asked. "When I think of all she's been through tonight, I just can't believe it. She looks as if she's ready to step onto the stage."

"We've all had a night to remember," Sunny said. "Wait a minute. Make that a night to forget!"

She went to stand with her arms around Rhea and Jacqui. "These are my two best friends in the whole world," she told Chase.

"I want to thank you, Rhea, for all the work you've done to make our wedding perfect, and I want to thank you, Jacqui, for coming. I wanted so much for both of you to be here."

"I needed to come, Jill," Jacqui replied. "I had unfinished business with the two of you. Now, I'm glad I did."

"In spite of everything?" Sunny asked.

"In spite of everything," Jacqui replied firmly.

She and Rhea went out to the balcony to give Sunny a few minutes alone with Chase.

"Do you think she told him the whole story about Cortero?" Rhea asked.

"I hope so," Jacqui replied. "You know how a lie always comes back to rear its ugly head."

The door intercom sounded, and Sunny spoke briefly to Cole Warren before she buzzed him in. But, when Sunny opened the door, to Rhea's surprise, he was not alone. Kevin Stacey was with him.

Later neither of them would remember who made the first move, but suddenly Rhea was enveloped in his arms.

"Oh, Kevin," she cried, "nobody told me you were coming."

"I wanted it to be a surprise," Sunny laughed and flashed Chase her best triumphant *I told you so* look.

Kevin was introduced to the congressman, but he did not let go of Rhea's hand. He hugged Jacqui, but as soon as possible, he and Rhea gravitated to the open door of the balcony.

"You look wonderful, Rhea," he said, looking deep into

her eyes.

"Things have gone well for me," she replied.

"I know. I visited the shop and the restaurant a couple of times when I was in Houston. Both times you were out, but I talked to Liz."

"She never told me," Rhea gasped in astonishment.

"I asked her not to," he said.

"But why?"

"I didn't want to upset you, I guess. Maybe I didn't want to upset myself. I knew I had to come to terms with the fact that you were not going to be a part of my life. Seeing you would have just been too hard."

"It was probably for the best," she admitted. "It took me a long time to really get my head straight. I even went into therapy for a while."

"I know. Liz told me."

"What else did she tell you?"

"The hardest thing of all—that you were seeing someone else."

"If I was, it wasn't serious. Do you know we've had an offer to sell?"

"You wouldn't, of course."

"I don't know. Liz wants to. That's what I have to decide this week in New York. I promised her I would think seriously about it."

"Have you?"

"Not yet. There hasn't been time."

"What would you do if you sold?"

"I thought about opening a bridal boutique and wedding consultant business—perhaps in another old house in Montrose."

"In that case, you'd need a good photographer," he proposed.

"Come in you two," Sunny called. "We've just opened a bottle of champagne."

Reluctantly, Rhea and Kevin joined them inside.

Chase poured the champagne, starting with Sunny who only got half a glass. "You're already a bit tipsy," he said.

"We all are," Jacqui confessed.

"We're allowed," Rhea laughed. "After all, we haven't all been together for five years."

"Of course, you are," Chase agreed and finished filling Sunny's glass.

As soon as they were all holding filled glasses, Chase proposed a toast.

"To my beautiful, brave Sunny. I will love you and hold you and keep you safe and happy, always and forever."

Sunny's eyes filled with tears. Rhea and Jacqui also had to wipe away tears. He knows, Jacqui thought, the exact thing Sunny needed to hear.

"To Sunny," Cole said. "I discovered her, you know," he said, beaming with pride.

"In a pig's eye!" Kevin objected. "How dare you take credit for discovering her?" he demanded of his friend. "I sent her to you. You call that discovering her?"

Sunny planted a kiss on Kevin cheek. "You originally put the idea of modeling in my mind when you took the first pictures of me. You helped me to believe in myself. And you, dear one," she said kissing Cole, "found me an agent and helped me get started. I owe a lot to the two of you. Don't think for one moment that I'll ever forget."

Then she embraced Rhea and Jacqui. "And to the both of you, I owe a debt that I can never repay. I'll love the two of you dearly for always." Sunny kissed them both.

"What is all this kissing?" Chase demanded. "And not one for the bridegroom? Did I ever tell you that I'm the jealous type? Come here, woman!"

Sunny melted into his arms, and Jacqui saw Rhea kissing Kevin.

Cole looked at her and whispered, "I feel like the odd man out. I'd better leave before I grab you and start kissing, too. I'm afraid my wife Melissa is not all that broad minded."

"Where is she tonight?" Jacqui asked.

"Working late like a good little executive, but I had better be on my way. See you tomorrow at the festivities."

Goodbyes were said, and Chase decided that Sunny needed her beauty sleep to be dazzling at the party tomorrow. They left on the pretext of his dropping her off at his mother's to spend the night.

Rhea surprised Jacqui by informing her that she was going back to Kevin's hotel with him. "We have so much to talk about," she explained. "I'll be back later."

Jacqui smiled her approval and spent the night alone, going back over the past few hours reliving the horror time and time again and praying that Rick Cortero's evil past would not cause problems for Sunny and Chase. Finally, she slept out of sheer mental and physical exhaustion.

CHAPTER FIFTY-ONE

Rhea and Kevin settled into the back of a taxi for the ride to his hotel.

"There's so much I want to say to you, Rhea. I even prepared myself for the possibility that you would show up with another man. Now, seeing you again, I know I'll love you always. Nothing has changed in five years."

"I've changed, Kevin. I know what a fool I was. I drove you away, and I trashed my friendship with Jacqui. Yes, I've been a success as a businesswoman but a total failure as a woman."

"You could never be a total failure at anything. You and Jacqui have patched things up, I see. I'm very glad."

"Yes, we're friends again." Bonded by an experience so horrible, she thought, that neither one of them would ever be the same again.

"Would you like something to eat?" he asked. "I'm sure we can find an all-night restaurant. After all, this is the city that never sleeps."

"I couldn't eat a thing." she replied

"I don't suppose you want a drink either," he said.

"No, I've had far, far too much already."

"What would you like to do?"

"I want to go to your hotel and have you hold me and tell me you still love me and that you forgive me for being such a fool five years ago."

"My beautiful, beautiful Rhea," he exclaimed. "Is there really a chance for us after all this time?"

"I didn't realize until tonight just how precious life is. I love you, Kevin, and I want to spend the rest of my life with you. I've forgotten all the silly reasons I had for thinking it wouldn't work. We'll make it work. How can anything this beautiful and good for us not work?"

They clung to each other as if they would never let go. When they got to the hotel, Kevin paid the driver and gave him an outrageous tip.

He held Rhea and told her all the things her heart was longing to hear. They made love passionately, then tenderly and sweetly. She thought about what Jacqui had said to her about Carter's love making up for every rotten thing that had ever happened to her and understood. She loved Kevin that much.

Rhea was so filled with happiness she couldn't contain her tears. Kevin cried with her, and they talked far into the night. He had to return to London; there were projects that he was committed to finishing.

"Three months—tops," he promised. "Then I'll be home for good."

"I'm going to sell the business," she said. "I've made up my mind. I'll call Liz the first thing tomorrow."

"Are you sure? You don't have to, you know."

"It's time," she replied. "Maybe I'll start another business sometime, but for now, I just want to concentrate on us. I want to sell, I really do, Kevin. I want us to start fresh. The house has a lot of memories, although you would hardly recognize it any more. I remodeled the upstairs, made myself an apartment, but the business encroaches too much on my personal life."

"I have one more job for you before you give it up entirely," he said. "My house. You once offered to make it beautiful for me."

"Your house? I thought it had been sold."

"I thought so, too. But the economy turned sour and the new owners weren't able to keep up the payments. Since I had guaranteed the mortgage, I had to take it back."

"Wonderful!" she exclaimed. "It would be great for a bridal shop. It would be a fantastic place to hold weddings and receptions—that immense staircase and chandelier."

"And a photographer's studio?"

"Of course."

"We wouldn't want to live there, would we?"

"No, we wouldn't. We would want our own place. I've had quite enough of a business in my residence."

"I agree. You'll start on the plans as soon as you get home?"

"What do you mean as soon as I get home? I already have a million ideas whirling around in my head."

"Put them away, my darling. I have plans for your head, and the rest of you, too. I don't want you thinking about anything except me for the rest of the night."

"Oh Kevin, it's really going to be all right, isn't it."

"You bet it is. I'll never let you go again."

Rhea settled into his arms happily, remembering all the time she had felt guilty to be there. It was right for both of them, as he had said that first day on the lake so long ago.

CHAPTER FIFTY-TWO

Jacqui watched Sunny throughout the festivities preceding the wedding, looking as radiant and happy as if she didn't have a care in the world. She was like a child, living just for the moment. For her, the past and the future did not exist.

Jacqui wished that she had more of that quality and remembered her seat mate on the plane from Arizona. He had asked for her phone number, saying he got to to the Phoenix area often and would like to meet her for dinner, but she refused. It didn't seem right. The breakup with Jonathan was imminent, but it had not yet occurred.

Perhaps she should have proffered the number. The man was attractive and a good conversationalist. She would be lonely when Jonathan left. No, she corrected herself. She would not be lonely—only alone.

She looked in the mirror and saw only plainness and could not understand why so many men seemed to be interested in her, why Spence and Greg and Jonathan had loved her. In her mind's eye, she was still the tomboy with braided hair and dirty jeans who climbed trees and could sink a basketball and swing a tennis racket with astonishing force.

She was a psychologist, and she helped people to overcome grief and fear and low self-esteem and addictions. She understood behavior and human needs. She taught college classes in psychology and, on occasion, had written for scholarly journals, but when it came to her own life, she felt like a fraud. She was only beginning to understand herself.

After Greg's death she had hauled her own grief and fear clear across the country from Texas to California and then back to Arizona. She had settled for Jonathan because he made her feel less abandoned, less afraid, after she had promised Greg that she would never settle. She had carried the fear all the way from Texas—the fear that she would never again know the passionate love she had known with Greg. It was time to let go of that fear.

A lump rose in her throat when she saw Rhea and Kevin look at each other. They were so much in love. Rhea had been given another chance. Jacqui guessed that in a way she, too, had been given another chance.

"Kevin is flying back to London as soon as the wedding is over," Rhea had said. "And I'm going back to Houston. I don't need another week in New York. I've made my decision to sell the business. I'm going to sign on the dotted line before Riker has a chance to change his mind. I called Liz, and she was overjoyed."

"Will you join Kevin in London?" Jacqui asked.

"No, he's leaving the magazine and coming back to Houston. He has several projects under way to finish, so I'll put my things in storage and just hang around somewhere until he gets back. Then we'll be married and take a long honeymoon."

"Hang around with me in Arizona," Jacqui pleaded. "I would love to spend some time with you. I want you to see my house, and I want to show you what my life is like now."

"Is it a good life, Jacqui?"

"Yes, it is. I didn't realize how good it was until the other night. I have a number of private patients, and I coach basketball part time. My girls won the State championship two years in a row. Promise you'll come and stay with me."

"Perhaps I will," Rhea said. "I think I'd like that very much."

CHAPTER FIFTY-THREE

The day of the wedding dawned beautiful and clear. The view of the city from Sunny's balcony was spectacular, but Jacqui longed to be back in Arizona looking at the world from her own deck. Wedding presents kept arriving until they threatened to overwhelm the spacious apartment.

Jacqui had seen little of Rhea. She was spending all her time with Kevin. Even Ruth complained that she hardly got to see her sister at all.

Jacqui had one brief conversation with Sunny about Court's death. "I know you think you feel nothing now, but the shock will wear off in time and remember, if you need someone to talk to, I'm always available."

"Listen, Doc," Sunny had said. "I feel no more remorse than if I had swatted a fly or squashed a bug. I made a choice. It was simply him or the three of us. I'm prepared to live with that. But if I'm ever bothered, believe me, you'll be the first to know. Remember, I'm a southern girl, and they don't call us steel magnolias for nothing."

"Well, just remember me if you need to talk."

"Pencil me in on your schedule for about twenty years from now. I don't plan to even think about anything connected to Cortero for at least that long."

Jacqui hoped fervently that she was right.

She scanned the newspapers for stories about their ordeal. There wasn't much mention of Rick Cortero, a petty drug thug from Houston. The story was about the heroic actions of actress

Sunny Houston just prior to her wedding to Congressman Chase Williams.

Rhea and Jacqui helped Sunny dress. "You should be on the cover of a magazine in this," Rhea said. "I've never seen you look so lovely."

"You're not just a little prejudiced?" Sunny teased, as she adjusted the headpiece that framed her golden hair that had just been styled. The filmy, cascade veil was perfect, and her face was framed in pearls and silk roses.

The flowers were delivered, and Sunny held up her bouquet of yellow roses with Casablanca lilies and stephanotis. "I'm going to throw it to the two of you," she threatened, "so be ready."

"Don't you dare," Jacqui cautioned. "Rhea already has her wedding planned, so be fair and favor one of your bridesmaids."

Sunny laughed mischievously.

"How did Chase's family take the story of your involvement with Cortero?" Rhea asked.

"Better than I expected," Sunny said. "At first, his mother took to her bed with a migraine, but when Chase's father heard how I struggled with Court over the gun, he slapped Chase on the back and congratulated him on marrying a real woman. I don't think the publicity is going to hurt either one of us."

The ornate cathedral was decorated with yellow roses and stephanotis and greenery tied with yellow ribbons at every pew. And, when Sunny and Chase recited their vows, they faced the guests from the altar with the wedding party around them. The priest was below in his embroidered white robe with his back to the guests.

Rhea and Jacqui seated together with Kevin daubed at their eyes with the Battenberg lace handkerchiefs Sunny had given them. Jacqui was striking in her emerald green faille suit with a long skirt and matching pumps, and Rhea wore an apricot chiffon gown with a draped collar that plunged to a deep v in the back, graced by a matching fabric rose. Sunny had thoughtfully provided white orchid for them both with streamers that matched their dresses.

Jacqui's thoughts drifted back to that night so long ago when the four of them, she, Caroline, Rhea, and Jill had shared Rhea's beautiful old house. The afternoons around the pool. The late night suppers. Who could have guessed that time would lead them down such divergent paths?

She thought again about Caroline's last words, "Forgive me, Jacqui, I was afraid of the wrong person." Did Caroline know of her husband's involvement with the young Jill?

She wondered if Sunny ever felt guilty about leading him to Caroline? But maybe it was the other way around. Who knows? Cortero might have been stalking Caroline, watching the house, without any of them knowing. None of them would ever know now.

Jacqui put Cortero out of her mind. She agreed with Sunny. Twenty years would be too soon to think of him again.

After photographs were taken, Sunny changed clothes for the reception, appearing in a yellow silk chantung mini dress with a detachable bustle. Yellow roses, Sunny Houston's trademark, were everywhere, and when they went into the candlelight supper, each guest was handed a single long-stemmed yellow rose, and a crystal bud vase was provided at every place setting.

The dance afterward in the elaborate ballroom lasted far into the night, with an orchestra playing songs from the forties and fifties. Sunny had changed again into a ball gown of Victorian design made of gold silk Dupion and trimmed with Guipure lace. She really looked like Cinderella with Chase as the handsome prince in his black tailcoat and matching trousers as they waltzed across the polished dance floor under the massive chandeliers.

Jacqui had expected the wedding to be magnificent, but she had not been able to imagine this grandeur. Everything went off like clockwork. The multiple toasts began with the best man. "May you always have stars in your eyes and visions of a perfect future in your heads. May you always hold hands in friendship and hold love in your hearts."

Jacqui looked at Chase and Sunny. She silently wished them no less than the love and no less than the happiness that she and Greg had known. But she wished them more time. She decided to write it to them in a letter thanking them for inviting her to the wedding. What she wanted to say was too private to share with everybody.

Rhea was with Kevin, Cole was with Melissa. Chase's parents were together. Each of the bridesmaids seemed to have a special someone. Only she was alone.

She knew that Chase and Sunny would spend the night in the

bridal suite at a grand hotel, although they had kept the location secret. In the morning they would again greet a select group of guests at a brunch given by Chase's parents in their Long Island home. It seems that the groom's mother had recovered from her migraine quite nicely. Then they would be off to cruise the Caribbean on a private yacht.

Jacqui decided not to stay over for the brunch, but to fly back to Arizona on an early morning flight. She was suddenly anxious to be home. She said her goodbyes and took a taxi back to Sunny's apartment.

CHAPTER FIFTY-FOUR

Jacqui stood on the balcony off the spacious living room, looking at an umbrella of stars in the night sky. She had felt alone, lonely, shut off from everyone's happiness. It wasn't exactly envy, she thought. She wished them, Sunny and Chase and Rhea and Kevin, truly the best. It had taken Rhea all these years to acknowledge the love between her and Kevin that had existed from the beginning of their relationship. They both deserved their new found happiness.

Jacqui had packed her bags, leaving out the clothes she planned to wear on the plane. Everything was ready. Tomorrow she would be whisked from La Guardia and set down in the Valley of the Sun at the Sky Harbor Airport. Perhaps Jonathan would be waiting. Perhaps not.

The last thing she heard on the radio was a story about Sunny. They played a tape of the conversation between Sunny and her abductor. It seemed that Sunny had managed to let the police eavesdrop on her final conversation with Cortero before he threw away her cell phone. Hearing the tape sent chills up Jacqui's spine. She knew why Sunny had not told her and Rhea about the conversation. She wanted to spare them the horror of knowing Cortero's plans for the three of them.

Jacqui had misjudged Sunny. She had more courage than anybody had given her credit for. That tape would be the stuff nightmares were made of for years to come.

She went to bed, but sleep did not come easily. There were too many things on her mind. She hadn't wanted to tell Jon on the telephone that she wasn't moving to San Francisco with him, but he knew, nonetheless. The confrontation would come as soon as she returned home.

Finally she drifted off into a dreamless sleep. She awakened abruptly and sensed a presence in the room. Someone was there, but when she turned on the light, there was no one. The room seemed bathed in a strange golden glow, but she could not find the source of it.

When she satisfied herself that she was in no danger, she went again to the balcony to look down on the sleeping city. The glow she discovered was coming from the sunrise. The incredibly brilliant sun touched the rooftops with liquid gold.

She still had the same sense of another presence, strong but soothing. She closed her eyes, and the golden light penetrated her closed eyelids. When she opened them, she felt as if a dam somewhere had been broken open, and the golden energy of the universe was pouring into her. Scar tissue from wounds she had carried deep within herself started to peel away, layer by layer, and dissolved into the golden light.

A deep sense of peace and joy, almost more than she could bear, permeated her very being as the golden light surrounded and enveloped her. She felt herself melting, turning liquid, blending with the light until she became the golden light, and she knew that she had merged into the essence of the Divine.

Time had no meaning. She could have been there an hour or a minute, but gradually the ecstasy subsided, ebbing until the golden light diffused into the morning. And she was left in the soft, pale glow of unconditional love.

The words from a poem ran through her consciousness. *At sunrise every soul is born again.* She felt the presence of God so strongly that it seemed she had only to reach out her hand to touch the wholeness of the universe. Her wounded soul had been reborn.

She thought of Greg and experienced a moment of pure joy, knowing that she had merged with his energy in the golden light. Memories of him were no longer more than she could bear. Now she cherished them.

She felt a lightness, an exhilaration, deep and profound peace. She wanted to pray, but no words came. Yet her voiceless prayer seemed to soar into the morning. She felt the urge to laugh from deep within the core of her. She wanted to shout with new found delight.

She let go of her envy for Jill and Chase and Rhea and Kevin. She knew in a way that she had never known before that love was the center of everything, including herself, and that it was time for her to go home.

She had made the right choice. She and Jonathan had come together out of mutual need, and the need had been fulfilled. It was time for him to move on. The San Francisco job would make it easier for both of them. The separation would be for the highest good of them both, and whatever painful feelings he harbored would pass.

As he moved out of her life, Jacqui knew that a new space would be created. She was beginning from a place of total self-acceptance and unconditional self-love. The painful lesson that Greg's death had taught her at so much cost—that life goes on and that love is everything—would always remain. She had been slammed into the ropes and knocked to the canvas. But she had gotten up and lifted her hand in victory. It had taken five years.

She would never let anyone tell her that women don't form strong and lasting friendships. She didn't know how long it would be before she saw Rhea and Sunny again, but she would always know that there was a bond between them that would transcend time and space.

Jacqui had been lifted out of the limbo where she had struggled, psychologically insulated from life since leaving Houston five years before. She was now a whole person again.

The gold and pink of the sunrise had faded. She looked at the cloudless sky with a new awareness, taking delight in the joy of the moment. In the distance she heard a bell chiming, and as the city began to come alive, she eagerly embraced the new day.

It was time for her to go home.